SICK WITH REVENGE

SICK WITH REVENGE

E. VAUGHN MOORE

iUniverse

SICK WITH REVENGE

Copyright © 2015 E. Vaughn Moore

All rights reserved. No part of this book may be used or reproduced by any means, graphic, electronic, or mechanical, including photocopying, recording, taping or by any information storage retrieval system without the written permission of the publisher except in the case of brief quotations embodied in critical articles and reviews.

This is a work of fiction. All of the characters, names, incidents, organizations, and dialogue in this novel are either the products of the author's imagination or are used fictitiously.

iUniverse books may be ordered through booksellers or by contacting:

iUniverse
1663 Liberty Drive
Bloomington, IN 47403
www.iuniverse.com
1-800-Authors (1-800-288-4677)

Because of the dynamic nature of the Internet, any web addresses or links contained in this book may have changed since publication and may no longer be valid. The views expressed in this work are solely those of the author and do not necessarily reflect the views of the publisher, and the publisher hereby disclaims any responsibility for them.

Any people depicted in stock imagery provided by Thinkstock are models, and such images are being used for illustrative purposes only.
Certain stock imagery © Thinkstock.

ISBN: 978-1-4917-4955-5 (sc)
ISBN: 978-1-4917-4956-2 (e)

Library of Congress Control Number: 2015900135

Print information available on the last page.

iUniverse rev. date: 04/07/2015

For Leah

PROLOGUE

Sean Swoboda's intelligent gray eyes followed his client as she stared intently through the two-way mirror at the pummeling taking place inside the interview room. With white-knuckled fingers curled tightly around the leather-covered handle of his attaché, he trailed Sage's steps and reluctantly peered through the mirrored glass.

Superintendent Manny Cofield wiped drool from the corner of his mouth and smeared the blood across his Gucci pant leg. Three heaving breaths later, he pulled his wide frame upright, giving an unobstructed view of his prisoner—a thoroughly brutalized Anthony Campbell. One of Campbell's brown eyes was a narrow slit surrounded by purple, wrinkled skin; there were rising welts around the less damaged eye. Various hues of pink and red colored his cheeks. His engorged tongue was swelling like a blowfish wedged between two bloated lips.

Every warped bit of Anthony Campbell's face was the result of the punch-happy work of the superintendent's meaty fists. The prisoner sat as if content with being tethered to a chair, bound by a length of thick, biting rope. With his open eye resting easily on Manny Cofield, he twitched puffy lips into a defiant, lopsided smile.

Outside the interview room, the attorney had seen enough. He leaned into his client's space until his breath blended with hers. A black, bouncy lock swung back from her temple with each of his enunciations.

"Sage, I am leaving with or without you, and I'm taking Jadia with me."

Sage, five feet four inches with skin tanned golden from a summer of Philadelphia sun, shifted away from the scene in the window and swept across Sean's patrician face. At length, she shifted left and studied her vacuous daughter, who was a five-foot-two-inch facsimile of her mother—ravened haired with Mediterranean blue eyes.

Sage followed the tween's disinterested gaze back to the double mirror. A thorny vine spiraled up her back. Maybe the psychologists were wrong about the sight of Anthony Campbell being a good thing for Jadia. Their well-presented philosophy of facing fears by returning to their source had never gained traction with anyone but Sean Swoboda and herself. At the moment, the idea was losing ground fast. Defeated dark blue eyes turned back to Sean. She swallowed, nervously clutched the large purse draped over her shoulder, and nodded.

"You're right. We should leave."

On the other side of the window, Anthony Campbell snorted. "So you're going to cut me?"

Sean's and Sage's heads both snapped to the mirror. The hunting knife was rolling in Manny Cofield's hand.

Tireless, chemically-induced bravado barreled through Anthony Campbell's battered mouth. "It's okay with me as long as you know that I cut back—and I cut deep."

Manny Cofield squinted at the prisoner's words. Cofield's two henchmen, who had receded deeper into the interview room and stilled when the knife was introduced, were now exchanging questioning looks. The superintendent straddled Anthony Campbell's lap, grabbed his jaw, yanked his oblong head to attention, and then kissed his prisoner's bloody lips with a lover's intensity before licking his own mouth clean. The hunting knife began to roll in his hand again.

"Where are the drugs, Campbell?" Cofield asked with unsettling calm.

Anthony Campbell didn't answer.

The superintendent slipped the knife under Campbell's front teeth, and dug into the gum. A beige tooth flew across the room, a mangled root tailing behind it. One of the suited men jumped back from the spray of blood. The other shifted his weight from one foot to another, grimacing.

Anthony Campbell's drugged body didn't flinch. An eye, the one not swollen shut, beamed at Manny Cofield. He turned his face aside and spat. Heavy with phlegm, the blood landed on the arm of the chair before oozing to the floor and pooling in the welt of Cofield's quarter-brogue shoe.

Manny Cofield's eyes glided from the red staining his shoe to the trepidation reflected on the faces of his underlings. The two tough guys had retreated until their broad backs were against the far wall.

"What?" Cofield blurted out, spittle hurling from his curled lips. "You just now woke up and realized you've been sleeping in shit?"

The suits proffered looks as blank as Jadia's.

"Get out!" Cofield blared, tossing his chin to the right to indicate the only exit in the bloodied room. "Lock the door and keep watch outside."

The blue door slammed shut behind the men, leaving the superintendent alone with his knife and his prisoner. Corded veins crossed Manny Cofield's scrunched forehead as, with grunts and sweat, he dragged the chair and its cargo backward, and pushed it flush against the blue door, blocking it.

As Cofield straddled Anthony Campbell's lap, Sean and Sage scrambled awkwardly to move their shock-heavy feet from the insanity in the window. Sean managed to gain purchase first, rounding his client and heading straight for Jadia.

"I let you in, Camp," Cofield's voice ranted from the window. "You betrayed me."

The superintendent went to work on Campbell's mouth again, then stood upright, a blood-doused hand curled into a fist around the dripping hunting knife. He spread a sinister, drooling smile at Campbell's widening gap. Beneath the surface of Jadia's hollow-eyed stare, the flicker

ix

of a grimace danced on her face. In that very quick second, Sean made his way to the tween and placed a gentle palm on her chin. He turned her gaze away from the window and smiled at her expressionless face. Then, with quiet steps, he led her to the exit and protectively stationed her between himself and the door. With one hand on the knob and the other gripping the attaché, he pivoted back to find Sage inexorably drawn to the mirror.

What Sage saw and what Sean couldn't see was that one of Anthony Campbell's arms was free. In that impossible few seconds, the prisoner snatched the knife from the surprised superintendent's slippery hand and stabbed him repeatedly in the chest. The superintendent stood as if he'd heard someone call his name. He stepped back once, twice.

Wobbling, Cofield looked down at Anthony Campbell, grabbed the handle of the knife protruding from his chest, and stumbled backward. He coughed, gagged, and side-waddled until his backside was pressed against the glass. He remained motionless there a long second, then slid down the window like sluicing rain until he was hidden from view.

Sean yelled to Sage from the opened door. She didn't move.

Anthony Campbell stood and looked straight into the mirror, milky eyes bulging with rage. He spotted Sage. A sanguine smear spread across his face. After one hair-raising second, Sage realized it was a bloody smile.

Anthony Campbell stepped to the mirror and peered out between cupped hands. A bloated tongue darted out and licked the mirror in a long, lascivious, bloody stroke, leaving a red streak in its wake.

Revulsion crawled up Sage's spine and gathered at the nape of her neck.

Sean grabbed Jadia's hand and quickly pulled her to the other side of the opened door. Jadia's chest was rising and falling fitfully. Sean dipped his eyes to hers and whispered, "It's going to be okay. Stay here. I'll be right back." He waited a beat to catch her flitting eyes, held them a split second, and then darted through the jamb to Sage.

"Sage! Let's go! Now!" Sean bellowed into her ear.

Anthony Campbell stomped to the chair, grabbed it, and dragged it to the back of the interview room.

Sage rammed her rear into Sean's groin, butting him backward toward the doorjamb. He grabbed her by the waist, using her momentum to drag her with him. In a countermove, Sage dug her heels into the floor, throwing her body into a power spin that morphed the world into a slow-motion whirl. Everything happened simultaneously.

With a gurgled grunt, Anthony Campbell hoisted the chair over his head. Sage spun, punched the air out of Sean with a two-fisted uppercut to the gut, and pushed him out the door. As he crash-landed into Jadia, Sage slammed the door, and pulled a second-generation 9mm Glock 17 from her large purse— the purse that, thanks to Sean Swoboda's carte blanche access to the prison, had been poorly searched by prison guards.

Anthony Campbell catapulted himself kamikaze style through the window. Mirrored glass shot out in a starburst. With ear-piercing clangs, the glass shattered on the ground, breaking into smaller shards and spreading like liquid mercury across the grimy floor.

The two henchmen charged through the blue door into the interview room and froze, their stunned faces trying to make sense of the gruesome scene.

Anthony Campbell crept toward Sage. A booted left foot crunched against sharp, jagged glass, while merciless shards sliced through the calloused skin of his bare right foot. Milky, slitted eyes locked on Sage.

He charged.

CHAPTER 1
AUGUST 1994

Sean stood in the firm's midtown garage, his large hands pinning vicuna suit panels to his hips. Ignoring the construction signs had not been a good idea. His only reason for being there and not racing down I-95 to the Philadelphia office was the file he'd inadvertently left on his desk after attending a late meeting the night before. He stood under the shadow of derailed plans, staring at his SL73 AMG, which sat unusually close to the ground. The only thing rarer than the custom SL73 was his frequency of driving it. Five hundred fifty pounds of torque. Five hundred twenty-five horsepower. Twelve cylinders—and four deflated tires.

Sean checked his watch: 6:22 a.m. He needed to be in Philadelphia by eight forty-five. The problem was that Philly was at least two hours away. With horn-honking, bumper-kissing New York traffic, forget about it.

The SL3 slammed shut and locked after he grabbed the attaché. In quick strides, he loped through the garage, bypassed elevators to a stairwell, and backtracked to the office. Loose change jingled in his pocket as he skipped up the steps in twos, gaining momentum until he landed on the third floor past the mezzanine level. He was barely winded when he punched an elevator call button for a ride to whispers he was

1

certain awaited him on the fifty-fourth floor. Over the past few months, the firm had been abuzz with scuttlebutt (of which he was the focus) about the recently assembled O. J. Simpson prosecuting team.

Sean had licenses to practice law in several states, including California. As a corporate litigation attorney, his typical caseload involved intellectual property rights, torts, copyright infringement and the like. His representation reaped multi-million dollar billings. Although crimes against persons was neither his forte nor his interest, the lure of the Simpson criminal case was the opportunity to exercise DNA litigation skills in front of a national audience.

According to his contemporaries and a Bar Review Magazine article, Sean Swoboda was the go-to DNA subject matter expert. His reputation as a DNA litigation mastermind had traveled to the west coast ears of Marcia Clark, head prosecutor for the O. J. Simpson murder trial. The County of Los Angeles District Attorney had wanted to utilize Sean expertise to help prove celebrity and former NFLer, O. J. Simpson, murdered his ex-wife Nicole Brown Simpson and her friend Ronald Lyle Goldman. To the ill-concealed chagrin of Sean's employers and his wife Lori, Sean Swoboda had refused Clark's last and final offer. Now he was the subject of open spite at work and furtive suspicion at home.

A few early birds Sean hadn't seen when he first entered the fifty-fourth floor now huddled with coffee mugs and water bottles in the large oval-shaped foyer near the firm's ostentatious mahogany double doors. They were the eager junior leaguers who may have lacked experience but who more than made up for it with enthusiastic drive and ruthless competitiveness.

As the mahogany doors performed their slow, disdainful close behind him, not one of the four junior leaguers assailed him with the usual daily gossip that customarily escaped hand-cupped mouths. Sean gave the quartet a curt nod as he brushed past them, heel-tapped through and anteroom with its receptionist station and bay of empty visitor offices, and pushed through a set of double glass doors that led to Partners' Row.

He quickstepped into the first office on the right and placed his attaché on the desk as he reached for the phone and called his client. He related the tire misfortune to the client and was listening to the reply when he sensed a presence filling the doorway behind him.

Sean spun around and caught sight of his colleague, the quick and savvy Ayde Carona—owner of the office he had intruded. She leaned against the doorframe, perked up the corners of her full, moist lips, and held a lone key that dangled from a metal loop.

"What?" he mouthed with a stern face as a tweeting voice emitted from the receiver. He quickly asked the client to hold, pressing the receiver to his chest afterward to mute the conversation with Ayde.

"I owe you, and I don't like owing," Ayde cooed in a discrete whisper. She was young, bold, brunette, and beautiful, and her long legs were advancing into the office with a determined stride. Her round, mocha eyes flirted unabashedly with his.

"What are you talking about?" His words had an annoyed edge.

"Christmas party?" she whispered in a how-could-you-forget tone.

"Christmas was a year ago," he whispered back, covering the mouthpiece with his hand.

"Not quite," she breathed. "We still have several months to go yet. Anyway, why wait when opportunity says now?"

He shifted his weight to one leg with a quick exhale. "I'm in a hurry, Ayde. Whatcha got?"

"A key." She clucked her tongue, gave him a lingering blink, and then added, "It's mine."

Sean stared at her blankly, a flicker of impatience squeezing between tight folds forming on his brow.

"You and Lori drove me home after the Christmas party last year? My date was on call and had to rush to the hospital so ..." She shrugged her shoulders. "I was kind of stranded."

"Ahh," he said, "that." His face relaxed. "You don't owe me, Ayde. That's what friends are for." The exaggeration hovered over them like a

Goodyear blimp. Sean and Ayde both knew the extent of their relationship was business: his choice, her dismay.

Ayde smiled. "It's my car key, Sean," she said, eyeing the phone he clutched to his chest. She leaned in closer and whispered, "Sounds like it could come in handy right about now."

"Uhm." Sean drew out the word. "Hold on a sec."

He moved the receiver to his ear, announced his return, and listened to his client's voice through the earpiece as he kept watch on Ayde Carona.

"You know," he said into the phone, "that plan just might work. See you in a couple of hours."

Sean rested the phone in its cradle, leaned his haunches on the edge of the mahogany desk, and folded his arms. Ayde stepped back to close the door, then closed the distance between them again, standing even closer this time.

"Please take it," she said, dangling the Ford Explorer key in his face.

"What's your morning look like, Ayde?" Sean asked, ignoring the swaying key.

Ayde retreated from his personal space and shifted her tone to business speak. "I'm working a segment of the Warner Brothers intellectual property case. A gang of their corporate attorneys flew in last night for an afternoon briefing, so there goes my evening. We'll probably be here all weekend." Ayde grabbed Sean's hand and dropped the key into his open palm. He squinted at it.

"This is not exactly what I had in mind," he said. He grabbed her palm, dropped the key in it, and gently folded perfectly manicured fingers over it.

"Is that so?" she said. She stepped closer. Her voice dropped to a whisper. "So what did you have in mind?"

Another step closer. She leaned into him. He smelled her perfume—light, fresh, pleasant. Her breath kissed his lips in minty puffs.

He inhaled a deep breath and studied her. Despite the bounciest, brownest hair, Ayde Carona had been the New York firm's golden girl for five years. She'd joined the team girded with the experience of some cf the toughest commercial trial and appeal cases in the mid-Atlantic states and was heralded as one of the country's top one percent of the industry. Best yet, she had earned the respect of the East Coast judge circuit. Ayde Carona was a formidable contender inside the courtroom and a savvy networker outside.

Like Sean, Ayde was one of the few non-partners with an office on Partners' Row, which was a sure sign the partners were fast-tracking her to become one of them. Sean, however, seemed destined to remain outside the partners' exclusive circle, no matter where he was seated.

Sean hadn't ignored Ayde since she joined the firm, but he hadn't exactly warmed to her either. Still, he couldn't help noticing her coquettishness. Ayde Carona's flirtations were like a car alarm incessantly shrieking in the distance: noticeable but not a showstopper. Besides, she was discreet and selective; she only flirted with him.

Sean also noticed Ayde's other qualities. She had quick wit, good humor, and she was exceptionally clever. She didn't discredit litigation capabilities with cheap antics of femininity, although she damn well could have—any tall, svelte woman with a face like hers could. But she didn't. Instead, Ayde Carona wore poise and grace and smarts like everyone else wears skin. Her tact and easygoing nature had the respect and attention of just about everyone in the firm.

Sean, on the other hand, retained professional distance from most people in the office—especially after being shunned from the partnership—but he couldn't be described as a total recluse. He loved law and litigation and, despite the O. J. whisperers, internal and external colleagues often sought his advice. Sean was irrefutably one of the top performers in the firm and on the East Coast. He billed high, and made his work look effortless. Most days filled him with priceless job gratification, a must because Sean Swoboda was independently wealthy.

Then there were the other days. Days when he was the subject of office gossip that speculated why he had been repeatedly passed over for partnership and, as a separate appendage, why he had rejected the opportunity of being a part of the O. J. Simpson prosecution team.

Through it all, Ayde Carona remained supportive; she had even gone to bat for him. And she gave no one outright support but Sean Swoboda. She referred to his counsel in the office and in court. She referenced his files for precedence when working cases similar to his. Ayde had recommended Sean to lead most senior counsel advisement boards. For the last five years, Ayde Carona had consistently done all this.

Sean's gaze raked over her, evaluating one feature at a time. The nose: perfect size for her oval-shaped face. Lips: full, moist, and inviting. Her eyes: spheres of mocha with translucent flecks of gold and bottomless pupils that took in … everything. Including him. Especially him.

Ayde smiled. "Well?" Warm, minty breath puffs tapped his lips again. "What do you have in mind?"

"I need you to drive me to the Philadelphia office. I'm meeting a client there." Sean grabbed the attaché and checked his watch: 6:31 a.m. "You should have plenty of time to get back for the Warner Brothers' briefing."

She stepped away again, this time to grab her purse from a nearby credenza. "How will you get back?"

"I'm not coming back. I'm taking the rest of the week off and staying in my Philly home. Lori's already there. Got some long overdue projects she's wanted me to take care of."

"Sounds like fun." Her voice sounded flat as she exited through the door Sean held open for her.

He nodded as she brushed by. "Yep. It will be."

CHAPTER 2

Sage Wirspa mindlessly fingered a covered button of her capped sleeved silk blouse as she stared at the rainbow-colored Apple decal on the Macintosh tower. She purposely ignored the steady stream of gotta-have-it-yesterdays dribbling onto the screen. Today's version of office uniformity was complemented with a pencil skirt and three-inch pumps. She had held the receiver, listening to Sean rattle on about a flat tire. Taking time to change it would plunge him into I-95 gridlock, and they would never make the ten o'clock appointment with Manny Cofield, and never get Jadia in front of a chained and cuffed Anthony Campbell.

Sean Swoboda himself had arranged the appointment via his wife Lori's contacts—*or something like that*, Sage mused as she listened. At some point in the recent past, Manny Cofield's initial hesitation had degraded to downright refusal. It had taken a lot of finagling for the Swobodas to turn the recalcitrant Manny Cofield around. He didn't like people in his prison business—especially not a juvenile victim.

And then there was the business of Manny Cofield not receiving the letter Sage and her former husband, Thomas, had written. It was all so— so strange, Sage thought. But then she had blown it off because they were finally in Manny Cofield's good graces—kind of. Things seemed to be progressing. Thomas and Sage's grandmother Oma were both adamantly against Jadia being present at the meeting. *So,* Sage thought, *one step forward, ten steps back.*

Sage couldn't understand the unrelenting resistance Thomas and her Oma clutched like they were junkies and screw-you Sage was their drug. It was the first time she'd done anything regarding Jadia without Thomas's expressed consent. The first-time compromise hadn't followed disagreements—it was Sage was going against the grain of joint parenthood. Well, damn it, it was the first time their daughter, her Jadia, hadn't spoken in four years. *Four years.* After Sean had described the complexities and impossibilities of arranging such a prison visit with a minor in tow, Sage realized how close she was to the appointment never happening. But it had to happen. And now, by the hair of Sage's chinny-chin-chin, it was going to happen.

As Sean talked about the flat tires, Sage mentally dismantled their original plan to meet at the prison, and she cobbled together various new scenarios. She presented Sean with each possible alternative, and all were rebuffed in curt, Sean Swoboda style. Except the last one. Sage offered to pick him up at his Philadelphia office. This was a major inconvenience for her because it meant burrowing through traffic from the South Street advertising and branding agency where she worked to the west Philly suburbs where she and Jadia lived with Oma.

There she would grab Jadia—that is, Jadia and the suitcases—and reverse the route through even thicker traffic eastward to Market Street on the front end. Then they'd make the one-hour trek to the new minimum-security prison—or, Sage thought, halfway house, jailhouse boutique hotel, recreation spot, or whatever New Age name the Feds wanted to give it—between Lancaster and Nottingham. On the return trip, Sage would chauffeur Sean back to Market Street. Afterward, she and Jadia would have to punch it to Philadelphia International Airport to catch a Caribbean flight.

Sage let out a long, airy sigh and stared absently at a notepad. Sean still had her on hold. Fine. She'd hold as long as he didn't delay her vacation. Her three-inch heels beat out a rhythm on the carpeted floor as Sean murmured with someone on his end. Then she propped an elbow the desk and pinched the bridge of her nose. Their words were garbled, but Sage was sure the other party was a woman. During the discourse, the woman had moved very close to Sean. Sage's eyebrows rose. The woman's voice was louder now but not very clear. Sage forced herself not to eavesdrop, and she directed her thoughts to the action items growing like white mold on the green computer screen.

CHAPTER 3

Ayde Carona eased the Explorer into a riot of Manhattan traffic in a well-practiced weave. Vehicles clogged the Lincoln Tunnel in a nudging roll and at length squeezed from it like toothpaste from a tube. The tunnel opened to Southbound I-95, an early morning sun, and a gust of muggy, August air.

From an open window Sean drew it in, shifted in the passenger seat, and thought of his upcoming vacation with Lori. They'd planned to spend it relaxing in their palatial New Hope home, which had been built to accommodate a shorter commute to Philadelphia while Sean built up his clientele. Thanks to the help of marketing and advertising expertise, the Philadelphia business mushroomed, almost immediately increasing the firm's gross profits by 18 percent. The New Hope home quickly transitioned into a mainstay, while the beloved Central Park West location gradually took a backseat. Now, revenue from Sean's venture accounted for more than 25 percent of the firm's total profits.

As the Philadelphia skyline rolled into view, Sean heard Ayde say, "I want to work in the Philly office," as she snaked the Explorer around an exit ramp pothole as they merged onto Market Street.

Sean looked her. He didn't want to have this conversation. His team was already in place, and he wasn't remotely interested in another harangue from the firm's bean counters about his existing headcount surplus.

He checked his watch: 8:46. "It's not going to happen," he said.

Ayde remained silent for a while as if contemplating the cramped streets. "I …" She paused, giving him a sideways glance. "I want to be a part of whatever it is you're doing here."

Sean tossed a steely glare at her. "The only thing I'm *doing* here is making a bigger footprint for the firm."

"Look. All I'm trying to say is you're a remarkable leader. You've got this great gig going, and I would like to be a part of it. See it through to the end, you know?" She searched his face and found a silent, flexing jaw.

"I have a proven track record," she continued. "My win ratio—"

"I know how good you are," he broke in, his voice firm. "I don't need a win ratio. I need grunt work. You're too talented and frankly too expensive for that."

As Ayde Carona slowed the vehicle to a stop at a light, Sean looked out the passenger window at corporate-dressed pedestrians holding attachés and disposable paper cups.

"I don't get it," he said, staring at discarded sheets of newspaper that were blowing around in front of prime real estate. "I'm not a partner," he said turning back to her. "You need to latch on to something big, Ayde. Philly fish are small. Fewer, too."

"And so are the steps to the top," she said. Her voice was soft, strong. The light turned green, and she accelerated further down Market Street.

A short while later, they were veering into the glint of Philadelphia offices. Exorbitant rent accompanied top floor offices that opened westward to a view of the Schuylkill River. The firm partners had given Sean a thunderous round of applause when he explained how he had negotiated prime real estate at a discount price. Their smiles had been broad, their claps clamorous and hearty. At the time, he had wondered if they were just happy he had found a place to go.

Ayde Carona pulled the car to the curb and set the gear in PARK. She met Sean's assessment with a hard stare. After a moment of silence, she turned away, pursed her lips, and drummed the steering wheel.

"Philadelphia is a temporary gig for me, Ayde." His voice held a clear edge that sliced the air, and she stopped the drumming.

"And I'm already grooming someone else to take the helm when it's ready to fly on its own. I can't trust an investment in you. By the time you shift gears and get up to speed on a Philadelphia path, I'd be heading back to the city for good, and you'd be on my heels. I won't allow it."

Ayde Carona faced him head-on in an unwavering gaze, her face pinched in silence. He checked his watch (8:57), and got out and closed the door. He leaned into the open passenger window.

"Hey. Maybe we can discuss this over dinner. A little wine and a bit of ambiance could help ease the tension between us. What do you think?"

She brightened, a smile spreading on her pretty face. "That would be nice."

"Great," he said before spinning off. Over his shoulder he yelled back, "Now remember, Lori and I are treating!"

Ayde Carona's smile faded into a stunned, open mouth.

CHAPTER 4

Sean's face remained characteristically still while something inside him smiled at the fresh memory of Ayde Carona's slackened face. She'd dropped him off in Philadelphia well over an hour ago.

He checked his watch. It was 10:14. Pre-Parole Transfer Facility superintendent Manny Cofield was late.

Sean head swiveled to his left, and he looked at his client, Sage. She stood erect, rigid with determination. At her left shoulder stood her daughter Jadia—twelve and post-traumatic quiet. The were in IR-1, the observation pod of an interview suite situated in a small, privately owned federal confinement facility, the kind recently dubbed a "boutique prison."

Swoboda and his clients looked through a dusty, two-way observation window at a feral, antsy prisoner slumped in a chair behind a pedestal table. This man had spent most of his life steeped in sexual deviance, unquenchable violence, and recidivism. No one needed court records or local and federal prison documentation to get the gist of the vile Anthony Campbell. The deep, telltale lines on the sadist's angular face spoke volumes of a wasted life—and whispered harsh echoes of Sean's own failures. Against the firm's advisement and Lori's ire, he had continued his attachment to Anthony Campbell—his bold nose, his angular face, and his rapes.

A late night in June, two months before, he'd been sitting at his desk, contemplating the County of Los Angeles District Attorney envelope trapped between his fingers, his head bent over the final offer. The corporate din of the stellar midtown Manhattan office had drifted down the firm's corridors past the impressive, hand-carved, mahogany double doors over an hour earlier.

Sean was among the few remaining stragglers on the fifty-fourth-floor office and the only one seated on Partners' Row. While exhausted associates quietly squeezed the week's last billing hours onto the firm's swollen receivables, Sean passed the time by tapping a corner of the district attorney's envelope against the leather-topped mahogany desk. Superimposed over the typed words, figures, terms, and conditions, Sean saw images of the Wirspa family: thirty-four-year-old Sage; her husband, Thomas, who was significantly older than Sage; and their twelve-year-old daughter, Jadia.

Under the muffled taps of the envelope hitting the desk, he heard the promise he'd made to the Wirspas, a promise he'd made in 1991—months after he'd first met Sage. It was a promise he had repeated every chance he got, most recently on June 13, 1994: the day Nicole Simpson and Ronald Goldman were found nearly decapitated and two weeks before Marcia Clark mailed overnight her last and final offer. A promise that eventually stood as wide as a continent between him and the chance of a lifetime. And this was all because of a pedophiliac drug dealer named Anthony Campbell.

Sean felt renewed fury surge inside him just as it did each time he thought about what Anthony Campbell had done to Jadia. He had kidnapped, raped, and held her hostage across state lines. The trailer Campbell had hidden Jadia in was stocked with enough child pornography and cocaine to keep him incarcerated for life, yet Anthony Campbell had been granted some sort of furlough and was within striking distance of a second parole. Sean doubted the prisoner was even wearing the federally required Central Inmate Monitoring System that should have been cuffed to his ankle.

Sean compartmentalized the rage and moved on. He found himself back in the firm's New York office that late night in late June, mentally tracing the signature inked on Marcia Clark's final offer. The tantalizing opportunity to become a part of the O. J. Simpson prosecution team literally laid in his hands in the form of an eight-by-eleven, off-white sheet of paper. Lady Justice, blindfolded and crowned with scales of justice, stared at him from her post on the County of Los Angeles District Attorney seal. Sean knew then what he knew now. It was an offer he had to refuse, and a refusal without forgiveness—least of all from his wife.

"Nail the bastard," she'd said when she learned about the offer. "Nail each and every last one of his wife-beating, murderous chromosomes." The gleam of power and fame lay ever at the ready in her light blue eyes.

Lori's voice still rang with fisted empathy in Sean's ears for two children who had lost their mother, parents who had lost their daughter, and a sister who had lost what seemed to have been her best friend. An attorney of the non-practicing variety, Lori saw no conflict between harboring an ardent belief in O. J.'s guilt and desiring gain from his celebrity. Membership on the O. J. Simpson prosecution team meant Sean could sport his DNA expertise like a litigation Olympian.

Sean blinked away his reflections, reeled his thoughts back the dusty prison system room, and, thumbing his ring, drew the scene in the window into clear view just as Anthony Campbell jammed a finger into his nose, dug around, and flicked off the harvest. Sean winced as he turned to his watch in disgust. The face showed 10:17.

Manny Cofield had yet to present his corpulent body to Interview Room 1. Sean dug his hands deep into his pockets, rocked on his heels, and cased the room as the pounding in his temples signaled that something was off-kilter. The meeting place had originally been a maximum-security facility, but a number of recent changes had relocated it to a private minimum-security facility. Sean drew in stale air, thinking that the underground maze he, Sage, and Jadia had traipsed through had obviously led them to a different building from where they'd started. He leveled his view back to the mirror. Everything about the case stank to a micro level, and it was becoming more and more rancid by the minute.

Sean massaged his temples. Maybe he and Sage both had made a mistake in choosing to stick to Anthony Campbell's case. Since the federal judge had not received Sage's protest letter, Manny Cofield was her last chance. *Their* last chance. As the superintendent, Cofield had the power to reconsider and revoke Anthony Campbell's parole. Therefore, if Manny Cofield didn't show up, the choice Sage and Sean had made to pursue Anthony Campbell over anything else, would be all for naught. Sage would have circumvented her family's strong objections in vain, and Sean would have squelched the opportunity to prosecute Nicole Brown Simpson's alleged killer for nada. He leveled a thoughtful gaze on his client.

CHAPTER 5

Trying to ignore the pain stabbing her pinking toe, Sage scanned the filthy interview room, her mouth filling with the taste of dirty air. A grimy cement floor underscored the occasion's harshness, as did her attorney's judging eyes. She swiveled her head away from him and was assailed with air reeking of dirty mops, moldy dust motes, and years of bad breath and body order. Her cerulean blue eyes darted from one filthy corner of the room to another. She didn't know what she had expected, but this wasn't it. She focused on the room behind the mirror where Anthony Campbell sat.

"Do you have a mobile phone?" Sean asked.

"I'm sorry?" She leaned closer to Sean, keeping her gaze fixed on Anthony Campbell.

Sean tilted his head downward to her ear. "I said, did you bring a cellular phone?"

"Who do you think I am? Rockefeller?" She glided her eyes back to Anthony Campbell and, in the same jocular vein, added, "That would be you bringing a phone, *Rockefeller*, not me."

"Just wanted to follow up on a hunch," he said, keeping his usual aloof composure intact.

Sage turned to face Sean. "Hunch?"

"Yes. I think we're at the wrong place."

Sage gestured with her head to the interview room. "If Anthony Campbell's here, this is the right place."

Sean gave the room another wary scan. "Good point," he said.

"Anyway, where's your cellular phone?" she asked. "I thought you were the first human to own one."

"The battery was dead this morning, and I couldn't find the charger before I left the house. My wife will find the darn thing and have the phone up and running by the time I get back to Philly."

A small smile crept onto Sage's face. "Sounds like she takes good care of you," she said.

"That she does," Sean uttered under his breath as Manny Cofield's absence tugged his attention.

Sean glimpsed his watch again and pivoted away from the mirror to survey the attaché he'd left open on a table that stood a few paces from the observation window. There were no chairs in the room. It was one of many odd things about the place, like the lackadaisical show of guards at the door and the inarticulate, malodorous janitor who'd given them directions. They'd traveled down two flights of aluminum, grated stair treads and across buff-slick white tile, through countless bends of narrow corridors. The sound of his hand-stitched Italian shoes and Sage's stilettos had echoed like a tribal war call. Then there was the dust-choked interview room filled with the noxious remains of the dourest penal conditions.

Under a muted yellow glow emitting from dirty ceiling lights, Sean looked over his shoulder at his client.

Sage pried her face from the window and tilted it toward Jadia's profile. "Jadia," she said.

Silence.

"Jadia."

A pair of blank blue eyes lethargically turned to Sage. Just then, the blue metal door inside the interview room swung open. Sean, Sage, and Jadia watched as two men, dressed in suits that rivaled Sean's corporate attire, filed into the interview room. Sean walked toward the window and took his place at Sage's side.

Keeping her eye on the men in the window, she said, "Who do you think they are?"

"A couple of men wearing Gucci," he said.

Her brow creased as she said, "Right, Rockefeller." She smiled, combed a restless hand through her short, jet-black ringlets, and then rubbed her daughter's shoulder.

"I don't understand why child molesters and rapists are eligible for halfway houses anyway."

"We may not like it, Sage, but the transfer was well within the limits of the law for prerelease." Sean lifted his eyes to scan the ceiling and walls. "You know …" He squinted as he peered through the two-way mirror. "This is kind of odd for an interview room."

"I noticed that," Sage said. "The entire setup is strange, just like when I protested Anthony Campbell's application for pro—" Sage paused, faced Sean, and then continued, "I forgot to tell you that I called the judge's office yesterday about the letter requesting a review of the dropped charges."

"You called the judge?"

"Yes I did, and the judge's office is holding to their claim that they never received it." Sage swiveled on her heels to face Sean head-on. She leaned a palm on the sill of the two-way mirror. "Thomas and I sent the letter the same day you told us about the Victim Services Office calling with notification of Anthony Campbell's application for early release. I knew we should have sent it certified."

Her naturally arched brows furrowed atop a petite nose as she briefly glided away in thought. She let out a labored breath before looking back at Sean and saying, "First you received the probation notification late.

Now this." She paused. "Were you able to trace the letter Thomas and I sent to the jud—"

Muted sounds of commotion and gruff voices could be heard from the windowed room, silencing Sage. She followed Sean's slitted gaze into the mirror. A man with raging, bulbous eyes and wearing a midnight blue suit almost identical to the two men flanking Anthony Campbell, had walked into the room behind the glass. The Gucci duo had given Sean pause, but not as much as Manny Cofield. Bordering tall, bordering bald, and definitely wide and menacing, he waved a nearly new suede Timberland in the prisoner's face.

A scratchy, tinny voice belying his wide girth howled, "Camp, does this boot belong to you?"

Sage leaned toward Sean and whispered, "Who is he?"

"That's Manny Cofield."

"The superintendent?"

Sean squinted at Manny Cofield's suit. *Gucci must be Cofield's mandated team uniform,* Sean thought as he absently answered, "Yes."

Manny Cofield was addressing the prisoner. "I'm not going to ask you again, Camp. Is this Timberland yours?"

Anthony Campbell said nothing.

Cofield thwacked Campbell's face with the sole of the Timberland, shouting, "Answer me!"

Campbell righted his face. A red blotch, shaped in a boot print, marked his left cheek. He studied Manny Cofield with the ease of person who did not have a care in the world. His gaze flicked to the boot then back to the wide man leaning over him.

"It's not my boot, Manny, but why don't we ram it up your ass and see if it fits. This way we'll know for sure," Anthony Campbell whispered with a cocked smile. The two guards closed in.

"Oh, I think it fits all right," Manny said. He took out a hunting knife and finished a tear he'd apparently already started inside the boot. He worked feverishly, ripping the sole and shaking it until small pouches of cocaine tumbled out and dropped on the table..

Campbell smiled and said, "How sweet of you to offer. I hope the shit is good."

"I'm sure you've already helped yourself." He dropped the dismantled Timberland on the table.

Campbell's milky eyes fell to the superintendent's crotch and held it in a lascivious grip. Then he sucked a corner of his bottom lip and brought his gaze to Manny Cofield's face.

"If I've helped myself to anything, it wasn't your stash. And that"—he tilted his chin toward the mutilated boot—"is not my boot."

Cofield closed the knife and returned it to the pant pocket. "It's not yours, huh?"

"No," Campbell persisted. His gaze slid to the mirror. Sage's heart jumped. She glanced at Jadia and unconsciously grabbed her daughter's hand. The twelve-year-old remained unmoved by her rapist's unflinching glare.

Sage nudged her right shoulder closer to Sean as she whispered, "Do you think he can see us?"

"He's just avoiding eye contact with Cofield." Sean stayed glued to the scene behind the mirror, but he watched with assessing eyes as Sage stepped closer to it.

"What is it?" He stepped closer to her.

"This mirror," she whispered. "It isn't right."

Sean eyed the mirror. The last time he'd seen a standard eighteen-inch thick, two-way security mirror was during law school. He'd be damned if this mirror wasn't the real thing.

"Don't worry," he said, running his fingertips along the sill. "This is bona fide, Sage." He stepped back, gently pulling her by the hand until she was between him and Jadia again.

Sage's head moved in a slow shake, sure the mirror was only a couple of inches if that. And she was sure of something else too. "He's looking right at m—"

Commotion exploded from the other side of the glass, snatching her words. She looked inside the room just in time to see the two men lift the table and send it, the drugs, and a right-foot Timberland soaring across the room. Campbell was thrown into the wall and fell in a to-and-fro rock on the floor. Sage followed the guards' eyes to Anthony Campbell's feet. The right one was bare, the left clad with a new-looking Timberland.

"You tried to be a smart-ass by taking off both your shoes and leaving this one on the transport bus so one of your buddies could pick it up later. It's your shoe, Camp. Or should I call you Cinde-fuckin'-rella?"

Anthony Campbell shrugged.

Sean kept his eyes fixed on the scene beyond the mirror as he cocked his head toward Sage and murmured into her ear, "Campbell can kiss any chance he had of parole good-bye. We're getting out of here."

Sage glared at Sean. "I'm not going anywhere. Not until I know for cer—"

Manny Cofield's roar reverberated through the glass. "Tell me who's holding the rest of my drugs, or I'll plant all the kilos on you."

Campbell jumped to his feet. "Don't go there, Manny." His head swayed and snapped like a rooster in Manny's face. "I'm up for release, so stop riding my dick."

Cofield nodded to his men. One held Anthony Campbell while the first tied the man's wrists to the chair. He leaned over Campbell. "Tell me where the rest of my stash is."

"Fuck. You." Spit flew from Campbell's mouth with each word.

Sage cupped Jadia's shoulder and drew her closer, unwavering eyes glued on the window. Then she leaned to the right toward Sean.

"His stash?" she whispered. "What does he mean by 'my stash'?"

Silence.

Sage repeated the question, then threw her daughter's profile a concerned frown. After a beat, she tossed her gaze over a shoulder just in time to see Sean snapping the attaché hasps. In the three heel clicks it took for Sage to close the distance, Sean had slid the attaché off the table and spun around to meet her blazing eyes.

"What are you doing, Swoboda?"

"Anthony Campbell blew any chances he had for parole. We're leaving."

"We're not leaving until I know for sure."

"You don't have a say."

"Uhm—I think I do. I'm driving, remember?"

Sean pivoted to face her.

"It couldn't be clearer, Sage. Anthony Campbell is headed back to maximum security."

Muted sounds of violent thuds and repressed grunts resonated from the interview room.

Sean Swoboda's intelligent gray eyes followed his client as she stared intently through the two-way mirror at the pummeling taking place inside the interview room. With white-knuckled fingers curled tightly around the leather-covered handle of his attaché, he trailed Sage's steps and reluctantly peered through the mirrored glass.

Superintendent Manny Cofield wiped drool from the corner of his mouth and smeared the blood across his Gucci pant leg. Three heaving breaths later, he pulled his wide frame upright, giving an unobstructed view of his prisoner—a thoroughly brutalized Anthony Campbell. One of Campbell's brown eyes was a narrow slit surrounded by purple, wrinkled skin; there were rising welts around the less damaged eye. Various hues of pink and red colored his cheeks. His engorged tongue was swelling like a blowfish wedged between two bloated lips.

Every warped bit of Anthony Campbell's face was the result of the punch-happy work of the superintendent's meaty fists. The prisoner sat as if content with being tethered to a chair, bound by a length of thick, biting rope. With his open eye resting easily on Manny Cofield, he twitched puffy lips into a defiant, lopsided smile.

Outside the interview room, the attorney had seen enough. He leaned into his client's space until his breath blended with hers. A black, bouncy lock swung back from her temple with each of his enunciations.

"Sage, I am leaving with or without you, and I'm taking Jadia with me."

Sage, five feet four inches with skin tanned golden from a summer of Philadelphia sun, shifted away from the scene in the window and swept across Sean's patrician face. At length, she shifted left and studied her vacuous daughter, who was a five-foot-two-inch facsimile of her mother—ravened haired with Mediterranean blue eyes.

Sage followed the tween's disinterested gaze back to the double mirror. A thorny vine spiraled up her back. Maybe the psychologists were wrong about the sight of Anthony Campbell being a good thing for Jadia. Their well-presented philosophy of facing fears by returning to their source had never gained traction with anyone but Sean Swoboda and herself. At the moment, the idea was losing ground fast. Defeated dark blue eyes turned back to Sean. She swallowed, nervously clutched the large purse draped over her shoulder, and nodded.

"You're right. We should leave."

On the other side of the window, Anthony Campbell snorted. "So you're going to cut me?"

Sean's and Sage's heads both snapped to the mirror. The hunting knife was rolling in Manny Cofield's hand.

Tireless, chemically-induced bravado barreled through Anthony Campbell's battered mouth. "It's okay with me as long as you know that I cut back—and I cut deep."

Manny Cofield squinted at the prisoner's words. Cofield's two henchmen, who had receded deeper into the interview room and stilled when the knife was introduced, were now exchanging questioning looks. The superintendent straddled Anthony Campbell's lap, grabbed his jaw, yanked his oblong head to attention, and then kissed his prisoner's bloody lips with a lover's intensity before licking his own mouth clean. The hunting knife began to roll in his hand again.

"Where are the drugs, Campbell?" Cofield asked with unsettling calm.

Anthony Campbell didn't answer.

The superintendent slipped the knife under Campbell's front teeth, and dug into the gum. A beige tooth flew across the room, a mangled root tailing behind it. One of the suited men jumped back from the spray of blood. The other shifted his weight from one foot to another, grimacing.

Anthony Campbell's drugged body didn't flinch. An eye, the one not swollen shut, beamed at Manny Cofield. He turned his face aside and spat. Heavy with phlegm, the blood landed on the arm of the chair before oozing to the floor and pooling in the welt of Cofield's quarter-brogue shoe.

Manny Cofield's eyes glided from the red staining his shoe to the trepidation reflected on the faces of his underlings. The two tough guys had retreated until their broad backs were against the far wall.

"What?" Cofield blurted out, spittle hurling from his curled lips. "You just now woke up and realized you've been sleeping in shit?"

The suits proffered looks as blank as Jadia's.

"Get out!" Cofield blared, tossing his chin to the right to indicate the only exit in the bloodied room. "Lock the door and keep watch outside."

The blue door slammed shut behind the men, leaving the superintendent alone with his knife and his prisoner. Corded veins crossed Manny Cofield's scrunched forehead as, with grunts and sweat, he dragged the chair and its cargo backward, and pushed it flush against the blue door, blocking it.

As Cofield straddled Anthony Campbell's lap, Sean and Sage scrambled awkwardly to move their shock-heavy feet from the insanity in the window. Sean managed to gain purchase first, rounding his client and heading straight for Jadia.

"I let you in, Camp," Cofield's voice ranted from the window. "You betrayed me."

The superintendent went to work on Campbell's mouth again, then stood upright, a blood-doused hand curled into a fist around the dripping hunting knife. He spread a sinister, drooling smile at Campbell's widening gap. Beneath the surface of Jadia's hollow-eyed stare, the flicker of a grimace danced on her face. In that very quick second, Sean made his way to the tween and placed a gentle palm on her chin. He turned her gaze away from the window and smiled at her expressionless face. Then, with quiet steps, he led her to the exit and protectively stationed her between himself and the door. With one hand on the knob and the other gripping the attaché, he pivoted back to find Sage inexorably drawn to the mirror.

What Sage saw and what Sean couldn't see was that one of Anthony Campbell's arms was free. In that impossible few seconds, the prisoner snatched the knife from the surprised superintendent's slippery hand and stabbed him repeatedly in the chest. The superintendent stood as if he'd heard someone call his name. He stepped back once, twice.

Wobbling, Cofield looked down at Anthony Campbell, grabbed the handle of the knife protruding from his chest, and stumbled backward. He coughed, gagged, and side-waddled until his backside was pressed against the glass. He remained motionless there a long second, then slid down the window like sluicing rain until he was hidden from view.

Sean yelled to Sage from the opened door. She didn't move.

Anthony Campbell stood and looked straight into the mirror, milky eyes bulging with rage. He spotted Sage. A sanguine smear spread across his face. After one hair-raising second, Sage realized it was a bloody smile.

Anthony Campbell stepped to the mirror and peered out between cupped hands. A bloated tongue darted out and licked the mirror in a long, lascivious, bloody stroke, leaving a red streak in its wake.

Revulsion crawled up Sage's spine and gathered at the nape of her neck.

Sean grabbed Jadia's hand and quickly pulled her to the other side of the opened door. Jadia's chest was rising and falling fitfully. Sean dipped his eyes to hers and whispered, "It's going to be okay. Stay here. I'll be right back." He waited a beat to catch her flitting eyes, held them a split second, and then darted through the jamb to Sage.

"Sage! Let's go! Now!" Sean bellowed into her ear.

Anthony Campbell stomped to the chair, grabbed it, and dragged it to the back of the interview room.

Sage rammed her rear into Sean's groin, butting him backward toward the doorjamb. He grabbed her by the waist, using her momentum to drag her with him. In a countermove, Sage dug her heels into the floor, throwing her body into a power spin that morphed the world into a slow-motion whirl. Everything happened simultaneously.

With a gurgled grunt, Anthony Campbell hoisted the chair over his head. Sage spun, punched the air out of Sean with a two-fisted uppercut to the gut, and pushed him out the door. As he crash-landed into Jadia, Sage slammed the door, and pulled a second-generation 9mm Glock 17 from her large purse— the purse that, thanks to Sean Swoboda's carte blanche access to the prison, had been poorly searched by prison guards.

Anthony Campbell catapulted himself kamikaze style through the window. Mirrored glass shot out in a starburst. With ear-piercing clangs, the glass shattered on the ground, breaking into smaller shards and spreading like liquid mercury across the grimy floor.

The two henchmen charged through the blue door into the interview room and froze, their stunned faces trying to make sense of the gruesome scene.

Anthony Campbell crept toward Sage. A booted left foot crunched against sharp, jagged glass, while merciless shards sliced through the calloused skin of his bare right foot. Milky, slitted eyes locked on Sage.

He charged.

"Shoot him!" The crumpled superintendent bellowed the slurred order to his henchmen from the other side of the broken window. "Shoot him! Shoot him!"

Cursing her aching pinky toe, Sage leveled the gun with two hands curled sweetly around the Hogue rubber grip. Sage had waited four years for this moment. She planted her feet shoulder-width apart, cupped the grip with both hands, slightly bent her elbows and knees to catch the recoil, and released the safety. Then Sage Wirspa nailed a copper tipped bullet to the center of Anthony Campbell's charging forehead.

Campbell was still smacking at the hole in his forehead when Sage crouched to pick up the shell casing. She heard a thump against the crunch of glass and looked across the floor. Anthony Campbell was down. She clutched her purse and reared her head to scream out four years of pent-up fury. The scream was stifled by Sean's fast-moving hand slapped over her mouth. He hoisted her upright and, without any further assistance, she darted out the door behind him.

Shots rang out from the room after the door slammed shut. Someone apparently wanted to make sure Anthony Campbell was dead.

CHAPTER 6

Sage, Sean, and Jadia's feet pounded on the buffed, slick basement tile floors. Sean led the way through a labyrinth of long, white-walled corridors, with Jadia's sandals pounding right behind. Sage brought up the rear—she was struggling to zip her shoulder bag as they ran. Then she clutched the pouch of the purse under her arm, steadying the still-hot Glock with hard pressure against her ribs.

Endless sequences of single doors lined the sterile hallways in the underground maze. The three hurried down interminable stretches, turning this way and that at intersections as Sean's memory guided their retreat to where they had entered. They rounded a corner, momentum throwing them into the outside of the turn.

Sean slammed against unforgiving steel double doors and grunted as he felt the stab of thick chains that had been looped through the door handles. The chains, like those used for ship anchors, rattled and dug into Sean's gut again as Jadia crashed against his back. Before he could peel his face from the white door, Sage skidded on the tips of pumps with outstretched hands, ramming into her daughter and her attorney before rolling off Jadia into a half-fall. Desperate hands grabbed Sean's as he helped her straighten up. In the same move, he checked on Jadia and found the young girl's eyes staring at the secure chains.

Sean tried the door, the heft of the chains bringing his efforts to a rattling, abrupt halt. With unspoken synergy, the three of them began to step backward until Sean spun all of them into a forward sprint, retracing their steps until they came to the closest intersecting corridors and then heading to the right. While regrouping and changing course, Sage kicked off her heels, slinging them ahead, across the slippery floor with her feet like a skeet trap shooter, then picking them up with her free hand while in chase. She padded the rest of the run in bare, runner's feet, a bruised baby toe aching all the way.

While the wrong turn had completely disoriented Sage, Sean needed very little time to regroup after the wrong turn. He led the entire way through the tangle of cold, lifeless corridors until they reached an exit sign.

Sean's heaving torso blocked the door. "Wait." His shoulder heaved as he looked at Sage and said, "Give me your car key."

"What?" she gasped out in confusion. Her rump rested on the wall as she leaned over and propped her elbows on bent knees. Breathing heavily, Jadia propped her own forearms on the wall and buried her forehead in them. Sage gave her the girl a motherly once-over, then twisted her own head up to Sean.

"Put on your shoes," he said.

She followed his eyes to her feet. "What?" Red-painted, bare toenails looked up at her. "Oh, yes. You're right." Sage stuffed a swollen, angry foot into a shoe. She was forcing the other foot into the second shoe when Sean held out his hand.

"What?" she asked, peering up from her hunched-over position as she poked the last bit of her heel into the shoe.

"Your car key. Give it to me."

"I'm lost." She stood upright, an unreasonable sense of possession welling in her. Sage had never shared the Bimmer, pop culture's moniker for a BMW. "Why am I giving you the key?"

"It might be best for you to keep Jadia company in the backseat."

Still breathless, Sage thought about it and, unable to come up with an argument that didn't make her seem petty, she reluctantly unzipped her purse and dug deep into it. As her fingers searched, Sean leaned into her.

"Besides," he said. "You have a gun." He thrust the words into her face like gritty slaps. As Sage's fingers curled around the key and pulled it from her purse, she countered with, "And it's a good thing, too, because the mirror was not as bona fide as you claimed."

Sean worked tight lips against his teeth.

Sage stood up and thrust the car key into his gut. He pulled the key from her resistant fingers.

"Do you have more tissue?" he asked, his tone biting.

Sage looked up and met titanium. "Sure," she said, pinching off the word. Her hand plunged into the purse again, rummaging until she felt a soft wad.

"They're unused," she said, shoving the stash into his hand. "Just bundled."

"No surprise," he said with enough acid to clean a battery. "Considering everything else you pack in there."

He cut off her attempt to respond by addressing both her and Jadia. "Dab the sweat from your foreheads and necks and regulate your breathing *asap*."

He waved away her second attempt for a comeback, taking a few of the tissues. "It might take them a while to realize someone was in the room." Dabbing his sweat-beaded forehead, he looked at Sage, steel shielding his eyes again. "Sage, they definitely know someone else was in the room."

After a beat, he stepped past Sage and lifted Jadia's chin with his forefinger. "Are you okay?" Jadia fell into his embrace. He squeezed her comfortingly, then pulled back. "Everything will be all right," he said, dipping into her gaze. "I'm going to get us out of here."

Addressing both Sage and Jadia, he ran a hand over his head and said, "We have to walk out as casually as possible. We'll pass the common area and head to the guard gate. Pace yourselves. Every once in a while glance at the wall art or the furniture—anything so you don't look anxious. Got it?"

"Yes," Sage answered for both herself and her daughter, giving Jadia's hand a squeeze.

Strolling through the common area, returning the visitor badges, and finally exiting went virtually unnoticed. Bystanders stood in corners, paced around them, and lurked in solitude, but no one paid attention to them. Guards were distracted by conversations as they passed the visitors' entrance. They headed straight for Sage's '92 black 5-Series Bimmer that was parked near the main gate.

Sean corralled Jadia and Sage into the scorching backseat, and then scrambled around to the driver's seat. He jerked the car into gear, eased forward, and then stomped on the accelerator, the growling engine masking the clicking sounds of Sage securing Jadia's seat belt. From behind the empty front passenger seat, she stared madly at Sean's flexing jawline and tightly clamped lips. Rubber burned against the sweltering tarmac, and the tires squealed in the thick August air.

With darting eyes policing the windshield, Sage squeezed Jadia's hand. As her heart tried to punch through her chest, she spun around to look right and left, left and right out the back window. She gave Sean a quick glance before her brief review of Jadia. The only signs of duress on the youth's lean body were the steep rise and fall of her developing breasts and the grip of her long fingers on Sean's headrest in front of her.

Tires spun and screeched, and rubber burned once again against the black tarmac. The car sped across rows of empty parking spaces and careened onto the remote two-lane highway that had led them there. In the Bimmer's turbulent motion Sage's feet involuntarily flew from the footwell and swung through the hot air. The first ping of metal piercing metal sounded as shots fired out in the distance behind them.

"Get down!" Sean yelled. He hunkered down and inclined his head as far as he could without losing sight of the fast-approaching road. Large knuckles curled tightly over the steering wheel as he jerked it from left to right and right to left in violent but controlled movements, careening the vehicle out of the way of flying bullets.

Swaying with the car's erratic swerves, Sage reached for Jadia's seat belt, barely touched it, lost her grasp in the car's swaying momentum, and tried again. On the fourth attempt, she finally unfastened the seat belt and pulled her daughter's head into her lap as she hovered over her like a protective cloak. A single shrill peal of rubber sounded as a shot grazed the driver's side door. Sage braced a palm on the back of the front passenger seat, trying to steady herself and Jadia as the car jerked violently from side to side.

A bullet sideswiped the passenger side, and Sage threw herself, head low, against the backseat and used her body to shield Jadia. As Sean serpentined the Bimmer back and forth, Sage stiffly pressed a shoulder into the backseat, slowly raised her head to the top curve of seat, held her breath, and then dared to steal a look through the rear window. A guard was running onto the open road to join two suited men, who were firing their weapons. He held a gun in his hand and a mobile phone to his lips. The suits stopped their fire, scurried back to the parking lot, and dispersed into separate cars.

Sean spun off and heard the squeal of the Bimmer's tires. He shot a frenzied look into the rearview mirror before glancing at the dashboard. Sage followed Sean's eyes to the road ahead just as more shots were fired. They both ducked their heads. Before spinning around to check on Jadia, Sage checked the speedometer—it read 97 mph.

The urge to jump into the front seat and jam her foot over Sean's for more horsepower was a force she wasn't sure she'd be able to resist for long. Another bullet sounded in the rear. Sean stomped the pedal to the floorboard, throwing Sage backward.

Sage pushed Jadia to the floor. "We need to stay low," she yelled over the roaring engine before stretching herself flat against the backseat with her head craning toward Sean. "Are you going to drive this baby, or what?" she barked at him through the space between the front seats.

"What?" Sean shouted back with his head angled backward toward her.

"Put the pedal to the metal, Sean! The Bimmer can handle it!"

"What are you talking about?"

"Nothing," Sage shouted. "Just drive!" She fell against the backseat, muttering, "I should have driven."

From the rearview mirror, the attorney shot an aggravated glance at her. Ignoring him, she spun up to look out the back window.

The engine revved, pushing them northwest toward PA-472 N/W. Sage studied the road behind them. Her hand absently reached down and stroked Jadia's long, black hair. She recalled that they had not signed a visitors' log. After Sean flashed ID and a letter, guards at the gate and in the lobby told them they'd be free to leave whenever they were ready. *Which should have been long before things got out of hand,* she mused guiltily as she eyed Jadia. Slowly she brought her mind back to the fact that their visit to the prison had gone exactly as Sean had promised it would go. He'd arranged for it primarily for Jadia's sake. No drama. Nothing that could trigger a meltdown before Jadia laid eyes on Anthony Campbell.

After only five minutes—minutes that felt like a lifetime—the danger of bullets joining them in the backseat had passed. Sage kissed the top of Jadia's head and helped her up from the floor. As Jadia sat up, Sage scooted to the middle of the seat and craned her neck around Sean's massive shoulder to see the dashboard. Sean had coasted back to the speed limit. *The freakin' speed limit!*

Reclining in the seat, Sage grudgingly secured seat buckles for Jadia and herself. Jadia pressed her head back against the seat with contemplative eyes. Sage's hands reach out and stroked her daughter's hair as she tried to block the sounds blaring in her own head. And, oh God, the smells— sweet metallic blood and urine-tainted death. Glass breaking. Bullets. Soles of shoes clattering like hooves in the corridor. Shoes.

Shoes!

Sage remembered the pair of flats she had stashed under the seat. The flats she had planned to wear to the airport. The same flats she was now slipping on sore, battered feet. She sat back in the seat and resumed holding Jadia's hand, resumed her thoughts. Anthony Campbell's prison life had been a far cry from the experience of most convicted pedophiles. Clearly Manny Cofield had been Campbell's benefactor. Sage recalled the Victim Services Office or VSO informing her of Anthony Campbell's conditional approval for a community correction program and his imminent transfer from Frackville, a maximum-security state institution, to a new minimum-security recreation spot between Lancaster and Nottingham. A halfway house of sorts, the VSO rep had called it.

"Halfway to what?" Sage remembered asking the representative on the other end of the phone. "Another rape?"

Sage scanned her daughter's face. Twelve-year-old eyes were plastered on the black ticker tape rolling under them. Sean swerved left on PA-472 W.

"I don't see anyone," Sage announced, although the quiet on the quickly passing barren road was not enough to convince her that they were no longer being pursued. She whipped her head to face forward again and ran a hand through silky, loose curls.

Sweat beaded atop Sean's nose and head.

"Maybe they ran out of time," he said. He looked intensely at her from the rearview mirror.

Sage connected with his eyes, saying nothing.

"Fortunately we were able to get a head start," Sean continued. "They would have been forced to take us out on the highway. I don't think Cofield wants to risk anyone else witnessing his atrocities."

Sage nodded and spun around to the back window again. She studied Jadia until her image blurred, wondering if Manny Cofield survived.

Ten miles of road spanned the distance between them and the minimum-security facility. Sage fought against the seat belt to see if anyone was following. The rear window framed a picturesque view of backwoods Pennsylvania with a ribbon of road undulating in the middle as if blown by the wind. All signs of a chase were gone.

The Bimmer rolled through the small town of Quarryville where route 472 was called Lime Street. At a two-way stop, Sean turned left on 372, and according to the sign, Buck was four miles, Lancaster fifteen.

They hugged the right side of 372, passing flatlands and farms and long stretches of nothing. Gas for a chase hadn't been Sage's plan, but she was glad she'd gassed up the night before. Plan A had been to get herself in front of Manny Cofield for a stop-release, get Jadia in front of Anthony Campbell for a healing, and then get both of them away for a tropical vacation.

Plan A-1, the plan she had not shared with anyone, was to kill Anthony Campbell if release seemed imminent, and *then* head for the tropics. But she had never been sure she could carry out the "dash one" part. Not until she saw Anthony Campbell peer out the two-way mirror and lick it. It was the pivotal point. A tipping point. A breaking point. Forgiving Anthony Campbell was one thing. Letting him live to ruin another girl, another mother, another family was quite another. Sage Wirspa was incapable of doing either.

The Susquehanna River ran like a crack through monotonous, flat farmlands. Cedars, hemlocks, and white ash flanked the shoulders like green piping along a murky seam. Everyone in the car welcomed the Norman Wood bridge and the ripples underneath it. When Jadia powered down the window to improve her view, they all sipped freedom and fresh air like drinking champagne.

CHAPTER 7

"Where are we going?"
"I don't know," Sean answered in frustration. "I'm just driving."

And that he did. Zigzagging through the southern section of the Pennsylvania state line, Sean tried to clear his mind and map a way out of the situation he had driven his passengers to a few hours earlier. After twenty minutes on Route 74, he swung left and stayed on Route 182 W for less than four miles, then veered to Croll School Road for half a mile, trying to stay as far away as possible from the federal prison system—*any* prison system. It went on like this for a long time as they moved with purpose but without destination.

The day was beset with challenges, with Sage Wirspa topping the list. After driving for another hour, Sean lifted his eyes to the rearview mirror again. The nook between the window and seat cradled Jadia's lolling head.

"Is she asleep or just resting?" he asked, keeping his voice as low as possible over the purring engine. Sage scooted to the edge of the seat.

"She's asleep," she whispered.

"The pros are that we didn't sign in when we entered, and by the time those goons came out with guns, we were too far away for them to read your license plate."

"But Manny Cofield was expecting us."

Sean waited a beat before he said, "I wonder." He clicked the blinker lever and veered around a slow-moving truck. "Cofield was antagonistic about meeting with us. Maybe he canceled and something snagged the communication. Stranger things have happened—like your letter never reaching the judge."

"But," she whispered, draping an arm over the headrest, "Anthony Campbell saw me."

"Campbell may have sensed someone was on the other side of the mirror, but clearly Manny Cofield did not."

Jadia stirred. Sage paused a few beats, looking out the window. Then she whispered, "Anthony Campbell did not sense me. He *saw* me. Sean, we both know that mirror was not standard issue. Cofield was angled away from us most of the time, and his men kept watch on their prisoner. Campbell was the only one who had the opportunity to pay attention to the mirror."

Sean knew Sage was right. The mirror fell apart like a pair of cheap eyeglasses. "Even so," he said. "The observation pod was darker than the interview room. Campbell shouldn't have seen anything."

"But he did. And if he saw me, he saw Jadia."

"If he was the only one who saw you, what difference does it make now? Anthony Campbell is dead."

Jadia stirred again, then abruptly sat up. Sage cast an accusing look in the rearview mirror.

They stopped at a Sunoco in Hanover where cash was used to pay for gas. Cash also covered their lunch at Hanover's Dutch Country Restaurant, chosen by Sage to honor her strong Dutch heritage and the now defunct St. Maarten vacation. Where they ate did not matter to Sean. What he was thinking as he opened the door was that a bullet-riddled vehicle was bound to attract undesired attention. The car would have to be ditched soon. He hoped Sage wouldn't greet the news by slinging lead, and he decided to delay telling her until later.

Under cover of the Dutch Country roof, he explained that all purchases would have to be made with cash because credit card transactions could be traced. He had plenty of cash on hand, he told Sage between bites, saying it was a darn good thing he liked to do things the old-fashioned way. Sage said she had stockpiled lots of smaller bills in anticipation of tipping island porters, hotel doormen, cab drivers, and excursion hosts. Other than uttering reassurances to Jadia that everything was going to be all right, Sean and Sage said little else during the meal.

In silence, Sean zipped the bullet-punctuated Bimmer over the state line into Maryland and continued southwestward in a random pattern. He cut across the northeast Maryland corner, then took the ramp onto 340 W, passing through that eccentric nook in the country where state borders between Maryland, Virginia, and West Virginia were located within a forty-mile radius.

Denser forest, taller trees, higher mountains, and fewer people rose in the southwestern horizon. The Bimmer traveled beside winding railroad tracks, under tree canopies, over low water bridges, and past street signs named Picadilly, Wardensville, Parkers Pike, and Moorefield. The sun swirled in its own odyssey behind their shoulders as they ascended the Appalachian range. On Mount Freedom Drive, the sun seemed to glow special. It was the kind of beauty that mesmerizes and boggles and lulls a person to listless bliss. Over six hours and nearly 240 non-highway miles later, Sage leaned over the armrest and spied the dashboard gauges.

"Sean," she said, settling back into her seat and lazily gazing at the leafy view out the window. "We're low on gas. And we'd like to go to tinkle town." The sun was beginning its retreat behind trees in Seneca Rocks, leaving the sky alit with salutatory hues as the Bimmer was pulling up to a pump at Harper's Old Country Store.

"I'm nearly cashed out," Sean said into Sage's ear as they walked from the car. Jadia was already out and waiting at the stairs to the store. Neither one of them wanted her to know how dire the situation was. At that moment, Jadia's face hardened. It was clear she was looking at the holes in the Bimmer.

Sage turned to Sean and said, "I've got you covered, Rockefeller." She flashed him the biggest smile he'd seen that day. The hardness in his eyes relaxed, and he shook his head with a smile that didn't quite reach his face, but she knew it was there. When they reached Jadia, Sage watched as Sean hugged her daughter. Together they stepped into the historical store.

They looked like a nice family, he supposed, but the car was an eyesore, and he and Sage stood out like penguins on glaciers. Sage's attire had taken a wrong turn hundreds of miles ago. They both had shed their suit jackets, Sean's draping the passenger seat, Sage's scrunched in a bundle on the backseat. Nearly everyone else in the Seneca Rocks area was dressed as rock climbers, cyclers, or hunters, making their faces easily identifiable, more memorable. They agreed to eat their meal in the car.

Before the trio split up to go to the restrooms, Sean instructed Sage and Jadia to purchase the sandwiches and chips they'd agreed to share. After his own bathroom run, he'd pay for gas and fill the tank. He already knew gas was as expensive as it was rare in the high country—they were burning through Sage's singles and his larger bills. Until he conjured up a viable plan, he'd have to keep the remaining funds wrapped in a tight wad.

After Sean gassed up, he parked the Bimmer on the side of the 1902 Hanover building, away from nosy locals and curious tourists. They ate in the car, then Sean palmed the gear and shifted into drive. The next second they were driving into the colorful, jagged horizon.

As they coursed up, down, and around the Appalachian terrain, Sean tried to strategize a way out of bedlam. *How far will Manny Cofield go to cover himself?* He hadn't seen any visible surveillance cameras on the property. *But how do I know for sure?*

At the bypass to US 20, Sean headed back east and prodded his mind for solutions. A few short moments later, daylight disappeared altogether as did the mountains—as did ideas. His firm would not be enthusiastic about protecting him. His unpopular decisions of not adequately shutting the doors on the Anthony Campbell case and subsequently turning down the one-off opportunity to be on the prosecuting team for the O. J. Simpson case had already made him a liability. A gun made Sage a liability. He peered into the rearview mirror at Jadia. She was such a sweet kid, he thought wistfully.

CHAPTER 8

Ayde Carona was distracted during the Warner Brothers briefing. The prospect of Sean Swoboda remaining resolute in not approving her transfer to Philadelphia presented a significant roadblock, and yet a more recent development had earned more of her attention than their impasse. Ayde pensively tapped her pen against a stack of Warner Brothers artifacts, one ear taking in the Latin-infused, opinionated, staunchly delivered words of overly talkative executives who seemed to go on ad infinitum.

Earlier in the day after she'd transported Sean to the Philadelphia office, she'd circled the block and parked further back from the building's entrance so as not to be seen. With fingers drumming the steering wheel, she'd watched the building's vacant recessed curb for eight minutes before an immaculate 5-Series BMW parked in her line of sight.

Ayde Carona had checked her watch: 9:03. Two and a half minutes later, Sean Swoboda walked out and slid into the Bimmer. Swoboda had said he was meeting a client. Back at the office, after running a check on the plates, Ayde Carona learned the client was Sage Wirspa of the Anthony Campbell case.

As the present meeting droned on, Ayde stopped tapping the Warner Brothers artifacts, her mind racing forward. *Why was Sean Swoboda so attached to the Anthony Campbell case even at the expense of his reputation?* She set the pen aside and looked up at one of the conference room executives until her attention and her gaze both drifted anew. Maybe Sean was not so much attached to the Campbell case as he was to Mrs. Wirspa. One more angle to investigate. She picked up the pen again.

Ayde considered going over Swoboda's head to garner more support for a Philadelphia transfer. Securing approbation from the partners would not be nearly as difficult as it was proving to be with Sean. She absently leafed through a pad of legal prose as she weighed the possible outcomes, the most undesirable being squandering Swoboda's trust—not that there was much of it.

No. Going to the partners will not work, she thought.

"Did you want to voice something, Ms. Carona?" she heard someone ask.

Ayde looked up, following the voice across the long cherrywood table. It belonged to one of the partners. He was frowning with reproving lips, and his haughty eyes were hooded with wrinkled lids.

"Yes," she rallied. "I was saying the approach we're considering won't work." Ayde Carona proceeded to explain the contention. She followed the succinct argument by recommending an alternate course, citing relevant precedent cases, and wooing her audience with the profundity, refinement, and complete shutdown effect for which she was renowned.

CHAPTER 9

Sean eased onto an obscure road. Sage craned her neck, looking past Jadia into the darkness. It was the kind reserved for suggested thunderclouds hovering overhead or perhaps a canopy of looming trees, shielding them from moonlight. She scanned the other side of the road, which was just as obscure. Then she looked ahead, following the twin glows beaming from the headlights. The narrow road had eventually become gravel and was flanked by unrelenting, lush vegetation. White ash and a motley group of striped, red, and sugar maples mingled indiscriminately with the ranks of dogwood. The road was leading to nowhere but more vegetation.

"How are we on gas?" Sage asked. She peeked over the front armrest at the dashboard's profusion of displays and indicators.

"We're low, but we're almost there."

"Almost where?"

"Four thousand feet high on a tiny spot in the middle-of-nowhere West Virginia where a friend of mine lives. His name is Greysen Artino—he was a classmate. We forged a close friendship. That's about it. I haven't seen him in a while, but I'm sure he'll understand why I didn't call ahead to announce our visit once I give him the reason."

"What do you mean you haven't seen him in a while? How long is 'a while'?"

Sean thought about his friendship with Greysen. Guarded, reserved, eclectic, Greysen was one of the most intelligent and introspective people Sean knew—and the only one he would turn to for help. Greysen was a solution man. In truth, Greysen himself was the solution.

They had met in law school and nurtured a close friendship. Study schedules and dissimilar lifestyles prevented frequent contact, but that had no affect on their closeness. After graduation, Greysen had left the country on an assignment he didn't talk about much. Sean remained stateside on a more traditional path that included a Manhattan firm and a wife.

Greysen and Sean were kindred spirits, always picking up the friendship where they had left off, no matter how much time had passed. Greysen had returned to best man Sean's wedding and left before the reception was over. As he negotiated a hairpin curve, Sean thought about the open door Greysen had extended after he returned a few years ago and found a spot on a West Virginia ridge.

Sean had taken him up on it, visiting a couple of times a year or whenever he needed a break from the grind or simply wanted to reconnect with an old friend. He always felt welcome at Greysen's open door. This time was different though. This time he was bringing company, a long story, and a hefty load of trouble. Even with that, Sean was confident Greysen would be a solid rock. Always had been.

In his reverie, Sean realized, for the umpteenth time since they left the prison facility, that he urgently needed to talk to Lori. But what would he say? How much would he tell her? How could he explain all this?

"Uhm, I saw him late last fall. This isn't a place you want to be in the winter unless you're planning to stay awhile." The trees reached to one another, blocking out the moonlight. Dark poured around them. At the last second, the headlights highlighted another hairpin curve.

Concentration shone through Sean's straining eyes. When the road was straight again, Sean spoke to Sage in the backseat. "I think Greysen will be able to help us, Sage. He has a lot of good connections."

"Yeah," Sage said sarcastically before collapsing back against the seat and folding her arms. There they were in the middle of nowhere, fleeing without knowing for sure whether or not they were being chased, and heading to a stranger's house.

After seven or so miles, Sean swerved left onto another dirt road. The car deftly shifted back and forth as it snaked through twists as if weaving its weary passengers through a night thick with dread.

"What's that?" Sage yipped. She released Jadia's hand and grabbed the headrest of the empty front passenger seat.

"The tank's on E."

"That's great."

"You're right," Sean retorted, coasting the car to a halt. "Greysen lives right …" He paused for effect and to put the car in gear. The lights turned off. "There."

Sage leaned over between the two front seats, squinting from left to right. Then she spun around to the back window, following with attempts to see through the side windows.

"Where?"

"Oh," Sean said apologetically. He switched the lights on again.

Leaning between the two front seats and squinting again, Sage followed the stream of light some one hundred feet away. A large hovel sat pitifully against a backdrop of climbing and crawling vegetation, which appeared as eager to devour the house as Sage was to get away from it. A stooping porch mourned for the old days when its sagging stairs had been young and firm. Chips of paint glinted in the car's headlights as if the house was pushing back tears. It had passed its rustic stage long, long ago.

"It's exfoliating," Sage murmured through barely moving lips.

Sean looked out at the pathetic house and then over his shoulder at her. A smile edged onto his face. "I'll admit it's past its awkward, rustic stage," he said, facing the house again. "But don't judge a house by its paint, Sage."

"You know, Sean," Sage whispered as she leaned over him and stared at the massive shack. Her tone was troubled. "Maybe—maybe we should have called the police."

"Sage," he said, turning back to face her. "We vacillated about telling the authorities ever since we left Harrisburg. We mulled it over and rehashed everything on our way here, but each time we got off the highway to make the call, we just got back on the road again." He paused, gray eyes piercing her. "And there's that other thing you and I need to talk about."

She blinked through the windshield at the sad house, remembering the ghastly look on Anthony Campbell's face after he'd stepped through the shattered mirror.

"I know," she finally agreed.

She felt the squeeze of the trigger and the hole the bullet made in Anthony Campbell's charging head.

"I know," she repeated.

CHAPTER 10

Lori Swoboda nibbled on a carrot while watching a plate of food rotate on the microwave carousel. She fixed her eyes on the spinning morsels, troubled by Sean's unexplained absence. Frank had no knowledge of her husband's whereabouts either. After explaining this to her three times, Frank had assured Lori the New Hope house was safe and in order; then he left. She filled her mind with the task of handling the steaming plate of free-range chicken, steamed organic vegetables, and brown rice the cook, Vanessa, had prepared a couple of hours before leaving. Labor-intensive gourmet meals were reserved for weekends when Vanessa's shift lasted at least two hours longer, and all night if Lori and Sean were in a festive mood and had invited friends to share in the gaiety.

After Lori finished eating her meal, she roamed from room to room, ensuring everything was properly placed—pictures, flowers, books, and lamps. Phones stationed about the house kept coming into insistent view. She called Sean's office, hating the uneasy feeling that she was checking on him.

There was no answer, and she didn't leave a message. He could be in the men's room. Or maybe he stepped out for a bite to eat.

A few minutes later, Lori was in the master bedroom on the west wing of the ranch home, naked and sighing under a spray of hot, mind-clearing water, and enjoying scents of jasmine and vanilla wafting from the foam sliding off her back. Shortly after the flow of water stopped, her skin was clean, the lights were out, but her mind was still on. Lori sat in a chair near the bed, no longer snagged by the tangled thicket in her mind. She turned to the nightstand and stared at the clock's red LED light that read 10:15.

Lori was tired of guessing about her husband's whereabouts. By the time she made her way to her husband's office in the southwest wing of the house, a layer of stress had rested on her face. Lori needed to speak with Sean. Now.

Lights flooded Sean's office when the motion sensor detected her presence. Seconds later, Lori was seated near the phone, dialing a number from the firm's roster. Silence ticked interminably as she waited for the first and only ring. The subtle white noise of open airways spilled into her ear, followed by another endless stretch of silence.

"Hello?" a sultry female voice answered.

CHAPTER 11

"I'm uncomfortable with this, Sean," Sage said, her neck craning forward from the backseat, her bleary eyes fixed on the house. She watched and waited as Sean pressed a lever and the front seat began to glide backward. He swiveled around as much as he could so they could make eye contact.

"Let's go in and think this out," Sean suggested. "We need to get our heads clear."

Sage blinked incredulously. "But—" The silhouette of a tall, well-built man appeared on the obscure porch, interrupting Sage's words and thoughts. Sean's gaze followed Sage's eyes to the porch.

"Greysen," Sean muttered, an audible exhalation indicating his relief.

"May I help you?" the man called out into the darkness.

Sean opened the car door and gleefully yelled out, "It's me, Grey—Sean!"

"Oh." His friend chuckled youthfully. "I see you now." He reached inside the house and turned on the porch light.

"You and Jadia wait here, Sage," Sean said. He eased back into the car seat and leaned over to Sage until he held her gaze. "I want to explain the situation to Grey." He looked back at the porch door. "This, uh—this might take a while. Do you mind?"

Sage looked at Jadia, whose head lulled in sleep.

"Take your time, Sean. The last thing I want to do is wake her."

Sean jostled himself against the seat until he could peer behind it enough to get a good look at Jadia. "Pass me my jacket," he whispered to Sage. Once the suit jacket was in his hands, he shook it out and draped it over Jadia. Sage caught his eye as he finished.

"You might want to put yours on too," he said. "The mountain chill is going to suck the warmth out of the car pretty quickly."

As Sage slipped an arm into her wrinkled suit jacket, Sean looked at Jadia again. A corner of his mouth twitched. He glanced at Sage, squeezed her hand, and said, "She's going to be fine. Just give it time."

Sqeeek-bang!

The screened porch door opened and closed.

Sage blinked back surprise and released a breath she had not realized she had been holding. Then she watched Sean unbuckle the seat belt and unfold from the car.

"I'm sorry for barging in on you like this," Sean apologized loudly as he slammed the car door closed.

"You're fine, Sean. It's okay," Greysen said with an easy Manhattan accent as he stepped off the porch and padded across the elongated lawn toward the car.

"I brought company," Sean warned.

"I can see that," Greysen replied as he crossed in front of the car. Sage looked at him. He stood every bit as tall as Sean—six feet two inches at least. Greysen was leaner and tauter than Sean's bulkier build, and he had a cap of thick, wavy, darker-than-dark hair. In the milky light cast from the porch, Greysen looked almost completely devoid of color and, in perfect parity, in absolute control of his faculties. He embraced Sean and patted him on the shoulder.

"Thanks, Grey," Sean said. He hesitated. "Uh …" The gravel ground under his feet as he pivoted toward the car and hunkered down. His eyes met Sage's, and he gave her an encouraging smile. He pulled in a lungful of air and stood upright, facing Greysen again.

In a low voice, Sean said, "I took a client and her daughter to what was supposed to be an internal investigation at a community correction center this morning and ran into trouble. Big trouble."

Greysen studied his friend with narrowed eyes, his mouth twisting slightly in thought. He looked around Sean at the car and raised his brows. Gravel crunched under his shoes as he circled the car in a slow inspection. He ran fingers along a bullet scrape and then rubbed the fingers together, feeling and testing the texture. Sage turned to gaze out the back window, watching Greysen crouch and unfold, then crouch down again to survey the bumper.

After the man completed his inspection in a tight circumference around the car, he rejoined Sean, who stood near the driver's door.

"Looks like the trouble you ran into had weapons," Greysen said, his face strong yet unexpressive.

Sean opened his mouth then closed it, his lips pressing flat against his teeth as he signaled to Greysen with his eyes. Sean walked away from the bullet-riddled Bimmer, Greysen falling into step beside him. They stood several feet from the Bimmer under a canopy of trees in the faint porch light. Sean recapped the reason for the prison visit and how Manny Cofield had gone manic while he, Jadia, and Sage were there.

Greysen fixed inquisitive eyes intently on Sean. Then he looked at the car. "There are enough slugs in that car to supply an army."

"I know," Sean agreed, taking a deep breath. "We're lucky to be alive."

The two men said nothing for a while, letting the cicadas' singing fill the silence. After a long while, Greysen broke the silence.

"This manic superintendent—what's his name again?"

"Cofield. Manny Cofield."

Silence.

"I take it you haven't been in touch with the authorities."

"Uhm, no," Sean said in an exhale. He glanced toward the back of the car where Sage sat. In his hesitation, he thought about the Glock.

The shots. He winced at the memory of Manny Cofield yelling, "Shoot him! Shoot him!" and closed his lids completely at the memory of Sage slamming the door behind him and Jadia so she could carry out Manny Cofield's orders herself. Sean glanced away from the car and stared at the gravel, digging both hands deep into his pockets as if digging deeper into his pensive mind. His chest heaved before he looked at his friend again.

"I'm not sure if contacting the authorities is the best course of action, Grey. Manny Cofield could be as dead as Anthony Campbell. I don't know. But either way I could not drag that poor kid through any more of Anthony Campbell's filth." Sean watched Greysen, whose eyes kept wandering to the Bimmer.

"The man is the embodiment of insanity, but he's not stupid. The operation he's running is ingenious. I'd bet on it that he fills the prison with fawning minions from the main house after they have proved their loyalty. As I mentioned before, Anthony Campbell had furlough privileges and wasn't wearing an inmate tracking device. These guys—felons—get both freedom and protection from the system, not to mention housing. Cofield gets 100 percent profit off drugs, money laundering, and ..."

Sean hesitated and caught Greysen's gaze. The two men looked at one another. "There are penal perks you don't even want to think about," Sean finally said.

Greysen cocked a lopsided, wry smile and shook his head. "What else do you know about Manny Cofield?" he asked, shifting his weight to one leg.

"Only that he scares the hell out of me."

"I don't blame you for that," Greysen said gravely. "Apparently the man's a loose cannon who walks around with a small army." He squeezed the bridge of his nose. "You can't do that without a lot of power." He paused and looked into the wilderness. "Or a lot of money."

There was another pause, then he looked at Sean. "The good news is that you and your client may not be on the top of his priority list. If he's alive, he has to explain to the authorities, rogue or not, why and how he lost control in his own kingdom. The public may sleep through a lot, but news of an unarmed inmate who was up for parole being shot is entertaining enough to draw attention and hold any of Cofield's extracurricular activities at bay."

Greysen walked over to Sean and held an unblinking eye on him. "The question is, who is his sponsor."

Sean responded, "What do you mean, 'sponsor'?"

"The penal system is enormous, a subculture in its own right. Its link to the Department of Justice and the feds is secretive and powerful. Anthony Campbell was within the confines of a state-run, secured, community correctional center, and he's dead."

Sean glanced at the car where Sage sat. "Even if she hadn't killed Anthony Campbell, Cofield's men would have. You don't trust the police, and you believe the people who are responsible for all this happiness are a part of an operation so big, so powerful, so pervasive that they might have connections with the FBI."

Greysen crinkled his face into a grim expression. "Privatization of government functions is nothing new or illegal, but what you experienced today—the mini–army assault and the rest of it—Cofield has masterminded something lucrative for himself, that's for sure. What I'm gleaning from your story is he's been getting away with a blatant disregard for the law, taxpayers' money, and human life for starters. So again I have to ask, who's backing him and why?"

"I knew something wasn't right," Sean said with regret. "We should have left long before Cofield came into that room." His mouth closed into a tight, grim line. He thought about Sage. The gun. Anthony Campbell sprawled atop blood, glass, and filth.

"State and federal private prison systems are contractually entitled to per diem or monthly rates per prisoner, so the more the merrier. One of two things happen when quotas aren't met. Either taxpayers pay for any empty beds or new crimes are created. Either way, it's a win-win for the private prison business. This Cofield character seems to be driven by much more than nepotism and kickback opportunities in the private prison's subcontract and supply chains. Sounds like he's got someone backing him."

"Grey." Sean hesitated. His sharp eyes were intent, his head held slightly askew. "There's more." He told Greysen about seeing no video surveillance.

Greysen thought about that. "Financial woes have strapped the state for quite some time, making repair or replacement unlikely. New private owners are probably slow to move on any expenditure that doesn't reap instant return on investment."

"That may be true, but I have a funny feeling Manny Cofield had other reasons."

Greysen nodded. "You're probably right. … How can I help?" he asked.

Sean looked at his friend. He had been practically a brother since 1973, Harvard freshman year. They were both well-heeled, native New Yorkers and had known of one another from the city's blue blood enclaves, although they didn't actually meet until law school. At Harvard, they'd shared the same classes, conservative views, and passion for law. They often headed in different social directions, but their friendship did not feed on togetherness. Rather, there was a commonality and connectedness, a bond extending far past the surface of fraternal orders. It was a brotherly love, the kind that remained steady and easy even after they had been carried in different directions by rivers of self-discovery, vocation, and happenstance. The bond of time and distance had drawn them closer and made their friendship strong and resilient.

Sean rocked on his heels, pulling a hand from a pocket to wipe his smooth head. He looked at the willowy shadows of Sage and Jadia nestled together behind the dark reflection of the car windows. Greysen didn't own a cell phone, and he didn't even have a landline. He had a pager. It wasn't even a real pager, just something he'd rigged so it couldn't be traced. Paging Lori was not an option. She had tossed their own pagers at the relatively recent advent of consumer cell phone accessibility.

"It's funny. Now that I'm here," Sean said, "I can't think of anything. There's nothing you can do. I don't think there's anything anyone can do.

I can't even help myself. I don't have my cell phone, and Sage doesn't own one. Can you believe that?"

Greysen laughed. "You were always a technology hound, Sean. You and fewer than 100,000 people in the US are way ahead of us by owning one—and most of those people reside in coastal states. There isn't enough bandwidth to service the wait list. So don't beat yourself up. There is no cell service out here—your phone would have been useless." Greysen scanned the blackened horizon. "The millennium will break before repeaters are installed in West Virginia. We're always one of the last when it comes to education and technology."

Sean nodded.

"Look, Sean," Greysen said. "This thing is bad, and it's ugly. It's getting under my own skin, so I can only imagine what it's doing to you. You're probably worried about Lori."

Sean stilled. "Grey, I don't know how to handle this without endangering Lori."

This time Greysen was still. He knew that Sean was right. Anyone remotely associated with him right now was in danger.

"Follow the money," Greysen said at length. His tone was ominous. He studied the darkness like he was doing calculus, then he said, "Anthony Campbell may have been a pauper dining with kings." He paused before adding, "Pen kings. Corporate kings. You never know."

Sean shot him a puzzled look. It caught Greysen's eye.

"I'm just speculating," Greysen said in a lighter tone. He spread his fingers and held out his large palms in a wide sweep. "Throwing out wildcards. Casting a wide net."

"Follow the money." Sean echoed Greysen's words. His smile did not reflect the fear in his eyes.

CHAPTER 12

In the car, Jadia had stirred awake. Absentmindedly, Sage grabbed her daughter's hand and drew her closer. They sat hip to hip as Sage's thoughts flashed from Thomas to Anthony Campbell's gaping mouth, then to Manny Cofield, and finally to the Glock.

She gazed into the blackness of midnight greenery as she tried to push the images into the lush darkness around her. On the opposite side of her vacant stare, across forty or so feet of barren, rocky yard and beyond the decaying porch and its decrepit banisters, the silhouette of a tall, lanky female stood eerie and statue still behind a ragged screen door. A dawning awareness of the woman's presence gradually replaced Sage's mental haze. Stunned from her reverie, Sage, too, remained unmoving as discomfort drifted over her like smoky gossamer.

CHAPTER 13

Ayde Carona checked her watch—10:15 p.m.—and stared at the office phone cradled in her hand. Someone had called her from the Swobodas' house. Correction: *Lori* had called her. She heard that unmistakable tempo of heavy breathing. And then the clumsy woman dropped the phone. Ayde heard the distant, feminine grunt of irritation as Lori fumbled to grasp the receiver and prevent it from falling to the floor. A loud clattering indicated to Ayde that she had been unsuccessful in her attempt.

No one but Lori Swoboda, Ayde thought. *But why?* she asked herself. *And why my office phone? Why at this hour? ... Lori's looking for Sean. But why in New York?*

She answered her own question: *Because he's not in Philadelphia. And so the missus thinks her husband is with me?* Ayde let out a loud chuckle. It echoed through the empty corridor and bounced off the closed doors of nearby offices. *Pray tell, Mrs. Swoboda, where is that hunk husband of yours?*

Ayde inspected the entire phone, smiling at the unseen special equipment hidden in that particular phone. She returned the receiver to its cradle and wrapped her long fingers over elbows propped on the desk.

Sean is not with me, but no worries, Mrs. Swoboda. I will get him. One way or another, I will get him. A determined smile played across her full lips.

CHAPTER 14

"At least you were able to hold them at bay," Sage heard Greysen say. His voice had startled her. During her reverie, Greysen and Sean had edged closer to the Bimmer.

"That's not bound to last long," Sean agreed wearily.

"Time will tell," Greysen said, standing up and stepping back to capture a more panoramic view of the damaged car. "By the way, the prisoner who was killed—what was his name?" Sage started again, panting as she braced herself for the image of Anthony Campbell's ragged, bloody mouth.

"Uhh, why don't we pick up on that a little later," Sean said, feigning nonchalance by jiggling change in his pocket as he walked closer to the driver's door.

"Okay," Greysen said. His inspection had covered the entire exterior of the car. "Come in and we'll discuss the details. Do any of you have baggage we need to bring?"

"Uhhh, no," Sean answered stepping to the car. "My attaché is it." He reached into the front car window to turn off the headlights and remove the keys from the ignition.

"All right," Greysen said. He opened the back door and squatted to look at Jadia. "There's plenty of food and an extra bed in the house," he explained as he studied her. His next statement was directed to all three occupants of the car. He said, "You guys look like you could use some rest … and some nourishment too."

Then Greysen directed a greeting to Jadia in a tone that suggested he somehow knew she would not offer a reply, and without waiting for one, he extended his hand to her. Sage watched her daughter turn and face the stranger, and she was surprised at her responsiveness. *A new voice*, Sage reasoned. Jadia studied Greysen's outstretched hand a moment before accepting his gesture. "Wait there. I'll be back," he called back to her.

Her door opened and when he ducked his head into the side of the car where she sat, Sage had her first view of his strong eye-catching features. Individual gray strands were woven into his thick, black hair like a school of white dolphins diving into a black sea. Fresh stubble molded perfectly to his face, and a deep dimple lay as if waiting to catch a tiny puddle beneath a gray-speckled patch on his square chin.

He was Sean's contemporary and, like Sean, every one of his forty-plus years was concealed within a toned, hard body. It was his manner that struck her, the way he lingered, assessing her in the same way he had appraised her damaged vehicle. They held one another's gaze until she said, "I'm Sage. Sage Wirspa, Jadia's mother."

Greysen said nothing, offering an outstretched hand. Sage grabbed the hand and held it as she slid across the seat and exited the car. She glanced over at Sean, who gave her a warm smile. When she tried to release Greysen's hold, he gently squeezed her hand tighter and said, "I'm Greysen Artino. It's a pleasure to meet you."

Releasing his hold, he turned to Jadia, saying, "And you, Jadia." He eyed the teenager briefly, smiled, and said, "Come on. Let's go inside. It's getting sticky out here." He grabbed Jadia's hand and began striding toward the slumping house.

Sean fell into step with the trio and whispered in Sage's ear, "Are you okay with this?" Sage shifted her head, answering with an expression that could only be described as amiably cautious.

Greysen held open the screeching screen door as Sean and Jadia stepped through a threshold that opened into a sizable foyer with a living room on the left and a kitchen on the right. In the second or two it took for the attorney and the girl to step up into the house, Sage took in what she could see beyond the door.

The scene was bathed in dirty light cast from dusty, naked bulbs that hung from the foyer ceiling. From what she could see, the furniture in the well-lit living room was the sort she'd seen on garage-sale lawns in neighborhoods where families had been suffering from unemployment and underemployment for generations.

Sage thought of paddle boards, and then her eyes focused on the oversized, dark-stained, flat-board armrests at the ends of the sofa. Finally, the faded earth-toned floral cushions caught her attention as her peripheral vision took in matching end tables topped with matching beige lamps. In the center of the furniture arrangement was a huge cedar chest that served as the cocktail table.

Sage tried to appreciate the almost-antique look of the chest, although she was sure any remnant of cedar was too faint for even her sensitive nose. Instead, the smell of reheated leftovers drew her attention to the right where a rusted chrome table—circa 1950—stood flanked by matching chrome chairs. The only thing atop the table now was a plastic napkin holder that was overstuffed with paper towels someone had squared. Like the rusted table, its chairs' cracked, yellow, plastic seats told of the passing of time: excessive wear and a bit of good old-fashioned neglect.

But even in the face of age and excessive wear, and in spite of the dim light, the place looked clean—relatively speaking. Sage didn't want to think about how many layers of skin the couch had collected in its fabric and spongy cushion. Instead, she dismissed all that she'd processed in that split second, and she let her eyes and mind drift to the prospect of food filling her hungry child's stomach.

She took one step into the house to join Sean and Jadia, who were standing deeper in the foyer past the living room door, on the far end of the kitchen's threshold. Her entry was blocked when a tall, lean woman stepped into her path from out of nowhere—the living room, Sage supposed—and waylaid her. The woman's body was like her expression—hard, sinewy, and fierce. Her upper lip sported an almost imperceptible pelt-like layer of wispy blonde hair. Blonde bangs hung over her brows like an awning. Her caramel-colored eyes, gorgeous in an oddly exotic way, blended with her tanned, prematurely wrinkled skin, and glared at Sage with disdain.

"The young lady is Jadia, Eli." Greysen's voice rang out over Sage's head. He stood on the porch behind her. "And this is Sage, her mother." He cupped large hands on Sage's shoulders to still her as he eased his six-foot-three-inch frame past the threshold and stamped Timberland boots against lackluster hardwood floors with deliberate authority. The afterburn of Greysen's touch dispelled Sage's thoughts of Anthony Campbell's Timberlands.

Greysen's face was stern, his lips pressed tight. He stared at Eli with one eye slightly narrowed as if warning her to behave. Eli edged backward in a way that denoted respect, not fear. With practiced dexterity, Eli directed reverence at Greysen and defiantly tossed a curt nod and toothy smile to Sage. Except it wasn't really a smile. It was more of a sly sneer.

"Hello," Sage said. Her feet moved with hesitation, but she pushed them on, stepping deeper into the house and palming the door behind her until it rested on her backside.

"And you remember Sean, don't you, Eli?" Greysen's voice was easier now … coaxing. Eli's softened expression did little to mask the agitation lurking behind it. Eli nodded at Sean and spared him the spite she had obviously reserved for Sage. Sean smiled back at Eli and grabbed Jadia's hand. Sage noticed Jadia's subtle lean into the attorney. Somehow it made Sage feel all the more alone in the face of Eli's blatant ire.

The group formed an uneasy gathering between the foyer and the retro kitchen. Air conditioning swirled crisp air around them for a teasing second before a blast of heat from the stove ended the reprieve. Sage felt a prickle of sweat break out on her forehead, but she wasn't sure it was from the heat in the kitchen. The awkwardness inherent with being a houseguest to strangers was almost as screwy as the weirdness of the prison visit, and right now, Eli's undivided attention was outranking the killers' chase because it was the thing most currently in Sage's face.

"Sage, why don't you and Jadia rest a little in here," Greysen said after whispering something in Eli's ear. Eli was standing near the counter with her back to her guests, tossing a salad. She made no motion or audible reply to whatever Greysen had said, and he, clearly not waiting for a reply, had spun away from her and was already in motion to clear the living room.

Sage stepped over to Jadia and winked at Sean as she grabbed her daughter's free hand. Mother and daughter followed the ruggedly masculine figure across the foyer and into the living room. It was impossible to avoid noticing the way Greysen's muscles flexed under his cotton shirt as he cleared a basket of unfolded clothes from the couch. Tight quad muscles popped through faded black jeans. And he was clean. The fresh scent she smelled every time he breezed by her told her that.

As he disappeared from view, Sage wiped sweat from her brow and smoothed back a lock of hair in the same stroke. She tried to ward off the heat and the insanity of feeling attracted to Greysen. She squeezed Jadia's hand, then leaned over and whispered, "Let's see if this dame can cook."

"Eli's warming enchiladas she made earlier," Greysen said. His sudden and unexpected reappearance startled Sage. He leveled emerald green eyes at her and said, "She always makes extra to freeze, so there's more than enough." He crossed her room, squatted at her knees, and asked, "Are you hungry?" He was so close. Sage wondered about her hygiene. The day had covered her with layers of nervous perspiration. And her breath—she couldn't check that because he was already in her face.

"I could use a bite." She pretended to look at Jadia as she deflected her breath.

"What about Jadia? Do you think she'll eat?" he asked. "Eli's also making a salad."

Sage tried to return Greysen's gaze, but the best she could do was shoot him a glance, then look at his hand on her knee. Warm, big—and, she imagined, packed with the kind of skills that makes a woman smile with pleasure. Sage looked at Jadia and, after a lingering moment, shifted her attention back to Greysen.

"Let's try her," she answered, a smile pressed against her lips.

"Greysen," a voice called from another room. It was Eli. Greysen swiveled on his heels and stood, blocking Sage's view of the doorway.

"Greysen, I need help with the food," Eli said. Her voice was closer now, spilling from the other side of the jamb. Greysen followed Eli's voice until he disappeared.

As the sound of his boots scuffing the floor faded, Sage stared at the small toes peeking from Jadia's sandals. She was thinking, *Those toes were supposed be digging in tropical sand today*, when a shadow appeared in the jamb. Sage looked up, expecting Greysen. It wasn't. From the doorway, Eli peered at Sage, a smirk pasted onto her pinched face. Sage smiled at her reluctant hostess before looking away.

"Food's on the table," Eli snapped. When Sage looked up to thank her, Eli was gone.

Sage and Jadia were the last to be seated at the table, which grew quiet when Sean and Greysen saw them approaching. Sean had been filling Greysen in on the reasons behind Jadia's muteness. He turned his attention to the food, quickly consuming the sizable portion of enchiladas laying in wait, and profusely complimenting Eli between bites. It didn't take long for Jadia to clear her plate either. The rape had stunted her interest in talking, but remained powerless over her appetite. She drank the last of tea and gave Sage a look that said, *The food was delicious and I'm satisfied*. This tiny bit of communication made Sage hopeful and thankful.

Sean wiped his mouth with a napkin and placed it in on his empty plate before excusing himself to the bathroom. In his absence, Sage felt lost. While Eli noisily banged around the sink and counters with her rigid back turned, Sage felt the burn of Greysen's stare.

"Is there someplace where Jadia can lay down?" Sage purposefully directed the inquiry to Eli. "She's exhausted and needs to close her eyes if only for a little while."

"Eli will get Jadia something to sleep in, and she can bathe if she wants to," Greysen said, pulling Sage's attention to him.

"Uhhh," Sage stammered as she searched the kitchen for Sean who strolled across the threshold as if on queue.

"I think we better stay here tonight, Sage," Sean said. He never broke stride as he grabbed the plate and glass he'd abandoned and headed to the counter. He looked over his shoulder at her as he slid the plate into the soapy water in the kitchen sink. Eli put a bowl in the refrigerator, stood beside Sean, and began to wash the dishes with more vigor than Sage thought necessary.

"We ..." Sean continued as he returned to the table and sat across from Sage. "That is, Greysen and I had a long talk before dinner, Sage." He glimpsed Jadia. "There's still a lot to work out though. I'll give you the details later."

"Eli," Greysen called. "Why don't you show Sage and Jadia to the guest room and bathroom."

"Sure," she agreed sharply, slamming the dishtowel on the sink counter. Eli pivoted toward the table and sneered at Sage. "Come on."

"Later," Sage mouthed to Sean as she and Jadia stood. He cracked a silent guffaw when she quirked an eyebrow. Spinning on her heels, she gave Jadia a hug, and they followed Eli down a narrow hallway opposite the foyer and headed toward the back of the house. The deeper they went into the hovel, the darker it became. It was as if Eli's bad mood began to blossom the further they got from Sean and Greysen.

"I can help you with the dishes after I get Jadia situated," Sage offered. She searched the narrow hallway for a light switch and found none. The last place she wanted to be anywhere with Eli was in the dark.

"I know how to wash my own dishes," Eli said, revealing a vague Southern lilt. With a finger as rigid as her tone, she pointed to the guest bedroom on the right and a small bathroom on the left.

"Okay," Sage said. She drew it out the same way Eli drew out resentment. Sage looked further down the hallway into the impenetrable darkness. She was unable to see what lay between them and the end, so she tried to use it as a change of subject. "What's back there?"

"That's the master bedroom," Eli said. The words gnashed like shark bites. She shot Sage a shark smile, revealing a row of long, straight teeth, stained with tobacco and dark beverages, and added, "That's where Greysen and I sleep."

Sage swallowed and watched as Eli pulled her mouth into a one-sided smirk. In the dark, the jaws of her angular face protruded more, and the soft cheeks underneath slacked into a gauntness that should have been reserved for Halloween. This was what Sage was thinking before she corrected herself. She wondered if she'd have these kinds of harsh thoughts if Eli were kinder, gentler—and if Sage herself had not felt a surge of heat every time she was near Eli's man.

Eli stretched a gangly arm behind Sage and blindly opened a narrow door, reached into an apparent hall closet—one Sage had not noticed in the dimness—and pulled out two stacked towels. After handing them to Sage, Eli faded deeper into the darkness further down the hall, and two minutes later, reappeared from it headfirst like a disembodied phantom. She was carrying two sets of pajamas, which she placed atop the towels Sage was still holding.

"Thanks," Sage said. She felt chewed up and spit out. "Since you don't need my help in the kitchen, Jadia and I will prepare for bed and retire, and I'll stay out of your w—"

"Good." Eli cut her off with a brief nod and left.

"What do you say we throw her to the dogs?" Sage whispered playfully to Jadia once they were secluded behind the closed bathroom door.

A twitching mouth was Jadia's reply.

"That was pretty funny, wasn't it?" Sage said. She'd learned that making a big deal of Jadia's rare reactions was the best to shut her back down again.

"You have a great smile," she said, and then asked, "Will you be okay?"

Without answering, Jadia reached over the tub and turned on the shower. As she began to disrobe, Sage gave the place a visual once-over. A claw tub in need of new paws and porcelain sat atop weary wood floors. Throw rugs that clung desperately to the last remnants of mauve gave the small space signs of life—feeble and wheezing, but life just the same. The good news was, despite age and wear, the bathroom looked and smelled clean in a frequently maintained way. The best news was the privacy plastic covering the high window, and the layers of paint that sealed both the windowsill and its iron sash locks.

Satisfied with the security of the room, Sage pressed the bathroom door's button lock and whispered to Jadia, who was now stepping into the shower, "Yell if you need me."

The moment of aloneness felt like a foot massage—Thomas's foot massage. Standing in the nearby doorway, Sage kept one foot in the silent, dark guest room, while placing the other in the hall in case Jadia needed her. The room's solace read like an invitation to the Fiji islands, all expenses paid—a sanctuary to silence today's pandemonium and tomorrow's uncertainty. Under the calming influence of the great room, Sage's racing mind and jittery nerves subsided.

"You're welcome to anything in my house, Sage." Sage spun around, knocking her shoulder against the doorframe in a jerky, clumsy twirl. She gasped at Eli's sudden appearance.

"Excuse me?" Sage said, rearing back from the acrimonious words spoken by Eli, who was now standing so close to Sage that she could feel the other woman's hot breath heave from thin, curled lips.

"I said," Eli drawled out, "you can help yourself to anything in my house." She drew a deep breath and hissed, "Except my man."

The shower stopped just as Sage's mouth formed the first word of a blistering retort, bringing a mix of disappointment and perspective. She really wanted to face off with Eli but self-corrected before her ego got too far ahead. After all, the shack was indeed Eli's house and Greysen was indeed Eli's man. Sage was merely a guest—unexpected, uninvited, and apparently, unwanted. Sage's very presence endangered her hosts' lives. Still, Eli's hostile attitude was becoming tiresome.

"Grow some confidence, Eli," Sage said with disdainful boredom. "Now if you'll excuse me, I have a traumatized daughter to attend to." Brushing past a stunned Eli, Sage crossed the hall and tapped on the bathroom door.

CHAPTER 15

Lori Swoboda blindly placed the phone in its cradle and eased back into the chair, into the room's blackness, its silence. She propped an elbow on the arm of chair and cradled her forehead. She had not come up with a logical reason to call Ayde Carona. Lori chided herself for acting based on conjecture and a knee-jerk reaction to her concern about Sean. Ayde Carona was beautiful—beautiful and exotic and hot after Sean, whether he knew it or not.

In the darkness of the room, and in growing self-examination, Lori sensed an inner ghost escaping from deep inside her. It was jealousy that had been caged up long ago—seventeen years ago. Jealousy. After seventeen years, it stretched lazily and seemed to come back to life. It was the ghost of the only other woman Lori Swoboda had been jealous of, and that ghost had come crashing back in. She didn't want to say the woman's name. Didn't want to think the name. It was so long ago—1977. A year after they'd graduated from law school. She and Sean had been seriously dating for about six months when she first saw the letters—copies of letters he had written to the other woman. Her Sean. Her love. Pining over another woman she had never seen. It had driven her crazy.

Sean's love for this other woman had been unrequited. His words to her, the groveling, the sickening way he had belittled himself by writing the letters in the first place and then making copies for his own reference as if they were artifacts. Where was his pride?

There was another thing. Sean was begging forgiveness. Apparently he had mishandled a business deal for this no-name woman and had caused a load of money to be lost. He felt guilty and wanted to make it up to the woman. Loving her. Begging her.

Lori had let it go on for three more months, not saying anything, pretending she didn't know. But on the first night of their honeymoon, Lori leveraged consummating their vows against the letters. She'd kept her virginity until, on the second night of their honeymoon, he'd finally, painfully, tearfully promised not to ever write the nameless woman again. Never.

Lori Swoboda spent the rest of their honeymoon and every week afterward making sure her husband never regretted his choice, forced though it may have been. She looked at the abandoned phone and bit her lower lip as the same hot jealousy whipped anew, but this time against Ayde Carona.

CHAPTER 16

Jadia and Sage, both freshly bathed and silent, lay side by side in the darkness on the full-size guest bed.

"Do you smell that?" Sage whispered to Jadia. "These sheets were hung outdoors to dry."

Silence.

And then the mellifluous sounds of crickets and cicadas and the occasional owl hoot drifted into the room through a slightly opened window. Sage listened as she felt the crisp air waft over her face. The sound of the floor groaning under the drag of a chair being pushed to the kitchen table sounded over murmurs. Sometime later, the front screen door screeched open, then slammed shut. Water trickled through pipes in nearby walls and then splashed into the kitchen sink. The kitchen door screeched open and closed again, then the refrigerator door opened and closed. The murmurs drew closer, their words distinct. A fresh wave of alertness crested in Sage.

"The couch will be fine," she heard Sean say. "I really appreciate your putting us up tonight. I don't know what I would have done if I hadn't thought about you."

"This is what friends are for, Sean," Greysen answered. "I'm glad to be here for you."

The sound of Greysen's voice made Sage tense—maybe because of Eli's warning. But the magnetism to Greysen rivaled her addiction to the Glock. The first feel of her fingers curling around the handle, and she was hooked.

"I need to head for that gas station you told me about," Sean was saying. "It opens early, right?"

"That's right. It's a tiny, one-pump station, and they open promptly at five o'clock. You can use the outside pay phone anytime. Take my truck."

"Nooo," Sean drew out. "I prefer to walk. I don't want to bring any more attention to you or Eli than I already have."

"It's a ninety-minute hike through mountainous terrain, or only five minutes by car." As Sage blindly listened in the dark, Greysen drew back a curtain just enough to peer through the window and train his focus on the Bimmer. "Judging from what you've told me and the trauma on Sage's car, it probably doesn't make a difference at this point."

A jingle of keys, a pause, then Sean said, "I'll leave no later than four fifteen. I need to talk to Lori. Let her know what's going on. Have her wire money. The sooner Sage and I are out of here, the better."

Greysen nodded. "Okay. Help yourself to coffee or whatever you find if you need a little energy before the journey."

"Thanks again, Grey. I mean it."

As the footsteps that Sage assumed belonged to Greysen drew closer, she lifted her head from the pillow and peeked at the lit space between the closed bedroom door and the floor. A few minutes later, the bar of light winked out. Sage eased back against the pillow, determined to keep a watchful eye open for the duration of the night. Underneath the bed, the Glock lay silent in her purse.

CHAPTER 17

"Lori." Sean's voice blew in his wife's ear like a comforting ocean wind—wet, warm, and salty. She dug her head deeper into the pillow and nuzzled into the phone as if it were Sean's chest.

"Lori," Sean had repeated. "Are you there? Are you all right?"

"I'm here, hon," she heard herself say. Why hadn't Sean called before she'd dialed Ayde Carona's office? "Where are you?" she asked. Her tone had dropped.

"It's, uh … it's complicated, babe," he said. "My meeting was extended and—" He coughed, a choke brought on by the realization he had not quite figured out exactly how to describe yesterday's calamity. "All hell broke lose, Lori," he said. "On an apocalyptic level. Seismic scale twelve."

Lori's breath quickened into the receiver as Sean spat out a condensed version of what happened at the prison facility.

"I'm okay, babe. Sage and Jadia are with me. But I need time to work things out."

"Let me help you."

Silence.

"Sean?" Her eyes darted in the dark. "Leave Greysen's place as soon as you can. The people chasing you could be on your heels." Panic could be heard in her voice. "They could be watching you right now. It won't take long for them to figure out where y—"

"I need cash," Sean interjected. "Plenty of it."

"You've got it." Lori's quick agreement came out in a rush. "Just get out of there."

"We have to be careful with the transfer," Sean said. "No one can know."

"What I mean, sweetie, is you already have it."

A hush fell on the line as Sean tried to work his way through confusion. "Uh—I'm sorry, Lori. I have no idea what you're talking about."

"After last year's World Trade Center bombing, I had a tannery design your attaché with a hidden compartment at the base of it. In it, you'll find small- and medium-denomination bills and reloadable debit cards." The line fell silent.

Sean rubbed his head, thinking about the heft in his attaché. He'd always wondered about that. "When did you do that?" Sean said.

"I arranged to have it done during our vacation last year," Lori said. "Most of the bills are large. It was the only way to pack power and efficiency without the weight, but there are smaller items in there as well." She chuckled a little. "There's even a toothbrush and miniature bottle of hand sanitizer in the compartment."

They both were chuckling now. Sean's relief was like his Harley Road King—relaxed and easy. Lori was relieved about one thing: Sean had not spent the night with Ayde Carona.

CHAPTER 18

Sage jumped at the sound of soft knocking.

"Sage," Sean said from the door. "It's five forty-five. Let's go."

Sage sat up, resting her weight on one arm and casting a crusty, groggy eye about the room. The other eye had yet to catch up with the whole waking-up thing. The room was dipped in black, and a strip of bright light shone from the bottom of the raised door. A hand swiped drool from her mouth, and the motion somehow brought reality into full view. Bullets and glass and knives and running. Yes, they were on the run. The bed belonged to a man and a—Eli's snarling visage flashed. *Yes,* she thought, forcing the other eye open. *It is definitely time to leave.*

Sage gave Jadia a gentle rise-and-shine tap, and Jadia blinked until her eyes adjusted.

"Be ready in a minute," Sage said to the door, wishing she had a toothbrush.

The sun peered like a red, omniscient eye above the horizon as Sean, Jadia, and Sage stepped onto the porch. Past the threshold of the dilapidated frame, she was careful to close the screen door so that it didn't wake their hosts. Sean had drilled this procedure into her a few minutes before. As if he needed to tell her that. It was obvious that Rockefeller thought her a heathen. The sun had barely risen, and he was already slinging insults.

The West Virginia vista that greeted them was amazing. Sage was glad to be out of Eli's dark house. Staring out at the clearing and beyond it at the bounty of trees and waves of cresting hills, she hugged Jadia and kissed her temple, taking in her daughter and the morning air as if it were her last whiff of anything good.

"Look, Jadia," she said, pointing beyond a circumference of lush mountains. "That ridge is wrapping around you and rocking you like your mama." Sage gave Jadia another squeeze and added, "Or Oma."

"Sneaking off without saying good-bye?" a voice asked from behind. Sage looked over her shoulders across the small span of porch toward the threshold. Greysen Artino's strong, handsome face and broad shoulders were little more than a shadow behind the decrepit screen door; however, nothing could hide his brilliant smile.

He opened the screeching screen door, then stepped onto the decaying porch, easing the door closed behind him.

"Good morning, ladies," Greysen said. Green eyes turned to Sage, then alighted on Jadia. "I hope you slept well." Jadia held his kind gaze with pressed lips that skirted a smile.

"You look as though you've been awake for hours," Sage said.

"I have." His large Timberland boots clumped across the splintered wood as he moved closer to her. Flashes of corpulent Manny Cofield, cocky Anthony Campbell, and the drug-packed Timberlands swirled in Sage's head.

"I spent the night stalking the forest." Greysen squinted, surveying the verdant bounty. "This is home to deer, ducks, bear, rabbits, wild turkeys, and Sasquatch."

Sage smiled. "Sasquatch? I bet he's a real party animal."

"She," Greysen announced as his eyes lingered over her body, "is probably the sexiest woman I've ever seen."

"She," Sage chimed in with Greysen's emphasis, "is one lucky girl to be here, sexy or not."

"You could join the party," he said. A hand swept over the broad expanse. "Just dive right in."

"If only I could," Sage said, stealing a look at the Bimmer.

Greysen's expression turned serious.

"I've got motion-sensors and night cameras all over this property, but nothing spells security like foot patrol. I didn't see or hear a peep from anyone all night."

"You were up all night?" she asked, wondering if her finger-brushing routine had tamed her morning breath.

"Grey was the all-nighter king in law school," Sean chimed in, smiling proudly and nodding as he made his way from the Bimmer. The rotting stairs buckled and creaked as he hopped up to the porch. "The next day, he'd function twice as good as anyone who had had eight hours sleep—and score twice as high on exams."

"Did anyone sleep in law school?" Greysen asked. The quip brought a round of laughter. Jadia leaned into her mother's embrace and looked at the two men. Sean said good-bye and escorted Jadia to the bullet-riddled Bimmer. Sage watched until she felt Greysen's gaze, homey and warm, pull her back to him like a musk-scented invitation. She let the sensation linger a while before gently gliding her eyes to his.

Sage took a breath and glanced at the car. Sean was watching them from the driver's seat, Jadia from the back. She breathed again and looked back at Greysen.

"Thanks for everything, Greysen," was all she could manage. She forced her eyes to stay on his. "You and Eli have been so gracious."

He hesitated as if to scope the very depth of her, then said, "I'd like to see you again." His smile slowly transformed into pursed lips and contemplation, pulling on her like a hook on its catch.

"Greysen." She raised prohibitive palms and said, "Besides your offer being very strange considering ..." She looked through the rust and dirt of the screened door, then back at Greysen. "Besides all that, I don't even know where I'll be or—"

"You know where I'll be."

"Right. And I know who you'll be with."

Greysen seized Sage with insistent eyes that could not be dissuaded. He reached into his pants pocket, pulled out a small piece of paper, and stuffed it into her sweaty palm. Cupping the hand, he leaned in until his breath reached her lips.

"I don't have a phone, but you can page me. I have a post office box. Write me, let me know that you and Jadia are okay." He paused. "And maybe we can talk."

He stood upright again and gazed at her.

"Sage," Sean called out. "We have to leave. Now."

Sage looked at him through the windshield of the ruined Bimmer, then back at Greysen.

"I have—"

"—to go," Greysen finished with a smile. "I'll walk you to the car." They covered the gravelly distance to the car in about twenty crunchy paces, marking time like a countdown.

Greysen stepped ahead to open the door. Sage, hanging back before rounding, flung her head back to take one last look at the house. The shack's better qualities began to emerge from back-road squalor. Sage had to appreciate it, even if she did not understand its inhabitants. An entire transformation began to take place. Old became rustic. Shabby became downright cozy. And everything around the house was beautiful— thriving. She looked up at the clouds and took a deep breath as if inhaling energy from the rising sun. With an arm rested on the frame of the open window of the passenger door, she looked at Greysen and said, "Thanks again for everything. G—"

Sss-q-u-e-e-e-k. Bang!

Sss-q-u-e-e-e-k. Bang!

In unison, their heads jerked toward the porch. Eli stood inside the house leaning in the threshold, slamming the screen door open and closed.

Sss-q-u-e-e-e-k. Bang!

The sound of the door slapped Sage with each swing. Under the threshold surrounded by worn wood and chipped paint, Eli brandished her insidious smirk.

Piqued, Sage glowered at Eli as she whispered to Greysen, "Is she on medication?" The pause drew her gaze to him. She found him gaping at her with tightly shut lips.

Sage began to say, "I shouldn't have said th—" Suddenly, there was a deafening roar, and in the next few interminable seconds, many things happened at once.

Fuming pressure packed with intense heat and a spray of glass and debris shot through the air. In unison, Sage and Greysen jerked up their heads and flew back. A mélange of stinging debris sprayed their faces, as Greysen, with primal instincts, grabbed Sage's shoulders. The blast spun them both away from the car. He fell backward to the ground, his momentum pulling her down with him. Pressure from the blast rocked and bounced the squeaking, growling car and violently jostled Sean and Jadia inside it.

Greysen and Sage rolled toward the back fender as aftershock waves surrounded them and the car. The car jounced and pitched to and fro, side-to-side. Jadia's screams and Sean's yowl chimed inharmoniously with the cacophony of glass shattering outward from the house, combined with the loud crack of wood splitting and the low howl of energy from the blast. Eli's charred and broken body went airborne from the porch, spinning in the wake of a disintegrating screen door. Several distinct *thwack*s announced Eli's body landing in pieces in a grassy patch that was disturbingly close to the Bimmer.

Sage's jaw and chest hit the ground first, followed in sequential order by every area of her body starting with her neck and going all the way down to her toes. She felt the impact and scrape of the rough road on her sensitive flesh and bone as the weight of Greysen's free-falling body pounded her to the ground.

Greysen felt the momentum of his body drag Sage under him across the course earth. His outstretched palms pushed against the protracting skid. The feel of road burn was accompanied by sounds that reverberated through their flesh and bones, along with overwhelming pressure. Wildly flapping and fluttering leaves added their own rhythmic sound. Pebbles, bark, and a cocktail of debris from the annihilated house sprinkled down like brittle rain.

After interminable seconds, Sage and Greysen finally rocked to a stop. Greysen lay across Sage like a protective lead mantle. One of Sage's cheeks was squished on rough ground, the other fanned by Greysen's harsh breathing. His breaths were hot, moist, and out of tempo. Something dribbled from his direction onto her neck. It slid along her skin, moving and feeling wet like saliva, not sticky like blood.

Smoke rolled over them like dusty tumbleweed, blinding them. Sage and Greysen coughed, and Sage spit out gritty sediment. Sean ducked his head below the vehicle's glass level and whipped his body around to check on Jadia. He found her curled in a fetal position, knees down behind his seat. Still hunched as far as his long body would allow, he reached between the front seats, found her chin, and pulled her tear-streaked face up just enough to ensure that she was okay.

"Everything's going to be okay," he whispered to her. Even to him, the words felt as empty and false. Slowly, Jadia's head rested on the seat. Sean stroked her back and braved a look out the window. Sage and Greysen were out of his view, still sprawled on the unyielding ground. Crackling sounds and the smell of fire and smoke pierced the air. An unshakable feel of warlike aftermath reverberated through the cores of Sean, Jadia, Greysen, and Sage, the explosion's ebbing energy marking everyone with a bit of violent perpetuity.

Greysen, stirring from a concussion-induced daze, had not yet begun to string together shreds of the last few seconds. He lifted back his pounding head just enough to inspect Sage. One of her eyes, stunned and weak, had squinted open. Sage's head spun in nausea at the sideways world where arbors, saplings, and foliage lay bent or broken in defeat like war casualties around the little house. Her eye closed again as the crackling, popping sounds of a mourning forest spilled into her ears.

Then the first inklings of reality began to work their way into Greysen's waking mind like the dusting of snow. The place he and Eli had called home had been consumed in just a matter of seconds. Greysen winced at the thought, then suddenly, and against a backdrop of sharp, shooting physical pain, he found himself pushing back awareness that the unthinkable had happened—his world had disappeared in thick, smoky air that rushed at him like a linebacker.

"Eli," Greysen croaked into Sage's ear. With scraped and bloody palms, he pushed his weight away from the ground—away from Sage.

"*Eliiii!*" Greysen called out into the vertical pillar of dirty smoke.

Sage opened her eyes again, wincing at the crumpled sideways world. Pain spread across her face as Greysen simultaneously rolled to the side and peeled himself off her back. He tried to stand. She lifted a braised chin and twisted her stiff neck to look back at him. Most of his brows and lashes were burned off or hanging in singed clumps.

For just a second, Greysen straddled the back of her knees while balancing on his own knees. Straining to see through the rolling plumes of gray smoke, he tried to stand. He faltered backward and landed on his haunches at Sage's downturned feet. Trembling and spitting out gravel, Sage raised to her elbows. As she began to belly-crawl toward the car, she heard the quick crunch of Greysen's scuttling feet, slipping with determination in the direction of the flames.

Heat from the blaze kissed Sage's skin as she inched her way to the car. She tried to push back the fresh memory of pieces of Eli's body taking flight. Pain from her own bruised body had not fully registered. She clutched the hot handle of the open car door and pulled herself to her knees. Heaving air, she anxiously looked inside, searching behind the passenger seat for Jadia. Jadia was hunkered, traumatized but physically unharmed, in a squatting position on the far floor, rocking and crying. Sage's outstretched hand stroked her daughter's hair for several beats. Then Sage craned her neck around the back of the passenger seat. She found Sean buckled in his seat and wearing the same remote stare as Jadia.

Sage couldn't see beyond the dashboard through the soot-obscured windshield, but she knew what had captured the attorney's undivided attention. His catatonic eyes were fixed on the spot where Eli had stood just seconds before banging the screen door. Raging flames spread and swept through and around the house, puffing out black billowing smoke. Sage pulled herself up to the running board and sat, shaking, with elbows resting on her knees, grimy hands clutching her singed hair.

CHAPTER 19

"Get in the car, Sage! Now!" Greysen shouted. He stood dangerously close to the flames. Sage's head snapped up so fast and hard that a bone in her neck popped. Greysen had turned back to the flames. He disappeared behind waves of smoke, fire, and heat for two beats, and then he reappeared, the fiery elements snaking around and up him like wispy medusa strands. He turned back to the inferno and raised a forearm to guard his face.

Sage stood when she saw him reaching into the fire as if expecting to grab and pull Eli to safety. A secondary explosion ignited, rocking the earth. Greysen stepped backward, lost his footing, and fell on his haunches. Ignoring the pain, Sage scurried toward Greysen in a wobbled rush, lost her balance, fell to her knees, and crawled the rest of the way to him.

"Come with us!" she shouted. In clumsy movements, she stood and plucked at Greysen's torn shirt, her fingers slipping through the sweat-soaked fringes. With determined hands she grabbed a resistant, hard arm.

"Greysen!"

Something popped in the distance. A beat later, Sage and Greysen were showered with another spray of debris.

"Come with us. Now!" Sage shouted. She hooked her arms under his armpits and tried to lift him up.

Faltering, Greysen freed himself from Sage's grip, propped himself on one knee, and guarded his face with a forearm. He breathlessly shook his head and squinted against the heat, staring at it—*into* it. A gust of wind blew the black and muddled gray smoke deeper into the dense vegetation, momentarily revealing the wide clearing awash in a blizzard of ashen destruction.

"No! ... No! I can't." He voice was ragged and tormented, and equally determined.

"*Greysen!*" Sage shouted defiantly. A gust of wind bore the fierce heat forward, driving both of them back until they crashed to the ground again. Another heat surge blew over them. Sage back-crawled her way to the car, then lifted herself and hoisted her heavy, breathless body onto the car door. Greysen stumbled to a stand and stepped defiantly back into the heat.

Sage pushed herself to her feet. She pushed deeper into the heat and called to Greysen's back. "We're probably being watched. Come with us, please!"

"No!" Greysen said, turning to face Sage.

Sage's eyes froze on Greysen's red-rimmed ones, then she took a frenzied scan of what was left of the smoldering house. Sage's gaze landed back on Greysen and the crackling wood, and he stared ahead, silence between them.

"Staying?" she asked incredulously. "Here? Are you insane?"

Greysen looked away, then back toward the flames, somewhere in the direction where Eli's body had landed. He was looking at—Eli. Sage could tell by the thick current of pain ripping his face and veiling his eyes. The thought of Eli drove her backward until she found herself falling upright onto the Bimmer's running board.

"No, Sage," Greysen said to the heat with dispassionate control. "I am not insane."

"Sage, get in the car!" Sean screamed across the front seat. Slouched in a panting hump on the running board, Sage glanced up at Sean. Then she pulled herself up and dragged her heavy body into the passenger seat.

"You've got to talk to Greysen," she panted. "He—he said he isn't coming."

"He can't leave Eli!" Sean said. "Can't you see that? Close the door so we can get the hell away from here."

Sage opened her mouth, but before she could utter a protest, Sean stepped on the accelerator. The car lurched forward, jerking Sean and Sage backward then violently swinging them to the right. Sage almost flew out the open door as it swung out wildly. The force threw Jadia from a fetal huddle. The car swerved, fishtailing as the tires spun, spitting out gravel and losing traction. As soon as it gained a hold, Sean stomped on the brake pedal, whipping himself and Sage forward with head-jerking force. Jadia, sandwiched lengthwise on the floor between the front and back seats, bounced back and forth. Sage palmed the dashboard with outstretched arms, eyes bulging.

"Dammit!" Sean yelped. He jammed the gear lever into PARK and punched the steering wheel until his knuckles blistered. After several blustering breaths, he opened the door, fought with the seat belt, and staggered out.

"Grey," he called out as he broke out in a drunk-like gait and rounded the back of the car. Sage spun around in her seat, watching Sean raise pleading hands.

"Grey, plea—"

Greysen spoke to the dying flames, cutting Sean's appeal short. "I'm staying, Sean."

Sean kept moving, baring the brunt of the heat with Greysen.

"She's dead, Greysen," Sean said. His sympathy carried over the lapping blaze. "And the house is gone, too. There's—" He stopped and swallowed dry, hot air. "There's nothing you can do. There's nothing anyone can do." Sean paused and placed a hand on Greysen's shoulder, his voice cutting the heavy air. "Eli's gone."

In denial, once more Greysen searched the smoke and fire as if what he sought was just beyond his grasp. Then he glimpsed her broken body beyond the flames as the putrid, sweet stench of roasted flesh wafted in the air.

"Yeah," Greysen finally said. His voice was now solid, controlled, unfaltering.

Under his hand, Sean felt Greysen's shoulder slacken in resignation. He pursed his lips, looked to the ground, then back to his friend before saying, "I'm sorry, Grey." Sean's voice broke. "I'm really sorry about Eli."

Sage got out of the car and willed her stiff, bruised body to move into the back seat with a squatting Jadia. The girl rocked on the floor, moaning with her head between bent knees. Gently Sage pulled Jadia into the seat and laid her daughter's tousled head on her grimy lap. Jadia's hair felt like the finest silk as Sage pulled it away from her daughter's beautiful face and forced her own back, wretched with stiff pain, to bend until her lips were at Jadia's ear.

"Shhh," she said. "It's okay. Shhhh. I love you. I'm here. Shhhh."

Sage unfolded and twisted to look out the window when she heard Greysen ask Sean, "Can we talk in private?"

It was sad the way Sean's head trembled; it was as if he had to force himself to maintain eye contact with Greysen. Sage craned her head, swallowed a grunt, and winced as she twisted further in the seat and watched the two men walk away from the dwindling fire and further from the car. She hitched an arm atop the back seat and followed their steps from the back window. Greysen limped, his seared face blotched with dirt and red patches. Sean, hands in his pockets, kept shaky pace at Greysen's side.

Jadia sat up and looked directly at her mother with an upturned chin. Her expression, relaxed anew, nearly serene, frightened Sage. She reached over the seat, grabbed Jadia's hand, and watched as her daughter slowly lifted her chin.

"Let's buckle up," Sage said. "We don't want to get thrown from the car when Sean's ready to take off." She gave her daughter a weak smile, parched lips cracking with the effort.

Just then noises of a quick click startled her. She flinched, her shoulders pulling up her chest with a jump. Jadia had fastened her seat belt and was looking at her. Sage narrowed her eyes, rubbed Jadia's cheek with the back of her hand, and said nothing.

A gentle current of crosswinds trapped the car with another wave of Eli's scent. The ghastly smell irritated Sage's sinuses and her nose hairs stiffened painfully. She wanted to get the hell away from there—with Jadia, Sean, *and* Greysen in tow. Trying to hold her breath, she looked through the sooty back window and over to where Sean and Greysen talked several yards away. The crackling flames distorted their low voices. Eli lay nearby.

At length Sean headed back to the car alone.

"Grey's staying," he said as he sat behind the steering wheel. Expressionless and mute, Sean started the car and punched the gas pedal, and they fishtailed away, spinning dust back into the maelstrom where Greysen remained.

CHAPTER 20

"Greysen is a former Special Service agent, Sage," Sean finally said after nearly an hour of mutually respected silence. They had rolled over long stretches of serpentine roads, and their breathing patterns were just now subsiding to normal.

"Or something akin to that," Sean continued. "Grey doesn't talk about it—these are my deductions. He's a survivor, and he knows what he's doing. That's all I know."

"I thought you said he was an attorney," Sage said. She was leaning forward, angling herself toward the driver's seat. "Didn't you tell me that you met in law school?"

"He is an attorney, yes. He's got a summa cum laude's worth of law under his scalp. He'd already signed up for …" Sean's words trailed off.

As Sage waited for Sean to finish, she glanced at the speedometer. They were going ninety miles per hour. She checked on Jadia and found fright scrawled across her daughter's face. Sage squeezed Jadia's shoulder and asked, "But then, what?"

"What do you mean?" Sean pressed harder against the accelerator.

"You were saying Greysen graduated and went overseas. Then what?"

"Sage, I really don't know. It's classified and personal. Greysen keeps it to himself. Like I said, I've only deduced a few things." He paused, glancing over his shoulder at Sage. "He's got connections from that part of his life—FBI or CIA or DOD or some other agency. He's going to work that end to see if he can find out who could be behind all this. In the meantime, I need to focus on keeping the directions Greysen gave me in my head."

Sean veered onto a road that was more remote than the previous one. The tires screeched loudly on two wheels before rolling on all fours again. Nearly thirty more minutes of quiet ticked before they swerved onto a two-lane highway.

"Shouldn't we head south?" Sage asked.

"No. We're backtracking," Sean said. "It's the opposite of what we would be expected to do because it's counterintuitive. Our first order of business is to ditch this car for a used one. The new ride might be a junker, but as long as it runs, we'll drive it. I'll drop you and Jadia off at a motel."

"Motel?" Sage squawked.

"Yes, motel," Sean repeated. "Greysen gave me an alias to use. As long as I use cash, they won't ask for ID. The other really great thing about this place is that it's deep in the backcountry of the good ole US." Sean smiled in the rearview mirror at Jadia.

Jadia's eyes smiled back at Sean.

Sage watched the exchange with a faint smile. Sean was on her side. He wasn't thinking about his career. He wasn't thinking about his wife. He wasn't thinking about how she'd blown everything with the Glock. This moment was about her, and he was telling her it was okay. She reached from the backseat and laid her hand on top of his on the gearshift, curling her fingers between his.

When he glanced over his shoulder in questioning surprise, Sage mouthed, "Thank you."

He nodded and refocused on the road. She gave the top of his hand a squeeze and let go. With quivering lips, she turned stinging tears toward the waving brigade of sugar maples stretched along the two-lane road.

CHAPTER 21

When Sage saw the two-door clunker Sean had purchased from the Richwood used car lot, she nearly lost it.

"Seannnnn!" she whined as they stepped into the '78 Capri. Piles of cash on the table of a tiny-town business owner went a long way—even if said bills, like the tiny town, did not add up to much. Sean had paid a junkyard owner cash to destroy Sage's 5-Series BMW framed license plate, anything with a VIN number, and the engine. The business owner was free to sell unidentifiable parts, but Sean had to ensure that no one ended up behind the wheel of the bullet-pocked vehicle. After that, he flash more bills at the tiny-town parents whose yard sported a one-car lot.

"It's a car, Sage," Sean said.

Later Sean paged Greysen from a pay phone outside the restaurant while Sage and Jadia waited in the car. Over forty minutes and full stomachs later, they sat in a hot car, waiting. At last Greysen rang back. Sean must have talked twenty minutes before he gestured for Sage to come over.

"Grey wants to talk to you," he said as she approached.

"Me?" she mouthed with raised brows. She took the beat-up receiver and watched Sean amble back to the car. Shielding herself from the booth's stifling heat, she remained standing as she stretched the cord and leaned against the doorway.

"How are you?" Sage asked without preamble.

Greysen's voice projected strong through an air of despair. Grief. "The question is how are *you*?"

"I'm doing fine—but I'm in good company. What's going on with you?"

"Things are quiet here." He paused. "How's Jadia?"

"She's faring well, considering. But, back to you," Sage volleyed. "I'm sure the fire department had plenty of questions about the house. They don't think you're responsible, do they?"

"Sage, this homestead is remote—miles and miles from anyone. Very few people knew the house was here, much less that it's now gone. Unless a plane happened by, I doubt anyone noticed a fire, and even if they did, they'd assume trash was burning."

"Oh," Sage stammered. She took a breath. "Well, what about …" Sage hesitated, not sure if or how to ask. "What about Eli?"

"I buried her deep in the woods."

Sage stepped deeper into the booth. "I uh, I was going to ask if you had notified her family."

In the brief silence, a gentle breeze came through the doorway of the booth. Greysen said, "Eli didn't have family. None who would claim her anyway."

Sage pressed the phone tightly against her ear, trying to come up with the words—any words—to console him.

"Greysen, I wish we would have never shown up at your place last night. … I'm just so sorry."

His reply was immediate. "Sage, none of this is your fault. It's okay."

"No, Greysen, it's not okay. None of this is okay."

There was silence for a minute, then she asked, "Where are you staying?"

"Tonight, in the woods. There's a soft spot around the grounds near Eli. I keep blankets behind the seat of my truck, and camping gear and equipment in the shed."

"We should have stayed with you. We can come back, you know."

He was quiet for a while and then said, "Considering everything, I am in a good place. I need to be alone to process and regroup. I'll be fine, so don't worry. There's a well nearby and plenty of edible plants in the woods."

Sage frowned and scanned the phone booth, silently marveling at his strength. "Okay," she relented. "But what about tomorrow?"

"I'll cross that bridge when I get to it. I'll be all right, Sage. If the guys behind the shooting and the bombing have any idea that you're alive, this will be the last place they'd look."

"Then maybe we should have stayed there," she said.

"Maybe. I don't know. I had a few of my contacts put some feelers out. I'll know a lot more within forty-eight hours. Sean has the details. I … I just wanted to know how you and Jadia were doing."

Sage noticed birds chirping for the first time. She thought of the endless ways everyone took things for granted. She stepped outside the booth and whispered, "Thanks," into the receiver.

"And, Sage?"

She waited a second, then responded, "Yes?"

"Don't hesitate to page me if you need anything or you just want to talk."

Sage frowned at the gravel. "What if *you* need to talk?"

Greysen said nothing.

"What if you need someone to tell you it's going to be okay?"

The line stayed silent.

Sage stepped inside the booth, sat on the hot metal seat, and closed the door. "Did I offend you?" she asked.

Silence stretched itself in a lazy recline. At last she heard him take a breath.

"Don't ever think saying kind words offends me."

Sage's forehead rested on the chunky keypad jutting from the boxy phone base.

"You don't need a reason, Sage. Just page me."

Sage kept a tight grip on the handle long after she'd hung it on the base. When she finally walked from the booth, Sean was leaning against the passenger door talking to Jadia who looked at him as if she were actually listening. When Sage was close enough, he pulled a lock of curl from her sweaty forehead and asked, "Are you okay?"

"I'm good, Rockefeller." Sean nodded.

"It's nice to know that you care," she said. "Thanks."

"I do care. And you're welcome." He pursed his lips. It looked like a smile this time. Sage met Jadia's bright gaze and wrapped an embracing arm over her shoulder. She whispered, "I love you."

"She's going to be okay," Sean said, regaining her attention. "*We're* going be okay."

Sage kissed Jadia's cheek and looked at Sean. "I hope you're right," she said.

"Yeah," he agreed as he opened the driver's door. "I hope I'm right too."

CHAPTER 22

"How about a change of clothes?" Sean suggested the next morning as he backed the Capri from the gravel parking lot of a greasy spoon. They had downed a hearty breakfast of sugar, syrup, and caffeine after staking out a phone booth in Moorefield, West Virginia for three wee early morning hours before Greysen answered their page.

"How about the money?" Sage countered.

"I have plenty, Sage. We're covered for a while—don't worry."

A short time later, as they left a small discount clothing store—one without cameras—Sage said. "I wonder what Greysen will do about clothes or food. Wild herbs can only carry him so far."

"Greysen is a survivor, Sage," Sean assured her as they traveled toward a different highway. Toward a different city. Toward a different motel. Staying in one place too long could make it easier for them to be tracked. "He's probably been in tougher situations."

"Yeah, you told me. Special Services, right?"

"Well, something like that is my best guess."

"We should have stayed together, Sean. All of us."

Sean didn't reply.

"Why doesn't Greysen have a phone?" Sage asked.

"Cell phones can be traced," Sean said.

"Even the prepaid?" Sage said.

"If they can trace the purchase. It's a chance Greysen doesn't want to take."

"I guess he has a point," Sage said. "The authorities tracked O. J. Simpson's cell phone and caught him coasting along an LA freeway."

Sean stiffened as if in pain. Sage did not know about the unpopular choice he'd made to swap the O. J. Simpson murder case for the Anthony Campbell rape case. It wasn't her fault she didn't know, but he wished she hadn't brought it up. He deflected back to Greysen.

"Greysen can route calls by going public so they appear to originate from a switch, not from a terminal. He feeds the call into a stream of thousands of bundles so it will bypass authentication."

Sage threw Sean a blank look as they veered off Route 55 and headed northeast on Route 29.

He could have said more. Could have explained how Greysen knew how to slip by the Fed's telephone gatekeepers, but the thought of doing so left him with the uncomfortable feeling of compromising a client-attorney confidence. Although he was not Greysen's attorney, he was Greysen's friend.

"Anyway," Sean continued, "Greysen gave me the sequence of numbers to dial. The mechanics are fuzzy. All I know is that when it's all said and done, the end switch randomly assigns the portal entry as a hub anywhere in the continental United States. The origination point is never recorded."

"I'm uncomfortable using Greysen's methods, so I bought the calling cards. Not quite the same, but I figure for the most part, Greysen's been returning our calls to phone booths. We haven't jeopardized his anonymity." He waited a moment. "We jeopardized most everything else though."

Sage closed her eyes, fighting with haunting images.

There was a lingering silence before Sean said, "Look Sage, your primary concern should be Jadia and yourself. Greysen is not the target here. The murderers aren't after him—remember that."

Sick with Revenge

"And they weren't after Eli either—you remember *that*," she rebutted. Sean gave her a sideways, reproachful glance, then drew his eyes back to the road as he veered onto a driveway and parked in front of a motel office.

As Sean paid for adjoining rooms, Sage absentmindedly peeked inside the large plastic bag on her lap. Sean had bought shampoo and other toiletries from a discount store. The prospect of a long hot shower was a nice diversion, but did not take her mind off the explosion.

"You seem a little insensitive to Greysen's dilemma," she blurted when Sean folded back into the car. "If it weren't for us, Eli would still be alive, and Greysen would still have a roof over his head. Don't you think we owe him?"

Sean slipped into silence and drove across the motel property to their suites. He pushed the driver's door ajar, then turned to her and said, "Sage, Greysen's strong, fit, and capable—results of genetic traits as much as from training and practice and perfection of his skills. He's a survivalist, but more than anything, he demands respect. There was no way he was going leave Eli there. We have to respect his wishes. As for Eli …"

His voice trailed to a stop when Sage yanked the door handle and clumsily tripped from the car. Jadia trailed behind her. Sean carried the remaining bags.

"If you don't mind, Sean, I'd like to take a shower."

"Sure," he stammered as he handed her their bags and a room key. "How about pizza a little later?" he proffered.

"Fine," she agreed, opening the hotel door for Jadia.

"Uhhh," he drew out thoughtfully, "I guess this is as good a time as any to ask you this." He peeked through the crack in the door to ensure Jadia was out of hearing distance, and then pulled it shut.

"What is it?"

"We need to get Jadia to a safe place until this is over," he stated in a factual tone.

Sage raised a hand to her eyes, squinting under her hand at Sean. He stood in the sun's backlight, cast in an alcove of shadow like a shrined deity. He reminded Sage of Thomas.

She found herself remembering how Thomas had sold her on the idea of boycotting television after Jadia was born. How Thomas had hopped up like he'd won the lottery to provide Jadia's 2 a.m. feedings. In her memory, Sage saw ruffled baby socks strewn like multicolored, deflated balloons across their unmade bed—the same ruffled socks Thomas kept stowed away until this day in his own sock drawer. When Jadia was a toddler, he'd brush her hair this way, then that way. Later, when she was older, he had searched for the best school in the metropolitan area. Now, of course, they shared home-schooling duties with Oma.

Sage visualized Thomas's stricken face when he'd learned Jadia had been kidnapped. She remembered how his eyes slowly closed when the authorities informed them that they had found Jadia in a Maryland forest with Anthony Campbell. For seven days, she'd been repeatedly raped.

"The only thing capable of stirring Thomas is Jadia." Sage snorted. "Kind of like you."

Sean steadied his thumb on his wedding ring, saying nothing.

"I meant it as a compliment, Rockefeller," Sage said with a weak smile.

Sean looked over Sage's head at the mountainous horizon, thought about it, and then recaptured her expectant gaze. "Jadia stole my heart the moment I saw her," he admitted.

He didn't mention he'd first seen Jadia pictured as a missing child on the front page of a Philadelphia newspaper. That he'd laid it on Lori's nightstand so she'd also see it. Or how six months and a private investigator later, he'd walked into the South Street advertising firm where Sage worked, requesting the most successful senior executive to manage his account, because he'd already learned Sage was both the best account manager and Jadia's mother.

Sage frowned. "I hope to God taking Jadia to the prison didn't set her back. What if the psychiatrists were wrong? What if seeing Anthony Campbell threw her into oblivion so deep we'll never reach her?"

Sean stopped spinning his ring and leaned closer to Sage. "Jadia's got more strength than the lot of us. She's going to be okay, trust me."

He leaned a little closer. "But she needs to be with her father right now. Thomas can give her the stability and security she needs."

Sage screwed her face into a scowl. "The safest place for Jadia is with me, Sean."

"Not now, it isn't," he countered, clipping the words. "Call Thomas, Sage. Call him tonight. If you don't, I will."

The next morning, Sage was haphazardly tossing clothes and toiletries into a plastic bag. She said to Jadia, "You've got to be hungry. I'll make sure we eat breakfast at a restaurant that serves banana pancakes."

Suddenly she stopped fussing and studied her daughter. "Jadia," she called, "are … are you looking at me?"

Jadia blinked casually. And smirked. Jadia was definitely smirking.

"You're listening to me, aren't you?" Sage dropped the bags on the table, then ran to the bed and sat beside Jadia. "What was it—the banana pancakes?"

Boom, boom, boom! The knocks fell hard and fast against the door. "It's me," Sean's voice rang out.

"I would have cooked banana pancakes morning, noon, and night had I known you'd react like this," Sage said to Jadia as she padded over to open the door.

"I just talked to Greysen," Sean blurted before she fully opened the door. He pushed past her. "We gotta leave now!"

"What's going on?" she asked, grabbing their bags.

"I'll tell you when we're in the car!" He grabbed Jadia's hand and ushered them both through the motel door. "I already checked us out."

Sean scrambled them into the car. Doors slammed shut, and he tossed plastic bags into the trunk before jumping behind the wheel. Skids and screeches sounded from spinning tires. The car rocked under Sean's maneuver.

Sage's dancing eyes alighted on the backseat. Jadia was struggling with the seat belt. She finally managed to insert it into the latch. Her body lurched one way and wrenched another in the swerving car before being thrust back, rocking, into the seat.

Sage whipped her bobbing head forward, and grabbed the dashboard for stability. Her gaze danced across the display. Seat belt light, cool engine, 6:30 a.m. The speed was 36 mph and increasing even before they had cleared the parking lot. Sean choked the steering wheel. Sage's eyes bounced to his flexing jaw, then to a sallow cheek above it, and finally to dry lips parted in a grimace. His square white teeth were grinding and shifting. He swerved southwest onto Route 29, skids sounding again in a horrid screech. Sage locked on the speedometer on the dashboard: 47 … 61 … The rackety Capri was vibrating under the strain.

"What's going on, Sean?" Sage asked, her voice shaking with fright.

Her eyes darted to the swiftly passing road. It pointed southwest, away from Capon Bridge where they were going to meet Thomas, and back to … Greysen.

"Are you going to tell us or what, Sean?" she yipped. He said nothing.

"What is going on?" She asked again. "Sean?"

As if suddenly awakened, Sean threw her a wild-eyed glance. "What?"

"What?" Sage blew harsh loud gushes of air through her noise. "What do you mean, 'what?' Where are we going?"

"We're getting as far away from that motel as possible." he finally answered.

"Why?"

Sean shot furtive glances at Jadia. "Maybe I ought to tell you later," he said.

"No!" Sage's voice shifted excitedly. "You tell me now! Tell me!"

Sean began to speak in tones barely audible over the car's engine. Sage squinted at his moving lips.

"The judge who presided over Anthony Campbell's trial—the rape trial—the judge you wrote and called? She was murdered in her home. Her body was found with a bullet lodged in her temple a couple of hours ago. Lori told me when I phoned her."

"The … it … I'm sorry about her death, of course. It sounds senseless, but what does it have to do with us? Her murder may have been the result of domestic violence or, or … I don't know, someone really upset about the outcome of another case altogether, or perhaps it's random. The possibilities are end—"

"Sage, a gun to the temple is classic execution-style murder."

Sean paused, glanced at the rearview mirror, and met Jadia's unnervingly still eyes. Shifting his focus back to the road, he cocked his head toward Sage's awaiting ear and spoke even lower. "Anthony Campbell's probation release was the last case over which the judge presided before she retired."

At the sound of that name, Sage looked toward the backseat. A dull, blank expression had plastered itself on Jadia's face again. Sage mustered a smile—doctor's recommendation—and strained to keep it on her face. She reached over the car seat, held her daughter's hand, kissed it. Jadia didn't seem to notice.

Sage muttered "banana pancakes" under her breath as she faced forward in the seat again.

"What?" Sean leaned forward in his seat and stared tersely at the road.

"Banana pancakes," Sage repeated, her voice as loud and annoyed as his—and just as scared. "Jadia needs banana pancakes."

"We're not stopping for banana pancakes or gas or anything, Sage." Sean's panicked voice rose. Fear smeared anew over his face. "We're not even stopping to piss. We're going to stay on this highway until we're the hell away fro—"

"From what, Sean? Everywhere we go, there they are. We were at the correctional center, there they were. Then you figured we'd go to Greysen's place, and that idea blew up in our faces. Now they've hit the judge. We can't outrun them so stop at the very first greasy-damn-spoon you see and order banana pancakes!"

She fell back into the seat, winded. "And slow down," she added between breaths. "This is not a major highway. Children live on this street."

The racing engine growled then settled on a rackety purr, tread rolling smooth on asphalt. An occasional vehicle whined past, going in the opposite direction.

Sean reclined deeper in his seat, jaw set. Jadia, expressionless, hugged the silence. Sage looked out the window at tall, bending grass. Her gaze rose in steep ascension up the trunks of sassafras and maples, and finally climbed in an abounding arc over the great expanse until her racing mind went blank.

CHAPTER 23

The sound of gurgling water replenishing the toilet tank filled the narrow restaurant hallway when Sage opened the bathroom door and tripped across Sean's shoes.

"What are you doing here?" she asked, righting herself. "I thought you were keeping an eye on Jadia."

"I was—I am," he said, pulling her aside. "Listen, Sage, there's more to the judge's murder. I didn't want to say any more in front of Jadia."

Rushing apprehension gripped Sage's stomach. "What is it?"

"There are a few more things you need to know about the judge." He hesitated. "And about other things. So first the judge. She was forced to retire because she illegally released court-sealed documents into her custody by signing her own name. The documents were in regard to Anthony Campbell's criminal dealings inside the pen. Rumor is she had planned to launch a clandestine investigation into Anthony Campbell's long history and untimely parole. Child molesters are usually killed in prison—if they're lucky. Anthony Campbell had no problems while he was there, which means he had protection. This judge must have been onto something." He paused. "I believe she was eliminated because she was getting too close to the truth. Your letter must have somehow inched her even closer. Greysen agrees."

Sage bit her lip in thought. "Sean, I'm still not sure this has anything to do with us—"

"There's more, Sage. Cofield's Gucci-wearing minions were found in a field not far from the prison with their penises in their mouths. Bombs at the prison killed the guards and a maintenance man. The media is labeling this a terrorist act, but you and I know better. Someone is cleaning up."

They stood under crude light between narrow walls stained with honey-brown tracks of dripping grease. Sage ignored the filth and rested a shoulder on the wall.

"What about Anthony Campbell?"

"His body has not been found, but he's presumed dead."

Sage pressed her lips together hard. "It's Glock time."

"It's *time* for Jadia to be with her dad," Sean retorted.

Sage thought about it. After a long wait, she grudgingly said, "You're right."

Sean nodded. "We're going to wait on the next word from Greysen."

"So we're *not* headed back to him?" Sage asked, groping for the hope that had just winked out.

"Uhm, no," he said. An elbow lifted above his head and rested on the wall. He palmed his head. "We were going in the wrong direction. I was kind of in a hurry."

Sage burst out in full-throated laughter.

A sheepish smile spread on Sean's guarded face before an unreadable expression returned. "We'll get back on track after breakfast, find a hotel in Capon Bridge as planned and, after Jadia is safe with Thomas, talk with Greysen tonight."

"Tonight? Tonight is … forever away." Sage's breaths came short and ragged. "I can't stand this," she said, shaking her head. "We're always lagging behind information. It's just a matter of time before it catches up with us."

Sean laid a consoling hand on Sage's shoulder. "Listen, Sage, we've got to keep our heads on straight. Evidently reliable sources are keeping Greysen apprised with solid information. We shouldn't make a move until we hear from him tonight. Until then, let's try to enjoy the banana pancakes I just ordered. It wasn't on the menu, but the owners happened to have bananas on hand for sundaes."

"Okay." Sage's smile was as forced as her agreement.

"And keep the Glock under wraps," Sean whispered.

"Whatever you say, Rockefeller." She gave him a hip bump as she swished past him, then threw a bug-eyed face over her shoulder. He belted out a laugh behind her.

Jadia ignored their return, instead focusing on the table, which was at that second being stacked with pancakes, eggs, bacon, fresh-squeezed orange juice, milk, and coffee. Jadia was lit up like shine itself.

Before they left the tiny diner, Sage dialed Thomas and confirmed the meeting place they had discussed the night before: Capon Bridge.

"US Route 50 and Capon River Road at midnight," Sage repeated to Sean after they had reached the western border of the West Virginia panhandle. "It sounds more like a movie title than custody arrangements."

CHAPTER 24

"Hey, Sage!" Sean yelled and banged on the bathroom door. "How long are you going to be in there? It's getting late. We need to get out of here!" He was in her room of the suite at the motel he'd found just ten minutes outside of Capon Bridge.

"We only have thirty minutes for dinner," Sean later admonished in a low whisper as he eased onto the highway, "if we are going to meet Thomas in time."

"Let's not talk about that now," Sage said. She gestured to the backseat. "I haven't discussed it with her yet."

"*What*—you haven't told her yet?" he silently mouthed with bulging eyes. "When were you plan—"

"At the restaurant—after you excuse yourself to go to the bathroom," she said with a bite. Without replying, Sean steered the car into another greasy spoon restaurant attached to a gas station.

As soon as they ordered, Sean excused himself, leaving Sage sitting across from Jadia.

"So, Miss Jadia." She smiled sheepishly when eyes just like hers looked up. "I want to apologize for everything we've been through the past two days. It got in the way of our vacation, and I am very sorry for that too." She got up and sat next to Jadia.

"I love you so much. I goof trying to express it. I goof trying to protect you. I goof trying to make you feel better. I am sorry I did not get it right for you, Jadia. I just hope one day you can look back on all of this and see that I tried. That I put my best, goofy foot forward. And I hope you will see that all my goofy effort was no less than a labor of love reserved only and especially for you." To her surprise, Jadia pressed her head in the crook of Sage's neck.

After a minute, Sage pulled back. "You're the best," Sage said.

Jadia quietly looked on.

"So," Sage said, shifting gears. "The good news is that your dad is coming for you." Jadia tightly wound her arms around her mother. Sage choked with surprise.

Sean folded into the booth. "Someone's happy." He grinned.

CHAPTER 25

Thomas was seated atop the hood of a green '94 Pathfinder when the '78 red Capri approached the coniferous ridge near Capon River Road and parked on the flat verge. The professor wore a pair of tortoise-rim glasses, corduroy pants, Hush Puppy shoes, and a sensible shirt. Athletic, he was a runner like Sage. Marathons, basketball, rowing, and biking kept his tall frame muscular. The gray at his temples was becoming more apparent, more distinguished, and still he looked like the same handsome geek Sage had fallen in love with nearly eighteen years before.

Even without his money or education, Thomas would have been easy to love. The guilt of having hastily and illogically relegated their love, their commitment—their family—to divorce, stabbed at Sage's chest in unmerciful repeat mode.

Thomas loped from the car and quickly closed the distance to Jadia. Jadia's embrace, warm and clean, sluiced over him like pure water falling from a fresh spring. A smile snorted itself somewhere in his throat as swirls of aromatic memorabilia filled his nostrils and memories filled his head.

The smell of cinnamon toast had wafted off Jadia for years. Then it was banana pancakes and maple syrup. Reeds from wind instruments. Horses and swimming pools. The little girl who loved them all made his life bigger than the universe. The past came at him from every direction, unending infinity rings from years past. They blanketed him, cocooning him in the sweet, inimitable chronicles of Jadia.

He could never have dreamed that the likes of Anthony Campbell would have entered their lives. Thomas shuddered at the thought.

Jadia lifted from his embrace.

"Jadia," he whispered, pulling back a second to look at her. He pulled her into his arms again, rocking her from side to side.

Sean studied the ground as if to give Thomas and Jadia privacy.

Sage shrugged into a smile.

Thomas and Jadia were both gleaming when they finally released their last squeeze. Sage and Sean strolled a short distance from the Capri to Thomas. Still smiling, she turned sideways, giving view to Sean.

"Sean," Thomas said. "Nice to see you again."

"You, too, Thomas."

With perfunctory nods, the men shook hands. Sage searched for curiosity in Thomas's eyes and found total disinterest. He really didn't want to know where she and Jadia had been instead of on vacation. What they had done. Whom they had seen. Or why Sean was with them. Thomas's only concern was for Jadia to be removed from the unsavory situation Sage obviously had her in. He'd get the details later, long after he'd resumed full control of his daughter. That expectation scared Sage far more than Manny Cofield's deadly cleanup effort.

"Thomas?" Sage paused, glancing at Sean. "It would probably be better if you didn't try to reach me at Oma's. She doesn't know about this and—"

"I understand, Sage," Thomas said, cutting her off without intonation. "We'll wait for you to contact us."

As Thomas held Jadia's hand, he eyed Sage closely. Weight loss wasn't necessarily a good thing for his former wife. Normally a trim size two, she was taking on a scrawny look with the lifeless hair and sagging-clothes theme she was currently sporting. Thomas inspected Jadia more closely, then Sean, wondering with deepening anger when any of them had last had a fresh change of clothes.

Thomas wanted to snatch Jadia up right then and there and run like the dickens to a safe place where he could help her heal. But he couldn't act on his impulses. He'd leave the erratic behavior to Sage, although it was an act of God for him to tamp down his desire to beat the hell out of Sean.

He gave the two adults another poorly concealed, scathing scan, then asked, "Are you two going to be all right?"

"Uhhhm," Sage drew out, looking dubiously at Sean's unreadable face. "Sure, we're going to be fine." Just then she remembered Jadia's recent spurts of cognizance. "Thomas, Jadia gets pretty excited about banana pancakes so—"

Thomas cut Sage short. "We'll have pancakes first thing," he said. Their daughter's state of mind was fragile at best. Thomas couldn't imagine what in the hell Sage was thinking.

"Call when you can," Thomas advised.

Sean stood in quiet darkness, hands in pockets, heels rocking. He watched Sage step with open arms to Jadia and envelop her in a lengthy embrace. Watched the surrealism with her as Thomas secured Jadia in the car before getting behind the wheel. Listened to the crunch of tires rolling against gravel as Thomas backed up and steered the car forward. And finally, he stared at a pair of diminishing red lights until they disappeared around the curve of the highway.

CHAPTER 26

"It's time," Sean said. He stood erect in the suite doorway between their rooms.

Lids, heavy with the want of sleep, flipped open. Sage shifted in the bed and drew in a deep breath. Until four that morning, they had waited to no avail at a phone booth near Capon River Road for Greysen to call, then they had driven an hour from US Route 50 to a desolate hotel.

"What's up?" Sage said, eyes still blurred.

Sean stepped into the room, seating himself at the nearby round table.

"We need to talk about Anthony Campbell."

Sage sniffed and looked around the room. She thought about how a nice, long run would get her blood flowing and sat up cross-legged on the bed.

"What about him?"

"Well, Sage, you shot him."

She scratched her neck and covered her yawning mouth, then said, "Who says I shot him?"

Sean pounded the table.

Sage flinched. "Geeze, Rockefeller, what's with you?" she asked.

"We need to talk about the gun, Sage, among other things." Sean watched as Sage crawled from the bed and crossed the room to join him at the table. He waited for her to say something. She didn't.

"My career is at stake. You and I both know I was unaware you were carrying a concealed weapon yesterday. Not that it matters much now."

"You arranged for Jadia and me to have access to the prison system without signing documents, without being checked for weapons. What about all of that?"

He nodded at the table, considering. "Totally unorthodox, true. Lori had a few friends in all the right places to make it happen. Explaining that could get some people I like in a lot of trouble, but it would be a lot cleaner than justifying your use of a gun to bring down a prisoner."

"Which makes the fact that you saw nothing in your best interest."

Sean frowned and leaned forward. "Oh, so you're concerned about my interest now? Nice to know. Too bad it didn't kick in before you smuggled a gun into a prison by using intelligence I entrusted you with." He paused, waiting for some reply. When he got none, he leaned back in his chair and said acerbically, "Classic."

"Okay, so Sage has been a bad girl. If your"—she pantomimed quotation marks with raised fingers—"connections could have kept the late, great Anthony Campbell from hurting little girls, I would have had no compulsion to bring protection."

"*I* was your protection." Sean pointed to himself and leaned forward again.

"Yes, you were. And you urged me to leave when Mr. Anthony Campbell was in trouble, because you didn't want to see him hurt. Yes, I know." She leaned over the table. "The problem was that a lot of somebodies had already been hurt, including and especially Jadia. I appreciate everything, Sean. The hard truth is that you couldn't stop him from being released. And here's hard truth number two: those who had the authority to keep him behind bars obviously had other priorities."

Sean leaned back in his chair, meticulously inspecting Sage. "So you killed him."

As Sean watched her, Sage inspected her nails. "Who said I killed him?"

Sean changed tactics. "How did you learn to move and shoot like that?" Sean asked.

Sage squinted up at him. "What do you mean?"

"The way you punched me out the door. How did you learn to move like a ninja?"

Sage broke out in cagey laughter. "Ninja? I seriously doubt it happened like that. No way. I have a callous from hell on my toe—a corn." She looked at her toes. "I don't know where it came from. It just popped up Friday morning. I guess the heels I wore weren't designed for—"

Suddenly she stopped and stood. "My heels!" The stilettos had been in the Bimmer that Sean had junked for cash, a fact Sage was just realizing.

"They're gone, Sage."

She sucked her teeth and headed back to her seat. "We're both under a lot of stress, Sean. You forgot what happened in that prison like I forgot my heels."

Sean leaned forward, pointing a rigid finger to the table. "Drop the act, Sage. I want to know where you got the gun and how you learned to shoot it, because I'm telling you, lady, there is no doubt in my mind you killed Anthony Campbell. Oh, and by the way, assault weapon laws were changed just this year, and detachable magazines are front and center on the list."

In the quiet of contemplation, Sage studied Sean's stern face. If Sean knew too much, it could hurt him; he would be complicit in Anthony Campbell's death. That was the problem. Still, she owed him something—actually, she owed him a lot. With a sigh, she looked at Sean and began to spill a few beans.

"After Jadia's rape, I studied the Brazilian martial art, capoeira, which focuses on speed, balance, and strength."

"I never heard of it," Sean said, sharpening every word with skepticism.

She spelled the word out for him then said, "It's not common in the States. I found an underground dojo, a place where judo and the like are taught, but this one was for capoeira. During that time I also became a member of the International Defensive Pistol Association or IDPA. There aren't any official clubs in Philadelphia. But with luck and the right pull from the right person, one can hitch a ride to an underground club. I piggybacked on a former police officer who's a friend and a certified Glock armorer—a biggie with the IDPA. He taught me everything Glock. From the history of the Dutch manufacturer to the polymer materials ..."

Under Sean's blank face lay shock and awe at Sage's ease. She could have been talking about shopping. A new hairstyle. Cupcakes.

Sean refocused on Sage's words. " ... safety precautions, how to clean, how to shoot, the various Glock generations and correlating specs—everything." She looked at Sean, hand raking her hair.

Sean cleared his throat, the shock of Sage's ease still rippling through him. "Did your detective friend sell you the Glock?"

"No. I didn't want him involved with any of my intentions."

"Bullet forensics will show exactly where the bullets come from. Grooves in fired bullets are like fingerprints. One print, one gun."

"Guns are traceable to a murder but not necessarily the murderer. Don't worry, Rockefeller. If anything traces Anthony Campbell's death back to me, it will not be the Glock." She bit her lower lip and raised her brows. "I don't want you involved any more than you have to be either, Sean. Feel free to draw your own conclusions, but there are certain things I will not answer."

"Like the Don't Ask, Don't Tell law Congress enacted last year." His tone was sarcastic.

"Yes, except *you* keep asking."

Sean nodded as a mixture of shock and amazement lay concealed under an unflappable blank expression on his face. Delicate, beautiful, privileged Sage was dirty to her elbows, a mother sick with revenge. He watched Sage rise and pull her purse from a nightstand drawer.

"I'm uncomfortable keeping the chamber empty," she said, slamming the drawer close with a foot. "I prefer to be ever ready, especially with a situation we're in now."

The Glock and cartridge were in her hand when she tossed the purse on the bed and headed back to Sean. The magazine hit the table with a tinny thud. Sage held on to the gun at length before lowering it to the table.

Sean looked at the Glock and the magazine, then leveled on Sage. "Did you kill Anthony Campbell, Sage?" he asked.

Sage was coming up empty, trying for the first time to gauge her feelings about what she'd done at the prison. Some vital part of herself had become a mere specter loitering in the recesses of her languorous mind, leaving her to feel nothing about the act they'd both committed.

She looked back at Sean Swoboda and answered, "Yes. I killed him."

CHAPTER 27

Sean and Sage had been on the road for seven days, hopping from hotel to hotel throughout West Virginia highlands. Their funds were tight. Low hanging gray clouds drooped bloated underbellies.

The morning was young: 4 a.m. on Thursday. Sean had called Lori at her sister's home in hopes she'd intercept an attempt anyone else made to answer the phone. It had worked. After they'd talked, his lips curved into a smile.

"What?" Sage said. Fatigued, she leaned against the passenger door and tried to shake off sluggish remnants from the doze she'd stolen while Sean phoned Lori. She ran her tongue across plaque-slick teeth, then cupped a palm to her mouth to examine her breath, giving rise to aromas of stale spittle, pepperoni, and poorly digested cheese from the pizza they'd ordered the night before.

"Nothing. Everything. I miss my wife."

Sage's hand raked a tangle of unkempt, black curls and thought about Jadia and Thomas. Two red taillights vanishing into the night. "I bet she misses you, too. Is she sending the money?"

"That, too," he said, taking a deep breath and throwing his head against the headrest. He looked through the windshield into the darkness. "I told her to keep it light. We don't want to play the wrong hand by withdrawing too much cash from her accounts."

A calm, pleased smile spread across his face as he said, "She's safe, Sage. No sign of anyone trying to kill her."

"Who?" Sage struggled up from the slump she'd resumed. Sean was feeling chatty, a rarity she did not want to sleep through.

He flashed a stony face at her. *"My wife,"* he said.

"Glad you got one," she quipped, stretching and yawning, "otherwise this situation could get weird. And where's the coffee?"

The smile reappeared on his face as he thought, *She's safe.*

CHAPTER 28

"Wait in the car. It's pouring out there." Sean said. Parked near the pay phone for nearly five hours after Sean had talked with Lori, they'd dozed on and off through stormy weather. A scowl punched his face when he noticed Sage curl fingers around the passenger door handle.

"What?" she said. "I can't talk to Greysen?"

"I'm paging him, Sage. It's a lake out there."

He peered through the rain-splattered window just as a flash of lightning illuminated the sky, and the sound of thunder crashed behind it.

"I'm not sure we'll hear the phone ring if he calls back," Sean added before he hopped out of the car.

Sage jumped when the car door slammed shut. Her heart raced, and her stomach was in a gassy knot. With sweating palms, she cracked the window and watched Sean soak up the rain. With a face set in determination, he sat in the booth, rain pouring in from every corner. Finally, he headed back for the car.

Sage searched the empty car for a towel or—anything. "You're soaked, Rockefeller. You'll get sick."

"I'll be okay," he said, shivering as he passed a hand over his drenched face. "I waited twenty-three minutes." Sean wiped his watch and said, "It's 8:53. Let's grab something to eat, then get rooms."

"So there's no chance he'll be near a phone before nightfall?" Sage asked absently.

"I seriously doubt it," Sean said. He grunted, turned the ignition, and engaged the wipers. "It was his call to change the pattern. I'm sure he has his reasons."

Sage covered a yawn, then shifted to Sean. "Why is Greysen hiding?"

Sean's dripping hand froze momentarily on the gearshift lever. He looked at Sage, then said, "You're not the only one who has secrets."

Silence rolled into the car like a fog. It accompanied the damp couple into the restaurant. After they ordered breakfast, Sean stood in front of the men's room hand dryer until his britches no longer felt swampy. The waitress was walking away with their empty plates he when reached for the check. Sage grabbed his hand.

"What was Greysen doing out there in the boonies?"

Sean pulled free from her grasp. "You mean, what was he doing out there in the boonies with Eli."

Sage left her gaze on his freed hand for a beat then leveled on his face. "Excuse me?"

"It's Eli. You can't figure out what Greysen saw in Eli. It puzzles the hell out of you, doesn't it?"

Sage's sharp gaze speared Sean. "What puzzles me," she groused, "is your insensitivity to Greysen's dilemma. I've said it before and I'll say it again—we should not have been there at all. Eli died and you left Greysen."

"But not before you and Greysen exchanged coy looks and whispers at Eli's door. You showed no respect for yourselves, Sage. Nor for Eli. And you did it right until the very second she was killed. Now you blame me for Eli's death. Guilt—it's a pisser isn't it?"

Sage stopped to catch her breath and her thoughts, and then added, "I'm glad Greysen walked me to the car. I'm glad he and I talked as long as we did. Otherwise, he would have been killed too."

Sean was quiet. Then in a low voice he said, "What were you two talking about?"

"That, Sean Swoboda, is none of your business," Sage said. She turned her attention to the restaurant window. The rain was easing up. At some point, their waitress reappeared and asked if they needed anything else. Without answering, Sean handed her a bill with the check and told her to keep the change. He planted palms on the table to slide from the booth. Sage turned from the window and laid a hand on his.

"Greysen and I weren't talking about anything to be concerned about, Sean." Once she had the undivided attention of his sculptured face, she continued. "He seemed genuinely interested in Jadia's well-being." She bit her lip and reclined against the puffy booth back, releasing his hand. "You were right about something," she said.

He waited.

"There was—I don't know—chemistry I guess between us." A delicate crease formed between her brows, changing everything else on her face. It was difficult to detect any unsavory intent on her part, especially because she was unsure it actually existed. Plaintive blue eyes drooped at Sean.

"Greysen and Eli are enigmas to me, but I certainly didn't want her dead." Under the weight of the memory—and the guilt—fingertips pressed her eyes closed. She muttered, "Geeze, I wouldn't have wanted that for anyone."

Sage opened her eyes to find Sean expectantly watching her. She swallowed.

"Stop blaming me for Eli's death," he said. "And for God's sake do not make me responsible for Greysen's decision to stay." He drew in a breath. "Lay off it and I—I won't pry into your private affairs unless it potentially or directly affects me," he paused and said, "or Jadia. She was there too, you know."

Sage nodded slowly, tucking her lower lip inside her mouth and saying nothing. She missed Jadia, wanted to get back to the good ole days of being a mommy. She thought about the day she'd been baking chocolate chip cookies, waiting on Thomas to come downstairs. Waiting on Jadia to come home from the neighbor's. Only two houses away. An entire life change away.

She focused her attention back Sean. They'd known each other a long time, but other than occasionally mentioning his wife, Sean didn't talk about his personal life much. "Do you have children?" Sage's question caught Sean off guard, but he supposed it was not completely unexpected.

"We tried," he admitted laconically. "Didn't work out. The alternative didn't work out either."

"Artificial insemination?"

"No. Adoption." His words were terse but not rude.

Sage searched his face. "It fell through?"

Sean stood and slid his wallet into a damp jacket pocket. "Something like that." To keep Sage from spilling more questions, he said, "Let's go."

His abrupt tone drew a puzzled look from her.

"Sure," she said, sliding across the vinyl seat. "Let's."

When they were sitting in the car, Sean held the key to the ignition and stared through the rain. "Promise me something."

She swept over his stern profile. "Okay."

He tugged his gaze from the windshield and looked at her. "If we ever get out of this, let's—"

"*When* we get out of this."

"Okay. *When* we get out of this, let's plan to meet for lunch or dinner. That way you can meet Lori." His lips formed a faint smile. "You'll love her."

"Sean, if she hooked you, she's got to be special. I like her already." Sage's smile faded when she saw Sean's disappear. "You'll see her again, Sean." Her voice was soft and, she hoped, reassuring.

CHAPTER 29

Fully clothed, Sage had awakened in yet another remote motel at 1:39 a.m. with no news from Greysen—or Sean! He'd left hours ago for the paging routine. She was exhausted and hung back. The book he'd promise to purchase while he was out lay on the table in her room, which meant Sean had returned and left again. Sage leafed through the *History of Coal Mining in Eastern West Virginia*, searching for a note, a card, anything to indicate where Sean might be. There was nothing. She returned the book to the table and, with her heart in her throat, padded to the suite door they shared and pushed it open.

Empty.

An explosion of fear rippled through her, and she lost all semblance of reason. She leapt into her shoes, grabbed her things, and jetted from the motel room in a trot. The plastic bag rattled as a sweaty hand cuddled the Glock inside the purse that was draped across her chest like a beauty queen's sash. After a while, the road became more desolate. There were no cars for nearly a quarter mile. No streetlights from the time she'd commenced her search for Sean.

Then she heard an engine. It was much closer than it should have been considering there were no headlights. Fear bigger than life sat on her like a sumo wrestler. Her heart beat rapidly. Her eyes darted from left to right, right to left. She didn't know which way to run.

Twin beams felt like steel and shone like lasers. High beams. She squinted, then darted into the woods. Sage tossed the plastic bags and freed the Glock from the purse. She hid behind a wide tree trunk and—going easy, very quietly slid the Glock glide. Her hand curled around the grip. The car stopped with the motor idling.

A door opened. Sage waited for it to close. It didn't. Steps sloshed across wet leaves but not quite off the pavement. With the Glock pushed out in front of her, she began to count. One … two …

"Sage?" a man's voice called. Her face pinched. *Rockefeller?*

"Sage, it's me. Sean. Put down the Glock." He laughed. Rare—and nice. "I know you have it."

The grip released the Glock. Sage threw a shoulder against the trunk and muttered, *Ouch*! There was the sound of a plastic bag being kicked, then picked up.

"Uhm," the voice rose to dripping branches, "I think you forgot something."

Sage left the cover of the bushes, disengaged the magazine from the Glock, and dropped it in her purse. With a sigh, she sloshed over the forest floor to the tall shadow. She held a hand to a brow as she tried to focus on the amorphous shape closing the distance to her.

"What are you doing out here?" Sean's shadow said.

"I'm looking for you. Still am, kind of."

He held her elbow and guided her until they were clear of the woods. They stood in the rays of the car's bright lights, facing each other.

"I woke up at 1:40," she started with one hand held over her pounding chest, the other pointing toward the ground. "And you weren't there." She hesitated to catch a breath and swallowed. "There was no letter, no note, no sign, no you. Nothing." She paused, blinking back tears and pushing reflux acid back down her throat. *"You scared me half to death!"* she screamed with a spray of spit.

"I scared you? You scared me!" he said. Anger oozed from deep folds in his brows. "When I realized it was you out here carrying your life in these ... these ..." He pointed to the bags he'd dropped on the ground and finished, "These plastic totes, I thought they had found you. I wondered if you were being followed. I ... I ... You scared religion out of me, Sage!"

"Yeah, yeah, yeah," she said. She spun around in hysterical relief. With closed eyes, she stilled herself then raked a trembling hand through her hair.

"Where were you?" she asked. Her voice was low, exhausted. And her eyes were still closed.

"Talking to Greysen."

Her lids flipped open. "At this hour?"

"Actually, I had spoken with him before—"

"Before you left the book in the motel?"

"No. The first time I went out, I paged Greysen and waited three hours before I gave up. That's when I came back with the book. I watched you sleep for a couple of hours, then decided to try paging Greysen again. By the time I returned to the bookstore, tons of people were in there. I kept going until I found a more remote area and drove for miles before I could find a phone that worked. When he called back, he said—you're not going to believe this, Sage—"

"Tell me! What did Greysen say?" Sage insisted, practically nose to nose.

"He said that it's over."

Sage's entire body fell slack in confusion. She stepped backward until the backs of her legs hit the Capri fender. "What's over?"

Sean looked over her head, past the hood of the car into the midnight air. With an imperceptible shake of his head, he leveled his eyes back on hers and spoke. "The entire abominable mess. Manny Cofield was found in Juárez, Mexico. He confessed and is in the process of being extradited."

Sage stared at Sean in wonder. "Confessed to what?"

"Just about everything—including the prison bombs." He paused. "Anthony Campbell had been reported as missing, which is the only reason the authorities raided the prison in the first place. Manny claimed he got into a brawl with his men over who was responsible for Anthony Campbell being AWOL. The authorities were anxious to hit him with the truckload of drugs on the premises and with aiding and abetting an escapee, so they didn't bother to look hard for anything or anyone else.

"The guns they fired at us were loaded with the same bullets used to kill the judge. Interviews with Cofield have led them to believe Anthony Campbell is also dead, although they have no leads as to where the body was disposed of—probably in the Atlantic somewhere."

Sean set the plastic bags on the hood of the car beside Sage. He stepped back and shoved his hands into his pockets, rocking on his heels until her eyes found his.

"If Anthony Campbell's body is in a shark's belly, your Glock will never enter the picture, Sage."

The air fell silent as Sage and Sean fell still. At some point, cricket chirping rose in the stillness.

"Do you think someone's trying to smoke us out?"

"I don't think so. According to Greysen's trackers, no one is sure Anthony Campbell was actually in the prison that day. Supposedly prison records documented his departure from the maximum-security prison that morning. But, like us, there is nothing supporting his presence at the boutique facility. As for us, it's evident Cofield and his men think we're dead. And there's one salient fact."

Sage waited.

"Greysen was able to confirm there were no video surveillance cameras on the property. The new private owners recently removed an older faulty system, but the contractors hadn't finished installing the new equipment due to purchase order discrepancies and invoicing issues."

Sage nodded her head pensively. "And everything was cleaned?"

"Everything. Doorknobs, the furniture, the floor. Completely sanitized with some pretty powerful chemicals that ate up the floors and walls. No sign of anyone or anything. Verdict? Manny Cofield is guilty, and his dead coadjutants, complicit."

Thinking it over, Sage lifted her rump and pushed herself up on the hood. "Too bad the cleaning crew was on strike when we arrived," she said.

Squinting into the headlights, Sean snorted a grin. Sage tried to return his smile but only mustered a weak head shake.

"How did all this happen?" she finally asked, peering up at Sean again.

He squinted at the headlights. "Let's talk about this in the car."

"Okay," she said. Her voice was soft, agreeable, and awash in doubt amid the fresh news. She joined him in a squat and helped him to gather belongings that had tumbled from the bag and her purse. Afterward, they sat in the Capri's plastic-and-nylon interior. Sage stared through the windshield at the abyss as Sean turned off the headlights and silenced the roaring engine.

"Why is it so loud?" she asked, turning to face him.

"I think it's as exhausted as we are."

He rested a wrist atop the steering wheel and studied the dashboard. "When Anthony Campbell was on the outside, he became hooked up with this—this cult. It turned out to be Manny Cofield's cult. Campbell's rapes, believe it or not, offended those who worked for Manny. You sell drugs, you steal, you cheat, but you don't rape little girls." Sean's eyes shifted to Sage and found her watching and listening attentively. "Manny protected Campbell for other reasons."

Sage thought about the way Manny Cofield straddled Anthony Campbell. The look on his face when his prisoner bucked his hips. The bloody kiss.

"Eventually," Sean continued. "Anthony Campbell became a nuisance with too many people, and he fell in disrepute with a lot of powerful people within that circle. When he was convicted, Manny made arrangements for the sentencing judge—the one who was killed—to ensure that Campbell was sent to his prison system. This way he could keep his lover happy, protected and under control. Campbell managed to get out of Manny's good graces. I don't think Campbell realized how ruthless Manny really was. I think Manny planned to blot out Campbell all along. Maybe he was waiting to get his fill of him."

Sean and Sage sank into their respective private thoughts.

"What about Eli?"

"What about her?"

"You mentioned Anthony Campbell, the prison bombings, and the judge—you didn't say anything about Eli."

Sean took a deep breath and nestled deeper into the seat. "Manny Cofield has said nothing about a house bombing, so as far as Greysen and I can tell, no one knows about Eli. Greysen wants to keep it that way."

"*He what?*" she blurted out. "What do you mean, he wants to keep it that way? An innocent woman is dead, Sean. An entire house burned to the ground. Greysen lost his whole li—"

Sean interrupted Sage with, "Eli's death was horrific, Sage, but there's another side to this. If Manny Cofield was behind the blast, then he believes we are as dead as he knows Anthony Campbell is. I'm not sure how much power he has, but either way, it's a good thing he thinks we all died in that blast."

Turning from her, Sean fingered his wedding band with his thumb, and he stared at length into the bleak scene beyond the windshield. "It's time to put all of this behind us."

After another stretch of pensive silence, he said. "We have to recondition our minds so that we can get back to normal, everyday life. It's going to take a while but—" Sean grabbed Sage's hand. "We have to. There's no other choice."

Sage studied their entwined fingers for a while, and she finally reciprocated with a firm squeeze as she met his gaze with a tight smile. With a breath, she freed her hand and peered through the windshield into the bleakness ahead.

The next morning, Sean dropped off Sage in front of Thomas's home at ten fifteen.

"Give my love to Jadia," he said as she opened the passenger door.

"Will do. Ciao, Rockefeller." She grabbed her purse and the bags and jumped out of the car.

CHAPTER 30

Sean listened to voices coming from the kitchen door inside the garage. Lori, sexy and unabashed, and believing her husband to be at home waiting for her. Her sister Anna's hallmark loud shuffle sounded against the pristine garage floor. He imagined her wearing the pair of boots her husband, Larry, loved—Russian bast shoes that wrapped around her muscular legs.

Just then, Sean, concealed on the floor of the backseat under a blanket, heard the Swoboda driver, Frank, exiting and rounding the car, his polished footwear tapping in crisp steps and clean rhythms against the pavement—*tap, tap, tap*. Frank helped Lori inside the backseat of the Mercedes. Then Anna hung back as Larry helped Frank place Lori's belongings in the trunk.

"Feel free to use our kitchen for salyanka anytime," Larry called after Lori lowered the window. A burst of laughter exploded from the threesome before the driver's side door closed.

Frank started the car and put it in gear. Lori pressed the lever to raise the window. Anna and Larry waved and retreated to the open garage. The car moved forward, tires pushing against the pavement. Sean's hand eased from the blanket and dove deep between his wife's silky smooth thighs. Lori's hand went to her heart, and she opened her mouth. A gasp threatened to morph into a scream when Sean's head rose from the blanket.

Pinned under her husband's hungry gaze, Lori curved her heart-shaped mouth into a sensual smile. Sean's large hand found its way to her round face with its porcelain skin and high cheekbones. The hand raked through her short, blonde, coifed hair until it rested on her delicate neck. Sean's eyes ate Lori, one body part at a time. He leaned into her face.

"I thought you were meeting me at home," she whispered in breathy happiness.

"You made salyanka?" he whispered, his lips moving against hers with every word.

A corner of her mouth pulled into a half-smile. "Room and board had to be paid some way," she whispered into his lips.

"I want some," he said, pressing a little harder against her lips.

"There's plenty." She cupped soft hands on his smooth head.

"I'm not waiting until we get home."

"You better not."

"Frank," he called out without looking away from his wife. "Power up the privacy window."

Before the custom-installed privacy window completed its glide across the tracks, Sean was working his way to Lori's panties, and he was pulling her down into the seat with careful, gentle ease.

CHAPTER 31

Frank was helping Lori inside her New Hope home when Sean advised him he could leave for the day with full pay once Lori was fully unpacked and comfortable. Vanessa was already at the house, back on duty since the prior day. Sean had arranged this once he learned Manny Cofield was behind bars without bail.

After Sean explained that Lori had already eaten, Vanessa brought a plate of canard à l'orange and a chilled glass of imported beer to Sean's office. He gestured for her to be seated and handed her a piece of stationery. It held instructions for her to hold all calls, mute every ringer in the house, and cancel all appointments for the week, including Lori's physical therapy visits. He explained he'd planned to work from home and that he would take care of his wife's needs. Vanessa was to perform an inventory to ensure ample supplies of Lori's massage oils and medications were on hand, and that the freezer was sufficiently stocked with Vanessa's five-star dishes. She was also to bring a case of wine from the cellar and replenish the wine cooler that was located on the ground level.

Sean handed her the list, ran both hands over his head, and fell back into the seat. Vanessa was a fortyish Puerto Rican whose cooking rivaled the best French chefs. After a week of greasy spoon cuisine, Sean found himself looking at his employee with appreciative eyes. Along with his wife's sensuality, the aroma from the duck and orange slices was the perfect welcome home.

"So," he said, sitting up in the chair, "here's a little something to go with the list." He pulled out an envelope stuffed with twenties. "After the list is complete, you can start another paid vacation. I would like my wife to myself for a while. We'll see you here next Monday."

Shortly after eating, Sean was in the master bedroom admiring his wife. She sat in a wheelchair, picking a bit of colored lint from her plush, white robe. Her face lifted when his shadow filled the doorway.

"You're as beautiful as the day I met you," he said as he turned the dimmer knob. Sean attributed Lori's uncanny attractiveness to her Russian descent. The accident that had put her in the wheelchair nearly six years before seemed to have slowed down her aging process. On the other hand, and as her confident smile reminded him, nothing could deter Lori's confidence as a businesswoman and master strategist. When closed the distance and leaned in, Lori's smile opened to his kiss.

"Do I smell orange?" she asked his mouth.

"No secrets shall be revealed this day, my dear," he teased, closing the kiss. He stood up and wheeled her through the extra-wide door of their bathroom, straight to a footbath.

"Sean," she gasped. "Thank you."

After the slippers were removed, he eased her toes into water heated to her usual specifications. The fact that Lori felt the warmth of water and the tender strength of her husband's sexual prowess had given the couple and Lori's physicians' hope—the hope that she might someday regain feeling.

As her feet soaked, Sean seated himself on a stool before her and commenced to detail every memorable moment of his absence, starting with the walk to the Interview Room and Anthony Campbell. Then the men dressed in Gucci and Manny Cofield. The knife. The teeth. The blood. Hearing shots fired—shots he attributed to Manny Cofield alone. As for Sage's Glock, he did not mention it. Once he completed details of the bomb at Greysen's house, he lifted Lori's feet from the footbath and replenished the cooled water with a warm, sudsy batch, and told Lori about the Capri, the string of motels, Thomas and Jadia, and the ride back to Philadelphia. By the time Sean finished the story, his large hand had found its way between his wife's thighs.

Grabbing his hand and stilling it between her legs, Lori asked, "How did you get to Philly?"

Sean's eyes rolled up to hers. "What?"

With a grip as strong as a man's, Lori held her husband's roving hand at bay and she said, "The SL73 sat on flats in the firm's Manhattan garage. When you called me from West Virginia, you asked me to arrange to have it towed to the climate-controlled storage facility you use in the city—the one that specializes in storing classic vehicles. So how did you get to Philadelphia without a car?"

"Oh that," he said, letting his hand slide from her thigh. He eased her feet from the water and rose to empty the dregs into the sink. "Ayde Carona gave me a lift."

Lori's face remained as placid as frozen lake water when she asked, "How did Ayde get involved?"

"Uhm," he said, thinking as suds swirled down the drain. "She overheard me talking on the phone about the flats and said she owed me from the ride home we gave her last Christmas after her date had to leave."

"What was she doing listening to your phone call? Does she barge into your office all the time?"

Facing the mirror, Sean stood and studied Lori's reflection.

"It was her office, Lori—" He held a hand up, heading off something she had opened her mouth to say. "I was running late. The only reason I stopped by the firm was to retrieve a file I'd inadvertently left the night before." He paused, setting the foot massage aside and drying his hands. Then he turned to face her.

"By the time I returned to the garage, the tires were completely deflated, so I raced back in. Ayde's was the first open office I saw. It was her office, Lori. I think she had a right to be there."

"And she runs to your rescue so she could drive you two hours to Philadelphia." Below Lori's placid, ageless face, her chest heaved up and down.

Sean pulled the stool closer to Lori and reseated himself. His hand reached and stroked her cheek. "She offered her car key, Lori. Only her key. And she offered it as a gratitude gift to you and me for the night we took her home after the Christmas party." He searched her face and leaned over to whisper into her ear.

"What are you thinking?" he asked, kissing her lobe. "Are you thinking how much I love you? How you are the only woman—"

"I'm thinking you should have accepted the offer to join the O. J. Simpson prosecution while you had the chance." Sean froze under icy chill of Lori's voice. A dreary thought climbed up his spine as he tried to recover from the air-sapping punch of her words.

He thought about the morning of June 17, 1994. He had spent the previous night in the New York condo alone. Lori had not been up to the trek and hung back in Pennsylvania. Her news had pained him because sleeping without her meant little rest. That was something he'd never wanted to get used to, but sitting through meetings drugged-eyed was no walk through the park either. Coffee, sugar—not even mocha-eyed Ayde Carona—were antidotes.

The meeting had been well underway when a late-arriving partner charged in, grabbed a remote, and turned on the television monitor mounted high in a corner. The disruption and his erratic behavior held the stunned room at bay. And the stunning—well, it had only just begun.

The black screen hissed static and flicked to a national broadcast transmitting the image of a white Ford Bronco cruising LA freeways with a fleet of law enforcement cruisers lagging behind it. A charged voice projected headlines over the plop-plopping flaps of rotary winged aircraft—some close, others in the distance. Their swift, flipping beats underscored tension mounting in the room. At length, the latecomer punched the remote's channel changer button and amped up the volume.

Sick with Revenge

Another *hiss* and *pop*—this time with a sound level that pierced ears. The Bronco again. It appeared from a different angle, from a different hovering copter. The man changed the channel again. Then again. The television showed a different copter, a new angle, and the same Bronco.

He changed it again—and again.

A hodgepodge of anchors, excited witnesses, the white Bronco, and legal subject matter experts had flashed. Pictures of O. J. Simpson, Nicole Brown Simpson, and Ronald Goldman were superimposed the right-hand corner of the screen. Goldman and Simpson family members were interviewed. Former O. J. teammates, coaches, and sponsors weighed in. News crawls streamed from right to left across the bottom of the screen. Everything and everybody on the firm's conference room monitor wanted a piece of the gruesome history playing out and a slither of the backstories within that history—O. J. the superstar NFLer, O. J. the loving husband and father, O. J. in car rental and orange juice commercials, infidelity, movies, divorce, remarriage, more children.

Then the bizarre string of events: O. J. was indicted, did not turn himself in, was a no-show, disappeared, rode around in a Bronco, and threatened suicide.

Over a thousand reporters had assembled in front of the police station, awaiting O. J.'s 11:00 PT arrival. Now it was 2:12 PT (10:12 ET). O. J. was a no-show. Somewhere Sean had seen the date stamped on the newsfeed: June 17, 1994.

The monitor now flaunted a close-up of the white Bronco. O. J. Simpson sat in the back, holding a gun to his head. Former teammate Al Cowlings drove. Signs of the inevitable trial being the most publicized in American history waved like its very own red, white and blue flag.

The meeting's latecomer muted the screen, and the conference room fell silent. No one looked at Sean. Aversion, pity, and the kind of sneering that cowers behind blank faces seeped into the room, slow and lethal like odorless, poisonous gas. O. J. was killing Sean, murdering his credibility. Professional relationships that were once strong were now weak, sick, and feverish from fumes drifting from one lone, toxic decision.

Sean had motioned for the man to unmute the monitor. A reporter's voice spoke to the conference room. Rotor blades applauded—*flap, flap, flap, flap.* Then Sean had stood and walked out.

Now, still reeling from Lori's barbed words, he pulled back from his wife's ear and looked at her placid face. Not that he needed to read it. She had spelled it out loud and clear. And it wasn't about money—they had plenty of it. For Lori, everything was about accomplishment. About not sinking into the ranks of plebes.

They were eye level now, Sean squatting in muted anger and ill-concealed shock. "We'll just have to find something to achieve," Lori said.

CHAPTER 32

"I look like a vagrant, I know," Sage said. She hoped the admission would move Thomas from indignant staring to inviting her inside. Instead, she remained standing in his Manayunk doorway and braving his icy reception.

"Good morning to you too, Sage," he said. His hand waved her inside.

"I guess it's going to be one of those days," she said. She scratched the back of her neck, brushed past him, and scanned the open area beyond the foyer for Jadia. Rustling from plastic bags disrupted the quiet in the spacious stone, colonial home. It was the house they had purchased after Jadia's abduction four years before. Hand-scraped hickory floors looked up at coffered ceilings in the living room. Beyond a center staircase, the great room held a vaulted ceiling, recessed lighting, and a gas fireplace and mantle. The formal dining room, used frequently when they had been together, displayed wainscoting and crown moldings. Oak stair treads with black iron spindles often served as a conversation piece.

A tray ceiling, recessed lighting, upgraded tile bath, and jetted tub were in the master suite. Granite counters everywhere made the home feel clean, even on the rare occasion Sage was not quite up to the task.

Oil-rubbed bronze hardware and fixtures appeared throughout the house. Beige carpeting kept bare feet warm in the rest of the home. Two nearby, large, suite bedrooms gave the Wirspas space and privacy without feeling Jadia was too far away to be heard in case of a crisis or emergency. Sage and Thomas had used the master bedroom's jetted tub together whenever Jadia was with his parents or Oma. Thomas used a fourth bedroom as an office. Modern art and pictures of Jadia covered the walls.

Thomas, at home during the university's summer break, closed the front door and circled around to face Sage. He assessed her with a discerning, concerned eye, and in a friendlier voice, asked, "Are you okay?"

"I'm good," she said, flopping the purse and plastic bags to her sides. "Really, I'm good," she said. Deep blue eyes searched the room then landed on Thomas's hazel eyes. "I'll be better when I see Jadia."

"You need to eat," he said.

Sage stared at the three-sided fireplace, feeling like a speck in an orb as she gave Thomas's non sequitur thought. "You mean I look haggard."

Thomas dipped his head to regain her attention. She looked up at him.

"I mean," he said, "you normally wear a radiant, healthy glow. Right now you look fatigued. You need to eat."

Thomas inclined his head toward the kitchen, and Sage followed him to the gleam of white-on-white appliances and cabinetry that made up the front right wing of the sizable home. "Okay—fine. What are we having? And where's Jadia?"

"As a matter of fact, Jadia and I finished eating breakfast not too long ago," he said. Thomas opened the refrigerator and stuck his head inside. "I'm sure the oatmeal is still warm, and it won't take me long to whip up a couple of eggs."

Sage made a quick scan of the kitchen. "And Jadia?"

After a long hesitation, Thomas stood upright, rested his arm on the opened refrigerator door, and locked his weight on a loafer-clad foot. He inhaled deeply and slowly breathed out.

"Thomas?" Sage rushed over to him and tugged on the loose-fitting shirt he wore over comfortable jeans until his tall physique swayed back and forth. "Tell me."

Thomas closed the refrigerator and sucked in air again. "Jadia's at the psychiatrist's office." He exhaled.

Sage looked up at sympathetic, determined hazel eyes.

"Dr. Warsel. I've told you about her before. She's part of a team with one of the best track records in the land," he continued.

Flourishing uneasiness spread through Sage like thorny weeds. She remained still.

Thomas hesitated, then waved a hand past the cooking island toward an oval, glass-topped table supported by an antique cast-iron base.

"This isn't good, Thomas," she said, after walking to the table and flopping into the chair Thomas had pulled out for her. "I can feel it."

"On the contrary, Sage; it *is* good. In fact, it's excellent." He sat and faced her as their knees nearly touched at the curve of the table. "Jadia's going to be staying with me for a while, Sage."

Sage shook her head. "What's this all about, Thomas?"

Thomas studied her before calmly saying, "It's about Jadia." He paused. "Now that I've had time to cool off a bit, I can talk about how I angry I was because you took her to a crew of inept …" He looked away and shook his head, then returned to her with brows curved down in a pained expression. "I went along with it until I had had enough. Sage, we agreed not to take Jadia anywhere or subject her to anything out of the usual without mutual consent."

"A vacation was planned, Thomas. It's not like you expected her to be in the Philadelphia metropolitan area. My God, we were just—"

"Don't go berserk on me; just listen." He leaned over the table, reaching for her hand.

"I can't listen to this, Thomas!" she snapped.

Then came the words flung from Thomas's mouth like rocks from a well-aimed slingshot. "You don't have any choice, Sage. You lost your vote when you went wherever you went, did whatever you did, and stayed wherever you stayed. None of it was good, and all of it was without my permission. You didn't call; you didn't show up. Not until you were desperate and had no other options."

His hand slid from hers.

"And Jadia saw it all," he continued at last. His eyes nailed hers. "*She—saw—all—of—it.*"

In the stillness that followed, images fluttered and fell on Sage's lap, melting like flurries in a hot room. The prison. Anthony Campbell. The shots. The chase. Bullets and bombs and—

Thomas interrupted her mental ramblings. "Anthony Campbell's dead, Sage. Did you know that?"

Oh shit! Oh shit! Sage thought. *Did Jadia tell? Did she write anything down? Did she draw pictures? The bomb? Eli?*

Trying to calm her rising panic, Sage finally said, "That's great." The words slopped out and fell flat on the table.

With raised brows, Thomas opened his mouth, closed it, and then tried again. "That's an odd thing to say," he said, scratching the nape of his neck. He hesitated in thought and looked away for a second. Then he added, "I supposed you're right." He searched her slack face.

"It's not all bad news, Sage." He reached for her hand again and cupped it. "Jadia's made profound progress."

"Tha—that's wonderful news," she stammered. She leaned over the table, reciprocating the squeeze with a pathetic smile. "So what's she doing—talking? What did she say?"

"Uhhh, nooo," he drew out. "It's kind of hard to explain. She's, she's responsive—very responsive by way of her facial expressions. As soon as I noticed, I scheduled an appointment with Dr. Warsel, who consulted Dr. Klein and Dr. Caesar. They assembled a team and—"

Sage interrupted. "Jadia's always been responsive to you."

"True, but it's not just responsiveness. She's initiating more interaction. It's subtle, but the doctors and I agree. There's a lot more of Jadia surfacing now—scads more."

Sage's smile bloomed.

"The doctors agree, Sage. Jadia's progress is the direct result of having a stable environment." With closed eyes, Thomas lifted Sage's hand and pressed it against his lips for several long seconds. A thumb stroked her forefinger, as his eyes opened to hers. In a breath he said, "The doctors recommend that Jadia remains in my custody. Legally."

Sage's smile fell. She withdrew her hand, stony blue eyes weighing in on Thomas. "She's only been here four days, Thomas."

"Exactly. And in less than a week, she's already shown more improvement than in the two years she was under your custody."

The words threw Sage against the back of the chair. "Two years of *shared* custody, Thomas," she said breathlessly. "You don't believe Jadia's improvement is the sole result of being with you, do you? She'd already showed signs of improvement."

"Really?" he said. He leaned back in his chair with folded arms. "You never mentioned it before."

"Thomas!" Sage stood, walking to the island and spinning around. "I told you about it just this week."

Thomas shifted in his chair to face her. "Oh, do you mean the night you handed Jadia to me in the middle of the night like she was a package in an illicit drug deal?"

Sage braced herself against the island behind her and ignored the comment. "Thomas, I was talking to Jadia earlier that day. I mentioned banana pancakes, and she just lit up. She, she, she, uhm … she blinked and uhm … smiled kind of with her eyes a little … and, and …" Sage paced back to the table, gesturing with her palms. "And that wasn't the only time. She had been showing signs of increased awareness since …"

Thomas stood and walked over to Sage. He shook his head. "A stack of banana pancakes, Sage? That's all you've got?"

Sage went back to the table and collapsed into the chair. "Custody, Thomas?"

"Full custody." The words flowed from his mouth like liquid lava as he eased down into the chair beside her.

"For Christ's sake, Thomas, just be patient!"

"I have been patient, Sage. I have been waiting with extreme patience for you to tell me what you have been doing. Tell me why you had our daughter out at half past midnight and why she was half-dead from exhaustion. I need to know so I can help her—so I can help us. We should be able to work through this together, Sage."

"Thomas, it was ..." No sooner had she started when she thought about the prison. Anthony Campbell's slit gums. The Glock. Eli's fiery body. The murdered judge.

"I can't," she mouthed more than uttered.

"Even if it means relinquishing full custodial rights to Jadia?"

The refrigerator kicked into a hum, a stream of water replenishing the automatic ice dispenser. Sage slumped deeper into the chair, staring at the bottom of the cabinets.

"I'll just spend all my weekends here."

Silence.

"I don't think that's possible, Sage," Thomas said.

Questioning eyes followed his rise from the chair. "Why not?"

He gripped the back of the chair he'd just abandoned, glanced at the ceiling, and then sat down again. "I've accepted a job at Harvard, Sage. I'll be moving to Boston in two weeks." A cold, bitter silence filled the room and languished as their eyes locked.

Finally, Sage nodded and stood. She paced away from him, then returned to the table, raking a hand through matted curls. "Okay, so maybe it's best for Jadia to be with you for the time being. But this Boston thing—"

"Purely coincidental," Thomas said, jumping in. "Harvard offered me the job some time ago. I had just accepted it a couple of days before your call."

"I can't believe this," she said, plopping back into the chair.

"Timing, Sage. It's all about timing. It's just—" His hand flew up, then dropped. "Timing." He paused. "Sage," Thomas continued, reaching over and wiping tears trailing down her cheeks. "You've always been a good mother—the best there is. The rape hurt us all, but I think something raw still sits at your core. It's affecting your decisions."

He paused, eyeing her. "Maybe you should talk to someone about how to move on." He paused again and said, "You're obviously dealing with some other crisis right now, too, so look at it this way. I'm helping until it's over."

"It *is* over, Thomas," she said. The words belied her confidence in them.

Thomas inspected her. Wrinkled, soiled clothes. Body odor. Pallid, almost gray skin. Mangy, oily hair. Breath reeking of a bad diet and an empty stomach.

"From the looks of things, Sage, it's not."

CHAPTER 33

"What time did you get in last night?" Oma said to Sage's back as the older woman stepped into the kitchen.

Sage was leaning over the counter and spooning honey into a cup of steaming tea as she struggled to remember. It was after eleven the night before when Thomas had yelled over his shoulder as he climbed to the second floor, "Don't forget to lock up after you leave." He had not been agreeable to reconciliation. "It wouldn't be best for Jadia right now," he'd said.

Sage tarried in that thought a long while before cabbing it to Oma's house and the suitcases she had left in the walk-in closet. Those suitcases had never made it to the car the day she, Sean, and Jadia had visited the prison. The day she and Jadia had been scheduled to spend a week in St. Maarten. Instead, they'd spent their holiday on the run.

"What a hell of a way to spend a vacation," Sage muttered in agitation to herself.

"What's that?" Oma asked, brushing with ageless sophistication and sass past Sage to head for a fruit basket on the far end of the counter.

Sage stirred the tea. "I said I'm surprised you didn't hear me come in."

After a bit of browsing the fruit basket, Oma said, "I took one of Jadia's sleep aids." Oma plucked an apple and tossed it in the air and caught it a couple of times as she headed back in Sage's direction.

Sage scowled at the kitchen window, thinking, *Why in the hell are you taking Jadia's tranquilizers?* With a sigh, Sage turned around and faced a smooth face that, coupled with a tall, svelte figure belied seventy-something years. Oma attributed her spry body and excellent health to yoga practices, but Sage attributed her grandmother's well-preserved appearance to undiluted Dutch ancestry. Oma wore fitted royal-blue rayon capris and a crisp, white button-down blouse. Thick silver hair framed her face in a short front sass and faded into a no-nonsense dark taper in back. Sage was met with electric, scrutinizing eyes, almost as deep blue as her own.

"I was expecting you and Jadia two days ago, but I figured I had that wrong."

Sage took a deep breath, wishing she could bat answers back at Oma without having to think so hard. Without having to lie. She said nothing.

Oma inspected the apple as if seeking its opinion, then squinted at Sage a beat before saying, "Yeah, well, I called Thomas Saturday night, and he said you guys were fine and not to worry. That you probably extended your vacation a day or two or something like that." She pulled a paring knife from a drawer and took a couple of steps to reach for the overhead cupboard for a bowl and small plate. Holding the knife with a fist she rested on the counter next to the plate and bowl, she looked at Sage and asked, "Why did you get in so late?"

"Taxi shortage."

Sage sat at the round wooden table and sipped her tea. She looked toward the kitchen sink, awaiting the eastern rays that would stream in the kitchen window over the faucet.

Oma interrupted Sage's thoughts. "Well, Jadia must be exhausted."

Again, Sage said nothing.

"How was the trip? You look awfully pale for someone who just returned from a week of Caribbean sun."

"Actually, it was overcast most of the time we were there. Dreary. Besides, you know how vacations are, Oma. They can wear you out."

Oma began peeling the apple. "Is Jadia awake?"

Sage glanced over the sink again. "Uhm, I don't know."

"I bet she's still asleep. We would have heard her by now." Apple peels spiraled and dropped on the plate in soft plops.

"Probably not." The words were spoken into the mouth of her raised cup. "She's not here, Oma."

Oma turned to Sage. "Where is she?"

"She's with Thomas." The words wheezed out like an egg blown from a shell. Sage picked up her cup of tea, stared into it, and then sat it back down.

"When did this happen?"

"This weekend."

"This weekend?" Oma tossed the paring knife into the bowl with a clang that rippled a while before fading out in a weak *clink*. "I thought you were in—"

"We cut our vacation short bec—"

"Why?" Oma's fingers tapped the apple stem.

"I'm getting to that, Oma. You remember how Thomas had been begging to spend a lot more time with Jadia? Well, things got a little rough while Jadia and I were gone—it's a long story, and I really don't want to talk about it. We cut the vacation short, so I decided now is a good time for Jadia to spend some time with him."

"And?"

"And, well," she stirred, then met her grandmother's expectant gaze head-on. "It turns out that Thomas has had plans for better, more expensive therapy for Jadia, which of course, you know I agreed with." She blinked at the sill over the kitchen sink. Orange and purple hues were pouring through the window. With caution, Sage looked back at her grandmother, then she said, "He wants her to stay with him until the therapy concludes, Oma. … and—" She took a breath. "He's moving to Boston."

Oma abandoned the apple completely. "He's taking Jadia with him?" Sage closed her eyes in affirmation.

Averting her eyes, Oma allowed her mind plenty of time to consider the painful idea of Jadia going away. Her long, slender hands continued to cut apple wedges. When she'd finished, she carried the core to the wastebasket, tore a paper towel from the dispenser, and dampened it with water to wipe her hands. She grabbed coconut yogurt and walnuts from the fridge and returned to the table, clear eyes on Sage. After a long pause, Oma mixed the yogurt and walnuts with the apples and slowly ate as she cast herself into deeper thoughts.

Sage felt the heft of Oma's eyes on her, and she forced her attention from the gleam growing in the window. Oma had pushed the food aside.

"What else happened, Sage?"

Sage thought about the Glock she'd hidden inside a sweater in an under-the-bed storage container. The Glock she'd used to kill Anthony Campbell. "Nothing else happened, Oma." The words dropped hard and flat.

The heat from Oma's stare could have blasted Sage up from her seat and out of the kitchen. Sage threw her head back against the lip of the chair and rolled her eyes to the ceiling. "Thomas has Jadia's best interest at heart."

After several beats, Oma nodded her head slowly. "You're right. Thomas has Jadia's best interest at heart." Oma reached over and grabbed Sage's stiff, unyielding hand. "Sage, you know I love you—I love you all. I know you think I side with Thomas, but I don't. If I side with anyone, it's Jadia because she is a child. She not only needs love, she needs both her parents to be level-headed." She paused as if weighing her next words. "And honest."

Sage trudged through a deluge of restrained anger at Oma's barb. Skirting around the truth was not her chosen morning ritual, especially because she obviously sucked at it. At every turn she was being punished for having the cojones to face off with Anthony Campbell and for protecting everyone else.

Oma was at the sink. Sage kept her ceiling vigil, and she listened to water piping from the faucet and the clink of porcelain ware and metal utensils as Oma tidied up. Oma turned around and perched a hip on the edge of the counter. "Perhaps you'll consider joining them."

Sage's eyes slowly slid from the ceiling to Oma. "Joining who?"

"Thomas and Jadia. Maybe you can stop working against Thomas and work with him to help your daughter heal."

Sage sat and thought about how Thomas had already doled out a "hell, no" on that idea. She was too ashamed to tell the truth, too ashamed to tell another lie, so she muted herself, and all the things she didn't say began to rattle ominously inside her.

"Don't take too long with this contemplation business, Sage," Oma advised as she sidled up to Sage. Sage took one last sip of tea, now cold and bitter, and listened as Oma added, "Because it's later than you think." Oma left the kitchen.

Sage picked up her cup and walked to the sink. Looking out the window, she studied the house next door across the wide driveway. Oma's sweet peas, crown imperials, and parrot tulips were in full bloom. From somewhere in the distance, her job drifted into her thoughts.

Oma stepped back into the doorway just as Sage whirled around, screamed a long string of expletives, and hurled the cup. The cup popped against a far wall. Porcelain shards sprayed in flight then plummeted in a noisy spread across the floor, underscoring Oma's long-standing suspicion that Jadia was not the only one who needed psychiatric help.

CHAPTER 34

"Welcome back!" Carlie exclaimed as she barged into Sage's office and plunged into one of the chairs. The narrow office walls volleyed the hefty woman's brassy voice. Sage, stationed behind a desk that faced the long wall to the left of the door, felt as if she were in the middle of two clashing cymbals. She'd cabbed it to work and supposed it would be her mode of transportation until she had the time and gumption to purchase a new vehicle. She swiveled around in the chair, giving Carlie a full frontal view.

"Whoa!" Carly yelped. "You look rough, girl."

"Uhh yeah, well, I'm just a little tired, Carlie. You know how vacations can be sometimes." Sage turned away from Carlie and pretended to busy herself by looking for a pen and pad she really didn't need.

"Hmm," Carlie hummed, shifting her large frame in the chair. "So how about Jadia? Did the change in environment do her any good?"

Original-flavored Listerine poorly masked Carly's onion bagel breath. She was wearing Design perfume today, which usually meant an after-work date was on order.

"Uhm, yeah." Sage spoke over her shoulder without really looking at Carlie. She waited for Carlie to go away. When that didn't happen, Sage bent down as low as she could go without being under the desk, still feigning a pen search.

"So uh, Carlie," she said to the floor. "I'm not trying to be rude, but I have to meet with a client in forty-five minutes, and I really need to prepare."

"Sure," Carlie said.

Sage breathed audible relief when her office fell silent. She sat up with tightly closed eyes, massaging her temple. Wanting to go back home. Hoping Oma would not be there when she arrived.

"But did you get some?"

Sage's eyes popped open. Her chair swiveled slowly around, and she found that Carlie was now standing in the doorway.

"Get some what?" Sage asked, still holding her fingers frozen on her temple.

"So you didn't get any, huh?" Carlie said. She gaped at Sage with anticipation.

Sage threw her head back, closed her eyes, and clutched the back of her neck, kneading it in a self-massage.

"You have my condolences, sweetheart," Carlie said as she sashayed out the door. Predictably, she turned her head back, then added, "Better luck next time."

CHAPTER 35
SEPTEMBER 1994

Per the written agreement drafted by their attorneys, Thomas paid for Sage's flight and hotel expenses to see Jadia in Boston each week—and Sage had to commit herself to therapy. Oma could not have been more pleased.

The therapist recommended Sage return to running or other exercise, but the work-therapy-Boston-work routine left little time for anything else. She did take a moment one evening to page Greysen and wait for his return call. To her relief, he was okay. The first clumsy conversation, and each subsequent chat, was filled with momentary bursts of their voices overlapping, followed by long lapses of awkward silence.

In all, the only thing clearly communicated was the desire for companionship. Mayhem had passed through a West Virginia mountain that one summer night, and it had given birth to a wobbling, flailing friendship fed by pager and phone.

CHAPTER 36

Finally the office lights were out, and Sage headed home. A while later, she found cars pointing in every direction atop Oma's lawn. Every make and model lined the curb and blocked the driveway. Trilling alarms went off in Sage's head, warning of the world's harshest realities and crippling her senses. Jadia's name seeped through her lips as she bounced her newly purchased replacement Bimmer over a curb and bulldozed onto the sloped lawn.

"Jadia," she gasped again, pulling the key from the ignition and jumping out before the Bimmer stopped rolling.

She screamed, "Oh, my God," as she threaded between cars speckling the lawn and headed for the door. "What's happened to Jadia?"

The sound of reckless laughter rushed her as she burst through the door and stepped inside. "What the hell is going on here?" she blustered. The group of aging noisemakers fell silent at the outburst.

With bulging eyes, Sage scanned the crowded room. Eight card players sat around two fold-out tables in the middle of the room, all staring at her with an "Oh" shaping their open mouths. The couch and the love seat held another set of them. More females of varying sizes, shapes, and colors spilled from the kitchen. All of them gawked at Sage as she stood, wild-eyed, at the door.

"Stop ogling me!" she shouted. "You should be ashamed of yourselves. You scared me half to death!" She stepped deeper into the house and blasted, "I saw all these cars ... and ..." Sage's narrowed eyes darted about the room of astonished faces. "And ... what else was I supposed to think?"

Oma stood with the dignity and grace she was born with, sharp blue eyes glaring at Sage. "What exactly did you think, Sage?"

"I thought something had happened to Jadia. Something ... terrible. The only time"—she pointed to the windows behind her—"that many cars are parked in front of anybody's house is for a funeral."

"Or a party," someone said with obvious sarcasm.

Another woman, one Sage barely recognized, stood and said, "Sage, you need rest, honey."

"With all due respect, miss," Sage said, wracking her brain to remember the woman's name. She waved a hand about the room. "What I need is for you and all your friends to leave."

No one moved—except Oma. The floor vibrated as she stomped her way to Sage. "Enough," Oma said, filling the air with restrained coolness. Her voice was low and loaded with potency like a torpedo. Her arm brushed against Sage, and she said, "We need to talk." Without breaking her stride, she continued toward the office, the only room in the house without people, certain Sage would be trailing on her heels.

"Don't worry, Oma," Sage whispered into her back. "When there's a real funeral, we'll invite them back."

Already, a few people relaxed back into their seats, most resuming their activities and hubbub as if Sage had never entered the house. The fact that they could so easily ignore her stifled Sage. Oma held the office door open and watched as her granddaughter stood in the doorway, surveying the room before she huffed into the room.

"What is it, Oma?"

"You know exactly what it is," Oma replied with her chin out. "Pull yourself together," she warned, cool eyes steady on Sage, "before you lose Jadia for good."

"Jadia?" Sage repeated acerbically. "Do you think this is about Jadia, Oma? This isn't about Jadia; it's about rest. I haven't had any in a few days, okay? This past weekend was the first in a month and a half that I wasn't hopping on a plane to Boston like a crazed rabbit, and how did I spend it? By running errands, playing handywoman, raking the leaves, cooking all the meals, going to my job—and working very hard, mind you. I worked late every night this week, this particular night being the worst and the latest. Then I get home at ten thirty, and what do I see? Cars, cars, and more cars. I thought something had happened. I had an anxiety attack and it's all because I'm tired, Oma. *I need rest. I want to sleep.*"

Oma studied Sage, her face expressionless. Then she said, "Maybe stress is affecting your memory, Sage. Handywoman? Raking leaves? Cooking meals? I pay for plumbers, electricians, and yardmen to do the work around here. You and I used to dine out or prepare meals together. Now I meet friends out, and you hardly eat at all."

In the ensuing silence, Oma stepped closer to Sage.

"But even if any of your claims were true, nothing justifies your behavior tonight, Sage. You're acting like a teenage brat on drugs—heavy drugs." Oma glared at Sage, shaking her head. She continued, "Do you know the real reason for your not having enough rest? You're too busy laying up at night feeling sorry for yourself."

Oma stepped even closer, now hugging distance from her granddaughter. Averting her head, Sage went stiff under her embrace, but the tall woman hugged tighter. Finally she released Sage and stepped backward to the door. A hand reached behind her and curled around the brass egg knob, and rested there.

"Think about seeing someone, Sage," she said to her granddaughter. "A priest. A preacher. Another therapist. You need to talk to someone who isn't as emotionally invested in your troubles as Thomas and I are."

At this, Sage's eyes flicked to her grandmother and stayed a beat. "Do you mind if we continue this in the morning, Oma?" Sage asked sardonically. "I'm really sleepy."

Oma shook her head and left.

Hours later, after the last of Oma's friends had left, a roaring, gurgling stomach dragged Sage from fitful sleep. Still fully dressed, she lumbered barefoot down wide, sweeping stairs and across the dark living room and great room to the kitchen.

"All that cooking I've been doing," she grumbled to herself as she scoured the refrigerator in vain, "and not a drop left for me to eat." The next beat, she was in the pantry with a hand curling blindly over a can of soup.

"I thought you needed to sleep so badly."

Sage's heart leapt at the sudden and unexpected sound of Oma's dull and humorless voice. She spun around and gasped loudly, holding the can of soup at her pounding chest.

Sage pushed words through a breathless splutter, "I was … I am. I mean …" Sage tried to calm her breathing. She brushed past Oma, saying, "Apparently I'm hungrier than I am sleepy. In fact, I'm too hungry to sleep." She stalked to the counter, back turned to Oma, glared at the electric can opener, and slammed down the can of soup on the counter.

After a long stretch of retaliating silence, Sage heard her grandmother move closer behind her. Oma whispered, "It's too bad you didn't figure that out before my friends and I ate all the food," she said. "I would have put some aside for you, but like I said, you haven't been eating much."

"Good night, Oma," Sage bid encouragingly, resentful eyes fixed on the opener.

"Good is the last thing this night is, Sage," Oma calmly said, stalwart dignity lacing every word. "The very last thing."

Sage's back remained stubbornly rigid as Oma turned and exited the kitchen. Sage jammed the can onto the magnetic clamp on the opener's latch and pressed the lever. The small motor sounded and the can spun around, flashing cursive letters that spelled "Campbell."

She flinched, glaring at the letters until she saw nothing but a white blur. Jadia's tranquilizers glazed over Sage's eyes as the can opener came to a stop. She blinked again, bringing the still tin back into focus.

Campbell.

"Die!" Sage hurled the opened can across the room, ran from the kitchen, and scuttled up the stairs, abandoning the chunky splatters of chicken noodle soup coursing down the wall and noiselessly spattering into salty puddles on the floor.

CHAPTER 37
EARLY OCTOBER 1994

The clock had been buzzing for over two hours before Sage heard it well enough to pull herself from drug-induced sleep and drag herself to work. Thursday morning meetings were killers. She'd sat through five such meetings since Anthony Campbell's murder—four of those since Jadia and Thomas had moved to Boston—and each subsequent session was worse than its predecessor. Oversleeping through a today's conference was a welcomed change from insomnia, she supposed. It meant two things. One, her slovenly mind would be too bedraggled to offend anyone. Two, therapist sessions and prescription meds weren't a complete waste.

"Well, good afternoon," Carlie greeted as Sage lumbered past. "Glad you could join us. Lucky for you, the boss has a few a.m. asses to kiss. He's been in a meeting with the corporate crew since seven this morning—an hour you obviously skipped today."

Sage backtracked to look at Carlie. "Really?" Red eyes scanned the mess on Carlie's desk for a clock. "What time is it anyway? I forgot my watch."

"Nine forty-eight."

Sage gave a detached "Oh" and resumed the lumber to her office. Carlie hopped up and with the agility of a much smaller, fit woman, rounded the desk to gain purchase in Sage's wake. Several feet later, they were both in Sage's office. Sage haphazardly tossed her attaché and purse into a guest chair and hand-raked her hair as she fumbled her way to the other side of the desk.

"Hey," Carlie called out, much too loudly for Sage's comfort. "Do you have that file—"

"Uhhh," Sage interrupted. She was standing behind her desk, wincing at Carlie's shrieking voice. "Look, I don't know how to put this ... uhhh ... let's see. Okay." Finally finding the right words, she nodded only once, because moving made her head hurt. "I'm not in the mood for your antics, okay? Not now. Not ever." She pressed the butt of her palm to her temple. "Do you know what I mean?"

"No, I don't know what you mean," Carlie said, biting into an apple she'd lifted from a fruit bowl she kept replenished on Jadia's credenza near the door.

Sage watched as Carlie took another bite of the apple. Apple spray dotted a line across Sage's desk.

"Sorry," Carlie said, attempting to clean the desk by smearing the droplets with a bare wrist.

Sage belted, "Carlie, please leave!"

With a jolt, Carlie stopped chewing, paused a moment longer, and then swallowed.

"You are in an evil way, woman," she said, swallowing again. "A very evil way." After a beat, Carlie looked at Sage and said, "The Niameck file. Did you—"

"Out!" Sage shrieked. "Out now, Carlie!"

"Okay," Carlie said with a semi-smirk. "Whatever you say."

When the doorway was clear, Sage carefully held the arms of the chair. No sooner had she lowered herself to the seat, than Carlie popped her head in again and opened her mouth to speak. At that second, Sage's phone rang. With pursed lips, she glowered at Carlie and lifted the receiver. Carlie spread her signature half-smirk, half-coquettish smile across her face, then disappeared before Sage said, "Sage Wirspa" into the phone.

"Sage, have you got it or what?" her boss roared through the phone.

"Got what?"

"Hellowww. Earth to Sage—the Niameck file, dammit! I told Carlie to have you in here thirty minutes ago! Niameck reps are here now. We're all waiting."

"On my way," she said, scrambling to get to the credenza. Fifteen minutes later, she scrambled to the meeting. Hours later, Sage returned to a blizzard of paper and a ringing phone.

"Yes," she answered, plunging into the seat and propping an elbow on the table with a palm on her forehead. "Yes?" she repeated.

"Sage? ... Hi, how are you? You sound a little ... Do you have a cold?"

"N—" Sage cleared her throat and tried to speak again. "No, I'm just a little tired." She hesitated. "Rockefeller?"

"Of course!" he said cheerfully.

"Wow," she said with as much animation as she could muster. "Long time, no hear."

"Yeah, well, I've been pretty tied up with a major project."

Sage knew about the project. It was the blat of local television and the blot across local newspapers. Philadelphia's own millionaire attorney Sean Swoboda was staging a run for president of the United States.

Sage screeched over the phone, "Rockefeller for president!" But as mouth cheered for Sean, her mind spun out of focus.

"Focused, huh?" She chimed in absently to something Sean had said.

"Focused. Determined. Obsessed. All the things that make for a lively ulcer." He broke into a hearty chuckle. Sage joined the guffaw as if she hadn't missed any of the conversation.

"We can only plan for these things, Sage," Sean was saying more seriously. "But there's no telling how they'll turn out."

"Yeah," she agreed. "Tell me about it."

"Sage ... are you all right?"

"Sure. I'm great," she lied. "Everybody's not lucky enough to have something to hold their attention like you. You have two things going for you: an exciting career and a loving wife."

"You have a good job, Sage."

"Hmpf."

"And you have a family—Oma and Jadia."

"Oma's too feisty to have, Rockefeller," she said with a quick mirthless laugh. "And Jadia's too far away," she whispered in a cracked voice. Sage forestalled any questions Sean might have presented by quickly telling him that Thomas had gained full custody of Jadia and moved to Boston. She explained how circumstances undercut her ability to contest either decision. She didn't have to spell out the circumstances. Sean knew the night in Capon Bridge had sealed Thomas's resolve to excise Sage's parental latitude.

The line Sean said, "You miss her, huh?"

"Like hell."

"So I take it you're spending weekends in Boston, right?" he asked.

"Until last weekend I was," she grumped. "Jadia's going abroad with Thomas. He's serving as an academic attaché on the psychiatric project Jadia's a part of. Subject matter experts around the globe are converging in Europe for a study that Jadia's a part of. She'll be there until Thanksgiving."

She swiped a clearing on her desk so she could look at the calendar. September 8, 1994. Three months before she'd see Jadia again. Staring mindlessly at the small numbered buttons on the base of the phone, Sage gripped the receiver tighter and said in a low voice, "I don't know if I was ever fit to take care of her."

"What are you saying, Sage?"

Her lips pressed hard against the mouthpiece, her increasingly loud words jabbing the air. "I'm saying that the psychiatrists Thomas hired sanctioned a trip to London as therapy, while the ones I hired said, 'Take her to the correctional center'!"

"Are you okay?"

"What?" she breathed into the mouthpiece.

"I didn't say anything," Sean answered.

"Well, who—"

"I did," Sage heard a gruff voice say. Sage looked up and found her assistant at the door.

"Carlie." Saying nothing to Sean, Sage covered the mouthpiece and stammered, "Uh, what … what can I do for you?"

"Nothing," she replied, furrowing her brows as she stepped deeper into the office and gawked at her boss. "I was bringing you this message when I heard your voice—three doors away." Carlie extended a small, pink message slip.

"I'm fine," Sage assured her as she stood to take the slip. Even after Sage resumed her seat, she felt Carlie's questioning eyes. Covering the mouthpiece again, Sage said, "Thank you, Carlie," and motioned for her to leave.

"Yeah, sure," Carlie said, hesitating and frowning before she backed out.

"Rockefeller?" Sage called into the phone.

"I'm still here," he answered.

"Sorry."

"No problem. Sage, where exactly in Boston does Thomas live?" She'd heard the question but her attention was on the message. Thomas had called.

"Uh, Sean," she said absently, "I have to go. I need to return this call right away."

"Is everything all right?"

"Yes, just business," she lied. She was trying to convince herself nothing terrible had happened to Jadia. Thomas rarely ever called her at work.

"Okay, but one quick thing before I let you go."

"All right."

"How about dinner tomorrow? You, Lori, and me. She's dying to meet you, Sage."

"Uhh ... well, I uh—"

"Oh, come on. You just told me your weekends are free. Unless you've made other plans."

"Nnnnooo, no. I'm not doing anything. I'll be glad to join you and your wife for dinner."

"Great. How about Ippolito's at seven thirty?"

"Sounds good."

"Okay. We'll see you there."

"Have a good evening, Sean ... and Sean?"

"Yes?"

"Tell your wife I'm looking forward to meeting her, too."

The switch hook was under her finger before she could take another breath. As Sage listened to Thomas's phone ring, she prayed, then made a mental note to call him on his car phone just in case—

"Wirspa here," he finally answered.

"Thomas?" Sage said as a gust of long-held air exploded from her lungs.

"Sage? Are you okay? You sound like you've been running."

"I was worried, Thomas. Has something happened to Jadia?"

"Will you please calm down and relax?" he urged in an aggravated tone. "If something had happened to Jadia, I would have told Carlie to put you on the phone right away. Geez, Sage, your behavior is—"

"Skip the lecture, Thomas. I'm not accustomed to my daughter being so far away and—"

"Out of your control, right?"

In the silence that followed, Sage swallowed the guilty verdict Thomas's words delivered. She'd disappeared with his traumatized daughter without telling him, and he was leveraging an opportunity to drive the point home. Sage sucked air before saying, "Jadia's all we have to talk about these days, Thomas. I can't imagine what other reason you would have to call my office."

"I am calling about Jadia, but it's not about the gloom and doom you spend every waking hour anticipating. I called with good news, Sage."

"I'm listening," she said, rolling her eyes and gripping the phone tighter.

"I just got word that the university wants to step up an experimental pro—"

"Will you get to the point, Thomas, I'm at work." The gaze she held on the paper-littered desk was broken when Carlie walked in and dropped a truckload of folders on top. If only the stack of work meant business was booming. The polar opposite was happening, and it was scaring her boss, who was responding with tyrannical behavior. "Things are piling up as we speak."

"Okay, okay," Thomas shot back. "Sage, you're pretty intense. I'm worried about you."

Sage bit her lower lip. Her voice calmed. "I am—I'm sorry, Thomas." Silence filled the line.

At some point, Thomas said, "Sage, what's wrong?"

Sage looked at the pile on her desk, then at the monitor. The cursor flashed like a metronome, sucking her into a vortex of spiraling thoughts and regrets until the screen blacked out. She was sinking and taking her work down with her. This year's bonus seemed more and more an unlikely event.

"Everything's fine, Thomas—really. Please tell me what's going on. I'm all ears."

"Okay. As you know, Jadia and I are flying to London tomorrow to join the psychiatric effort I told you about. Originally, financial backing was secured for one semester but—as of today—funding was approved for the entire academic year, and more is headed down the pipeline for an extension through the summer months."

Sage frowned at her Macintosh screen, lost for words.

"The holidays are still on, though," Thomas continued. "It's important to keep family traditions, especially for Jadia's sake. I already told my parents like I'm telling you now. Don't cancel your Thanksgiving flight. We'll all be together as planned."

"Everything is—" Sage stopped. The work on her desk and the shock of the news laid her thoughts flat. "This is, is, uh … wow," she stuttered. "I uh—"

"It's about timing, Sage. That's all."

"Yes, for sure. I'm happy for you, you know. And if this will help Jadia, all the better."

"This is happening to all of us, Sage," he said with a smiling voice. "It's a good thing. A very good thing."

Sage knew he was right. It was a very good thing. And yet … And yet she felt diminished somehow, kind of like color fading from a photograph. Somewhere in the past, her fading away had been set in motion and had continued in such small degrees that she had not even noticed until it was too late.

"Thomas?"

An apprehensive voice filled the line. "Yes?"

"Thank you for being such a great father."

Silence strung itself out. Sage could feel Thomas suppressing a grateful, albeit embarrassed smile. Thomas was nothing if not humble. Then he changed the subject.

"I'm sorry you're getting this news so late. I had a strong feeling funding for the extension would be approved, but I've been wrong before."

"Rarely," Sage whispered.

"What's that?"

Before she could answer, another line rang in Thomas's office, and he abruptly said, "I gotta go, Sage. If you need me, call my secretary. She's going to be checking messages day and night because of the time difference. I left strict instructions for her to patch you through immediately if you call."

The dial tone sounded in her ear before she heard her own voice, scratchy and hoarse, whisper, "Good bye."

CHAPTER 38

The phone was on the third ring. It was past the end of a phone-ringing, boss-shouting, Carlie-griping day. Sage debated at length whether or not to answer it before she finally decided to reach under a pile of disarrayed papers and lift the handle. Sheets of paper feathered to the floor. On the fourth ring, another folder slid to the edge of the desk, and more folders toppled to the ground. It would have been just as easy to unplug the damned thing and hurl it across the room.

"Sage Wirspa." Sage's voice was bland.

"Sage, did you forget about dinner tonight?"

"Excuse me?" she said, reaching for a file on the floor.

"It's Sean ... My wife and I—"

"Oh, my God!" Her eyes wandered, searching the desk for a clock. "I completely forgot," she confessed, rummaging through reports and memos until she felt the hard edges of the oval-shaped timepiece. "Oh, my God," she repeated under her breath. "It's eight forty-five. We said seven-thirty, didn't we?"

"Don't worry about it, Sage."

"Oh, my God, I got so ... Please, please apologize to your wife for me. I have so much work to do ... I just ... I'm sorry, Sean."

"Sage, please. I'm just glad you're okay. I was concerned, that's all."

"How did you know I was here?"

"I called your house. Your grandmother said she hadn't heard from you, so she assumed you were still at work."

Sage's mind flashed to the night of Oma's girl party. The party she'd crashed. The guests she'd insulted. The Oma she'd disrespected. "Oh, yeah. Yeah. Right. Oma. Right. Right," she babbled.

"Maybe next weekend?" Sean requested.

"Huh? ... Oh, yeah. ... yeah ... Sure. That'll be great."

"Okay. Let me know if you can't make it."

"I'll be there, Sean," she promised. "If the load here gets better."

CHAPTER 39
LATE OCTOBER 1994

Sean rose from his seat at the table and greeted Sage with a kiss on the cheek.

Sean said, "You look wonderful!"

Sage knew he was lying. She had stolen a quick look at her reflection in the window and—yep, the Philadelphia winds riffled her hair and the restaurant lighting accentuated her tired, insomniac skin. They dined at The Fountain at the Four Seasons partially because it was just a few blocks from Sean's office and touted as having the metro area's best French food, which was his favorite. He was already seated at a table with a street view when she arrived. A scattering of Thursday night pedestrians drifted past one another in the cool, late evening.

"Where's your wife?" she asked after their orders were taken. She sipped iced water from stemware and looked around the room for a beautiful blonde to waltz through the entrance or stroll back from the ladies' room. During their "accidental vacation," as Sean coined it (meaning the time they'd spent on the road after the visit to the correctional center), he'd shown her a bust of his wife; a wallet sized picture, which only showed Lori's head and shoulders.

"Lori's got a sick child," Sean said.

Sage nearly choked on a piece of ice that slipped from the glass into her mouth. "Wh—what?" she coughed.

"Are you all right?" Sean asked. He was out of his chair and heading toward her side of the table to assist.

She waved him back. "I'm fine. Sit down, please. You just caught me off guard, that's all. I thought you and your wife didn't have any children."

"Oh ... oh, I see." He chuckled. "We *don't* have any kids, Sage. My wife volunteers at the children's hospital. She called me just before I left the office. The ward nurses had contacted her about a little girl who may have a week or so left to live. The little girl's been calling Lori's name for story reading. With the campaign underway, this may be Lori's last opportunity to see her. On my way here, Lori called me on my cell saying another volunteer had called in sick, so they're short tonight. They asked if she could stay to help out. So it looks like her late arrival unfortunately has morphed into an out-and-out cancellation."

After the server delivered their beverages, Sage said, "Lori's commitment to the hospital is admirable."

"Lori loves children." He laughed. "Volunteering at the hospital is the only activity she does not expect to reap votes."

Sage laughed with him.

"Seriously though," Sean said after the waiter took their orders, "and with all that, she attends fire marshal balls, distributes leaflets at the local grocery stores, organizes lunches with newspaper publishers. She's championing the Accelerant Detection Canine Program."

"Hmm," Sage said, pulling a glass of water from her lips. "Puppies saving lives—who would have thought?" She paused, thinking. "Oma may have told me about that. I'd forgotten." She pinched a corner of her mouth. "I've been doing a lot of that lately."

"You've been through a lot, Sage. You need time, that's all. A vacation—a real one next time."

They sat in silence until the server arrived with their food. Sage saw strain melt from Sean's face as his ambrosial plate was presented. He'd ordered salt-cured, roasted Muscovy duck breast with brown butter; spiced red jewel sweet potato; dried cranberry and escarole salad with hazelnut vinaigrette; and acidic plum game reduction.

Praises were expressed by both of them as her plate was presented: vegetarian autumn buttercup squash and carnaroli risotto; smoked mozzarella; Micro True Leaf Farms arugula; shaved burgundy truffle; pine nut pesto; and of course, sage oil. They dined and talked of current events, car shows, and technology.

"I'm glad we finally got together," Sean said, resting his fork and knife on an empty plate. "I'm driving to the city tomorrow and staying for three weeks, giving seminars at NYU and Fordham."

"Really? You're in high demand, Rockefeller," she said before sipping water.

"Well, I wouldn't say all of that," Sean answered. He sipped water and added, "But things are picking up. As soon as the seminars are over, Lori and I will be knee deep in pre-campaign travels. Our last stop will be in Orlando the first week in December."

"How convenient. Florida in December?"

Sean laughed. "Yes. It's too bad we won't be able to stay. Lori's planning soirees all through the holidays. They will be squeezed between political shindigs here and in the city. We'd love for you join us at our place or tag along at the various parties. It will be fun. Bring Jadia—and Thomas too."

"It looks like our holidays will be in Boston. Thomas's parents have already arranged to extend their Thanksgiving stay to help decorate for Christmas and prepare holiday meals. Oma may join us. It's hard to keep her away from Jadia for long." She hesitated before adding, "Jadia's in Europe with her dad now."

"You don't say."

"I do say," Sage proffered with a sad smile. "They're in London today. Paris tomorrow. The trip has something to do with meeting other victims and the professionals who support them, exchanging lessons learned, and letting the kids know they're not alone in their experiences. Everyone's fallen head over heels for Jadia."

"That's—" Sean grinned. "That's really impressive." He paused, seriousness shadowing his face. "It's been a heck of a year, Sage."

"Yes," she agreed. "The year 1994. I can't say I'll be sad to see it leave."

Sean pensively stroked the nap of the linen tablecloth. Then he added, "Jadia's one lucky kid to have so many people love her. I'd probably fly to Boston to see her myself if I weren't bidding for the '96 ticket."

"The '96 ticket." Sage repeated with awe gleaming in her eyes. "It's really happening, isn't it, Rockefeller? You're monopolizing all the local headlines." Her face split into a wide smile. "And you fit the part so well. You're not only smart and successful, you have a beautiful wife who's community minded, and it's obvious you're taking good care of yourself." She eyed the shaped of his arms under his crisp, white shirt and smiled. "You've been working out, which is great. America wants a fit president—Richard Simmons is all the rage, you know."

Sean breathed in Sage's jocular air with a warm smile.

"You have certainly given yourself plenty to look forward to," she said.

"Plenty to keep the '95 calendar full you mean."

"Exactly."

"Speaking of a full calendar," Sean said, his face turning earnest. "I'm not going to be around for the next few weeks, and I thought maybe you'd want the number to my mobile in case—" He hesitated, choosing his words carefully. "You know … in case you needed anything."

The server returned, collected the dishes and used silverware, smiled through their refusals for dessert, then left.

Sage averted her eyes just for a second, then laid them gently on Sean. "I know you're concerned about my well-being, Sean. I'm not 100 percent yet, but I'm getting there—closer every day." She forced a smile. "It's sweet of you to make yourself available to me, especially after the way I've been behaving lately. You probably thought I was avoiding you."

"It's okay, Sage. I understand." Sean reached inside his suit jacket and whipped out a business card along with a pen. "The campaign number is also on the card. Call me if you ever need anything. In fact, maybe you can join me in the city one weekend while I'm there. If the timing's right, you can meet Lori."

Sage waited a beat before she said, "I'm leaving town myself, but my travels are strictly for rest and relaxation." There was a pause. "My flight leaves bright and early tomorrow morning."

"Oh," he said, returning the pen to an inside jacket pocket. He handed the card to Sage. "Where are you going?"

"That's the beauty of it. I don't know."

"You—don't—know." Sean repeated each word with emphasis.

"I really don't." She paused, tilting her head. "You've heard of those mystery flights advertised on the radio, right?"

It took a beat for Sean's face to light with full understanding. "Ohhh!" he sang out, throwing back his head with a broad smile. "Yes," he said as he nodded. "You're right, there's beauty in the unknown, isn't there?"

"Yes! You and Lori have to try it at least once, Sean. There's no planning. No hassles. You just get on a plane and go!"

Sean picked up his glass and lifted it to his lips, meeting Sage's gaze at the rim. With words jamming in his throat, he pulled a large gulp. The realization that Sage still did not know about Lori's paralysis occurred to him. It had been six years since her accident, and many years since he'd explained it to anyone. It was common knowledge.

These days, news reports talked about Lori being confined to a wheelchair primarily to laud her accomplishments, energy, and drive. Plus, Lori had a natural knack of drawing even the camera's attention to her beautiful face. People wanted to hear what Lori Swoboda had to say. As for Sean, pride, not shame, kept him from talking about it much. Pride in Lori's drive and resourcefulness. And she had always been an undeniable beauty, sitting or standing. If he were going to talk about anything, he'd talk about those things, not about her wheelchair.

"When will you be back?" Sean asked.

Sage took a deep breath, squinted, and then said, "I don't know that either."

"Wouldn't the folks at your job like to know the date of your return?"

"Not necessarily," she said, averting her gaze toward the window. Pedestrian traffic had lightened, and the street had grown darker. A couple strolled by, holding hands.

"Did you resign?"

Sage shifted back to Sean. "No. I'm, uh—I'm on medical leave, Sean. Doctor's orders."

Sean stared at her a long time, his face inscrutable as he watched the server place the check wallet on the table. After the server left, Sean asked, "Is it serious?" His voice was low, filled with concern.

Sage ran a hand through her hair. "I've been seeing a psychiatrist, Sean. Prescription: complete solitude for thirty days."

He pursed his lips and nodded as he reclined against the chair. "Is this doctor one of Jadia's new pals?"

"No, this one specializes in adult issues."

Sean nodded again, saying, "Sure. Of course." His eyes were steady, his voice low.

"I needed to talk to someone, Sean," Sage whipped defensively.

He turned down the corners of his mouth and stared at the remnants of food on his plate. "You could have talked to me."

Silence.

"Look, Sean, I have not nor do I intend to say anything about what happened at the correctional facility, if that's your concern. So, don't worry, okay?"

He quickly scanned the restaurant as though checking to see if anyone heard. He wouldn't bring up Sage's Glock any more than he'd mentioned Lori's wheelchair. There was no need. The wipe had gone so clean, he had been an invisible man that day. All of them—Jadia, Sage, and he—had been invisible. Cofield's minions had been castrated. The judge was dead. Bombs at the prison killed the prison guards and the maintenance man. Manny Cofield was in jail, and glad to be there from

Sick with Revenge

what Sean had gleaned, because it beat the alternative. Sean didn't think about it anymore.

He rested an arm on the table and leaned forward, saying, "I wasn't as much as thinking about that, Sage. It's buried so deeply in my head, it's like it didn't happen."

Sage blinked into the silence. After interminable seconds, she leaned forward and whispered, "But it did happen."

"I know, I know. Look. When I said you could have talked to me, I meant we've known each other a long time. We're close friends, and friends talk to one another. It's unnecessary for you to spend hard-earned money on an expensive shrink."

The server refilled their water glasses and retrieved Sean's credit card.

"Thomas pays for anything my insurance doesn't cover," Sage explained after the server left.

Sean leaned back again. "Wow."

"Yes," she agreed. "He wants me to get well, Sean." They went quiet for a few beats.

Sean spread a warm smile. "Thomas is a good guy."

"Yes, he is. He knows Jadia needs me in her life." Sage's lips twisted into a wry smile. "Jadia's laughing now."

Sean's brows jumped up. "Is that so?"

Sage snorted a quick chuckle. "It's sporadic, but, yes."

Sean nodded his head in an approving smile. "Jadia's lovely, Sage."

She bit on her lower lip. "Sean, may I ask you something?"

His expression slowly eased into the staunch persona that suited him so well. "What would you like to know?"

"About the adoption you mentioned while we were—" she paused. There was no skirting around being on the run. "Well, anyway," she said. "Do you feel comfortable sharing what happened?"

Sean tossed her an unreadable, protracted stare. "It wasn't an adoption," he finally said. His gaze drifted downward to the white tablecloth. "It was an adoption attempt."

Her hand reached out to touch his. "Sean, if this is uncomfortable ..."

"We were doing fine without children for the first eight years or so of our marriage." Sean gave her a lopsided smile. "Lori knows how to keep things interesting, so you could say we were happy and we knew it and we clapped our hands."

Sage laughed at Sean's play on the children's rhyme song. Sean covered his glass when the server approached with a pitcher of water.

"None for me either," Sage said. The server retrieved the wallet with the signed receipt.

"In fact, I think we're done for the night if that's all right." The server nodded acquiescence and left. When they were alone again, she said, "You were saying you and Lori were happy."

"Yes, we were. We still are. But there was a time when we suffered, although our marriage did not. We'd decided to have a family." He paused, staring at the tablecloth again. "Try as we might, we didn't get pregnant and eventually learned we couldn't have a baby in the conventional sense. I tried to console Lori, but I can't think of a time when I felt so helpless. We both immersed ourselves deeper in work, and I took DNA classes. Eventually we found ourselves taking baby steps toward adopt—" He stopped.

Sage smiled, understanding he hadn't meant to use the term *baby steps*. Her encouraging eyes never left his.

"Well," he said, focusing on the table for a long second before moving on. "Had we known that stated wait times for an American newborn were padded, we probably would have put more pep in our steps. I tried to manage Lori's expectations while keeping my own in check, but we were both excited about the prospect of altering our lives, surviving the pangs of our inexperience, and just enjoying parenthood. We were looking forward to getting to know the little fella."

Under Sage's soft, emphatic laughter, an indiscernible smile skidded onto Sean's lips and disappeared.

"We had no qualms with a six-month wait, probably because; number one we were a little arrogant in believing our status—our money and connections—could circumvent the process; and number two, we never imagined we'd end up in the three-year zone even without external influences ..." Sean's voice trailed, taking him with it.

Sage encouraged him to continue. "So, were you and Lori able to see any children during that time?"

"We saw two. We found ourselves at a hospital nursing window staring at a brawny baby boy. He'd jam a fat fist into his mouth and—" Sean paused at the painful memory, and he quickly continued. "Two sets of parents showed up." He paused to wave off a server. "It was the only time I've had a chance to say, 'You'll be hearing from my attorney.'"

Sean's laughter dissolved into a sad smile. His eyes found their favorite spot on the table.

"We tried to adopt a second time." He paused, gave the table a few light finger taps, and shook his head. "She glowed. She'd kick and grab at the air. One look at her, and my heart went on instant lockdown, bolted closed for life—and she was in it."

Sean looked away for several beats, then blinked back to Sage. "We named her Lauren. She would have been Lauren Nicole Swoboda had the adoption gone through."

After a few deep breaths and several finger taps, Sean's palm quieted on the table. "She went into cardiac arrest before we left the hospital. Before her twenty-fourth hour."

In the stretch of soundless reflection, condensation trickled down their glasses. At some point, a small hand with French manicured nails rested over Sean's. He looked at the soothing hand, abandoning his reverie like jilting a lover.

"You are a wonderfully rare man, Rockefeller."

A warm smile popped onto his face. Sage stroked the back of his hand.

"And you'd make a great father." She withdrew her hand with a pat and a smile. "You shouldn't give up, you know. Your passion is still there, alive and kicking. I can tell you're still intent on being a dad."

"*We*," Sean said with emphasis. "*We're* intent on being parents." Lori hadn't talked about it in years, but Sean believed Team Swoboda stilled tracked baby-Swoboda.

Sean and Sage laughed, the sound of hearty chuckles somehow making it seem as if the pain Sean shared had faded with the discussion of it. As if they had never shared the prison experience. As if Sage hadn't Glocked Anthony Campbell.

"Here's to your political future," Sage said, lifting her water in a toast.

"And to happiness," Sean reciprocated with his glass. "For Jadia and for you."

CHAPTER 40

The next day, Sage arrived at the airport three hours early, anxiety riding her like a racehorse. That plus Oma-avoidance ruled the day and the week and her life. They hadn't said much since the big bridge-day fallout, but Oma had encouraged the therapist-sanctioned trip, saying a thirty-day reprieve would be panacea for them both, and adding that she didn't care where Sage was going as long as she felt and behaved better when she returned.

Sitting in the relatively quiet airport, Sage became restless and decided to call the house to check the messages. She knew Oma would be at the Buddhist temple, the place where she spent Friday mornings practicing yogic meditation. Sage didn't expect messages, but checking the machine gave her something to do. Slapping the empty change purse on the phone booth's tray, Sage rammed a hand deep inside her purse, scouring for coins. She came up with paper clips, condiments, safety pins, receipts, lint, and lots of pennies. But no silver coins. Plunging into the purse again, she pulled out her wallet and fished for a calling card.

"Friday, October 28, 1994. You have no messages." The robotic male voice was repeating the announcement when Sage hung up. As she returned the calling card in a random slot in her wallet, Sage noticed a tightly folded piece of paper packed between the folds of cards. She pulled it out. It held a number and a note that read, "Maybe I can get to know you. P.S. If you ever beep, add 513 to the number you're calling from so I'll know it's you." Flitting unease rose and dipped in Sage's throat.

"Greysen," she whispered to herself before she flipped the tiny note over and read his name. It had been over a month since she'd last paged him. Forcing herself not to think, she snatched the calling card from the wallet and dialed Greysen's pager, then sat in the open booth for what felt like hours, waiting for him to respond. When the phone rang, her heart jabbed her chest. The handle was in her hand before it rang a second time. Then there was her breathless whisper, "Hello?"

In the ensuing stretch of silence, Sage thought about how, since the day of the prison visit, time had spanned across her life like a nail screeching across a blackboard.

Suddenly, Greysen's masculine blue blood, East Coast accent poured into the earpiece. "You took long enough."

That insufferable silence fell again, but this time Sage scrambled to end it quickly. "How are you?"

"I have nothing to complain about."

"Nothing to complain about," she repeated pensively. The line was quiet again.

"Why did you call, Sage? Is everything all right?"

She hesitated, forming a response. "Calling seemed like a natural thing to do."

An announcement blared through the airport's PA system.

Greysen's voice rose through the earpiece. "Where are you?"

Sage plugged a finger in her ear. "I'm at the airport, waiting on my flight." The announcement was over. The airport was filling with a low but growing murmur of activity.

Greysen asked, "Where are you going?"

Sage closed her eyes, allowing his voice to pool in her ear. She explained the psychiatric visits, the rather mandatory thirty-day leave, and the mystery flight deal, and she caught him up with Thomas and Jadia's life in London.

"Anyway, I haven't gone to the ticket counter yet," she continued. "My flight doesn't leave for a couple of hours. I'm waiting until the very last minute to know the destination—tired of having expectations, you know."

"A woman after my own heart."

"I packed light," Sage said, breaking another long silence. "All I have is a duffel bag with must-have toiletries, a bikini, and a pair of shorts if it's hot; a jacket and a pair of thermal underwear if it's cold. I'll shop for the rest when I get to my destination."

"In that case, it wouldn't be a problem for you to come here."

Sage's brows fell. "Excuse me?"

"I'm inviting you to stay here with me for a while. It's cheaper."

As a voice over the PA requested, "Ticket holder Frances Sanchez, please report to gate 12 in terminal B. Frances Sanchez, please report to gate 12 in terminal B," flashbacks of the charred remains of Greysen's home flooded her mind.

"Greysen, I really appreciate the offer but I have to kindly refuse you. My doctors prescribed rest and relaxation, not roughing it in the woods."

A gust of cackles rose from a group of boisterous teenage girls walking past the open phone booth. Greysen spoke when the line cleared. "I didn't invite you camping, Sage."

Sage shifted her butt in the hard metal seat. "What's the difference?"

"Plenty. Why don't you come and see?"

A silver glint bouncing off the keypad caught Sage's eye. "Greysen, I don't know you."

The din of airport conversations, rolling suitcases, and beeping carts filled the air around Sage. Greysen said, "You called me."

"To find out how you're doing."

"Sage, you said calling seemed the most natural thing for you to do. Inviting you to visit is the most natural thing for me to do."

The line fell silent again. Sage belatedly rethought her decision to call him, regretting how she'd unwittingly cornered them both. "It wouldn't seem like such a bad idea, Greysen, if I had met you under different circumstances." She gripped the phone tighter and swallowed.

"What happened back then wasn't my fault, Sage." His voice was calm, clear, intelligent.

A rush of anxiety filled Sage's mind and spilled over into her words. "Do you think I don't know that, Greysen?" she snapped. "We're to blame—Sean and me—for showing up at your place that night with hell piggybacking on us, and—" She saw the broken body of Eli again, flames and all. "Oh my God!" she cried out in muffled hyperventilation. "I'm going insane."

"You're not going insane, Sage."

Sage cupped the phone to her mouth, embarrassed by her outburst. Her voice dropped to a neurotic whisper. "No matter how much I try to get a grip, I keep losing hold of myself."

"Sage, Sage. Calm down," he ordered. "Calm down."

The line grew quiet, then she blurted out his name, "*Greysen!*"

"I'm here."

"I see her every day."

"Who?"

"Eli!" she shrieked. She'd never told that to anyone—not even her therapist. She couldn't. Even if she could, she was sure she wouldn't have. It took Eli to help her understand Jadia's shutdown. Really understand. Some things are too horrific to paint with words. Sage rested an arm on top of the phone box and buried her head into it to shield her face from the curious passersby. She thought if she cried, she'd feel better, but tears remained out of her reach.

"You definitely don't need to get on that flight, Sage. You're in no condition to be anywhere by yourself. Why are you doing this?"

"Doctor's orders," she whimpered.

"That shrink only told you to do this because you never said what's really bothering you."

Sage sat ramrod straight, suspicious eyes sweeping the airport. "How do you know I didn't?"

"Because I asked Sean to tell you not to. Because, if you had, someone would have been here by now, excavating Eli's body and hunting me down. Because Sean's career—his presidential aspiration—is at stake. And because, if you had, you wouldn't have called me today. You'd be running and hiding for your life—or you'd be dead. You don't want to do that to Jadia, Sage."

Sage exhaled, darting eyes settling to stare at her lap. "No, I don't."

"You need to talk to someone."

She suppressed a smile. "You sound like Oma."

The line grew quiet. "Who?"

"Oma. She's my grandmother. And it's a long story."

"And I have plenty of time to listen. Like it or not, I'm the only one besides Sean you can tell the truth to. You've got all this pent-up energy trapped inside you with no place for it to go. It's giving you warning signs, letting off a little steam like a volcano threatening—no, promising—to erupt."

Sage looked over her shoulder to scowl off a rangy man who'd been lingering behind her too long. Indignation rattled in her throat as she rotated back to the phone. "How do you know how I feel?"

In the stretch of silence that followed, another announcement droned, taking the entire airport captive audibly. Greysen delayed a little longer, then answered softly, "Because the same memories plaguing you haunt me too. So it's mutual. I need you as much as you need me."

Sage quietly ran a finger along the slick, curved angles on the side of the phone base. "Sounds like the blind leading the blind."

Greysen's laugh belted through the receiver. A reluctant smile spread on Sage's face.

"My flight is nonrefundable, Greysen," she explained.

"I'll reimburse you for all your expenses."

Sage ran a finger along the cold, smooth, shiny metal coiled around the phone cord, tugging at it gently as she weighed the offer.

"I can take a cab to the Greyhound bus terminal and leave my car here where it's safer.

"Does that mean you're coming?"

Sage hand-raked her hair and said, "This is crazy."

"Right. So let's do this."

Closing her eyes, Sage thought about it for a brief moment, then blurted out, "Okay, I'll come."

CHAPTER 41

A tall, well-built man with benignly rugged features stood at the desolate stop where Sage stepped off the Greyhound and dropped a small duffel on the asphalt. Dark hair, neatly trimmed black shadow with specs of gray, and unmistakable style greeted her expectantly.

The bus hissed and veered off, leaving them in front of an abandoned redbrick building—the town's makeshift bus stop. Sage gasped thin mountain air as she spoke the words she'd rehearsed on the long ride from Philadelphia. She was only able to choke out a medley of spastic facial expressions.

"Is something wrong?" Greysen asked, trying to suppress a laugh.

"Only if you count sleeping with strangers for eighteen hours wrong."

Greysen let out a loud chuckle, exposing straight, white teeth. Lines fanned from radiant green eyes. "You're in a mood, aren't you?"

Dodging his gaze, Sage said. "I think it's stress."

"I have the perfect remedy for that," he said with duffel bag handles held firmly in his hand.

Sage's sun-constricted eyes glided from the early morning sky, and she focused on Greysen's face. "What would that be?"

"A hug." He placed the bag on the ground. The next instant, she was well within his embrace, pressed firmly against his hard, roped chest, and secured by his buffed arms. The smell of him—aftershave, mouthwash, and mountain pine—ushered her right back to Eli's living room when he'd knelt down and spoken to her, and stirred the same feeling of ardor. Then she saw Eli behind the raggedy door, sneering and—then breaking up in the air. The effect of this memory was to pulverize any sexual reactions Sage was having to Greysen.

Greysen gently released the embrace until they were face-to-face again, and he whispered, "Hello."

"Hello," she whispered back.

"Better?"

She pulled her head back from his chest and gave him a slow nod. "Much."

"It was good for me, too." He winked at her and turned to look away in the distance. "My truck is over there, right down the road behind a shed." He hoisted the duffel on his shoulder and took off walking.

"Behind a shed," she repeated in a mutter as she lagged behind him.

"What's that?" he asked, turning to one side and then to the other before he spotted her.

"Nothing," Sage lied, stepping up a bit to catch up with him. "Look, Greysen, if you want to have your secrets, it's fine with me. All I want is peace of mind." She looked up at him, glad to see a cheery grin as she rounded the abandoned building with him and approached a buffed black Chevrolet SS pickup.

"You definitely travel light," he declared as he tossed her bag onto the truck bed.

"The last time I was in this neck of the woods," she explained as he unlocked the passenger door, "all I had were the clothes on my back."

He held the door open for her, but before she stepped in, he gently grabbed her shoulder and said, "It's not going to be like the last time—I promise."

She looked up at him and wondered how he could make such promises when he had not been able to prevent the maelstrom she and Sean had brought during their first visit.

"I just have one question, Greysen."

"What's that?" he asked, shifting his weight to one foot and resting an arm atop the truck doorframe.

"Where are the malls?"

He laughed and helped her into the truck. They rode about three miles, then angled left onto a descending dirt road as Greysen asked, "When's the last time you saw Sean?"

"Funny you should ask. Sean and I had dinner Thursday night." She eyed Greysen closely. "I guess you know he's vying for the next presidential bid."

"Yes. It was probably Lori's idea, but when I spoke with Sean several months back, he was taking on the charge in full-Sean fashion. He's got the right backing behind him—and the funds. He might just pull it off." He glanced at Sage and smiled. "We shall see."

"The camera will love him," Sage said, smiling back. "He looks terrific."

Greysen downshifted as they neared a hairpin curve. He waited until he cleared it, then asked, "Did you tell Sean you were headed here?"

With a bobbing head, Sage eyed Greysen before saying, "Would it have been a problem if I had told him?"

"No," he answered, shaking his head. "I'm curious, that's all."

"About what?"

"About you—your lifestyle, your friends, your family, your job. And I have to admit I'm curious about your relationship with Sean—how you met, what he means to you."

She took a deep breath, then said, "That's a tall order."

"I'm not pressing you, Sage. I'm just curious, that's all."

"Mainly about Sean and me."

"For now, yes, because he's our common denominator. He was my best friend in law school, and apparently your relationship with him goes beyond customary client-attorney bounds."

"Okaaay," she dragged out. Sage then chronicled how her friendship with Sean had evolved, starting with being assigned to managing a marketing campaign to Sean volunteering to help if needed with any issues regarding Anthony Campbell's parole.

"Of course at the time, neither one of us would have imagined a need would arise. If the system worked right, Anthony Campbell would not have been up for parole for another decade. When we were surprised by the news of Campbell's imminent parole, Sean stepped in like a charm. He wanted to personally make sure Anthony Campbell got what he deserved."

Greysen looked across the cab at her, a small smile creased his face. "That sounds like Sean. The protector."

Sage shrugged and flashed him a reciprocating smile as she nodded in agreement.

The corners of Greysen's mouth relaxed and the smile faded. "Had Sean met Jadia before the rape?"

Sage shook her head. "Sean hadn't even met *me* before the rape. I keep a couple of pictures on my desk and credenza. He'd comment from time to time that Jadia was a beautiful child. Eventually, Sean met Oma and my former husband, Thomas. Sean and I still weren't exactly friends yet, but he became our family's confidant. When he finally met Jadia—" Sage paused, remembering how Sean's face had lit. "It was like she made him happy somehow."

Sage went on to explain how Sean had referred Thomas and her to a team of psychoanalysts who specialized in child hysterical dysphonia and how he and Lori had used their influences to move Jadia's name to the top of the Victim Services Office list."

Greysen shot her a look. "So you've met Lori?"

"No, I've never met Lori," she said thoughtfully. "But I gather she makes it her business to develop strong relationships with leaders in the community by supporting their causes. And it's not all about the dollar. From what I hear, Lori Swoboda is not afraid of rolling up her sleeves and applying a generous amount of elbow grease."

"You have to admire *that* about her," Greysen said grudgingly. "Lori can't walk anymore but she still cracks a whip."

"Lori can't walk?"

Greysen met Sage's shocked look with one of his own. How was it possible for anyone not to know about Lori Swoboda's confinement to a wheelchair? He pressed a hard gaze on the road and told Sage about Lori's paralyzing accident. Sage shook her head when he finished.

"Talk about overcoming hardship and adversity," she said. "Maybe Lori should be the one running for president."

Greysen floored the pedal and changed the subject. "Sean's always wanted children, Sage. I think maybe he looks at Jadia as a surrogate. It's the only thing that adds up."

The truck jostled its passengers as it negotiated a long patch of undulating, uneven road dappled with potholes and jutting rocks. Sage grabbed the hold bar and asked, "What do you mean by 'adds up'?"

For one quick second, Greysen turned his rocking head from an upcoming curve to Sage. "Sean forfeited a chance to be a consultant on the O. J. case so that he could be available to help you. He's a DNA savant, one of the few in our craft. I couldn't understand why he would give up such an opportunity when there were plenty of attorneys capable of handling a case like yours. I had my suspicions when I met you and Jadia that night. Now I know for sure."

Greysen's words belted Sage in the stomach and knocked the wind out of her. Her voice eked out something inaudible and unintelligible.

After she used a shaking finger to power down the passenger window, she retreated from Greysen's intense stare. Passing sugar maples, aspen, and white ash waved leaves of orange, yellow, and red. Hemlock held its steadfast green. Crisp, cool autumnal air flowed into the cab, splashing freshness across Sage's confounded face. She sucked in the air, trying to catch her breath.

Other than overhearing heated office debates, she hadn't kept up with the O. J. Simpson case. Ever since Jadia's abduction, she, Thomas, and Oma banned news reports. Eventually they gave up on television altogether.

But it was the daily talk of the office, so it was hard to completely ignore. The jury had just been selected late last month—September—and already the attorneys working the case had become instant household names. The prosecutors announced a plan to seek life without parole. Sean could have been a part of Marcia Clark's team. He'd given that all up—for her. For Jadia. For her family. His sacrifice had started long before they'd gone to the prison. Long before she'd used the Glock.

She shook her head at the aspen. Bass trees began intermingling on the lush hillside as she mumbled, "I—I didn't know." She turned from the forest and planted a confused gaze on Greysen. "I had no idea."

Greysen said nothing as he turned right onto an even rougher road.

CHAPTER 42

"So what do you like to do?" Greysen said, mercifully changing the subject. "Any hobbies, passions?"

"Marathons."

"You run?"

"Well, I've been out of commission long enough now to say I *used* to run. It's been a while since I've done serious exercise of any sort." She knew exactly when it had stopped. The day of the prison visit.

"I'm told I inherited the running bug from Oma. She used to jog frequently, but yoga's her exercise of choice now." Sage propped her elbow on the door and held her chin with a fist as she admired more fading foliage on the rolling hills.

"Oma. Your grandmother, right?"

"Yes, my grandmother," Sage said, still staring at the picturesque view. "Anyway!" She snapped her head around to face him and quickly changed the subject before he had time to make additional inquiries about Oma. "What do you eat? Rabbits? Squirrels? Coon? An occasional delicacy of fried frog legs?"

He belted out a laugh. "You make it sound vulgar."

This time it was her time to laugh.

"Every once in a while, I crave turkey legs too."

"Turkey legs? You're joking, right?"

"It's almost been a year since I've had any, but I feel a hankering coming on."

"So why don't you indulge yourself?" She looked out the window again at the great passing outdoors and said, "I'm sure there are plenty of wild turkeys running loose around here. There sure are plenty in Philly."

He spit out hearty, sidesplitting laughter. Sage wondered if he'd lose control of the vehicle. "Yes, I'm sure we can drum up a bird or two for your liking. Do you hunt?"

Sage thought about the only gun she'd held besides the ones she tried on for size years ago when she first pistol-shopped. She'd bought it, studied it, and practiced with it for one sole purpose: Anthony Campbell.

"I guess it's hypocritical to eat animals and snub those who kill them." She eyed Greysen closer. He was handsome.

He looked at her, mirth all over his face. "I don't mind doing your dirty work, Sage," he said. Then he put on his best southern accent for her. "I'll shoot 'em dead, gut 'em, skin 'em, and clean 'em for ya."

Sage thought about Anthony Campbell's body sprawled out across the glass-littered floor, blood spreading across a sea of mirror chips. "You know, Greysen," she said with a deep breath, "I think I'll skip meat today."

Greysen laughed again. "We can always hunt mushrooms and nuts. Wild blueberries make a mean breakfast."

"I'm sure wild blueberries are the rave in these parts, but what about grocery food? Hunting food the modern way won't emasculate you," she said. "We can stop by the store—" She looked out and around at the vast wilderness. "I bet there's a store somewhere around here." She frowned and kept talking. "I'll even go in with you for moral support. You can buy a few, I don't know, dozen or so packages of turkey legs and put them in your freezer." She laughed at what she considered to be a great idea and a funny one too. Then, under Greysen's quiet scrutiny, she remembered his house had burned. Her face dropped. The frown deepened.

"Greysen, I'm sorry. Your house—"

"Uhh, that's not it, Sage," he interjected, pausing. "I uh, I …" He stopped again and puffed air into his jaws before blowing it out. "I prefer to stay under the radar."

Under a canopy of confusion, Sage stared at Greysen's profile as he fixed his gaze on the road. After a while, she inhaled deeply and turned her attention to the road. A moment later, she shifted back to him and asked, "How long has this been going on?"

"Since I returned to the States a few years ago," he answered candidly. Greysen explained how he would conceal his truck behind shrubbery and read a book while Eli walked about a mile to the grocery store.

"We handled most things that way and mail-ordered the rest to her post office box. Now that she's gone, I'm forced to get gas for this truck on my own. I go to far too many places than I'm comfortable with."

"Why are you living like this?"

Greysen stared ahead for the longest time, behaving as though Sage had said nothing.

"Never mind," she relented. "Do you have a book somewhere in here?" she asked, opening the glove compartment. Except for an envelope, shriveled and yellowed from age, and a windshield scraper, it was empty.

"Sage, don't be ridiculous. I can't let you walk."

"You said Eli did it."

"That was impromptu conversation. I wasn't suggesting that you do that." He sighed with exasperation.

"Where's your book?" she asked, reaching under the seat and blindly scouring the floor.

"I have plenty of fresh fish, and I've already stocked up recently. Besides, we're practically where I live, Sage," he said as he pointed to an area on the right beyond a sweep of headlands. "It's up that road."

Turning right at the bluffs limit, onto the grass where there was only a hint of road, Greysen adeptly maneuvered the truck onto parallel tracks of previously flattened shrubs. Ever so vaguely, Sage could see where tires had scarcely worn the ground. And then there was the clearing. It was as big as a football field, with a beautiful, well-crafted log cabin in the middle. Hills with trees that pointed to the sky like quills on a porcupine surrounded the house and created a natural fortress.

"This is where you stay?" she questioned skeptically.

"This is where I live. It's my home."

"I ... How ... Wh ..." she stammered before giving up and looking at the house again. "I don't understand this. Please explain it." She threw a hand to her mouth. The picture-perfect cabin seemed in complete harmony with the timber that surrounded it. Eventually she realized Greysen had not replied, and she faced him again, demanding an answer as she glowered at him.

His eyes made a slow sweep of her face before he finally said, "I built it, Sage."

With a dropped jaw, Sage looked at the splendid cabin, then back at Greysen. "But when? How?"

"It's been complete now for about six years or so." He huffed and paused. "I mail-ordered every scrap of material that went into that cabin. It was the most expensive, painstaking endeavor I've ever undertaken, and the entire process took years. I did most of it, inch by inch, in minute increments because I didn't want to attract attention. And I hired contractors from outside the surrounding counties to do the work I absolutely couldn't do. They were the only ones I trusted not to tell." He looked at her. "I paid them well and had them sign nondisclosure agreements."

Greysen turned away and uttered under his breath, "Eli didn't know about the cabin." A long stretch of silence ensued before he looked at Sage again.

Her eyes dragged over his face. "How did you keep all of this from her?"

"One day at a time. One dig of the shovel at a time. One log at a time."

Sage's blue eyes sliced into Greysen. "You had this all along—but you lived in that God-forsaken shack?"

"If I hadn't been, then this place would have been the one bombed, right?"

Sage averted her gaze when she felt the accusing heat in his voice.

They sat in stifling silence. A flash filled Sage's vision. It was Eli with that derisive grin welded on her burned face. Why Greysen had kept the cabin from Eli was none of her business, but she couldn't help wondering if Greysen treated everyone with the same aloofness.

"Does Sean know about the cabin?"

Greysen's lids slowly slid closed, rested, and then opened when he said, "No. No one knows, Sage. I couldn't trust anyone. Sean—"

"Sean's your friend—your *best* friend. You said so yourself."

"I said he *was* my best friend. That was a long time ago. After law school I had to live up to a commitment I'd made during my undergrad years. Once that was underway, I couldn't trust anyone. Not then. Not now."

Running a hand through her hair, Sage stared at the cabin and bit her lip. Fear clawed at her back. No one knew where she was. A cellular would have been a lost cause even if she had one. She remembered the night Sean had driven her and Jadia to these very mountains and Greysen saying there weren't any cellular towers in the area. The memory reminded her of how Greysen had helped them that night and the loss he'd sustained the next morning. A loss he would never have had if she had not shown up that night. She was thinking maybe Greysen should be afraid of her and not the other way around. Sage drew a breath and slid her eyes to Greysen.

"Let's give this a try."

CHAPTER 43

With Sage's travel bag in tow, Greysen lead Sage to the porch. It stretched the length of the wide house and held quietly firm as they padded across it to the door. Inside, Sage's mouth dropped. Light flooded into the spacious living room from skylights. Dark-stained oak paneling climbed from carpeted floors to a wooden, vaulted ceiling lined with bold crossbeams. A river-rock fireplace climbed to the pinnacle of the A-framed wall and was flanked by paneled glass that beckoned guests to bear witness to the spectacular view. Cedar and the scent of warm vanilla wafted through the immaculately clean house, wrapping Sage in homey comfort.

Sage's head rotated in awe until it landed back on Greysen, who beamed at her expression. "It's gorgeous." Nostrils flared in her uplifted nose. "And it smells wonderful." Sage breathed in the scented air as they walked toward the open view. She could see a kitchen off to the right.

"I pour vanilla extract into a small tin and set it at the edge of the fireplace when I'm heating the house," Greysen explained. "September nights are pretty cool up here. Yesterday's scent is still lingering."

"A trick you picked you picked up from Eli, I bet," Sage said, forcing a smile.

"No, my mother."

"And I guess you got your sense of decoration from her too."

"You're right. The home-building skills are from my dad."

"Contractor?"

"Made a mint off of it in the city. Being a respected Manhattan attorney didn't hurt business. He built a lot of strong relationships before shifting into contracting. People trusted him."

Strolling around, Sage admired Greysen's consummate craftsmanship and his taste in furniture—all cedar and leather.

"How did you do all of this without anyone noticing?"

"I kept it small and—"

"And amazing," she interjected.

His face cracked into a flattered smile.

"And like I said in the car, mail-ordered. I purchased the materials intermittently in such minute quantities, I'm sure this must have cost me a million dollars."

"Surely you're exaggerating."

"Maybe, but you get my point."

"Yes, I do," she said, stepping across the living room and inspecting a spacious kitchen on the left wall. "Money talks," she commented as she circled around to face him.

"That it does," he agreed. "I invented a name and offered double cash on deliver to a couple of dozen suppliers for the wood alone. I did the same thing for the other materials, then like I said, built one little tiny bit at a time."

Greysen led the way down a hallway on the left side of the living room to a bathroom, then an empty bedroom just big enough for a full bed, explaining that he could always expand later. She backed out of the room and followed him into a roomy master bedroom that held a majestic, king-sized, cherry wood bed, layered with thick mattresses. It was covered with a white down comforter and sprinkled with a potpourri of throw pillows. A large cedar chest sat on the far side under a window covered with thick drapes.

"This house started as a project," he explained as he set her bag inside the threshold of the bedroom door. His eyes glided from one corner of the room to the other as he continued. "Just something to do. Slowly, it became my sanctuary when I needed a place to go."

Sage gave her brows a quick lift. "I'm sure it has served its purpose."

Greysen pushed his lower lip tight against his teeth. Sage shifted uneasily under the stare of unreadable eyes.

"I can't wait to find out if you're as good with a stove as you are with a hammer."

"Does that mean you're staying?" he asked, his warm tone hopeful, inviting.

"At least until dinner." She smiled.

He smiled back.

Long after dinner and hours of talking, Greysen said, "Getting to know you might be out of my budget, Sage." She burst into laughter as she remembered how he'd stared as she loaded her plate with a second helping of baked pork chops, rice, carrots, and salad. She rose from her chair and began to wander down the long hallway toward the bedrooms, with Greysen ambling close behind.

She looked over her shoulder and said, "Hey, I earned my keep. I washed dishes."

"Totally unnecessary after you licked everything clean."

Their guffawing was bouncing off the walls when Sage's hand curled around the doorknob of the guest bedroom. His hand covered hers as he brushed between her and the door. "Where are you going?"

Her blue eyes lifted to his greens and rested there a moment. "It's late. I thought I'd prepare for bed."

He gently uncurled her fingers from the knob and held her hand. "You're my guest, Sage. Take my room."

"Uhm—" Sage stopped, looking down at her captive hand.

Greysen's head dipped down, pulling her attention back to him. He tilted his head to the guest room door. "There's no bed in that room."

"No problem," she said, freeing her hand from his and raking her hair with it. "I'll make a pallet on the floor."

"Not in my house and not on my watch, you're not."

Flustered, she finally blurted out, "Why can't I take the couch?"

"Because we both won't fit on it," he answered sardonically. "Will you go now, please?" Her eyes followed his hand as it extended toward the master bedroom. "Your bag is waiting for you in there."

"Okay," she gave in, gazing back at him. "You win."

"Good. Get used to it."

After that night, Sage did as she was told and got used to it. She got used to his pajamas—she hadn't brought any—and his spacious, feather-soft bed. Then there was his delicious food and his wonderful, plutonic company. On the second day, they started a jogging routine. Greysen didn't own a television because he found it counterproductive. He spent his time sticking to a strict exercise regimen and learning about technology, photography, and medicine.

Sage often found him studying a plant shoot he'd never seen before. He'd photograph it and record notes in a journal for later reference. He talked about building a greenhouse to cultivate rare botanicals, and perhaps produce that would not otherwise survive in cold climates. During warmer temperatures, he maintained a garden. During one of their many long talks, he and Sage strolled to the back of the cabin where the remnants of a vegetable garden lay, nestled at the foothills of conifers and colorful bluffs.

"Gardening season is over, but during the spring and summer months I spend a lot of time working this land. It's therapeutic. Out here I have everything I need; I'm self-sufficient."

Sage scanned the vast countryside, shielding her eyes from the strong afternoon sun. The thin air smelled of damp earth, rotting wood, and mushrooms. She inhaled, closing her eyes; her skin prickled under the thousand touches of nature. Her lids opened to Greysen's gaze, which she'd grown to savor as much as the mountainous air. Without Eli and stress to block her view, she felt like she was looking at him for the first time. There was something intrinsically refined in his manner—urbane; fit, but not rugged; strong, but not robust. And his accent was as New York as any. He was everything she'd remembered about the city—the little she had liked about it anyway.

"What are you doing here?" Sage said to him.

It took Greysen a minute to tug himself from his ocean-deep dive into Sage's eyes. And it wasn't just her eyes. It seemed to him that her subtle curves were packed neatly in a lean body made to run. And her wit could slice through with cutting truth or crack someone to pieces with perfectly timed humor. Greysen felt that she understood him without groveling over him. She respected him, as he respected her. She pressed him, but she also knew when to back off the inquiries. And—she was waiting for an answer now.

"Do you mean living in the mountains?"

Her eyes climbed his tall body. "Well, yes. You're trying to be incognito, but you stick out like a sore thumb."

"I would stick out anywhere," he stated. "But for all practical purposes, I am nonexistent. Not real in any real sense of the word."

Sage stepped closer to him. Light lanced through the tree leaves, playing shadows on his face. Her hand reached up to his unshaven face. He breathed audibly at her touch.

"You're pretty real to me," she practically whispered.

A short time later, Greysen and Sage walked slowly back to the house, hand in hand.

The next morning, Sage rose from Greysen's bed and felt her way through the dark. Careful not to make too much noise, she crept toward the door and tiptoed to the living room where he had slept all night. The couch was empty; not so much as a ruffled pillow was on it. The kitchen was empty too when she searched it. Mild panic ratcheted through her gut. She stood and waited for what seemed like forever. The sound of whistling streamed in from outside, and she darted to the porch just in time to see Greysen opening the truck door.

"Whoa!" he said. His eyes lazed over her appreciatively. "After you didn't hear me in the shower, I figured you'd be out for at least a couple more hours." He smiled and strolled around the truck, closer to her.

"Where are you going?" she questioned, slowly descending the porch stairs.

He looked around, appreciating the burst of autumnal psychedelics playing against West Virginia mountains. He looked back at her.

"Uhm, look. Breakfast is still on, but I need to run an errand. I'll be back within an hour and a half. If that's too long to wait, I'll be glad to cook now and go later."

"Where are you going?" she repeated as she stepped further from the porch.

He planted fingers on his belt. "Sage ... it's uh, it's Sunday."

She stood a few feet from him and waited. "Okay. ... Are you going to church?"

He sucked in air. "No."

She shrugged a wide, questioning smile. "So where *are* you going?"

Keeping a few feet from one another, they stood in silence. She wondered if he had heard her. Then she got irritated because she knew he *had* heard her.

"I'm going to visit Eli," he finally said. "I've been doing it every Sunday since she died. There are sparse patches of wildflowers along the way. They're kind of scarce this time of year, but I manage to find enough to pick. I drop them into the creek that flows a couple hundred feet from the woods in back of her house. This way her grave isn't marked, and my sentiments won't attract the wrong attention."

Studying him in silence, Sage bit her lower lip. Then she looked over her shoulder at the empty house a while before returning her gaze to him.

"Does this bother you?" he asked. He drew fingers to his nose and pinched the bridge.

"No, no," she lied, shaking her head vehemently. "I was just wondering if you felt like company, because—" She glanced back at the house again, then said honestly, "I really don't want to be alone."

He grinned and asked, "Do you really want to come? It's near the spot where Eli's house stood."

"I certainly do," she called back as she dashed for the house. "Just give me time to take a quick shower!"

"Would you like breakfast before we go?" she heard him say behind her as she hopped up the stairs and opened the door. "I'm in no big rush now that you're going with me."

"No," she said in a softer voice. She shifted toward him, adding, "Besides, I hear wild blueberries are great for breakfast. We can pick some while we're out."

CHAPTER 44

"Eli was standing right there the last time I saw her alive," Greysen said as they sat in the truck. He pointed to a clearing carpeted with rubble. Sage had last seen it covered with smoldering debris. She hooked an arm in his as they drew to a slow stop.

"That was the last time either of us saw her alive," Sage added, aiming for anything that sounded remotely consoling.

After shooting her a blank stare, he said, "Yeah. Right."

They lingered in sudden and harsh silence a while before Greysen gently pulled his arm from her hold and grabbed the paper bag filled with the bouquet of wildflowers he had picked from patches of perennials that lined the road along the way.

"She's buried behind the woods," he said as he stepped from the truck and slammed the door closed. The sound of it banging against the body of the truck poignantly reminded Sage of Eli when she had stood on the porch and sneered at her and Greysen—well, sneered at her. Eli had died with look of hatred on her face even as she was thrown through the air. With that thought, Sage quickly fell into step with Greysen.

"She was creepy," she mumbled, hoping that the sound of leaves crunching under their feet would drown out her voice.

"I see her," Greysen said, pointing to rays of light peeking between trees at the far edge of the woods.

"What?" Sage exclaimed as she lurched and grabbed her chest.

"There's a sizable creek just beyond the woods," he explained. "Eli's over there." As though on cue, rushing sounds of gurgling water echoed through the woods and flooded their ears.

Sage elevated her voice over the deafening sound of those waters. "It sounds huge."

"It is," he agreed, "for a creek." After fifty yards or so, they stood on the crest of a slope overlooking raging waters that seemed to be in as much of a hurry to get away from there as she was.

"I brought Eli here because the water reminds me so much of her," Greysen explained, sitting on a mound of dirt that she presumed was Eli's grave.

Sage hesitated before she joined him in a squat. "Makes sense. Water can be treacherous." Saying nothing, Greysen stared at Sage through the breeze.

Fiddling with a small rock, she bit her lip. "Ahem." She cleared her throat, reaching for words that might sound comforting. None came.

Greysen's silence was like a dull knife, mercilessly and painfully plunging into her. He spoke to the water, "I loved Eli."

"I can see that," she said, fingers digging deep into the browning grass. "Look at where we are."

"But I wasn't *in* love her," he confessed.

Sage inclined her head to Greysen, squinting against the morning sun as it reached for its apex behind him.

"I come here—" He stopped and licked his lips as he gathered the words, "I come here to meditate and to keep the hellish reality of my life and Eli's death in perspective."

Sage studied the ground, then tipped back up to him, listening.

"I also come here to let Eli know I cared for her." He squinted at Sage and said, "You must think I've flipped," and turned to the water again.

Sage leaned closer to him. "Greysen, I find your words—your story—touchingly innocent, something the rest of the world has lost." She paused. Then she said, "I believe Eli was happy."

Blinking pensively at the water, Greysen took a deep breath. He said, "I often ask myself how many more Sundays I will spend here."

Sage scooted closer to Greysen until their hips touched. She ran a hand through his barely graying hair and whispered, "Keep Sunday dates with Eli until you feel better."

Greysen waited a beat, nodded, and looked at the sky. Then he took off his shoes and rolled up the legs of his trousers. A large hand clutched the bag of flowers as he stood. Sage watched as he ambled with practiced dexterity down the steep embankment. Rapid water splashed vigorously and smoothed coarse black hair on his muscular legs as it soaked the pants roll.

He tilted the bag and sprinkled the creek with the multicolored flowers until the bag was empty. The madly rushing water seemed to pause a moment and accept the flowers with engulfing swirls, then moved hurriedly back on course, taking the bouquet with it. He climbed the hill back to the mound, resuming his place next to Sage.

They lost track of time, listening to the rhythmic cacophony of nature, Greysen squinting against the glint of the rushing waters, Sage doodling silt. At some point, Greysen shifted his body to Sage and inclined his head. "I can't help thinking about how you and I met. How it all came about. Sean seeking refuge in the mountain. Your car punched with bullet holes."

Sage glanced away, guilt wracking her, then she forced herself to return to expectant green eyes.

Greysen continued. "When we were talking the other day, you said you and Sean were scheduled to be at one prison facility, but at the last minute you received a letter stating the locale had been moved."

Sage waited.

"Who sent the letter?"

Sage grew still, reluctantly disinterring the fresh grave of memories she'd buried alive. "Gosh, I don't remember specifically. It had a government seal on it though."

"Do you still have the letter?"

She blinked, thinking. "Sean has it. Thomas and I arranged for all communications regarding the case to be sent to him as our attorney. Why?"

Probing eyes locked on hers. "I'm trying to connect dots. Anthony Campbell had not met the mandatory minimum sentence. He was on parole for drugs and child pornography crimes when he'd kidnapped and raped Jadia."

Sage's eyes darted away from Greysen as if trying to find a place to run. Her entire body tightened with the urgency of *gotta do something now*!

"Hey," Greysen said, craning forward. He lifted her chin with a thumb and forefinger. "Are you all right?"

A forced smile curved under her sad, racing eyes. "I'm fine," she lied.

"I'm just saying, Anthony Campbell couldn't have skated through the parole system without help, and that help didn't come without plenty of reason. A couple kilos of coke could have provided some motivation, but when the cost of an empty prison bed is factored in, the Anthony Campbell saga smacks of much more."

Confusion pinched on Sage's face. Greysen explained.

"Private prisons make money from per diem or monthly rates based on occupancy. Each occupied bed yields income. As the customer, the government pays for imposing bed occupancy quotas upon private prison companies. As the contractor, private prison companies promise performance, usually based on 90 percent or above-occupancy rates. If this win-win scenario for private prisons fails, crimes can be invented and prison terms extended to ensure beds are occupied. And if that doesn't work, taxpayers ultimately fill revenue gaps."

Sage chewed her lower lip and said, "So it would have been more lucrative to keep Anthony Campbell in prison?"

"Yes. Unless there was a lot more at stake than meets the eye."

"And you suspect there is." It sounded like a statement. Sage meant it as a question.

Greysen hesitated before answering. "I'm just speculating, Sage. Throwing out wildcards. Casting a wide net."

Sage was bitterly thinking, *Great, I killed a pedophile and, in the process, pissed off his super-bad-guy owners and levied yet another burden on taxpayers. Way to go, Sage.*

CHAPTER 45
MARCH 1995

The Swobodas' cook, Vanessa, entered the room and placed two hot plates of rolled flank steak and prosciutto on the table, then she returned to the kitchen. As steam rose from mashed potatoes and broccoli, Sean shook out a heavy linen napkin and stated, "The food looks delicious."

They ate for a while, not saying much until their hunger pangs had been diminished. After returning his wine glass to the table, Sean retrieved his fork and knife and spoke.

"I'm tying up loose ends in the Philadelphia office and shifting gears back in the city. I'm taking you with me to Manhattan tomorrow so you can begin setting up shop there and getting our condo ready for the shift."

Lori picked up a glass of water and sipped. She replaced it on the table with a little cough before saying, "No, Sean. I can't go. I've made campaign commitments that require me to remain in Philadelphia. There are six black-tie dinners alone between now and April—"

Sean cut her short. Their eyes met.

"You had me at no." Sean's voice lanced air. He thought his days of sleeping without Lori were long gone.

Picking up her glass of wine and giving it a whirl, Lori said, "The campaign comes first, Sean. It has to." She pressed the rim of the glass to her lips, then pulled it away and set it on the table. Her eyes met his. "I suppose our schedule will have to be changed to accommodate the unavoidable separation."

When Lori talked schedule, she meant sex. Sean Swoboda, though faithful to the hilt, was a greedy man when it came to his Lori. He reengaged in a slow and thoughtful chew. Sean finished the last of his meal and wine, silent—and hopeful.

✱ ✱ ✱

"Do you want to talk about it?" Lori said. Hours had passed since dinner. She straddled him in bed, her lifeless legs flanking each side of him. He rested inside of her, deflated as she twirled greying hairs on his broad chest. Muted light filtered into the dark bedroom from outside lanterns and pagoda lights. Sean looked over at the digital clock on the nightstand—2:08 a.m.—and hoisted Lori away from him until she was laying comfortably in his embrace.

He dipped his head to plant a kiss on her cheek. "Are you okay?"

Lori leaned over and licked his nipple. "Nice and comfy." She paused. "Sean, do you want to talk about it? It's okay if you don't."

"Talk about what?"

"The O. J. case."

Sean had known what Lori meant. She was obsessed with the Simpson murder trial. But the subject first and foremost in his mind was their looming and apparently inevitable separation. Lori should have whittled down Philadelphia commitments a long time ago, certainly after all the Christmas and New Year holiday hoopla was over. The year 1995 was supposed be a time of togetherness for Team Swoboba. Instead, he was going to New York alone in just three and a half hours.

Sean stared at the tray ceiling, the weight of anticipated loneliness dripping from the coffer like molten lead. He thought of Jadia being so far away in Boston. About how that had affected Sage. He hadn't spoken to her since they met at the Four Seasons for dinner last October. It was the end of March now, so that had been what—five months ago? Lori's visage grew stronger under his gaze as his thoughts of Sage faded.

Lori was saying, "If you don't want to talk about it, it's okay. It's just that today, well yesterday actually …"

As Lori droned on about the O. J. trial, Sean drifted off to sleep.

CHAPTER 46

SEPTEMBER 1995

"Hey."

Sean looked up from cleaning out his desk drawer in his Manhattan office and found Ayde Carona leaning against the doorframe. He took note of the Versace blouse under Ayde's tailored jacket and gave a mental nod. She looked like a supermodel carrying an impressive lawyer's attaché.

"Hi there," he said, closing the drawer.

"Long time, no see."

"It has been a while," he said, lounging back in the leather high-back chair and stifling a yawn. "So are you coming or going?"

Ayde Carona displayed the attaché. "I'm just back from court. Parts of the Warner Brothers IP case are still alive and kicking."

"Intellectual property can be complex," he said as he watched her stroll deeper into the office. "The firm nailed it by assigning you to the case."

"How have you been?" Ayde sat the attaché upright on the table.

Sean thought about it. A red-eye had just flown him in from Columbus, Ohio. Now he had to stop by the campaign's SOHO headquarters, then dinner with Lori and a long night with her if he was lucky (and he damned well better be), and then he'd be on a chartered flight to Iowa in the morning.

Against Lori's advice, Sean had opted for a political sabbatical after the Anthony Campbell case had closed rather than tender his resignation. Some of his more high-maintenance clients had resisted the potential resignation and, because he needed their campaign funding, he relented. This equated to being a part-time lawyer in conjunction with following a grueling, early campaign trail. He'd been withstanding this trek nonstop since 1995 rolled in nine months ago. He lacked sleep and was too frequently separated from campaign headquarters and his wife, although separation from Lori seemed to be mostly of her own devices.

Sean focused on Ayde and said, "Jury's still out." He joined Ayde Carona's unabashed laugh, basking in unspoken relief of being away from and not having to talk about the campaign, if only for a few minutes.

He swiveled in his chair and followed her gaze to the wall of floor-to-ceiling windows behind him. He stood and stepped closer to the view.

"Look at that," he said, motioning for Ayde Carona to join him. "Seventy degrees and a clear September sky." As Ayde Carona approached, Sean shoved his hands in his pockets and angled himself against the window. He threw back his head; enjoyed a long, deep pull of air; and looked at the looming New York towers.

Ayde Carona smelled delicious. He thought about getting the name of the perfume she was wearing to buy a bottle for Lori.

"It's beautiful," Ayde Carona said, glancing out at the high-rise buildings.

"Yes it is," he agreed, dipping his head to peer down at her. For a long while they said nothing, glancing at each other and the skyline in turns until they burst into another fit of laughter.

"You were smart, Sean," Ayde Carona began after their chuckles subsided, "to refuse Marcia Clark's offer join the O. J. prosecution team." She swept a hank of hair behind her ear. "I didn't say anything before because it wasn't my place, but I've always believed you did the right thing." She looked at the skyline in thought, then turned back to Sean. "You saved the firm embarrassing press. Our competitors would have eaten it up."

These were the first—no, the only—supportive words Sean had heard regarding the O. J. Simpson trial since Nicole Brown Simpson and Ronald Goldman were killed. The words felt good. Ayde Carona felt good.

"I don't like second-guessing fellow attorneys," she continued, "but I can't help thinking the prosecution's fatal flaw wa—"

Sean's cell rang from an open attaché laying on the credenza. He whirled around, following the direction of the ring. As he headed to answer it, he mouthed, "One second," to Ayde. She passed his back as she returned to the guest seat in front of his desk.

"Yeah," he answered, his back still turned. A lengthy silence ensued.

"Lori, Lori—slow down," Sean said into the phone finally. "First of all, babe—hello, I missed you. How are you?"

The creak of the chair filled the room. Sean turned around just as Ayde Carona was lifting herself. He pointed to the phone, mouthed "wife" as he sat on the edge of the credenza, and waved Ayde back into the seat. He folded one arm over his chest as the other held the phone to his ear.

"Yeah, we got in this morning, and I've been at the firm all day. I've been calling but—"

A few seconds ticked as he listened. Ayde lifted again. He waved her down.

"Okay. Okay. That sounds good. So, babe, I have to take the first flight out to Iowa tomorrow morning. I'll see you at dinner tonight. Reservations are already made at—"

Ayde picked up her attaché. Sean gave a soft snap of his fingers and shook his head "no."

Ayde mouthed, "Okay." She sat down again and gently opened the attaché.

Sean smiled and gave her a thumbs-up, then spoke into the phone. "I'm meeting with the field department head as soon as we arrive in Iowa tomorrow to straighten all that out."

Ayde had clicked open the latches. The springs flung back, hitting against the attaché with a loud snap. Her eyes popped to Sean, and she mouthed an "ooops!"

He gave her a smile, then focused back on the phone. "It's the only storefront we have in the nation that's experiencing those issues. ... Lori, we discussed this. I preferred to speak to the finance chairman after I arrived. You jumped the gun by calling. ... Yes, but there is a lot to be said about the element of surprise. ... I needed to get a face-to-face read on his initial reaction. ... Why don't we discuss that and the GOTV issues tonight at Daniel? I've already made reser—"

He turned his back and lowered his voice. "We made plans, Lori. I only have one night." He let out a long sigh.

Ayde Carona bit her lip and peered up at the back of his head.

"The only place you *need* to be is here."

With measured motions, Ayde Carona quietly replaced the files inside her attaché. The latches closed with loud clicks.

"I don't understand the change in plans. ..." Sean spun around when he heard the clicks. He held up a finger and shook his head at Ayde Carona, who was now standing with attaché in hand. She smiled, shrugged, and began to tiptoe out.

"Me? ... I don't know. I've been eating crap all week so I, unlike you, will probably stick to the plan and head to Daniel. ... Okay, you're right. I'll definitely eat at Daniel. ... Yes. ... Yes. ... Okay. ... Yes, I'll call you as soon as I get home. Keep your cell nearby while you're schmoozing. ... I know it's for me, babe. I'm grateful. It's just that I miss you. ... Love you too. Bye."

Sean snapped the lip of the phone closed, stared at his shoes, and took several long, deep breaths before realizing Ayde Carona was gone. He checked his watch and made a call. Afterward, he threw the files he had been studying into the attaché, locked it, and tucked it upright under his desk. He'd have his driver pick it up and bring it to the apartment later.

Sean grabbed his suit jacket, pocketed the cell, and sidled to the door, giving the room a once-over before he closed the door and headed down the long hallway. Just before he reached the reception area, he peaked into the last office on the left—Ayde Carona's office.

Ayde's head popped up as his shadow filled the threshold.

"Hey—you're off?" she said, looking up from her computer.

He ran a hand over his smooth head and shoved a hand into his pocket. "I'm sorry about the extended phone call. I thought I could get on and off. I didn't quite realize Lori needed to squeeze an entire dinner conversation over the phone—last minute, uhmm, calendar changes." He had started to say "schedule" changes. That used to mean sex between him and Lori. Now "schedule" meant nothing. He gave his nose a quick stroke and leveled gray eyes on Ayde again. "I apologize for holding you hostage."

"It's okay," she said, smiling. She stood, grabbed her attaché, and rounded the desk to join him at the doorway.

"I understand," she said. "The campaign sounds like a pretty tough ride." Her face fell serious. "You've got this, Sean, and you don't need anyone to mother you." She studied him a little longer, then added, "Still, I hope your next stop is home. You look beat."

In the passing silence, Ayde Carona tucked in her lips, leaned on the doorframe, and folded arms under her full breasts.

"I'm not nearly as beat as my campaign staff," Sean said after a second of retrospection. "They're determined to make this happen for me. I'm headed downtown to say hello—and ordering a pizza on the way so it should be there by the time I get there."

"Are you dining with your staff?"

"No. I need better fare than that tonight. Trying to keep in shape on the road is hard enough."

"You look great, Arnold—I mean, Sean."

He grinned at her humor. Thought a minute. Then, more seriously said, "Would you like to finish our conversation over dinner? The reservations are already made and uh—well, I think this is my last time in this office. I completed electronic transfer of my files. Deanna's shipping the last of my personal effects to my home within a day or so."

Mild shock moved Ayde Carona's body off the jamb. She stood upright, arms sliding from their folds as she considered.

"We can call it your farewell dinner," she proffered, with a gleaming smile.

"Sounds like a plan," Sean said.

"Which means I'm pay—"

"Nothing doing. I'm treating. Reservations are for seven at Daniel. Do you know where it is?"

"Sixty-fifth, between Park and Madison."

Sean raised his brows and propped a half smile.

"Sean," Ayde said, tilting her head. "Daniel has been one of the city's hot spots since they opened last year."

While Daniel was opening its doors a year ago, Sean had been spinning off a campaign. Everything since—cities, people, speeches—had been a blur.

"I only know about Daniel because my campaign manager highly recommended it, but it sounds like you've been there a time or two."

Ayde shook her head. "No. Never."

"Good. It will be a first for both of us."

The campaign's designated driver pulled to Daniel's curb at 6:49. Sean was out of the limo and across the walkway with his hand on the restaurant's Gallic door before the driver could exit and round the car to assist him. Ignoring the driver and the restaurant doorman who had appeared late on the scene, Sean pivoted back for a perimeter scan. A rare, broad smile spread across his face when he spotted Ayde Carona. He abandoned the door to greet her.

"Glad you could make it," he said before guiding her by the small of her back to the restaurant where the doorman awaited, holding an opened door and showing the kind of exaggerated attention anyone would have after being lax on the job and still jonesing for a big tip.

CHAPTER 47

"There he is," Lori Swoboda said to Frank as she saw her husband head to Daniel's door. As she powered the window down to wave at Sean, she barked at Frank, "Hurry up and get me out!"

"Sean!" Her voice rose over New York's hubbub of yapping pedestrians and honking horns, making a direct line across the street to her husband.

As Sean turned around and scanned the perimeter, she waved and said to Frank, "Hurry! I think he sees me."

Frank secured the gear in park and adjusted his hat as he placed his hand on the door handle and glanced up the street at the man in front of the Daniel. Yep. That was Sean Swoboda. The height. The bald pate. The expensive suit. The power stance. Definitely Mr. Swoboda.

Lori Swoboda and Frank both smiled when they saw Sean's head crane their way—and then stilled as a long-legged stunner greeted him. Lori watched her husband—*her* husband—placed his hand on the small of Ayde Carona's back and escort her to a dinner reserved for Mr. and Mrs. Swoboda. Reservations intended for Lori Swoboda. Lori had called the restaurant for directions and all but whipped Frank into defying physical and traffic laws in order to arrive on time. Just in time. Perfect time to see Ayde Carona's expensive stilettos step into the Daniel with Sean.

As Lori Swoboda looked out of the Town Car's window, her fingers slid down the door lock spindle along the door panel to the powered lock button. She pressed the power button once. Then again—again—again. With each press of the power button, the door lock spindle popped up and down—*pop, pop, pop.*

Behind the steering wheel, Frank's expressionless face looked into rearview mirror and stared at Lori Swoboda's disturbed reflection.

CHAPTER 48

The two attorneys were seated side by side in a private room Sean had reserved for himself and Lori. It was the only way to ensure no interruption considering his growing celebrity on the local front. They were seated close, just as he had arranged, except the close proximity was intended for his wife, not his colleague.

"Tell me about your family," he ended up saying. He watched with an expectant eye as Ayde sipped water a waiter had poured from a glass bottle of mineral water. The Daniel maître d', who spoke flawless English with an elegant accent, interrupted to describe the chef's specials and recommend pairing wines. Ayde ordered oven-baked black sea bass with Syrah sauce; Aleppo pepper; roasted parsnip; and Yukon Gold potato confit. After complimenting her choice, the maître d' shifted with a slight bow to Sean, who ordered duck terrine with hazelnut; Sauternes gelée; apple coulis; frisée salad; and aged sherry.

Having dodged Sean's inquiry about her family, Ayde sipped the champagne he preordered to accompany the golden Osetra caviar they shared, and she looked around the elegant settings of their private digs.

The last thing she wanted to talk about was her family. She was as guarded about her childhood and family as Sean was about everything.

"So is it anniversary time for you and Lori?" she asked. "This restaurant is pretty upscale swanky even for a presidential candidate." She smiled and added, "The private room is a very nice touch."

"Not our anniversary," he said with eyes steady on hers. He lifted his flute and sipped. They both had foregone wine to respect Ayde's personal limit of one drink, and Sean's required early rising the next day. "Time is a precious commodity for me these days. The original plan was to have a bit of time alone with my wife."

Ayde blinked and tabled the flute. "I am really sorry that the evening didn't work out as you planned," she said. "I know I'm no consolation prize." She didn't mean the last part, but she felt sorry for him.

"You're great company, Ayde," Sean said.

"I wasn't fishing for a compliment, but I must admit that's one of the best ones you could have given." Ayde smiled, relieved Sean wasn't regretting the invite.

"No, you're weren't fishing, but I thought I'd let you know. If I had a daughter, I'd want her to be like you." He tucked a stray hair behind her ear. "I'd be so proud."

"Father?" Ayde didn't know about the failed attempts at pregnancy or the close-call adoptions. She couldn't have known he saw her smarts as the part of himself he had always desired to extend via a child of his own.

Instead, Ayde envisioned a wheelchair and the pretty blonde woman sitting in it. She had learned from office gossip that Lori was the daughter of Russian immigrants, an inactive attorney who had a reputation for being formidable in the courtroom—and any room. Like Ayde, Lori spoke five languages, Russian and English being the only tongues they shared. The reason behind the wheelchair had always been referred to as "an accident." It had happened a year or two before Ayde joined the firm, making it about six years ago. Perhaps the heroic, almost dreamy way Sean stood by and protected his wife was his redemption.

She reached across the corner of the table and squeezed Sean's arm. "I really admire the way you demonstrate love for and loyalty to Lori," she said. Leaning back against the chair, she picked up a glass of water and said, "You like to growl and stamp, but deep inside, you're just a teddy bear. What you guys have is—well, it's old-fashioned romance. The real thing."

Sean studied Ayde Carona at length, and then signaled the maître d' to bring the check.

Humid wind slapped them around a bit as they stepped into the late evening air, leaving Ayde with sexy bed-hair and skin layered with dewy freshness. Buzzing, blaring traffic clashed with layers of pedestrian din like ear graffiti. Amid the overwhelming sounds, the presidential candidate and his former colleague found a small, quiet sidewalk spot to close the evening.

"Thanks for dinner," Ayde Carona said.

"My driver can take you to your car. I don't like the thought of a lady in a parking garage late at night."

"No need. The Explorer's been under the weather, so I've been cabbing it."

"This is 1995, Ayde. Explorers are called SUVs now—sports utility vehicles." He smiled and winked at her. "So your *SUV* is in disrepair?" he asked.

"Yes," she said. "The SUV's in disrepair. She's been sick a lot lately." She stepped to the curb and raised her head to hail a cab, then she looked over her shoulder at him and said, "Maybe it's time to trade her in for a new one." She shrugged, as she turned back to the traffic to continue the search for a cab.

"Ayde," Sean said. His voice was low—and close. She looked over a shoulder at him, hand gliding down as she turned to face his stony, handsome visage. "I love my wife," he said. "I have never cheated on her—never had an inkling. I don't plan to start now."

"Sean," Ayde said, stepping away from the curb as a Checker taxi pulled close. She extended her hand to Sean's biceps. "I don't want you to."

"Hey, lady!" the cabbie called from the curb. "You want a taxi or what?"

Ayde Carona glanced over her shoulder at the taxi, then back at Sean. She smiled at him, raising waggling fingers to hip level in silent good-bye before spinning around just as the taxi was pulling away.

"Ayde," Sean said. A car blared the "Macarena" song, and then two cars later, the tune blasted again like one baby's cry waking another. The "Macarena" was everywhere. People on the streets combusted into unified dances. Ayde pivoted back to Sean, a curious smile on her face.

Sean grabbed Ayde Carona's hand and said, "Thank you."

Her brows rose. "For what?"

"For the ride to Philadelphia that day."

She smiled. "I owed you. You and Lori gave me a lift me home after the Christmas party back in '93, remember?"

He ignored this and continued his thread. "And for sticking by me at the firm. For going to bat for me with every single partner in there. I'm forty-four, Ayde, and I've been with the firm since I interned in law school. You must have been what—ten or eleven when I graduated?"

"I'm thirty, so that's about right. But if you wanted to know my age, Swoboda, you should have just asked me."

Sean smiled, then continued. "I've had a long, rather exceptional career with the firm. Worked with a lot of people. And yet you were the first, the *only* person to root for me. You supported me whether I was wrong or right, friendly or—" He paused. "Or not so friendly."

A consumer jet streamed over their heads while, on solid ground, Sean threw a reflective glance up at the restaurant awning and said, "You know what I like about you, Ayde?" She waited. His eyes were trained back on hers, and he once again decided she was one beautiful lady.

"You're not afraid to be in the line of fire. Least of all, mine."

Ayde Carona smiled again. When Sean released her hand, she pushed on her heels and slowly backed away one measured step at a time. Their eyes remained locked until she spun away and blended in with pedestrian traffic. Sean watched until her shrinking image rounded a corner and disappeared.

CHAPTER 49

In a car parked across the street, Lori Swoboda watched her husband stare at Ayde Carona's long legs until they disappeared into pedestrian mire. She looked up to see Frank's placid eyes watching her, mocking her, in the rearview mirror. *Does he really think I need his pity?* She'd have to deal with him later. She lobbed an empty plastic water bottle at him and missed. He didn't duck. He did not so much as wink. It was as if he had been expecting it. As if she were that predictable.

Nearly two years had passed since the firm's 1993 Christmas party when she had seen the hungry way Ayde Carona looked at her husband, the way his gaze glided over and lingered on Ayde Carona's long legs. Worse, the way Ayde Carona looked at her, Lori Swoboda. Light brown eyes packed with pity. Did Ayde Carona think Lori Swoboda needed her pity? Lori pitied the fool who pitied her.

CHAPTER 50

The Central Park West condo, stripped of anything that was non-Lori, seemed for the first time foreign to Sean Swoboda. Leopards lay on the sofa in the form of pillows and throws; zebras had sprawled on the bathroom floor; a cheetah lay in their bed. The walls, overwrought with books, closed in on him like looming judges and sentenced him to a lifetime of dust. The velour chair he sat on after hanging up his suit jacket offered no more comfort than a witness seat. And him, feeling imbued with and trapped by Ayde Carona. Her scent stuck to his nostrils like a faithful companion.

Sean loped to the master bath, showered, and dressed in a pair of Neiman Marcus steel-black lounge pants. The refrigerator light shone on three bottles of beer, seven bottles of Perrier, and an opened container of almond milk that he was sure had expired. His hand grasped a cold neck of Perrier. He stood, leaning against the refrigerator and looking at numbers glowing green from the microwave: 9:03 p.m.

A red-eye to Iowa was already staring him in the face. *Take a number,* he thought as he trekked to the office, feet stealing the wood's cool. He sat behind the desk, a refuge from Lori's African safari. The campaign's driver had already retrieved and delivered the attaché he'd left at the firm. According to the quiet new-hire, security had given him no trouble thanks to the all-clear call Sean had made.

Under bright desk light, Sean worked for the next hour and a half. After placing his attaché near the foyer table, staging for tomorrow's flight, he returned to the office for a once-over. He couldn't afford to forget anything. Standing in the doorway, he scanned the room. Something caught his eye. A black velvet photo album lay flat on an empty space of the bookshelf. He walked over to it, surprised he hadn't noticed it before. He opened the album. Adroitly placed against acid-free, weighted paper were newspaper clippings chronicling the O. J. Simpson trial. Each month had its own header page.

> July 1995:
>
> *July 24*, Monday: Frederic Rieders, a forensic toxicologist, says he found evidence of blood preservative in two pieces of evidence, implying police planted the evidence.

Sean flipped the thick album pages, skimming over headlines like

> *July 28*, Friday: North Carolina judge blocks O. J.'s defense attempts to force screenwriter to hand over taped interviews of Detective Fuhrman; defense says tapes reveal Fuhrman is a racist who …
>
> *August 2*, Wednesday: Microbiologist John Gerdes …

Sean's fingers curled to slam the album shut, but he found himself lingering on the pages like

> *August 9*, Wednesday: Ito ends defense effort to question two reporters about DNA evidence leaks.
>
> *August 10–11*, Thursday–Friday: Michael Baden, ex– New York City medical examiner …

He stopped reading and exhaled a gust of air, nursing his ire. And then he skipped to Lori's most recent entry.

> *September 5*, Tuesday: Five witnesses, including McKinny, testify to Fuhrman's use of racial epithets within last ten years. At hearing with jury out of room, Fuhrman invokes Fifth Amendment protection in further testimony.

September fifth had been yesterday. Lori found it important enough stock his library with an ode to what she saw as his failure, but shirked behind political nothingness to avoid being with him today. Sean slammed the album shut and tossed it back on the shelf. He padded across the carpet and sat behind the desk on a swiveling, creaking chair. Sean settled his haunches into the soft leather and stared at the tilted keypad of the Nortel single-line desk phone: 11:07 p.m.

He stared at the telephone. Another sigh later, his fingers bypassed speed dial, taking the long, scenic route to Lori. As signaling tones pitched in his ear, Sean threw himself back against the chair, swinging his long, muscular legs over the desk to prop his bare feet.

Lori answered on the first ring. "Hello?"

"Hi, babe. Man, I miss you." The line was quiet. He frowned at his flexing toes. After a long stretch of nothingness, he asked, "Are you okay?"

"Yes, I'm fine. I was just thinking ..." Her voice trailed.

"Yeah, you were thinking what?"

"I was thinking I should have joined you for dinner."

His toes froze. Quiet. Expectant.

After a long wait, she said, "I know it's my fault." She sighed. "And now we won't see each other for another four days."

In the ensuing silence, Sean thought, *The hell you're sorry—you were here yesterday with no problem.*

"It's okay, babe." He twisted opened the Perrier and took a sip to help him swallow the lie. "Don't worry about it."

"So, did you dine at the Daniel?"

Quelling a choke, he said, "Yes. I, I uh—I ended up at the Daniel just like you advised, babe. I invited another attorney from the firm. We ate, talked shop, and I left. Lori—" Sean cut her off as he heard her prepare to say something. "Babe, we need to talk. Don't start on O. J. or the campaign. We need to talk about *you*."

"Me? What about me?"

"You don't—" He took a breath and leaned over the desk. A forefinger found its way to the rim of the bottle and circled it. "We don't talk like we used to."

"We talk all the time, Sean."

"You used to volunteer for the children's hospital. You'd talk about all the—"

"The campaign is all-consuming, Sean. You know that. By the way, I heard it through reliable sources that you've inspired another millionaire to vie for the 1996 Republican nomination. The candidacy announcement is slated for later this month."

"Which millionaire ? We're a dime a dozen these days."

"Steve Forbes."

Sean blinked. "You're kidding. He doesn't have a chance."

"I know. He—"

"Stop right there, Lori. No campaign talk tonight."

Sean counted six dead-air seconds.

"Okay," she said with soft reluctance. This was followed by more silence.

"You used to love current events," he said, easing back into the chair. "You read the paper every day like a news addict. I'd come home, and you'd update me on cultural trends and international events. I miss those days of my Lori being Lori. Right now we're falling into unfamiliar territory, babe."

"Sean, I'm lost. You're confusing me."

Lori's stonewalling chipped away Sean's cool like a building razed one brick at a time.

"Maybe this will help. A few months ago when I tried to talk to you about Jackie O's memorial service, you shooed me off with some excuse about not being in a Dem mood. Our friends were there, Lori, and called to ask why we—"

"You know we were ramping up the campaign when Jackie passed, Sean. I mean, who *are* you and what have you done with my husband?"

Sean pursed his lips and swung his feet from the desk to the floor. Icy grays sliced to the bookshelf where the black velvet O. J. album lay in wait for the next press release.

"What have you done," he said, chomping the words with gritted teeth, "with my wife?"

Under the hiss of the white noise that followed, Sean picked up the Perrier and slammed it back on the desk before the bottle met his lips. Carbonated bubbles belched in the bottle as Sean relished the burn inside him.

"My wife," he continued with emphasis, "would have celebrated in a lavish way when the Child Protection and Obscenity Enforcement Act was passed. Instead, the woman parading around as my wife harangues her husband about a calendar he looks at almost every moment of the day."

The hush expanded like a black hole. Lori collapsed it with a whisper: "July fifth."

"What?"

She cleared her throat and spoke louder, clearer. "July fifth. The Child Protection and Obscenity Enforcement Act was passed this year on July fifth. Sean, the campaign demands dou—"

"Lori, this is not a quiz," Sean broke in, killing the non sequitur. "I'm not questioning a goddamn calendar date. I'm questioning your lack of enthusiasm for things that used to be important to you." He paused for effect. "Like children."

Sean threw back a gulping swallow of Perrier. He squinted as the bubbles popped in his mouth. The silent receiver pressed hard against his ear. The slick bottle was back on the coaster. Sean frowned at the silence.

"Do you still want children, Lori?" The question was tinged with anxiety he wished he had tamped before speaking.

Lori said nothing.

Sean uprighted himself as silence drew itself out like a long story.

"Let's deal with one hurdle at a time." Lori's words crackled like static. "We can broach that subject again after you're president."

"That *subject*?" Sean repeated, sitting upright. His voice was on the edge of a boom. "I didn't ask you about a *subject*, Lori. I asked you about children." He pinched the bridge of his nose. After a long pause, he quieted his voice and spoke.

"I guess now is a good time to let you know I'm getting tired of you brushing me off like I'm a piece of lint."

"I'm sorry, Sean." At the sound of the poorly crafted words, Sean tapped the wet neck of the Perrier bottle.

"Yeah, I'm sorry, too," he said. His sudden realization of Lori's clear and obviously long existing desire not to have children was a measure of the plight their marriage. *When the hell had all this happened?*

"Have a safe trip tomorrow," Lori said. "I'll work on clearing the calendar so that we can get in some alone time when you return."

Another long silence filled the line.

"I—" Sean stopped, unable to add the *love you* part.

"Love you, too," she said. The line clicked dead.

Good ole Lori, he thought. *Always filling in the gap—with crap.* The conversation with Lori blotted out his resolve to revive their beloved sex schedule

Sean finished off the water and tossed the bottle in the recycle bin. Then he tidied the office, shut off the lights, set the alarm, and charged the phone. For the first time since their marriage, he was quite okay with crawling into bed without his wife.

❋ ❋ ❋

Across the street, Lori Swoboda sat in the backseat of an idling Lincoln Town Car, watching her husband's moving shadow that was cast against the bay window.

CHAPTER 51

"I love that song 'Take Me Home, Country Roads,'" Sage said. She stared at the creases of the wilted bus ticket in her hand, the date bolded in large font—September 6, 1995. She'd been on an all-day, overnight ride with strangers, and finally she was seated next to Greysen and listening to his truck radio.

"Of all the versions, I think John Denver's original take on it does it best. Now every time I hear it, I think of you." She looked at Greysen's profile, the magnificent combination of genetics and of an environment that included years of learning, loving, losing—living.

It had been eleven months since she'd seen him. A year since she'd dipped into his palette of smeared colors and fuzzy shadows—his secrets. She had never forgotten his laugh. His smell. The resolved expression that shadowed his face whenever he spoke of Eli.

Greysen and Sage had talked on the phone nearly daily since her visit in October 1994. Eleven months of healing and placing events, experiences, and memories in perspective; of storing them on a shelf for future reference away from the heart's window and mind's front door. Sixteen months from the last malevolent stink of Anthony Campbell.

Sixteen months from Eli's explosive death. Sixteen months, and still the mysteries behind the events lingered.

"You and John Denver may be singing about West Virginia together, but does he know you kept your New York twang and East Coast gait stashed away for a rainy day?" She took off her shoes, rested her feet on the dashboard, and stretched. "We're gonna have to toss ole Johnny boy out the window—'Native New Yorker' is your song."

"I'm glad to see you packed your sense of humor," Greysen said. He touched Sage's thigh—the first for that kind of tactile intimacy—and eyed her with a tilted head as he drove. "But just for the record. I didn't like disco then, and I don't like it now, so please find another song for me."

Sage caught his smile and held on to it until they reached his cabin. As he shifted the gear into park, Greysen fought another smile, then gave up after Sage tried to tickle him into telling more about himself. A corner of Sage's own dubious mouth lifted. "Yeah, well, all joking aside, you're going to have to start sharing," she said. "Is everything in your life a touchy subject?"

Under the heat of her scorn, Greysen found uninhibited, make-your-lungs-open laughter. The cackles plopped on her like giant snowflakes in a desert, simultaneously confusing and delighting her.

"I'm glad you're getting your humor on," she said, feigning interest outside the cab. "Just let me know when you're finished."

"Hopefully, never," he said. "It feels good to laugh."

Sage beamed and shifted toward him. "Good deal."

Much later, Greysen spoke to her in a more serious tone. They were seated on the sofa. "I have another one for you," he said, referring back to their conversation in the truck. He stood and reached for her hand and helped her stand. Filled with anticipation, she followed him toward the back of the house, where he led her to the bathroom and motioned her through the open door. Inquisitively staring at him, she smiled, shrugged her shoulders, and then walked past him into the bathroom. Inside, she beheld a tub filled with steamy water that was dotted with more of the same variegated wildflowers he had sprinkled in Eli's creek.

"You're not saying much," he said, wrapping around her.

"That's because I'm too stunned for words," she answered with an unsteady voice. "I—I don't know how to take this."

"The last I heard, you remove your clothes, step in, carefully sit down, and swish the water all over your body. Soap would be good too." He grinned and inclined his head toward her.

Sage ran a hand through her hair and said, "Oddly enough, Greysen, this reminds me of the flowers we left in the creek near El—"

"I want you to relax," he interrupted.

Sage swallowed anything she had planned to say, glanced at the water, and then looked back at him. "Sure," she outwardly agreed, forcing a smile. "Thank you."

Greysen left her in privacy, gently closing the door after handing her a huge, plush towel. Still baffled and now alone, Sage slowly began to peel off her clothes as she stared at the towel, then the water, then she looked back at the door. Taking a deep breath, she balked, then tore her eyes from the door and resigned herself to the bath as her toes dipped into the warm waters. An hour and a half later, Sage walked into the living room. She was wrapped Greysen's oversized terry cloth robe, and she resumed the position she'd established on the floor during her first cabin visit the year before.

"Thanks again, Greysen," she said, draping a panel of the robe across her shapely, outstretched thigh. "You even thought of razors and shaving cream." She looked at him. "Very considerate."

"How was it?" His eyes roamed her svelte body.

"It was wonderful," she raved. "I didn't realize how much I needed it. And this robe … How do you keep it so white and soft? Don't tell me that you have laundry service through mail order too?"

"I've never worn it."

"Greysen!" she protested.

"It's okay. I wanted you to wear it. It's looks good on you."

She slowly shook her head in amiable disagreement and smiled. After reflecting a while, she said, "You know, when I first saw those flowers in

249

the tub … it was really … an incomparable experience. But now—now it seems so perfect."

"It's funny how time can change things, isn't it?"

Returning his gaze, she answered, "Yes it is," before bursting into laughter.

"What?"

"Time really does change things. I was thinking about Jadia. She was such a curious child. That was redundant, I know. But all her idiosyncrasies—and the questions! Let me rephrase that. The really funny thing was my struggle to answer them, like, When is tomorrow? And, Why is why?" Greysen and Sage chuckled and nodded their heads, then Sage blurted out, "Oh, oh! This one really stumped me. She was six and asked me, What is sex?"

"No!" Greysen howled in laugher. "What did you do?"

"I took her to the local library and told the librarian that my daughter wanted to learn about sex. The poor woman had to get out of her seat and stretch over the counter to see Jadia, and once she did, she clasped the clothing across her chest and paged her assistant."

"Better her than me," he said, still smiling and shaking his head. "Kids. Where did she ever get that from?"

"Apparently she had heard the word *sex* at school. She's always been the type to follow through on anything she learns."

"Ohh, ohh, ohhh," he grunted as though in pain and wiped a tear from the corner of his eye. "She sounds lively," he said, busting into a chortle again.

"She is," Sage said, "or *was*." "Is" was no longer appropriate, she thought. From *is* to *was* with Anthony Campbell in between. It was a quick, four-word story: is; Anthony Campbell; was.

"Jadia," Sage said, corralling her fury, "was vivacious and energetic, and now she can barely express—*anything*. She stares without really looking." Her eyes darted to Greysen. "Sometimes I wonder what she's thinking." Sage lay on her side and propped herself on one elbow, exhausted from recollection.

"I know exactly what you mean." Greysen's voice sounded equally exhausted.

Sitting up again and studying him closely, Sage scanned Greysen's face. "Do you know someone like Jadia?"

"I did." He paused. "Her name was Eli."

Sage's eyes dropped from his. She tried to ward off quick flashes of Eli's flying body, her sarcastic grin, the smell of burned hair and flesh.

"I guess I never thought of her as being any other way," she whispered reflectively.

"She wasn't always that way. She had been a thriving, ebullient woman—and happy."

"And you knew her then?"

He slowly shook his head and drew in a deep breath.

"No. But I have pictures. Tons and tons of pictures that she carried in a box when I met her. It's funny, but she didn't even notice when I took them and stashed them away for safe keeping. Or maybe she just didn't say anything about it. Those pictures tell her story, Sage."

"What happened?"

"I don't know." His voice scratched the air like a dull razor scraping across a coarse beard. He looked away from Sage and stared into the fire.

"I met Eli after I bought this property. I hadn't started building yet, so I was sleeping in tents." He glanced at Sage.

"Ever the survivalist," Sage interjected.

Greysen picked up a twig from the log rack and rolled it between his fingers. "I inspected the area at night, stealthily learning the lay of the land. I was about fifteen miles out one night. It was dark, and I was too far to see her house, but I saw the light from it. I pressed on, pinning it to the map in my head like I did every other building, mountain, and waterway. A few minutes later, I was at the creek, and there she was, sitting on the mound rising above an outcrop of rocks and pebbles. Her favorite place.

"The last night Eli was alive, she wanted to make love." Greysen's words drifted over the flames' soft roar. "I—I refused her."

Ambient heat rolled from the hearth in the stillness. Sage stared at the flames and thought about that night and shook her head imperceptibly. She said, "You were on the lookout for people who may have been pursuing Sean and me, Greysen." Her head snapped to his profile. "You had no way of knowing—"

Greysen cut Sage off. "Spurning her had nothing to do with being on guard that night." He snapped his head to meet Sage's awaiting gaze. "I had never turned Eli down, Sage. We just didn't do that to one another."

Pointing a finger to a nebulous spot somewhere in the distance beyond the house walls, he said, "That night was the first for anything like that to happen between us. And it turned out to be the last time." He dropped the finger.

Sage bowed her head and wove her own fingers through the carpet fibers. The room remained quiet. The conversation, once rigorous and radiant, died down like flames in the hearth, awkwardness now glowing like embers.

"When I came in the next morning, she was furious." Greysen took a deep breath, then continued. "I ... I tried to explain that I just needed a little time. And Eli kept asking me, 'Time for what?' but I never answered her, Sage. I never told her. I couldn't tell her." They could hear an occasional pop of the last of the kindling burning in the fireplace.

"You can tell me," Sage gently offered. Her words ushered in a hush.

His gaze latched onto hers. "I just needed time, Sage."

She waited out his pause.

"To get my mind off you."

Sage opened her mouth. Then she closed it. Panic awakened. Nightmarish visions flared across her mind. Sounds resonated. Eli's squeaking door slamming repeatedly in Sage's head.

Sss-q-u-e-e-k. Bang!

She noticed Greysen crawling closer—but the sounds. So loud. She continued running fingers through the carpet. Saw his face drawing whisper close to hers. Felt the warmth of his breath on a cheek. She fiddled carpet fibers. Still heard the door. Still saw the flaming body and then—Greysen's lips were on hers. Sage hesitated. Redolent sounds and flashes vanished when she felt a strong hand gently grabbing a tuff of her curls, another gently pushing against her back until the soft mounds of her full breasts were pressed gently against his hard chest.

They made love. The knowledge of Eli having never stepped foot in that cabin, making it all the sweeter for Sage. Afterward, she tucked herself into Greysen's hold as they lay, naked and spent, across rumpled mail-ordered sheets.

"Tell me more about Oma," Greysen said.

"Oma," Sage repeated in a sigh. "She a devout yoga practitioner with cropped hair and preternaturally smooth skin. She loves her friends and doesn't suffer fools. Physically, she's tall, slender, elegant, and sprightly. I'm not the only one who says she looks fifty. Just imagine a lithe version of Rachel Welch."

"Wow," he said.

"Yes, wow. And she keeps her men in line."

Greysen laughed and said, "Well, at least you got it honestly."

Laughing, Sage sat up and playfully whacked him with a pillow. "And don't you forget it!" As their chortles faded, she fell back against the bed and rested her head on his chest.

His fingers stroked her flat stomach. "Sounds like you and Oma are pretty close."

Sage stared through the dark at the ceiling, before saying, "She and my grandfather raised me. Opa died before I graduated from high school."

Greysen stroked Sage's arm. "What about your parents?"

She shifted, nuzzling deeper into the mattress. "What about them?"

"Well, where are they?"

Sage was quiet.

"Okay, let's start with your father."

Sage waited a beat before saying, "He died in the Vietnam War before I was born. My mother gave me a picture of him when I was six." She thought about it. Her mother became pregnant at fifteen years old by a nineteen-year-old transplant from Louisiana.

"I always had my doubts about that picture," she recalled, blinking and pondering. "I mean, I never met or even heard of anyone else in his family. Not his parents or any of his siblings, cousins—so that picture could have been taken from a magazine or it could be one of those marketing shots placed in frames to boost sales. Who knows. Who cares. All that mattered to me was that he was perfect. How could he not be? He just sat there in the picture, looking handsome. As for my mother, she also died." Sage noticed the way Greysen's brows hung heavy over his eyes, and she took a deep breath.

"Greysen, I really don't want to talk about this. My parents are long dead."

"Okay," he agreed, clearing his throat. "Tell me about Thomas."

Something creaked in Sage in that deep place where a first love goes. Where the father of her children was. Sage swallowed. "He's an awesome father," she said. She commanded her voice to drop its regretful tone, but it behaved like a drive-through clerk, getting the order all wrong.

Sage stifled Greysen's next words with a kiss that grew into another round of lovemaking. And that's how the rest of the visit went. They'd talk a while, make love a while. Walk the grounds, make love. Get firewood, make love. Sage almost forgot who she was and why she was there. The days and nights were indistinguishable, feeding into one another as Greysen and Sage fed off each other.

"It's already September seventeenth, can you believe it, Greysen?" Another Sunday had rolled around, and it found Sage kissing Greysen's roped shoulder and whispering, "It's Sunday. Would you like to get an early start on visiting Eli?"

Rolling over, he groggily answered, "I'm not going to the creek today, sweetie."

He opened his arms and Sage fell into his embrace, saying, "Why not?"

"Because I feel better," he explained. "And I have you to thank for it."

"Greysen," she moaned as he kissed her neck.

"Thank you," he whispered. "Thank you," he repeated as he rolled on top of her. "Thank you," he said again as he found her mouth and kissed her hard, strong, and long.

CHAPTER 52

"Time is flying," Greysen noted one night after they cleaned the dinner dishes.

"Please don't remind me," she said as they took their places on the floor, his back pressed against the sofa, hers against the perpendicular love seat. A small fire kindled quietly in the hearth as if trying not to disturb the couple.

Greysen grabbed Sage's foot and began to massage it. "I was thinking that maybe your doctor would agree to extend your leave for another week," he said.

"Happiness and shear satisfaction are written all over my face, Greysen. I can't fake this. Things have been flowing quite nicely."

He lifted her feet to his lips and whispered between pecking them, "So let's not stop it. Extend your leave."

She pulled the foot from his grasp, then moved closer to straddle him. She cupped his face in her hands. "I had a generous thirty-day leave. I have to get back to my job. My grandmother." A long, regret-filled sigh escaped from her lips. "I never gave her the apology she deserves, and I need to thank her for pushing me to get help. Most importantly, I have to regain custody of Jadia. Greysen, I have a life out there."

Greysen's thumb rose and stroked her lip. "A life doctors felt you needed to break from."

Lifting herself from him, Sage eased to the floor and leaned back against the couch. Their shoulders touched. Greysen studied her face as she kneaded his thigh with one hand and twisted the carpet fibers with the other.

"Greysen," Sage said softly.

"Yes?"

She returned his look. "Why are you hiding?" A stillness crept into the room.

"I'm not hiding, Sage. I'm right here."

"But you won't tell me why you're here. Why you were nesting in a silo with Eli. Why didn't she know about this cabin? Who do you call every day? Why does a man of your ilk give up a chance for a successful career for no discernible reason?"

"That's quite a bit you're asking for, Sage."

"That's because I've been here a month practically, and I know no more about you now than when I arrived." Silence ensued.

"Okay, let's take this slow. You can ask me one thing—today." Greysen held up a forefinger. "One, Sage." He leaned back against the sofa panel, waiting.

She rubbed her eyes and thought of Sean. How he'd protected her secrets.

"I lied about being in a prison facility and lied about what I witnessed while I was there. I lied because Sean said ..." She paused. "Sean said it was your idea for us not to tell anyone. Is that true? And how did you learn so much about Anthony Campbell's involvement with the underworld and its connection with the judge's murder? Who are the mysterious people you contact, the ones who give you information? Where are they?"

Greysen's brows punched together like two bumped fists. He leaned away from the sofa back and turned to meet her eyes. "I said one question, Sage. I'll answer only one. Sean told you the truth. Going to the authorities would have endangered your lives. I have good reason to believe someone was tracking you."

Sage gave a resigned nod. She realized how silly and hypocritical she was being. She too was hiding. Holding back. Keeping secrets.

"We don't know each other," she whispered. There was a long, languorous silence, then Sage stood.

Greysen kept eye contact with her but said nothing. Finally she tugged her eyes from his and looked toward the bedroom where they had shared so much of each other. She looked at him one last time and ambled to the back of the house, where she stayed for a couple of hours—long enough to cool down and regroup.

Greysen didn't hear her when she returned and stood at where the dim hallway light dissipated into the open living room. He was squatting near the fireplace, stoking the red, glowing embers with a poker. She watched his distracted eyes travel light-years away into the flickering flames.

"Greysen," Sage called.

He didn't answer.

She padded in his socks deeper into the room and touched his shoulder.

"Greysen?"

He lurched, then looked at her as if returning from transcendental meditation.

"I uh, I don't have any flowers," she stammered. "But I managed to run a tub full of steaming hot water. I think we both could use a little relaxation." She smiled and shrugged. "What do you think? The bathroom's nice and warm."

Greysen ran a thumb and forefinger along the corners of his mouth, assessing eyes leisurely roving over her, head to toe and back. He accepted her extended hand and hefted himself from the floor as she stepped into the folds of his arms.

Their lips brushed and then worked themselves into a deepening kiss. Afterward, Sage nuzzled into Greysen's body-wrapping embrace and listened as he said, "I think I'm about to lose the best thing that has happened in my life."

She leaned back.

"Since Eli, you mean?"

"No, I mean you're the best thing that's happened period." He pulled her back into his arms, then whispered, "Don't leave."

CHAPTER 53

Nearly a week later, Lori Swoboda began living up to her promise to spend more time on Central Park West with her husband. On Monday, September 25, 1995, the country was seized by celebrity jailhouse fodder and racial divide. No one noticed when Manny Cofield walked out of prison due to a vaguely referenced technicality. Several days later, Lori Swoboda was unable to stop herself from adding clippings to the black velvet photo album.

> *September 8,* Friday: Appeals court rules Ito cannot even give vague hint about Fuhrman invoking Fifth Amendment.
>
> *September 11,* Monday: Defense refuses to rest while appealing on Fuhrman; Ito orders prosecution to begin rebuttal; five photographers testify about pictures of O. J. wearing gloves like ones linked to crime.

September 12, Tuesday: Glove expert says he's "100% certain" gloves were same.

September 13, Wednesday: State crime lab expert says most sophisticated DNA test finds Goldman's blood in O. J.'s Bronco.

September 14, Thursday: Prosecution forensics expert Douglas Deedrick rebuts defense contention that there was a second set of shoe prints at the murder scene.

September 22, Friday: Simpson gets a chance to address the jury without being cross-examined. He says he "did not, would not, could not have committed this crime."

September 26, Tuesday: Clark begins her closing arguments by blasting her former star witness—Mark Fuhrman—as a racist but cautions that does not mean he planted key evidence at Simpson's home.

September 27, Wednesday: Christopher Darden wraps up the prosecution closing arguments by portraying Simpson as consumed by a jealous rage. Cochran then takes up for the defense, hammering home the theme, "If it doesn't fit, you must acquit."

September 28, Thursday: Cochran invokes history and the Bible and wraps up by telling jurors, "God bless you." Barry Scheck says jurors cannot trust any of the DNA analysis on blood because of police contamination and tampering.

Sean felt himself being bent and contorted like a willow under the pressure of wet tropical gales each time he noticed a new clipping, and with each addition, he became a tad happier to be on the grueling campaign road.

CHAPTER 54

It was 3:57 a.m. and chilly. Sage was wide awake, thirsty, and needing to pee.

She wrapped her plush white robe over Greysen's oversized pajamas, took care of bathroom business, and downed a glass of water as she looked out the kitchen window. Stark darkness shrank her enthusiasm to jog off her in-your-face energy buzz. She was trekking down the hall to the bedroom and thinking maybe Greysen could help her burn off a little energy when a door she had previously thought was a storage closet caught her attention.

Sage looked at the door until curiosity—or sheer nosiness, she guessed—led her hand to the knob and a second later, propelled her body through the doorway. Disturbed dust stirred defiantly around the small room. She flicked a switch, and a floor lamp swamped the space in lackluster light. Carpet covered the floor, and a narrow window faced the door. A closet opened on the left. Empty walls surrounded a group of boxes on the floor. Sage was stoked by the prospect of running across at least one photo of a younger, saner Eli.

She scanned the room, considering the effort—not to mention embarrassing snoopiness—of disassembling stacks, unpacking, repacking, and restacking someone else's personal belongings without either his knowledge or permission. She argued both sides of a debate: waiting to ask Greysen for Eli's pictures, or wading deeper into the room until she was stooped at vendor printed box labels that were handwritten to identify the contents.

Most boxes contained the records of online orders. Linen. Clothes. Toiletries. A few office supplies. She was turning a box atop a stack near the wall, looking for identifying markings when something wedged between the stack and the wall caught her eye. It was a flat box shaped like a thin attaché case—handle, studded edges, and all. After gingerly shimmying the stack of boxes aside, she cleared a space behind it, then sat down cross-legged next to the cardboard attaché. Latching straps wrapped around the two-piece box like a pair of buckled suspenders.

Sage unbuckled the latches, lifted the lid, and rested it on the tall stack of boxes. Inside lay three manila envelopes, stained, softened, and dog-eared with age. She lifted them to keep them in order after inspection. She blindly set them inside the lifted box top, eyes glued to the bottom lid where a lone, white 8x11 photo lay, facedown, protected in an archival polypropylene sleeve. With the care of handling an archeological artifact, fingertips reached in the box, turned over the photo, and looked at it only one beat before croaking a gagging cough at the woman staring back her.

※ ※ ※

"There you are," Greysen's voice said cheerfully behind her. "I've been looking for you." He crossed the room.

Sage was standing at the sunlit window with folded arms. A crease dented her brow. Hours of staring at the woman in the now sleeve-free photo had not lessened the shock of discovering it. The woman was somewhere in her late twenties. Blonde. Tan. Gorgeous. She was definitely not Eli.

Greysen grabbed Sage in a feet-lifting bear hug from behind, then turned her for a face-forward embrace. He nipped her a good morning kiss and pulled back.

"I was snooping," she said with a smile so weak, it barely existed. "Those pictures of Eli you told me about …" Her voice trailed. "I'm sorry for prying, Greysen." She glanced around the room, then back at Greysen. "I'm embarrassed."

Greysen nodded somberly and pulled her into his arms. "It's okay." He reared back, stroking her cheek. "Privacy is a touchy subject, and I'm touchier than most about it. It's for good reason, Sage."

Sage nodded under the reproach, then ran a leery eye over Greysen.

"But here's a secret for you," he said with a playful grin.

Sage waited.

"I don't keep Eli's pictures in here. They're in my closet."

Sage nodded again.

"So," Greysen said with a smile and a clap. He rubbed his hands together. "What would the lovely lady like for breakfast?"

"The thing is," Sage said, ignoring his question, "I was looking for Eli, but I found something else."

Greysen cocked his head in surprise, then looked around the room. "I only use this as storage." He focused back on Sage. "I haven't been in here in months. What did you find?"

Sage sidled past him and crossed the room, disappearing behind a stack of boxes. She came out holding the photo facedown as she headed back to Greysen.

Greysen smiled and eased closer to her. "What do you have there?" he asked with an outstretched hand. He gingerly took the picture and then froze as he looked at it. The tip of his finger felt along the back of the acid-treated paper as a wistful shadow spread over his face like fog. He had not forgotten about the picture—of course, he hadn't. It was just that he had stored it away—it and the horde of rioting feelings that accompanied it like a band of rowdy, loud drunks. And now they were milling about, trying out their new freedom, boldly wearing its name.

Greysen's dry mouth was now muttering the name: "Cheney." A silence as stifling as the dust fell on the room.

Sage's haunches plopped against the sill. "Cheney?" she repeated, with way too much inflection.

Greysen felt the weight of two sets of eyes: Sage's and the woman in the picture, Cheney. His lips forced a dry, tight smile. "Cheney Dumasque," Greysen confirmed, the name barely passing his cracking lips. His eyes never left the photo.

Cheney's azure eyes held Greysen captive. He felt himself falling, plummeting into the memory of her laughter. Into the smell of sun-ripened raspberries. More laughter. He imbibed the chuckles and her scent until he was overcome with memories. Cheney had been tantalizing, afresh with sharp-edged wit. Brimming with social gravitas. Washing away the world's ills with overwhelming cheer. All aglitter with life, but now, just a photograph on paper. A subject for senseless rumination.

As Sage looked down at the upside-down Cheney Dumasque, a sickly trickle dripped in the pit of her stomach. "So," she said, feigning a bored sigh to masque the shake in her voice. "Were you and Cheney friends?" She hesitated before casually adding, "Lovers?"

Atop his face, a smile struggled to survive under the crush of a weighty frown. His sad eyes seemed to sink deeper into Cheney's picture. Greysen was soaking up the look and feel of Cheney. Cheney had been unlike other women he'd known. Mesmerizing. Intelligent. Independent. She had been a designer of men's clothing—so ahead of her time—and she'd made a pretty big name for herself. It was unheard of for anyone her age to have pushed so deep and high in the textile and design industries. But Cheney had been insanely talented.

An anvil slammed against Sage's chest as she watched Greysen's reluctant, marginally conciliatory eyes finally leveled back on her. As soon as she'd presented the photo, he'd retreated inside himself. A different Greysen had climbed out.

"Both," he said. "Cheney and I were friends and lovers." He paused as if deciding whether or not to say more. His pained face fell back on Cheney.

Sage felt her quivering organs implode. She cleared her throat. "So, uh, what happened between you two?"

Greysen pressed his lips together, swallowing. "She died. That's all."

His eyes descended back on Cheney like birds returning to nest. "We were engaged," he said. The words punched Sage into a quiet, gasping slump.

Sage whispered over a riotous tumble of her own private, distracted thoughts. "That's funny. Cheney never mentioned you to me."

It took several beats too long for the message to reach Greysen's adrift brain, but when it did, he snapped from reverie. "What did you say?"

With a deep breath, Sage drew shock-weary eyes back to him. "I said Cheney never mentioned being engaged. She never even mentioned a Greysen for that matter."

Greysen studied Sage's face as though readying himself to fatally swat an annoying gnat. "You knew Cheney?"

Sage's breathing was audible. Her disturbed gaze dropped to an upside-down Cheney without answering.

Squinting with marble-hard eyes, Greysen repeated, louder this time, "You knew Cheney?"

Silence.

The crease deepened on Greysen's confused face. "Cheney's been dead seventeen years, Sage."

Her eyes snapped to him. "And don't I know it." She bit off the words.

Smoldering impatience cut deep on his stony face. "How—How did you know her, Sage?"

Sage ran a hand through her hair and glanced at the picture. She looked back to Greysen. "She was my mother." The words blew out like crisp, cool air—laced with poisonous gas.

Greysen's eyes widened on a blanched face. The hand holding Cheney's picture fell limp, fingers grasping the corners of the paper.

"Sage," Greysen called as he reached for her. She was shrugging him off when a torch shot straight through her head like a distress signal. She leaned forward and screamed, "I'm Cheney's daughter. *Who in the hell are you?*" she asked.

Greysen stepped back, hands flying up in surrender. "I don't know," he said ruefully. "I—I'm just me."

She sidestepped away from the window, sliding her back against the wall. Her face twisted into a one-sided grimace. "I've been sleeping with my mother's lover." She coughed out, "Fuck!"

Surrealism whirled around them, filling the room, warping and melding past, present, and future like a Dali painting. Greysen's Adam's apple bobbed as color drained from his face.

"Greysen." Her voice was whisper low, and her eyes were glued to the floor. "Are—are you my father?"

"What? No!" He approached her again.

Sage shrugged him off. "How do you know?" she suddenly asked as if she'd been waiting for the denial.

He ran a hand over his face. "Sage, I was nine when you were born. I met Cheney when I was twenty-three, in my second year of law school. She was twenty-eight ... and ... and she already had a child."

Sage sighed, shaking her head, her face crumbling with many emotions, the primary one being *I slept with my mother's lover.*

Greysen felt ill-equipped to console Sage as he, himself, was trying to gain purchase on the idea of Sage being Cheney's daughter. He'd known about Cheney's teenage pregnancy and marriage to a man she'd said she deeply loved, but Cheney had been a master at compartmentalizing. She'd kept her most precious gems—fashion, Greysen, and her daughter—separate but equal. It was a quirk he adored, admired even. He'd finally met someone as guarded as himself.

Now he thought about it. He had wanted to meet the daughter and the rest of Cheney's family, but Cheney's rites-of-passage clause forestalled the event until it was a nonevent. *Geez, she never let me see a picture of the little girl. And the daughter's name wasn't Sage.*

"Her name wasn't Sage!" he belted out like a game-show contestant. "Cheney's daughter's name was not Sage, and she didn't live in the city. She lived in, in—"

"Philadelphia," Sage interrupted, leaning forward. "Cheney's daughter lived in Philadelphia with Cheney's mother—that would be Oma—because the daughter (that would be me) hated New York." Sage fell, a heaving lump, back against the wall.

Greysen blew out a gust of air and spun full circle on his heels. He held palms in front of his chest, facing the other.

"But her name was not Sage. It was …" Greysen searched the ceiling. "Oh, Mother of Jesus, what was her name? … Ma … Ma … Magilly! That's it." He snapped his fingers. "Magilly." Greysen heaved breaths of relief.

They dipped into silence, Sage imperceptibly shaking her head. "Galy," she corrected. Her voice sliced the air with a soft, sharp edge.

Greysen looked at her, his chest still heaving. "What?"

"Magaly. Mah-gah-lee. My mother called it my nom de plume. My full name is Sage Magaly Wirspa. Dumasque is my maiden name." She paused, sighing. "I was my mother's Galy. To everyone else, I was simply Sage." Sage clasped a thick tuff of locks at the crown of her head. Her lids briefly closed with a long sigh.

Greysen's face wiped blank when heard *nom de plume*. He remembered how Cheney loved everything French—all *je t'aime*, and *tres* this and *tres* that. He made a careful study of Sage. He was looking at, had fallen in love with, and had awesome sex with Cheney's daughter. His lids closed.

"But you don't even look like her," he mumbled under his guilt. Greysen's words brought an icy hush. His lids opened to find daggers waiting for him.

Sage stood upright. "Greysen." She spit out the name as if being force to chew sand. "You only see what you want to see."

Greysen's mouth slit open as Sage stormed past him. Behind his back, he heard her kick a box and shout, "Fuck!"

"It's funny," Oma continued, the thread irrevocably broken. "Cheney kept having premonitions of dying on train tracks, so she boycotted subways. Then she got the job designing costumes for a theater company. First time. Last time ..." Oma's voice had trailed off again. She twirled her spoon, then stabbed it into the flesh of an orange wedge. As it bled clear, Oma propped slender elbows on the table and held a strong chin atop intertwined fingers. "Sage, your mother had gotten it wrong. The dreams were warnings of light tracks, not train tracks." Without saying anything else, Oma had picked up her spoon and resumed eating.

❊ ❊ ❊

Sage pulled her eyes from the travel bag. Her mother had led parallel lives, keeping her only child from one such life with the acuity of a skilled strategist. As soon as Sage got to Philadelphia, she was going to ask Oma if she knew anything about Cheney's so-called fiancé. Sage wove her reverie with the thread of Greysen's story.

"I'm having a hard time believing my mother sat around, pining like a lovelorn idiot while you disappeared into the sunset and stayed there until she rotted. I'm sure Mother was not the only pretty thing in your collection plate."

Greysen took on a look he'd give a recalcitrant teen. "I understand you're hurt and repulsed," he said. "And you're probably not the least bit concerned with how our discovery is affecting *me*. I assure you, shock, shame, disbelief, rage, sadness, confusion—did I say disbelief?—have teamed to literally knock the wind out of me." He stood, keeping his eyes latched on hers until he was looking down at them.

"I need time to catch my breath. After that, I would like to shower, and then I'd like to share a cup of coffee with you so that we can discuss this like adults. It would be nice if you're still here after I've recovered enough to give you the conversation you deserve and answers you seek. But if you're gone, I'll understand."

Pinned in place by a pair of deeply probing eyes, Sage found herself unable to argue the point, but by the time Greysen had showered and shaved, she was no less ready to leave.

"I loved her, Sage," he said as she hoisted the travel bag and watched him cinch his belt. "And she loved me. Give me some credit."

"Credit for what? Passing the straight-face test?"

"513."

Sage winced, trying to make sense of what she'd just heard. "What?"

"513. It's the suffix I told you to append to the call-back number whenever you paged me. I used that number because that's the day of Cheney's death."

Sage looked away as she caught her breath. The tracks fell on Cheney on Friday, May 13, 1977.

"There were letters too," Greysen continued. "Cheney must have kept them."

"Uh-huh. That's kind of convenient, Greysen, to send me on a paper chase for letters belonging to woman who's been dead almost twenty-years. How about you show me the letters she wrote back to you?"

Greysen grimaced into a pause. Then, "She uh—she couldn't write me back."

Sage rolled her eyes and hoisted the bag on her shoulder. "Let's go, Greysen."

"Sage, will you hear me out? I was on a hardship tour. I worked with a clandestine agency similar to the military's Special Forces team. I had to protect myself, my parents, and Cheney. I couldn't tell anyone exactly where I was or what I was doing." He paused as if waiting for Sage to interrupt. She didn't.

"I was assigned to work in a small town in Italy called Siena. It was the most beautiful place I had seen, but it rained constantly. I labeled the return address Siena Rain so Cheney would always know the letters were from me—I never signed them."

Greysen searched Sage's blank face. She said nothing.

"Read the letters, Sage."

"If I find the letters, I'll read them." Her tight lips, tone, stance—her entire being—were shackled in committal. "Now will you please take me to the bus stop."

Greysen glanced at the clock on the nightstand, then he said, "We'll never make it. The next bus is early tomorrow morning."

"Great," she snarled, remembering the bus schedule. Greysen was telling the truth.

"And uh—"

"What?" she snapped.

"You're still wearing my pajamas."

Sage squeezed her eyes shut.

After a long hesitation, Greysen nodded once, stepped past her, and left the house. She spent the day and most of the night alone. She scattered a few of her clothes on the floor and used them as a pallet to sleep in the dusty room where, the day before, she had found her mother's picture. She found it again and ran a finger along the silhouette of Cheney Dumasque's still image. As the hours droned on, she found herself alternating between long, mindless takes of West Virginia's unvarnished panorama of colliding oranges, reds, and yellows and her mother's timeless, flawless beauty. Eventually all colors succumbed to rolling black and she fell asleep.

Sage didn't hear Greysen return to the house, and she was surprised to see him asleep in his bed after she awakened and padded in socks to his room. Moving cautiously, she crept around his room until she found his watch, a pair of his thermal underwear, and lamb fur-lined gloves. Tiptoeing, she returned to the photo room, shoes in hand, grabbed her bag, and slinked into buffeting night winds.

She was not sure how long she'd been running on narrow foot-trodden paths and through the trackless forest—forty-five to fifty-five minutes, maybe—before the sky began to grumble and light the universe with jagged, incandescent light. Sage ran faster, slogging through waving walls of rain, clenching a cramping stomach, until she broke free from the dense canopy onto asphalt—the halfway point. Five minutes after arriving, she wondered if the bus had beat her. She tilted her head back and caught rain with a wide-open mouth as she thought about Cheney. The roar of an approaching vehicle interrupted her reflective stupor. The bus. Sage waved arms like a marooned islander desperately signaling at the only chance of being rescued.

"Oompf!"

Someone grabbed her from behind, locked her into an unbreakable masculine hold, and then dragged her to the side of the abandoned building. She scuffled, all kicking feet and flinging arms.

"It's me! It's me!" the man declared.

Sage gritted her teeth and tried to shimmy him off.

"It's me!" His voice boomed through the pounding rain. "Will you calm down! It's me—Greysen!" Sage forfeited the fight, her back falling in a slump against his chest. They both heaved in air.

"Greysen," she said, trying to catch her breath. She grabbed her soaked chest before asking, "What are you doing?"

"I can't let you get on that bus, Sage." She bucked him off and spun around. Rain pellets sprayed from her drenched body.

Squealing rounded the corner from the approaching bus. Sage scooped up the travel bag and ran, clearing the sharp corner of the building. The driver's face was a blurred blink under rapid, sweeping windshield wipers. The bus came to a hissing stop. She was inches from doors folding open when Greysen yelled out, "She's dead, Sage!"

Sage froze in place, her dripping stare latched to the driver's perturbed expression. *Jadia.*

"Who's dead?"

Greysen said, "I just received word fr—"

Sage felt the weight of Greysen's presence behind her. He was very close.

"Who's dead?" the gasping whisper repeated.

The driver yelled across the rain. "Step it up, lady. I don't have all day."

Greysen eased closer. Sage felt breaths, warm and wet, beating a rhythm behind her ear. Strong hands alighted on her shoulders like feathers. And then came the one word she had never expected: "Oma."

CHAPTER 56

Sage winced. Surely she had misunderstood.

The bus driver yelled over the crackling rain, "If you have any luggage for undercarriage storage, forget about it. You blew that chance. Now are you getting on the bus or what?"

Sage shrugged Greysen off and rushed up the stairs. The driver put the bus in gear.

Greysen grabbed the balance bar and planted a soaked Timberland on the first step. He leaned his weight against the folds of the door so it couldn't close.

"Your grandmother was killed, Sage."

Sage stopped and, after a beat, looked over her shoulder. "Wha—"

"Someone put a bullet in her temple early Sunday morning while she was in bed, asleep. She was executed in the exact way the judge was killed."

A wailing sprang forth like a hot spring from the abyss of Sage's being, but she swallowed it down to ferment with the rest of her anger. She turned around in slow, mechanical movements. She shot an icy glare at Greysen. They stared at one another for a beat until Greysen let out a breath and said, "Your grandmother's murder was either a message, insurance for your return, or both."

Greysen stepped back, deeper into the downpour, and held out a hand for Sage to follow. "It's not a good idea to leave, Sage. Not now."

His image blurred in the downpour as she stared unblinking. Then she moved, zombie-like, off the bus and stepped into the rain. The driver rammed the doors closed and pulled off.

Under the gushing sky, Greysen gathered Sage into his soggy embrace and stared in bewilderment into the fabric of his jacket, her dripping arms hanging limp. She'd hollowed out completely by the time they'd walked into the house. With the life force of a mannequin, she mimicked Greysen: disrobe, bathe, dress.

Over cups of coffee and plates of picked-over breakfast food, Greysen spoke softly to a dazed Sage. Somewhere during the truck ride home, her anger had abated along with everything else. He explained that Sean had called Thomas, looking for Sage. He told him about Oma and instructed him to remain in Europe. Paying last respects to Oma did not merit the risk of joining her in death. Jadia was not a target, Greysen authoritatively assured Sage, but there was no sense in tempting chance.

At the table, Greysen explained how he'd awakened to find her gone, and panicked until he realized she'd trekked to the bus. He'd wanted to respect her wishes to be alone—he of all people understood the need for solitude—but empathy meant squat under the knowledge that Sage was in a poor frame of mind, roaming the West Virginia mountains. He'd driven ahead of her to the makeshift depot and held his breath for her to clear the forest, biting at the bit to go in and retrieve her from it if she had taken too long to show. Sean had paged fifteen minutes before the bus arrived.

"Sean paged," she muttered to a cup of untouched, cold coffee.

"What did you say?" Greysen asked.

Tired, dry eyes looked up at him. "You said Sean called—that he paged you. How did he know about ..." Her eyes wandered around the kitchen as if the toaster might pop out the right words. " ... about what happened?"

Greysen took a long look at her, then said, "After contacting Thomas, Sean called your office to see how you were doing. He'd been concerned because you had been stressed lately. Anyway, one of your coworkers told him about your grandmother and that they were looking for you."

"Carlie," she interrupted in a whisper.

"Yeah. I think that's who he said. Anyway, Carlie explained that no one, including the authorities, could find you. They had even contacted the airlines and the psychologist who recommended your leave. Your coworker told Sean a few of your grandmother's friends got together and arranged the funeral because you were unreachable. After a few days, he reached out to me, hoping my sources could locate you."

"Did you tell him I was here?"

"No. I was too busy giving him instructions on how to stay safe. He's in the public eye now, more exposed." Greysen also thought, *And I don't trust anyone else knowing your whereabouts.*

"Instructions?" Sage repeated.

"Yes. Where to go, who to contact. Fortunately, he's also away from Philly on the campaign trail, but someone who is aware of your close relationship with Sean may be using your grandmother's death to tease him out too. He'll have to alter his campaign plans for a while, but if he makes it to the points where I directed him, he'll be okay."

Sage's wandering eyes drifted to the coffee, then finally back up to Greysen. "How will you know for sure?"

"I told him to page me when he gets to the final destination. So if you want him to know you're here, you can tell him yourself."

Shivering, Sage peered through the kitchen window at the sheets of rain splattering through the gathering light and listened as Greysen told her about the funeral Oma's circle of friends had arranged in Sage's absence.

Sage's delicate state of mind and not-so-delicate outburst had prompted Oma to reassign executorship of her affairs in the event of debilitation or death to her closest friend. A Buddhist devotee, Oma's unrelenting support of a tiny church with a crenelated stone facade and striated interior walls in the heart of Philadelphia earned her a spot in its aged graveyard.

"She loved that church," Sage mumbled to the window.

CHAPTER 57

"I uh ..."

Greysen and Sage had finally reached a point where they could talk without emotional weeds sprouting, vining, and choking the conversational thread. She needed to know more about Greysen's relationship with her mother. Anything to help her piece things together before she read the letters Greysen had written Cheney—if she ever found them. Greysen blew air through his cheeks and leaned his haunches against the bureau stretching along the bedroom wall. He looked at Sage, seated and waiting on the bed, and tried to speak again.

"I met Cheney in 1974 at one of my parents' annual Manhattan soirees. I—I was born and raised there. I had just ended my first year of law school. One of my father's contemporaries happened to be a designer whose wife had befriended Cheney. Cheney had accompanied the couple to the party. We ..." He stopped, breathing into the memory. "As soon as our eyes met, I knew she was going to play a big role in my life."

Greysen continued telling the story of how he and Cheney had sequestered themselves at the party. How he'd spent the rest of his spring break at her apartment. How, by the end of the summer, he'd bought a large condo for them both. How she refused to move into it because she enjoyed her own cramped, SOHO tenement and unencumbered freedom. How every summer, weekend, and matriculation break after that, he was either in New York or she was in Boston. How being five years her junior was a moot point—they just fit and that was that.

Greysen paused, riding on a surf that took him right back to Cheney. "We were in love," he said.

Sage's stomach curled on itself at the renewed knowledge of Greysen loving her mother. In fact, things were worse—Cheney was Greysen's first love.

She lay on her back, her shoulders finally relaxing. She rested a hand on her forehead. The fingers of the other hand gently touched Greysen's as she pulled him down to lay beside her. "You're not alone," she whispered.

"Neither are you," he whispered back.

For a long time they said nothing else. Finally, without preamble, he spoke into the dark. "I didn't know Cheney had died until I returned stateside for Sean's wedding." He felt Sage's body stiffen, but he kept talking. "She wasn't my wife or a blood relative so her lawyer's plea for the government to let me know had gone unheeded."

They stared into the silence at the ceiling.

"I had promised Sean I'd be his best man. I was going to give her a ring during that brief reprieve from my job. Problem was, by the time the wedding came around, Cheney was dead. Sean's wedding turned out to be a time of grief for me. Maybe that's why I'm not so fond of Lori—who knows." He took a breath.

"After Cheney was gone, I saw no need to come back to the States, but—" Greysen paused for several long breaths, then spoke to the dark again. "After the wedding, I visited my parents, said good-bye to them, and practically ran back overseas. For years, I invested my earnings, skirted along the fringes of nonexistence, and jettisoned mainstream American life. I didn't want it. Didn't want to have anything to do with it or anything else I associated with Cheney's death. I spent twenty years of running and trying to get over it."

The rustle of a pillowcase sounded under the weight of Greysen's head shifting toward Sage. "I wondered about Magilly, er, Magaly—sorry—from time to time, and I hoped she and her grandparents were okay. But I have to admit, I didn't try to find her. She didn't know me." He paused. "It was better to let her and her grandparents grieve and live in peace."

He paused and shifted his gaze back to the ceiling. Then he continued the story.

"As I earned and saved and invested enough money to live several lifetimes, I watched America from afar, relying on newspapers and syndicated broadcasts to paint the picture of what was going on back home. It was hard to look at sometimes, but I love America and forgive her foibles like a child forgives an imperfect parent."

Greysen grew quiet again, staring at the dark as if it were a patient audience. He felt Sage hanging on to every word. Several beats later, he spoke again.

"One day I woke up and found myself wanting to be back home. The urge came on fast and hard. By that time, my parents were dead, leaving me with even more money. I had to find other ways to blind myself. I'd seen a lot of fucked-up things while on missions. I didn't want to see anything else fucked up. Maybe that's why I planted myself deep in the heart of West Virginia. It was one of the few places I could bury my head in the sand—or mountains."

In the quiet darkness, the warm, just-showered scent of Sage's body wafted over him. *Maybe it is just best to tell her good night and drop it,* he thought. He turned to her, hoping—what, he wondered. Damn. She looked so good to him. If he was supposed to feel guilty because she was Cheney's daughter, he was failing big time. He loved her, no matter whose daughter she was. Knowing she was hurting was killing him. He lifted himself on an elbow and looked through the shadows at her smooth, olive face.

"Sage, my life with Cheney was a long time ago, and I had no idea you were Magaly when you and Sean appeared at Eli's door that night." He stroked her cheek with the side of his forefinger. "I'd be lying if I said I'm glad I didn't know, because I fell in love with you."

His head dipped to her face, and his lips met hers.

CHAPTER 55

"I'm leaving," Sage said, pivoting toward the door. She stormed into the bedroom. Greysen planted his foot in the doorway when she tried to slam the door closed. She ignored him, pulling her clothes from drawers and stuffing them into her travel bag. She zipped the bag, dropped it on the floor, and then plummeted upright onto the bed. Sean was right—everybody has secrets. Clearly, Cheney had been no exception.

Greysen interrupted the mounting silence. "Cheney and I planned to marry after my two-year assignment, but she died …"

Sage heard Greysen, but she was no longer listening. As his voice trailed from her consciousness, she thought of Cheney dying almost two decades ago. She was remembering something Oma had told her a couple of years ago while they were eating breakfast.

* * *

"So when the theater track lights fell on Cheney …" Oma's voice had trailed off that day in the kitchen. She had stared into her bowl of fruit and yogurt as if the Fuji apples and blood oranges were offering condolences.

CHAPTER 58

Under the canopy of night, Sage tasted the sweet of her mother's memory, the savory of Greysen's sex, and the bitter of his ill-defined history with Cheney. No, she didn't blame Greysen for loving Cheney, nor her for loving him—if there were any truth to it. Sage was determined to find the letters Greysen had written to Cheney—and to visit Oma one more time.

The mattress wobbled under Sage's light weight as she eased from Greysen's bed and crept to the closet where the few clothes she had packed for West Virginia a month ago were now hanging to dry. Light from Greysen's clock disappeared behind his side of the mattress the further she walked from that side of the room. Like a storm gathers strength, the darkness grew in intensity and practically blinded her. She felt her way through the stark obscurity, groping for Greysen's heaviest sweater and warmest shirt. Her jacket was still wet from the previous morning's deluge, so she grabbed his parka.

Greysen stirred, rustling the sheets as she lugged her clothes and sneakers across the room, slipped past the door, and headed for the living room to dress. His scent filled her nostrils as she slid her arms into the oversized jacket and hefted it over her shoulders. She savored it, taking a moment to luxuriate in the memory of their sex.

He was going to hate himself—and her—for trusting them both enough to fall into such a deep slumber. His snores rang throughout the house as she scribbled a note explaining she was borrowing the truck to take herself to the bus depot. "I'll park it in an inconspicuous place," she promised, knowing full well he'd be able to find it in a shed down the road from the bus stop along with the key she would hide in the tire well.

CHAPTER 59

The chill inside Oma's house was the result of much more than a malfunctioning furnace. The air was heavy and cold with the unquestionable certainty of death.

Sage had entered the house from a crawl space underneath the southeast corner of the house. Years ago, Oma and she had stuffed a man-size hole—the results of a fly-by-night carpenter's hack job—with steel mesh to stave off pests and trash. Now, Sage was pulling herself through the hole and praying a killer was not inside, waiting for her.

Oma's thick window treatments covered every pane in the house, blocking drafts and all aspects of light. Sage blindly worked her way through solid darkness, blindly reaching for walls, thresholds, banisters, furniture—*anything* to help secure purchase across creeping floorboards. Cringing, flinching and sweating all the way, she inched past the rooms of the ground floor, and up the stairs, and finally down the long hall to the closed door of Oma's bedroom. Icy fear crept up Sage's back and rested like a thorny tiara atop her pounding head.

From a nightstand, grainy red light emitted from a digital clock radio with the discomfiting look of neon blood. Sage shivered with eerie unease as she stepped toward Oma's closet. Quavering lips, trembling hands, and tottering feet accompanied her across the threshold and deep into the walk-in. Finally, she reached the back of the closet.

Toes stretched and tipped, and Sage reached up to a shelf filled with Oma's hat boxes, stylish handbags, and a rolled yoga mat until she felt the outline of a large, rectangular box. Under the delicate pads of her interrogating fingers, she felt the rise and fall of rough textured paisley, a material her mother had loved because of its Indian and Persian origin.

The memory of Cheney's laugh spilled from the box and flowed like liquid wind chimes into Sage's ears. She stilled, garnering fringes of childhood memories and easing under them like climbing under blankets on a drafty winter night, afraid that even the faintest noise of breathing would hush her mother's laughter.

From the thick of Sage's mind arose an unseasonably warm May day in 1977 when Oma had driven to New York after receiving a call from an attorney there. It was no big deal when, against all family customs and norms, Oma had not invited Sage to accompany her to the city because this day—the day Oma drove to New York—was a school day. Besides, as far as Oma and Sage had known, Cheney was not in the city. She had been on tour in Europe, trying to recover from the theft and illegal sale of her most promising male couture. Oma and Sage had assumed Cheney was still abroad, but Sage had returned to the States two weeks ahead of schedule, and resumed a theater job; she had not yet told her mother and daughter that her quest to recoup her losses had not gone well.

Oma had returned from New York with a stilted face and a lone box that was covered in woven paisley. Sage had watched, baffled, as Oma approached the porch stairs; she looked like grief personified. Sage hardly recognized the sad, hunched woman who ascended the risers with limp arms. By the time her grandmother's feet had planted themselves on the porch landing, Sage's face had taken on the same weighted countenance, for as surely as the words had been spoken, Sage had come to know the ineffable: Cheney was dead. Her mother was gone.

Now, seventeen years later, Sage was sure the box held Greysen Artino's letters. With grim concentration, she slid the hefty box from the shelf and inched her way back to the bedroom. She closed the closet door, dropped to her knees, and crawled to the nightstand, dragging the box across the carpeted floor. Squinting with eye strain, she removed the lid and began holding envelopes to the red light. One-by-one, letterheads garnered from the Department of Vital Statistics, insurance companies, estate handling firms and other official-sounding offices, peered up at her from stationery yellowing with age.

The thought of Oma having been murdered in that very room less than a week ago began to imprint Sage's brain. She rubbed tired eyes with the heel of her palms and contemplated abandoning the box and taking a permanent timeout from the house she had shared with her grandmother. But she couldn't leave. Not yet. Not without knowing for certain if Greysen was telling the truth or lying. She took a breath, haphazardly grabbed an envelope from the back of the box, and held it to the clock's red light.

She blinked. She needed to be sure she was reading the words correctly. And—yes! The tight, small script she had grown to know as Greysen's distinct handwriting read, *Siena Rain* in the upper left-hand corner of the envelope. Sage snatched another envelope from the back of the box and held it to the dim red light as she squinted and looked at the return address. There it was again, Siena Rain. A trickle of sweat streamed down the curve in her spine. She reached into the box again and snatched another, and then another, and another. They all read the same: Siena Rain.

There were more; bundles of letters Greysen had written practically two decades earlier. Pursing quivering lips, Sage stashed four letters from rainy Siena in the deep pocket of Greysen's oversized parka. The other correspondence—official docs and all—were returned to the heavy, elongated box. She dragged it across the floor until she and her bounty were under the bed. Killers were known to return to the scene of the crime, but all she needed was a few hours sleep and then she could think straight. She was so afraid. Too afraid to sleep, she thought. Just then it dawned on her—Jadia's tranquilizers were on the nightstand, behind the clock radio. Oma had been taking them because she couldn't sleep. Sage felt her eyes sting.

"Oma probably never heard her killer," she whispered to herself. "Never even knew anyone was in the room."

She slid from under the bed and reached up to grab the bottle of tranquilizers. If she were going to die, she rationalized as she opened the bottle and dry-swallowed two pills, she wanted to be like Oma and sleep right through it. She resumed her spot under the bed, staring at the sheath of blackness above her, and waited for the tranquilizers to dislodge from her throat and drop to her stomach. Instead, the resurging thought of Oma being buried in less than twenty-four hours began to peel away fear and the desire for sleep, leaving nothing but renewed determination to see her grandmother one last time.

Sage scooted away from the bed, leaving the box tucked away. She jumped to her feet and opened the drawer of the nightstand. Inside she found the thick wad of *rainy day* cash Oma had kept inside the hallow of a skein of yarn. Sage grabbed it and quietly closed the drawer before snatching up the plastic container of tranquilizers.

CHAPTER 60

Sage's emersion from the house was quick, quiet, and unnoticed. She navigated an alley underworld with its narrow, gravel crossroads that connected one main street to another, one neighborhood to another. These were the capillaries beneath the community's outer skin, the dirt that was swept under socially acceptable rugs.

Dogs barked and howled in varying volumes, pitches, and intensity, and at distances both near and far. Their yelping woofs offered Sage neither companionship nor protection. An occasional drunkard tottered and rummaged through trash. She herself resembled a hobo, so the few scrummaging vagabonds she encountered paid little attention to the ambling woman wearing scruffy clothes that appeared to be bottom-pile donations. Here and there, one offered Sage a jittery, territorial glance while another one ignored her completely.

She kept to the perimeter of the alley, in its darkest trenches. A dark colored car creeping along the fronts of houses on one of the main streets caught her attention. She began sprinting between alley garages, stopping and craning her neck around vinyl siding and vertical drains pipes to watch and time the car's disappearances and reappearances. After a while, the car faded into the night and didn't return.

Sage breathed a little easier, but the business of tracking the vehicle had distracted her from a more immediate threat. As she turned back to alley life, she noticed, much too late, a pack of four thugs. She was sure they hadn't seen her sprints and dodges, but their presence forced her to emerge from the alley's shadows.

Instincts told her this crew would pounce on even feigned mousiness, so if she were going to pretend anything, it would be fearless confidence. She smoothed the parka and straightened her back. The four stood under the yellowish glow from a lone light whose fixture was mounted high on the triangular truss atop the stand-alone garage. It cast a performer's spotlight on the quartet, and she half expected them to break out in harmonized a cappella.

Their rowdy din of combative camaraderie lowered like a decrescendo moves toward silence; one by one, they noticed her. They eyed her with menace and suspicion as she approached, their dead silence making her even more aware of their attention and, to a much greater degree, of the semiautomatics they showcased. A couple of the dealers raised brows with wide-eye wonder, while their colleagues narrowed their gazes as if preparing for action in case it was necessary. In fact, that's exactly what they seemed to be doing—staging for action. Action she hoped had nothing to do with her.

Sage kept her pace, glancing once and trying to contort her face in respectful disinterest as she passed them with a steady and straight-on-the-path gait. Predatory edginess downgraded to simple wariness, and gradually, loud obnoxious bantering resumed. She supposed Uzis provided the thugs the same false feeling of calm that the anxiolytic compounds in her veins were giving her.

Sage faced her destination, gradually retreating to the shadows. By the time she reached the church grounds, the tranquilizers were producing nausea and haziness, but so far there was no hint of sleep. She paced across a short, curved path made of cobblestone laid in 1803 when the original

Saints of Calgary Presbyterian Church was built. It had burned in 1822 and was re-erected in 1823. When bodies of the deceased were no longer held in state at the homes of survivors, Saints of Calgary began a tradition of leaving the church doors open until 10 p.m. on wake nights. The custom continued, although wakes and funeral services were extended to only the few remaining members grandfathered to the privileged during the church's 1944 rededication.

Sage bypassed the front door to negotiate unkempt foliage, mounds of blown leaves, cracked and uneven sidewalks, and a portico crawling with dormant ivy vines. She made her way to the bottom of three cement stairs below the kitchen door in the back of the church.

As Sage crested the stairs to the kitchen door, she briefly turned back. Shrubbery, annuals, perennials, and a mixture of deciduous and conifer trees were obscured by the darkness. Fallen leaves still carpeted the ground. Obstructed visibility was worsened by a rolling mass of thick, rainless clouds, but Sage knew the kitchen door gave view to two rows of tall hedges flanking a long, narrow walkway that led to a lych-gate. Beyond the lych-gate was the cemetery where Oma would be buried tomorrow.

Sage shifted her gaze back to the kitchen door. Nearly two centuries of wear and misfortune had shaped the knob into an uneven, hammered ball. Sage's hand curled around its irregularity and fought against the spindle's resistance with a firm twist and upward jerk. The door creaked open and gave an oily squeak as she eased it closed. Sage ignored her heart's surge. Once inside the rickety edifice, she locked the door and sidled across the kitchen's linoleum floor and the foyer to the small chapel. In the door of the tiny sanctuary, she spotted a tiny wheel of the catafalque that held Oma's coffin.

She went in. Swallowing and perspiring, she shut her stinging eyes for a second and genuflected on a kneeler before the coffin. At least one of tranquilizers had finally started doing its job. There was no consolation for Oma's still body. Pride and a measure of feisty defiance was set in the upward tilted chin—her final expression. A tiny smirk lingered as if relishing in a private thought. Sage rubbed a long, lined finger of her grandmother's cool, tightly folded hands. Hands that had often patted Sage's own. Hands that rocked baby Jadia to sleep. Hands that shuffled and cut a deck of cards like any Vegas pro.

Under dim light, Sage wiped tear streaks from her placid face. She eased backward and sat in a nearby pew in front of Oma. She pulled an envelope from the parka and slid out a letter. As she unfolded it, her eyes studied the stone walls of the old church and the stained glass dotting them. Then she slid to the floor to be out of sight—just in case. The letter in her hand read:

> Cheney,
>
> I hope these words bring you a cheery smile. As for me, let's just say, I'm keeping the faith—as you often reminded me to do before I left the States. The pace is unbelievable over here. We work seven days straight, and sometimes I have to hide in order to get sleep. As usual, it's rainy and cold, but I've been taking vitamins and drinking plenty of juice and doing a lot of wishing that I were with you.

Life here means taking one day at a time, which is not different from any other place, but that truth seems even worse here as it would be <u>anywhere</u> without you. There are so many things that I want to say, but words are ineffectual unless I demonstrate them in person. Hopefully I will soon be able to do just that. All you need to know now is that I miss you terribly. And I love you.

Skipping to the second and last page, Sage searched for a signature. There was none, just as Greysen had said. She quickly folded the letter and pulled out a second one. Like the first one, it was brief and packed with emotion. Each letter was the same. Sage was on the third letter when she stopped reading midsentence and gazed at Oma's lifeless face. She thought about early childhood summers with her grandparents. Oma and Opa had lived in a fully paid-for home in what was still considered a prestigious Philadelphia neighborhood.

Sage had favored her grandparents' lush, suburban lifestyle over the crammed streets of New York. She had asked to live with Oma and Opa. Cheney had caved. Afterward, Sage had a few spectacular years with Opa before he passed. Oma and Sage had worked around their grief and created a revised bliss that Cheney frequently dipped into between fashion shows and intercontinental flights. Then Cheney died.

Sage looked at her grandmother's lifeless face, then glanced down at the letter in her own limp hand. Sean was right. Everyone had secrets, and Cheney had kept a biggie. Sage was concluding with growing certainty that Oma had known about Greysen. That both Oma and Cheney had decided to keep a young girl, who had seen enough change, wrapped in protective, shiny bliss like an unopened gift. That Greysen would have been introduced upon return from his clandestine missions. That—

The sound of a car's motor interrupted Sage's musings. She hit the floor and scrambled under the pew. Fear pounded against her chest. Clammy, clumsy fingers nervously folded the last letter she'd read. She was stuffing it into the envelope and listening.

Then she froze. The creeping sound of tires slowly burring against tarmac slithered into her ear like a snake undulating between tall blades of grass. She felt the car getting closer. The street grew absolutely silent. Sage stuffed the last letter in a pocket with the rest and craned her head above the pews. She checked the stained-glass windows for headlights. There was nothing but a motor's murmur and creeping tires. The headlights had been shut off.

Panic scrambled up Sage's back. She scuttled from under the pew and belly-crawled past the coffin to the kitchen, then back to the door that opened to the cemetery. Lifting up to a squat, she set the latch so the door would lock behind her, then she silently exited the building. Outside, the sound of the motor crept closer to the front of the church and then stopped. She crawled along the outside row of tall hedges flanking the long, cracked, narrow walkway until she was past the lych-gate.

She moved faster, hunkering as she dashed between tombstones and mausoleums, heading toward the far back corner of the fence.

Years ago, a bunch of neighborhood kids had built a furrow there so that they could crawl into the cemetery at night, smoke dope, and "party with the dead" as they were known to say. All Sage had to do was get to the hole under the fence, crawl out, and she'd be free. She moved in the direction of the spot, slipping over wet leaves. Then she stopped behind a tree and squinted over her shoulder across the stretch of tombs at the church. In the distance, through the small, lit, back windows, she spied the prowling silhouette of a man. He was gripping a pistol and searching one of the rear rooms. Sage scrabbled up again, keeping low as she dashed for the spot in the fence.

Then she found it—jammed with concrete.

The fence was too high and in bad repair for Sage to scale. She looked back at the church just in time to see the kitchen door swinging open. Rushing for cover, she crouched down behind a rambling cross, smooth with age and probably the biggest headstone in the cemetery. Burying her face in the leaves, she bit her lip, trying to get up enough nerve to move again.

She looked to the church. The lights were now out. The kitchen door open. Fine hairs on the nape of her neck stood erect. Her woozy, tranquilizer-steeped thoughts were on the Glock. The very Glock she had, in unreasonable determination to see Oma one more time, left hidden between blankets in Greysen's cedar chest in his master bedroom. Sage shook off self-flagellation—but the fear and the trepidation hung on like clawing kittens. Sage scrambled to her feet, then collapsed, belly-flat on the ground.

"God help me," she whispered, looking for refuge as her head sporadically bobbed around. Swooning, she blinked, not certain of what she was seeing. Just beyond the tree was a mound of dirt hiding a freshly dug grave. *Self-interment.* She stifled a grunt before rolling toward the grave. Her eyes strained against the pit's dark abyss. There was no liner—an earth burial. Four wide straps of a lowering device crossed the grave widthwise and wrapped around the apparatus's parallel bars.

Sage positioned her feet at a corner of the grave and attempted to slide between the straps, but a foot lost purchase. Her fingernails were packed with recently excavated soil as she clawed in vain at the loose dirt on the grave's perimeter. She pulled a grassy grave skirt down with her as she tumbled into the six-foot pit.

Fading in and out of consciousness, she covered herself with the grave skirt and listened to the blustering wind as it blew and scattered leaves and dirt. She faded again, eyes rolling behind lids as she lay in the pit of the grave, completely concealed under the skirt and wet leaves. Her breathing slowed. She slipped closer to unconsciousness once more.

There were sounds of feet moving rapidly across wet leaves. The man with the gun was zigzagging his way between massive headstones and shadowy trees. Half-open was as far as Sage could push her lids. The scrunching footsteps were closing in on her. Then the steps stopped, pivoting against boggy earth.

Sage's eyes rolled, and she popped them open. The man was moving again, each wet step swishing to a fade as the pull of drug-induced unconsciousness became utterly irresistible. Sage dropped into a deep sleep with the vague notion that Jadia's prescribed dose was one tranquilizer pill no more than twice a day—not two at once.

CHAPTER 61

Tap. Tap. Tap-clink. Tap-clink-clink-clink-thunk. Thunk-thunk-tap-clink-clink-tap-tap.

Sage woke with a gasp. It was raining—no, snowing. And, oh my God, it was sleeting too. She sat up—or tried to. When she shot upright, she rammed her head against something hard and unyielding. Without mercy, it thunked her back to the equally hard ground. Icy fingers that felt as if attached by thousands of gnawing midges gingerly reached for her forehead and found a knot—big, round, and packed with hurt—already pushing itself outward from her head.

Her toes were numb. Limbs and torso—both rousing dormant aches. Panic closed in, suffocating her. She had to remind herself to breathe. As she sucked in air, dim awareness subtly unfolded, and she began to recognize the tangy, sickening sweet stench wafting in her nose as death. Understanding began making its way to the surface of Sage's throbbing head.

The grave in which she had slept, the one she thought was intended for Oma, had actually been reserved for some poor unknown, whose time had expired in the city morgue before anyone came forward to identify the body. The women's missionary guild at the church considered it a public service duty to house at least one such unknown a year. Oma had headed the guild.

Sage gaped at the wooden coffin above her and presumed the poor soul's fellow drunkards, paid to carry out the duty, had probably taken an early morning break to sip on a pint of cheap liquor. Nibs of early Saturday light pointed down the sides of the grave, helping her retinas to acclimate to the light. Ignoring thumping temples and a throbbing forehead, she struggled to her knees—successfully this time—and used icy cold, stiff fingers to dig two pairs of holes, big enough for her to step in and hoist herself out. The space between the ground and the pine coffin was too small to squeeze through, so she shed Greysen's parka, his sweater, and two sweatshirts beneath it, then stuffed them through the small opening.

As she pushed the clothing as far from the grave as average-length arms would reach, pungent ripeness packed her nose. She didn't smell too fresh, but that's not what made her dry heave. What made her heave was the scent thrown off by the putrefied body packed in the porous box beside her. She pressed her cheek into an impossible squash against the wall of dirt and squeezed her head between the box and the hard ground. Then her stomach lurched, and she ducked back down, hair tangling in gravel and moist, cold earth. Bits of the grave wall crumbled over her bent head as puke spewed from her mouth and splattered into the pit of the grave.

Sage wiped her lips and looked up at the Saturday light. The gap between the wall and the pine box was wider now. With a grunt, she squeezed her head through the space again, hardly getting bare shoulders through before she could go no further. She grunted, veins popping on her face and arms as she pressed her weight against the heavy, reeking box. Stale breath plumed into the frigid grave air, against the shower of falling sleet. She grunted and strained until the coffin finally moved.

Exhausted, she collapsed forward with her head in folded arms, catching her breath before emerging from the grave. Quickly grabbing the parka, she scurried a few feet away to the tree she had spotted the night before, then hid as much of herself behind it as possible while she shivered and pushed filthy, frigid fists through the arms of the parka. After she checked the jacket pockets for the cash, she reached inside to make sure she had the letters. They were crumpled, but all were there.

The same fear that had pushed Sage into the grave the night before was now catapulting her across the graveyard. She sprinted between headstones and dashed between trees until she made her way off the church's property, where she slowed her pace and began to walk through concealed alleyways until she found herself spilling into bustling downtown streets—into too much daylight. There was too much visibility and too many people milling about—swinging attachés, carrying disposable coffee cups, biting into bagels, tucking newspapers under their arms, and staring at the addicted refugee—Sage.

She shivered against a marble wall, unaware of the dirt furring on Greysen's oversized parka; the damp leaves clinging to her limp, muddy hair; or the red lining the whites of her eyes like roads on a map. Her eyelids grew heavy. Jadia's tranquilizers were staging another wave of the time-released drug. She wanted to slide down the marble into a crouch, but the onslaught of passersby grew heavier than the lead on her lids.

She swept the street, suddenly aware of nature's call. A nearby McDonalds was her only choice for relieving her bladder. After that was taken care of, she tried to wash the grime from her face, hair, and nails, hiding in a stall whenever someone else entered the bathroom. A little later, she stepped from McDonalds with washed-over filth and stench.

Sage's head snapped to the sky, and she scanned its brilliant blue color with eyes rimmed with gunk and brimming with fear. The rising temperature had evaporated the last blast of wet, wee-hour cold, but the chilly fall air gusted in violent bursts. She focused on a fresh batch of fast-walking professionals who double-timed their pace at the sight of her. Opting for cold over the intolerant, judgmental glares, Sage took off Greysen's jacket and folded it over her arms. She combed a hand through her littered hair and spied a distracted cabbie.

It wasn't until she slammed the door closed that she realized she was in front of the Four Seasons where she had dined with Sean just three weeks earlier. She remembered how he hadn't said anything about the Glock or about giving up the chance to be a part of the O. J. Simpson trial just to help Jadia. To help *her*. She wondered if Sean had called Greysen yet. Whether his body was on a sterile slab, stiff with the starch of death, or if it was rotting, undiscovered behind underbrush.

Come on, Sage, she coaxed herself, *Sean's somewhere safe and enjoying a campaign trail breakfast with his wife.*

The pull of the driver's sour look in the rearview mirror forced Sage to banish the overwhelming reverie from her mind. Rapid fiddling fingers found a pocket in the folded parka and fished out two twenties.

"Greyhound, please," she said, plastering the bills against the Plexiglas, then stuffing it into the driver's drawer. "Keep the change."

Under the Greyhound's arctic air-conditioning vent, Sage snuggled back into Greysen's parka. The bus's brakes chuffed then released to begin its endless, zigzagging line of small-town stops through Pennsylvania and finally, West Virginia. Sage swaddled the excess material around her. Greysen's Siena Rain envelopes gave a soft *scrunch* under the weight of her arm as she leaned against the window and fell asleep.

❋ ❋ ❋

"I found the letters." Sage's announcement startled Greysen. He was chopping wood in the garden in back of the house and swung the ax at her as he spun around. She threw herself backward and fell to the ground with a squeal, glad she'd dodged the blade.

"Sage?" he called, craning and squinting to see the face inside the hood.

"Don't you know your own parka when you see it?" She tried to sit up, but the bulk of the parka made it hard. He flung the ax behind him and rushed over to help her. "Don't get too close," she warned. "I smell like the dead."

Greysen stared and leaned over her. The lines radiating from his eyes deepened, and he took on a look she'd never seen before. Sage fell quiet. A large, calloused hand reached out and pushed the hood from her head to get a good look at her. Pinned by his intense scrutiny, she watched and waited as he detailed every inch of her. The back of his knuckles gently stroked her temple. A calloused thumb tenderly rubbed the thick lump that sat above her brows.

"I just couldn't see it before."

"That's because it wasn't there, silly. I kind of knocked myself around while I was gone. I have a bump on the back of my head too."

Greysen snorted a broad smile. Sage crooked a grin of her own, wincing and rubbing the back of her head. A beat later, Greysen's gaze became serious again. He shook his head imperceptibly.

"I was talking about your eyes," he whispered. "They're exactly like Cheney's."

"Mr. Perceptive," Sage said, propping up on her elbows. "Anyway, I'm a brunette. She was a natural-born blonde." She narrowed her eyes, craning her neck to look at him.

"True," he said, holding her gaze as he stood upright. He held out a hand and pulled her up. "But you have her eyes."

"And her taste in men, undoubtedly," she whispered. Her briny words hinted at humor.

Greysen's face stilled.

"I'm sorry about taking your truck," she said. Sage dusted herself off, then added, "And your clothes."

"You can pay me later," he said, suddenly grinning like a Cheshire cat. He paused, his eyes taking in all of her for the first time. Dried mud. Grimy fingernails. Scratched face and hands. Crumbles of leaves littering her hair. His parka, battered and stained with Sage's Philadelphia experience. Worry appeared on Greysen's face. He found her eyes.

"Sage, are you okay?"

"I'm hungry," she said. "But first—a long, hot bath."

A while later, after Sage had showered off the grime, Greysen sat on the bathroom floor as she lay submerged in a tub of steamy water dribbled with wildflowers he had gathered while she was gone.

"How did you know I'd be back?" she asked, scooping one a bloom and admiring it as it rested in her drenched, cupped hands.

"I didn't."

"I see," she scoffed jokingly. "I guess these flowers were intended for the next stranger who happened upon you, huh?"

"No," he said, holding the smile. "I knew those were the last of this year's growth, so I picked them just in case you did come back."

She looked at him and nodded. "Thanks." She eased deeper into the water. "They smell lovely," she added, squeezing water from the sponge and watching it run down her arm.

Greysen cleared his throat and took a deep breath, then said, "Sean called."

"Thank God," she sighed with closed eyes. "Did you tell him I was here?"

"No, because you weren't."

Sage's eyes flashed open. She looked at him without saying anything.

Finally he continued. "He asked me if I knew how to find you, if I had heard from you. I answered no to both counts."

Gently placing the sponge back into the water, she sat up and looked at Greysen with blinking eyes and said, "You didn't? Why not?" Her voice trembled with bewilderment.

"I don't know. Instincts, I guess." He sat squatted beside the tub, leaning closer to her. His eyes glided over her face, leisurely soaking her in, one trait at a time.

"The less each of you know about the other, the safer you both are." He ran a finger along her jaw in a slow and gentle stroke. The decision whether or not to share his suspicions that perhaps Sean and Cheney may have known one another fought within him like rivaling siblings.

"Sage, do you mind telling me once again how you met Sean?"

Sick with Revenge

Sage's wet, soapy hand reached up to grab Greysen's wrist and stop his stroking.

"Why?" she said. Her voice was quiet, suspicious. Sean was her best friend. He'd sacrificed his career by retracting the offer to be a part of the O. J. Simpson prosecuting team to help Jadia. To help her. Then he risked it again after she'd killed Anthony Campbell.

"I found out that Manny Cofield was released from prison on an obscure technicality. I'm thinking Cofield's has powerful friends. Maybe someone in Sean's circle is behind this, Sage," Greysen said.

"Sean doesn't know anything, Greysen. He would have told me." Sage's hand held firm on Greysen's wrist.

Greysen felt the ground getting shaky underneath him. Her trust in him was tenuous at best. He knew he had to tread carefully. Sage's loyalty to Sean was strong and pitted like Patriot launchers against threats. And there was Sage's hypersensitivity to Greysen's history with Cheney to contend with—which is why he hadn't brought up the letters Sage had returned with.

"I am not insinuating Sean has done or knows of any untoward behavior, Sage," Greysen said. "I'm just trying to piece together bits of information that were strewn from every direction at my doorstep. Manny Cofield gets out of jail, and then your grandmother is murdered in the exact way as the only judge who had information that likely connected Anthony Campbell to Manny Cofield to you, and possibly—probably—to Sean Swoboda.

"I don't believe that was a coincidence, but the people alive with the only real clues are you and Sean. It's important for me to understand how you and Sean met, and I also need to know about any tangential relationships surrounding that meeting." *And it's really important to know if Sean knew Cheney.* But he didn't say that last part.

Greysen had mentioned Cheney to Sean often, but he'd kept her under wraps mainly because law school had him pinned down. Greysen and Cheney had spent most of their time together with him studying and her in his cheering section, cooking, washing clothes, and giving him more love than he could have imagined possible. If they did anything social, it was during the summer months and breaks when Sean was away with his parents. If Cheney and Sean had met, Greysen was convinced it had to have been after he'd left the States.

Greysen forced himself to refocus and breathe nice and easy. He needed Sage to align with him. *If I lose her trust at this juncture,* he mused as he imperceptibly forced air through his nostrils, *I'll never get it back.* He leaned into the interminable wait.

After a long while, he felt Sage's soapy fingers loosen from his wrist. Her hand laced around his and curled into a lock of solidarity. A small smile slowly curved on her face. *That's my girl,* he thought, returning the squeeze. And then he listened.

"Sean and I met in 1991 when my boss introduced us," she said. "I had been employed for the advertising agency on South Street for several years. I was the senior account executive and top-billing employee. Sean was working for a top law firm based in Manhattan and had recently established an arm in Philadelphia."

Greysen sat on the floor, long, muscular legs stretched out and crossed at the ankles, parallel with the tub, as Sage recounted the start of her friendship with Sean Swoboda.

"We need to talk to Sean," he gently said when she finished. He cupped her face. "I think we all need to sit down and make sure we've unturned every stone."

"No," Sage said. Her voice was low and firm.

Greysen hoped the shock did not riddle his face. He studied her unwavering eyes a second, then asked, "Why not?"

Sage thought about Sean's bid for president. About how he'd already risked his career to protect her even after she had put everything he'd worked hard to achieve in jeopardy. Enough was enough. It was high time she'd start reciprocating the friendship.

"Sean's in the midst of a presidential campaign, Greysen. Leave him out of this. Besides, I think the bad guys are a lot more interested in me than him."

She had a point, Greysen thought. Sean was a public figure now, and there had been no sign of anyone chasing him. Instead, Oma was targeted. Greysen studied Sage a moment, zeroing in on the knot jutting from her forehead, then he asked, "What happened in Philly, Sage?"

Something about Greysen's question triggered a stir of emotions. Her resilience yielded to grief about Oma's death and tearful relief of her own escape. Greysen grabbed tissue from the bathroom counter and returned to his spot near the tub. It took her a while to dry her eyes and calm down enough to talk to him, but eventually she told him the whole story—well, almost the whole story.

She didn't mention the Glock. The Glock was quite a different story. A longer story. While Greysen was outside, collecting firewood from the front side of the cabin, she'd moved the Glock and magazines from the cedar chest and stashed them in the travel bag so there'd be no way for her to forget them. That part of the story she'd leave out, but words describing the rest of the story about Sean streamed fluidly from her lips as Greysen listened without once interrupting. Afterward, he dipped his fingers in the bathwater and washed new streams of tears from her face.

"Did you contact Sean's wife while you were in Philadelphia?" he asked. His voice was a steady whisper, his face ever close to hers.

"Uhhhhh—no," she sniffled. "I thought about it, but I—I don't know. Like I said, I didn't want to get anyone else killed, and I didn't know how long I could stay in Philadelphia before they sniffed me out. This seems to be the only place I go that they don't know about. I still can't figure out how they knew I was in the funeral home."

"They probably didn't," he stated, dangling fingers in the water. "My guess is they're tracing the use of your bank card. That tipped them about you being in Philly somewhere."

Sage thought about it. She always used cash for her bus tickets, but she'd used the card when she disembarked the bus in Philadelphia to buy water and a sandwich before heading to Oma's house.

Greysen continued. "The man or people chasing you probably busted into the house and discovered you had been there, but you were long gone by then." He lifted her chin and told her, "It's a miracle you're alive. It's a good thing you had enough cash to get back."

"Saved by the grave and a skein of yarn," Sage said acerbically. Then, with more gratitude, she added, "And by the grace of God."

Greysen wasn't sure if he believed in God, but just then he felt the need for one. "Yeah well, if God is trying to keep you safe, he's got his hands full right now." He paused. "I think he knows how badly Jadia needs you." Greysen eyes latched onto Sage's. "And how badly *I* need you."

He looked at her another beat, stood and dried his hands on a nearby towel, and said, "The three of us need to talk, Sage. You, me, and Sean."

Sage opened her mouth, but no words came out.

Greysen squatted back to eye level with her. "I agree we do not want to do anything to taint Sean's career or political aspirations, but sooner or later the sniffers will trace your trail to here. I gotta get you out of here and put this thing to rest once and for all. In order for that to happen, we need to talk with Sean."

Greysen stood and left the bathroom. Sage stared at the diminishing bubbles.

CHAPTER 62
OCTOBER 1995

Sean Swoboda walked into his Central Park West home office. He'd been in television stations and radio stations and behind podiums in seven cities for the past three days. His eyes roamed the room as he closed the distance to his desk. Something to his right on a shelf of the built-in bookcase drew him in like it did every time: the black velvet photo album. Except it wasn't a photo album. It was Lori's chronological ode to his mediocrity. A shroud masking everything he had done or ever would do. A challenge of whether or not he was good enough to contend for the United States presidency. All according to Lori.

Sean thumbed his wedding ring and doubled back his steps to the bookshelf. He enjoyed the soft feel of the velvet under the tips of his fingers and, without notice, his mind wandered until it reached Ayde Carona. She was all rah-rah Sean. Backing him at the firm without ever taking credit. Staying behind him without being too close. Out of the way and yet always within reach. Dinner at the Daniel had been lovely, mesmerizing, and enchanting.

He opened the album cover so he could read Lori's most recent additions.

October 2, Monday: Jury begins deliberations shortly after 9 a.m. PT, breaks to hear the testimony of the limousine driver who picked Simpson up on the night of the murders, and returns a verdict.

October 3, Tuesday: Verdict of not guilty is announced, and O. J. Simpson is set free.

The prosecution Lori had so badly wanted him to be a part of, had failed. Sean closed the album and replaced it on the shelf. O. J. was free—something Sean's instincts said he, himself, would never be.

CHAPTER 63

Sage squinted, then blinked her eyes closed from the dawning light filtering in from … somewhere. She had no memories, no emotions, and by far no thoughts. After a long while, Sage's groggy mind forced her eyes open again, and she tried to sit up. Her strength failed, and her heavy, aching head plopped down on plush pillows. The pillows topped a thick mattress of the ultimate supreme variety. Sage cast her eyes about the white-on-white linen blanketing the bed. An equally white duvet, generously stuffed with down, rested in billowing folds at her feet.

Her lid-heavy gaze browsed the room that felt, looked, and smelled like a stress-free private spa light softening wall sconces, and a wall of windows hidden behind a thick layer of damask. At that moment, it occurred to Sage that the dawning light was seeping in from behind the damask. She saw French, leather folding chairs stationed in corners opposite the bed and low shag rugs spotting a wood floor like an arching archipelago.

Sleepy eyes lifted to cathedral-arched, beamed ceilings with a hand-scraped, faux finish. Her head rolled lethargically on her neck until a tall, white, tufted headboard stared sideways at her. To her left lay a pile of decorative pillows. The place felt safe, elegant, prestigious, and disturbingly unrecognizable. Worse, she had no idea who she was.

Frustration and fear glazed her eyes.

Crunching sounded near her elbow when she shifted. Barely visible under one of the many decorative pillows was a newspaper. She leaned over and pulled it out, confused eyes zooming in on the red ink encircling the periodical's date: Friday, October 13, 1995. She panned the wall of floor-to-ceiling windows where dawn was straining to peer around the damask. *Dawn of which day?* she wondered. She focused on the date on the paper again. Another red circle drew her attention. An obituary.

> Sage Magaly Wirspa, 35, died Wednesday, October 11, 1995. Ms. Wirspa was recently preceded in death by her grandmother, Doreen Marie Dumasque, and is survived solely by her daughter, Jadia Marie Wirspa. A private memorial service will be held at the Saints of Calgary Church tomorrow at 7:30 p.m.

The people, the places, the words meant nothing. Rigid joints and muscles pulsed sore as she reread the obituary before mindlessly dropping her arms to her lap. As the newspaper slid back to the bed near her thigh, Sage sat upright, wincing as she clutched her tight chest. Her neck, stiff and tight, cracked as she gave the room another once-over. Nothing rang familiar.

She snatched the newspaper page and read anew the small print at the top of the page: *PHILADELPHIA EAGLE*. Concentrating, she tried to remember something—anything—about Philadelphia, but other than being a place on the map, the city didn't ring a bell. Her mind raced in a mad frenzy, desperate for a wisp of memory. Bemused, she looked at what she was wearing. Sheer black stockings and a lined, tailored, two-piece suit, which was accented with leopard skin print cuffs and collar.

"What the … Who?" The muttered words fell flat on her chapped mouth. She leaned over the bed to upchuck what turned out to be only a dry heave. While the newspaper slipped from her limp hands onto the floor, she sat upright, swinging unsure legs with a wince on the side of the bed, looking around the room. She blinked at the black stilettos set on the floor next to the bed and scanned the room. On a closet door hung a tailored coat that matched the suit she was wearing. Wobbling, she leaned and grasped the side table, stepping with barefoot uncertainty. She hugged the wall until she found strength and equilibrium, then tottered to the bathroom door and lifted the coat from the hanger, studying it outside and in. It was fully lined and labeled Elie Tahari.

Sage whispered the name as she ogled the tag. "Elie Tahari. Elie Tahari." The coat was brand-new and the name, she surmised with reason as unsure as her wobbly steps, was probably hers.

The corners of an envelope slipped under the coat pocket caught her eye. Sage's mind whizzed from the Elie Tahari name to the envelope's contents. She fell to her haunches, snatched it up, and scrambled to open it.

Wait a minute! Wait a minute! Sage fumbled with the unopened envelope as she turned it around to read the addressee.

Cheney Dumasque
302 Forty-Ninth Street
Apt. 28D
New York, NY 10016

"Cheney. Cheney. Cheney."

She repeated the name over and over until it sounded like muddled nonsense in her mind. A barrage of blurred faces, buildings, sounds, and smells bombarded her mussed head. Faces that didn't want to be recognized. Buildings that didn't want to be located, and the smells—she sniffed the air. Nothing.

Sage groaned and grimaced before crumpling in a vertiginous swirl to the floor. Bended knees pointed to a door that undoubtedly opened to a bathroom, and it somehow inspired her to summon enough strength to move. After a few beats, she arduously stood and tottered like a drunken woman through the doorway. A huge tub stood with its four claws planted atop a mosaic of black-and-white Victorian hex porcelain tile.

Sage looked around the room until she found a strange thirtysomething woman staring back at her from the mirrored walls. The woman, as unfamiliar as everything else in the place, bore a small but strong frame, and stood at medium height—five feet four inches. Maybe five feet five. Resplendent blue eyes. Lightly tanned, creamy skin barely visible under a veil of pallor. And the blackest hair she'd ever seen—or ever remembered seeing. The hair hung to her shoulders in loose curls and was in bad need of a cut.

In time she ignored the stranger in the mirror and padded across the cool tile past the tub. Beyond it, in the far reaches of the pallor, stood a shower, and beyond that was an L-shaped walk-in closet as big as an average-size department store. Rich brown cabinetry brought a masculine look to the spacious wardrobe. White storage bins brought a crisp, clean feel to the space and profusion of drawers.

Empty drawers and empty space—except that Sage spotted a large suitcase and a smaller travel bag beside it. There was no purse. Losing her balance only once, she dashed to the far corner and opened the large suitcase. It was filled with men's clothing, confusing her. She riffled through the smaller luggage and found what she assumed to be her own clothing. Casual. Clean. Still no purse. No ID.

Sage stepped back and held the knob at length before finally closing the door. Its squeak repeated over and over in her ear.

Sss-q-u-e-e-e-k. Bang!

Hands pressed against her pounding temples.

The violent clue. Something very violent. Standing in place, she blinked and tried to remember more. Strangely enough, dangling teeth. Right then, Sage felt a rush—an uncanny feeling of more violence. Panting, she stood and tried to remember. Then *poof*! It all left. Still panting, Sage rushed to the counter, lowering her face into the sink and splashing water on it until her breathing calmed. Her tongue lapped water streaming from the faucet until she lifted her head just enough to notice a toothbrush, still wrapped in store packaging, and toothpaste atop a stack of fluffy white towels.

After brushing her teeth, Sage found herself tottering out the bathroom and reaching for the newspaper page that had slid across the floor. Searching around again, she retrieved the paper and stilettos from the floor, and then stood for a beat with the coat, not sure what to do next. Then she limped to one of the French chairs, which almost tipped over when she fell into it.

Her brain was scrambled with disembodied voices. No names. No faces. No places. Her mind strained to bring the voices closer to the surface of her mind. They were on the edge, fluttering like mad butterflies, their flapping wings tickling her recall. She raised the envelope again. The leopard cuffs caught her eye again. She wondered if she had a job. Surely she did—and it had to be a good one too. Look at how she dressed. She slipped on the shoes and the coat.

The unopened envelope. She held it up again. The upper left corner reserved for a return address read "Siena Rain." Her eyes and the hand holding the envelope dropped as she searched her head for answers.

Scrambling. Unscrambling. Scrambling.

Befuddled and suddenly much more terrified of the strange environment than her own anonymity, she jumped up and stuffed the envelope and the Philadelphia clipping into the deep coat pocket.

CHAPTER 64

"Nice place," Sean said, between bites. He sat on a leather barstool appreciating the tapering columns, corner blocks, and wainscoting of the West Forty-Ninth Street condo.

"Thanks," Greysen's voice rumbled blandly.

Sean and Greysen feasted on enough fried rice, orange chicken, lo mien, and steamed vegetables to feed an army. They sat across from one another on barstools in a kitchen alcove spanning the entire length of the condo's lower level. Sean was suited in Ermenegildo Zegna, Greysen in casual Versace. Sean's jacket was draped over the back of his barstool, his attaché opened on the massive granite-covered island that stood between the two men. A group meeting awaited Sage's arrival. She was upstairs, under the influence of Jadia's tranquilizers and, Greysen suspected, an inadvertent, non-life-threatening overdose of Oma's sleeping pills and other unknown pharmaceuticals she hadn't noticed were stowed in one pharmacy container.

Sean reexamined the Viking stove behind him and dug a pair of chopsticks into a box of orange chicken—his favorite if he had to eat Chinese food.

"How long have you had the place?" he asked, swiveling back to face Greysen.

"About twenty years," Greysen said after stretching out a delayed answer.

Sean's chewing slowed. He shifted around to face the massive living room space behind Greysen.

"Twenty years?" he muttered almost inaudibly. "But that's when ..." His voice trailed.

"I bought it shortly after meeting Cheney," Greysen confirmed.

"Cheney was the card you held closest to your sleeve," Sean said as he thought about it. "You always had a thing for secrets. You can't blame *missions* for that."

Greysen shrugged. He didn't want to talk about his relationship with Cheney. That subject was sore enough with Sage. The original purpose for inviting Sean to the condo was to corner him into explaining—in front of Sage—what the hell he was doing getting rich off boutique prison investments, how his prison connection played into the scheme of taking Sage and Jadia to see Anthony Campbell, and what his relationship was with Manny Cofield. Razor-sharp eyes sliced back to the man across from him.

"Well, what's the story?" Sean pressed.

Greysen sniffed a relenting laugh. "The story is that Cheney and I fell in love as soon as we met. Well, you already knew that much. Anyway, Cheney's place was small and cramped, and I lived with my parents between Harvard breaks. This condo is the result of me wanting Cheney to be close and comfortable. She insisted on keeping her place—loved her own space." He paused, taking inventory of the kitchen. "We spent most of our time together here."

Sean grabbed a glass of water and changed the subject.

"Lori's at the tail end of entertaining a group of Jersey community leaders. The dinner's a powerful meet-up with executives who have interests in what's going on here in New York—and particular interest in my campaign. She'll be here in about—" He chewed a piece of orange chicken and checked his watch. "Oh I'd say an hour or so."

Greysen tapped his chopsticks against the granite. "You called Lori?"

"Grey, you pulled me from a critical campaign event without notice and without reason. I had to let her know something urgent was up."

Greysen studied a box of steamed rice, then pushed his plate aside. Sean reached into his attaché and scooped up a brick-shaped cell phone.

"You're looking at $900."

Greysen mouthed an *ouch!* shaking his head.

"It's called the Simon Personal Communicator." Sean powered the phone, studied it a bit, and then began tapping the keypad before holding it to his ear. After a while, he shook the phone at Greysen and said, "No signal."

"Ahhh," Greysen said, wiping his mouth with a napkin.

"Did I mention I can send and receive electronic mail on the Simon? That, my friend, is technology. Welcome to the nineties."

Greysen balled the napkin and tossed it on his plate, saying, "Does Lori know about your relationship with Simon?"

"Oh, she not only knows, she has one too." Sean stood the phone on the counter. "Simon's already discontinued it. That's how fast technology evolves."

Greysen rubbed his eyes, debating whether to bring up the subject of Cheney again and telling himself once again to stick to the plan, but he couldn't stop his brain from looping one fact—Sean must have known Cheney. It was the only explanation behind's Sean's cloying attachment to Sage and Jadia. He decided it was probably the only reason Sean had met with him at all.

Tapping the side of the barstool, he forced himself to ask Sean a question, even though he wasn't sure he really wanted to hear the answer. "What happened between you and Cheney after I left the States, Sean?"

Sean's face was inscrutable. He said, "That was what—eighteen, nineteen years ago?" Greysen waited without answering.

Sean sat the phone on the slab. "Nothing happened between Cheney and me, Greysen. I had started at the firm and needed a fresh look. Cheney was recommended. We became friends. She fared okay after you first left, but eventually she needed a friend, Greysen."

Sean took in Greysen's hardened face. Then he added, "Actually, what she needed was an attorney."

Greysen's eyes sparked with anger. "An attorney? Why?"

Sean stood, shoving his hands in his pockets. "Lots of heavy bidders were vying for a particular set of designs in her portfolio." He paced the length of the island and stood stark still as he finished the story.

"They could have hired her, but the risk of the Dumasque name superseding their own was too high. Cheney was savvy. She had a firm grip on New York's loftiest crowd, but she didn't want to find herself digging at the bottom of financial or social buckets. She knew how tenuous social standings were for newcomers. She knew the big boys could have her blackballed, so she caved.

"Cheney asked me to refer her to an attorney who specialized in the textile industry. One who knew the language and culture of the fashion design industry. She wanted to ensure absolute protection against shysters—her word, not mine."

Greysen rested a tight fist on his end of the granite.

"I told her I'd represent her."

"You what?" Greysen burst out, pounding the granite and hopping from the barstool. "You were a gifted student, Sean, top of the class. But textiles? You had a smattering of knowledge at best. You should have referred Cheney to a subject-matter expert in international commerce and—"

Sean intercepted Greysen's thought. "You don't think I know that? I thought I could do it, but I—I dropped the ball." He paused, staring at a box of leftover Chinese food. "I missed a clause that in effect nullified the entire contract. Cheney expected compensation and credit for her work. She received neither."

Sean closed his lids at the memory of Cheney's waiting and suffering. When the lids opened, he found Greysen seated with slumped shoulders, elbows propped on the granite, head dropped in his palms.

Sean said, "I fell in screw-me love with her."

Greysen's head lifted. He pushed himself from the stool, angry eyes raking the man seated on the other side of the island.

Sean winced. Then he thought about something and caught Greysen's eye again. "Cheney didn't blame me for her hardship." He stared at the counter, then back at Greysen. "Or you."

Sean let that sit a minute as he studied the bulky Simon phone. He drifted back to Greysen. "She was looking forward to the wedding because it meant she'd see you again."

In a thatch of memory, Greysen was on a flight over the pond, returning for Sean's wedding. For two years the plan had been for Cheney to accompany Greysen's mother and father to the airport. Instead, Muth and Fath had come alone, greeting Greysen with postmortem news of Cheney's death. Greysen didn't blame them for that—they'd been unable to contact him.

Later at the wedding, Greysen didn't want to risk dampening the festive mood of the couple or their guests, but he never understood why Sean had not proffered one word of condolence. Not even an iota of acknowledgment. Now he knew it was because Sean had fallen in "screw-me love" with Cheney.

A shrilling ring intercepted Greysen's reverie. Both men looked at Sean's $900 cell until it sounded a second shrill. Sean grabbed his prized Simon and thumbed the keypad as he sidled to the balcony and closed the sliding glass doors behind him.

Still roiling, Greysen hung back, running a frustrated hand through thick waves. He heard Sean say, "Lori! ... Lori!" through the sliding glass doors. "Speak fast before I lose the sig—" The call dropped. Sean snatched the phone from his ear and watched as the battery's thirty-second light flashed.

Greysen's thoughts turned to Sage. He stepped to his spot at the counter and sat on the barstool before swiveling it around and peering at the stairs. He needed Sage to wake up soon. Something whirled across the long kitchen and spun past him, causing him to duck and leap from the stool. Sean had hurled the phone in a fury. The durable brick-like device ricocheted off the butler's pantry and crashed somewhere near the alcove of the coffee bar. Greysen pivoted to Sean with a *What the hell?* expression.

Sean shrugged saying, "No wonder it's discontinued," as he snapped his attaché closed.

For a few moments, Greysen studied the corner where the phone had disappeared, then he swiveled back to the counter. "Why involve Sage, Sean?"

After a long pause, Sean eased onto the barstool. "I didn't just love Cheney. I loved Galy, too."

✳ ✳ ✳

For some time now, Sage had been standing at the landing at the crest of the stairs, staring at the date on the envelope: May 20, 1977. She caught at the sound of unintelligible words, the hairs on the back of her neck prickling.

"At least," Sean continued, "I loved the idea of Galy. Cheney kept her under wraps, but I knew Galy—Sage—lived with Cheney's mother somewhere in Pennsylvania. When Cheney died, I wanted to find Sage, pay for her college tuition if she needed it—help her in some way." Sean paused and swallowed. "I did not know Cheney's maiden name, and I could not find a listing under Sage Dumasque. She was probably too young to have an extension in her name even if her grandparents had granted her a separate line. But Cheney had told me, as I'm sure she told you, that her mother was a libber who retained her maiden name after marriage. I found out later that Sage had decided to do the same. So by the time she was old enough to have a listed number, she was hidden under her husband's identity." He hesitated, looking at Greysen. "Sage married young—one of her college professors, but I guess you know that."

Greysen nodded yes and returned to the barstool.

Sean nodded back, drew a breath, and continued. "It was impossible to find Sage without a last name, and all I knew about her father—this Dumasque guy—was that he was from Louisiana and that he had died in Vietnam. Cheney had been tight lipped about him and never mentioned his first name. It wasn't until Jadia was raped that I realized who Galy really was." Sean stopped. His eyes met Greysen's. "Their faces were all over the tri-state papers. I saw those eyes—Cheney's eyes—and I knew exactly who I was looking at."

Greysen pursed his lips and looked away, Sage's words, "You see what you want to see," erupting in him and clouding his mind like volcanic ash. He saw what he wanted to see. Unaware of Greysen's distraction, Sean continued.

"After all those years, Cheney's daughter was still in Philadelphia, and she needed help."

Greysen froze. "No, here's what happened, Sean," he spat. "You found out Sage's daughter had been raped and then you skulked around her home, her job, her friends, and her family until you found a way in. You didn't help her, Sean." An accusing finger pointed across the island. "You *stalked* her."

Sean's face set in frosty coolness. He stood and shrugged on his jacket. Then he dragged the attaché across the granite as he slowly and deliberately rounded the island, closing in on Greysen until they were nose to nose.

"And you *fucked* her, Grey. Just like you *fucked* Cheney."

"If you would have told me Sage was Cheney's daughter, I wouldn't have—"

Sean brusquely cut him off. "Don't blame me for your lousy lack of control, Grey. You got an erection the moment you laid eyes on Sage. Oh, and by the way, that was *before* Eli died."

Greysen's fiery eyes burned into Sean. "Take care of your own house first, Sean, then come see me about mine."

A puzzled expression flickered across Sean's face. "What's that supposed to mean?"

"It means the beautiful, conniving, controlling, wheedling Lori Swoboda manages you. Always has and always will. It means she's figured out clearing political paths for you is no different than washing tracks from your briefs. It means maybe she's a freaking nutcracker because you always leave her wanting. And it means maybe, Sean, your lovely lady figures she's not the invalid—*you* are."

Sean's eyes lit with white-hot rage. Then he charged.

CHAPTER 65

When she heard a man's howl, Sage jerked up, ramrod straight. Something crashed and then—grunts, curses, smacks, punches. Sage walked backward away from the men's voices and the falling furniture until her back was pressed hard against a cool wall.

Rice, chicken, and chopsticks went airborne, the barstools toppling in one direction, the men crashing in another. Sean knocked Greysen to the floor. Greysen fell on his back with an "umph!" and the two men skidded together across the floor. As they skimmed the floor, Sean pounded Greysen with payback punches while they slid like a wayward train over the slippery black-and-white kitchen tile and then onto the slick, waxed wood in the open living room.

Sean's head thumped against the tiered base of one of the round obelisk-shaped columns like a mallet. With a crack, he ricocheted off the punishing wood and a trickle of blood oozed from a small cut above his right eye. Greysen sat upright on the floor, restocking his lungs with air Sean had knocked out of him. Wincing, he hoisted himself on a sore knee and—

"Umph!" Sean's head had cleared, and he scrambled to his feet and rammed into Greysen with a momentous blow to the jaw, followed by a left jab to the head. Greysen grunted as he fell back under the punches, but he managed to block Sean's next blow. In the same move, he slammed his forearm against Sean's throat, blocking airflow and thrusting him uncontrollably backward.

Sean impotently clawed at Greysen's face. Greysen reared back out of reach and gave one final shove, tumbling Sean backward so that he landed on an awkwardly twisted foot that sent him yowling to the floor. The trickle of blood was now drying in a zigzag above his right eye.

Greysen's battered knee buckled when he tried to stand. He was negotiating the other one when—"Oomph!" Sean had popped up like a jack-in-the-box and pounced one-footed on Greysen, throwing him to the floor with a thud. He landed atop Greysen's hips—not exactly what he was aiming for. Neither was the grueling agony he felt as his foot twisted at the ankle. Ignoring the pain, he threw an arm over Greysen's chest. His fingers clawed for ... anything.

"Argggh!" Sean growled.

Sage spun into a tiptoed run back into the bedroom. She searched everywhere for a phone—in nightstand drawers, under the bed, behind sconces. She circled the bathroom, stepping to a linen closet she hadn't noticed before because its door was camouflaged as a full-length mirror.

When she'd searched the luggage in the huge walk-in closet, there was a gun—a Glock. The blurred memory of its smooth, cool barrel and loaded magazine called to her. She answered it like a ringing phone, deft hands cradling it with the familiarity of a long-lost lover. With both hands wrapped around the handle and arms straight in front of her, she let the Glock precede her back to the landing.

Below, Sean pushed to his knees to gain on Greysen, but not before oxygen and realization collided in Greysen's stunted brain. He was still shaking fog from his head when his knee jumped in the game and went straight for Sean's crotch.

"Ohhhhh!" Sean lurched forward, headfirst, as he nursed his inner thigh with clutching hands.

Greysen missed the balls. *Damn!*

As the men scuffled, Sage stood in front of a lavish fireplace, searching their bruised faces for recognition. Neither one looked vaguely familiar.

"Okay gentlemen, that's enough," Sage said loudly. With a two-handed grip, she leveled the gun down at them.

The unaffected voice landed on Sean and Greysen like a bombshell. They frantically disentangled and scrambled away from one another, each with his own share of battered body parts and bruised ego. In shared disbelief, the breathless pair stared at the Glock pointed at their recently conjoined bodies. They knew Sage meant business.

Two sets of eyes moved cautiously from the muzzle of the gun to the woman holding it.

From his perch on the floor, Greysen ogled Sage. Black curls framed her oval face and danced freely around her shoulders. Something was wrong. Sage wasn't quite … Sage. For one thing she stood rigid, her shoulders crouched with primal, elemental readiness. And there was the other thing. Sage was actually holding a Glock and managing it with skills. Worse, Sage was looking at him like she didn't know him. He tested the waters with a smile and waited.

Sage looked at the tall men with angry disdain. She heard the one with green eyes say, "Sage?" The other—bald and handsome—asked, "Are you okay?"

"Sage is dead," she said with eyes as blank as her voice was detached.

She watched as the men looked at each other, and she heard the bald one whisper, "What's wrong with her?"

Greysen spoke through clenched teeth, "She's experiencing drug-induced amnesia."

Sean gaze shot to Greysen, then to Sage, then back to Greysen. In an agitated, loud voice he demanded, "What drugs? You gave her drugs? Why?"

Silence and Sean's seething anger jammed the room.

"Why don't you tell her, Greysen?" Bald and Handsome yelped. His gray eyes flashed, black pupils pinched tight.

Sage's lips pressed against clenched teeth, not understanding. Caged words struggled to escape. "Stand up," Sage ordered.

Greysen stole an incredulous look at Sean as the stiff men began to unfold in winces and grunts to their feet. "She took the drugs of her own volition, Sean." The whisper came just as they completed the painful rise.

Sage cocked her head in vacant impatience as Pusher—the new moniker she'd coined for Green Eyes—recounted a story she neither understood nor believed. He was looking right at her and giving her some cockamamie story about inadvertently overdosing on different prescriptions stored in one pharmacy container. He said he had phoned the incident and her symptoms to a local pharmacist, who'd predicted she should be all right. According to Pusher, she had collected the container from her grandmother's house in Philadelphia. Sage recalled neither the people, places, nor drugs Pusher had referenced. Now he was taking a breath and glancing sideways at Bald and Handsome.

Sage looked at Pusher.

With a clenched jaw, Greysen looked away from Sean and met a clearly pissed-off Sage. *Fuck!*

"What are you looking at, Pusher?" Sage snapped, each word a broad stroke of hate.

"I'm sorry," he said contritely. "It's just that you have an uncanny resemblance to Sage Wirspa."

Her mind blew back and stirred around in a maddening eddy. In the spin, she saw a newspaper slowly unfolding to an obituary: "Sage Magaly Wirspa, 35, died Thursday, October 11, 1995."

"Sage is dead."

The weight of Sage's deep-seated belief in the words shot through Sean like bullets.

"What *is* your name?" Greysen asked.

"How about we stay on point," she volleyed. "So you drugged me? Did you sleep with me, too?"

Sick with Revenge

"Yes," Sean intoned. "Why don't you tell her about that?"

"And why don't you tell her," Greysen growled, "how you screwed Cheney over?"

"I was talking to you, Pusher," Sage said. Her finger hooked the trigger.

The Glock's squared eye met Greysen's shocked gaze. His palms flew up in a halting gesture.

Sage lifted the gun higher, moving her aim from Pusher's heart to his mouth. "I suggest you speak now or forever hold your peace."

In the split second that followed, everything in the condo went still as if prostrating under the weight of oppressive dread.

"Boy, Jadia sure did like those banana pancakes," Sean chirped with alacrity.

Sage's attention snapped to him. She hunted for the reason for the sudden, inexplicable connection she felt with the man.

Flashes of straws. Falling straws. A young face with the deepest, bluest eyes sucked strawberry milk from two straws. Or maybe it was a shake. The little girl was giggling.

"Jadia," Sage repeated to herself. Something sweet and warm like vanilla sugar swirled inside her. Jadia. Fuzzy realization brought on kaleidoscopic images, broken bric-a-brac of memories folding and unfolding in polychromatic radiance.

She saw a tumble of the shiniest raven hair falling from a ponytail. A happy, gurgling infant with a tuft of nearly blonde hair and the starkest, bluest eyes looking up expectantly. An extraordinarily handsome man tickling an eight-month-old as happy chuckles spilled from both of them. A toddler laughing, talking, pointing to something at a zoo. A young girl whose front teeth barely pierced the gums. A gregarious preteen shopping with her friends for their first concert. Thomas chaperoning …

She looked at Bald and Handsome. "Who—"

Bam! Bam! Bam! Bam! The knocks were sudden, loud, and urgent.

A moment of silence seized the room. Sage looked past Bald and Handsome and the Pusher to the door at the other end of the long, open room. Both men twisted their torsos to look at the door behind them.

Bam! Bam! Bam! Bam!

"Were you expecting anyone?" Sean whispered to Greysen.

"No," Greysen whispered back.

More knocks. Urgency cranked with each pound. The entire far wall shook. "Open up," a voice barked from the other side of the door. "It's the FBI."

Frowns ripped across Greysen's and Sean's faces. Each looked at the other accusingly.

"Don't move!" The order came from Sage. Her voice was deep, raspy. It rang of "I-am-not-taking-any-shit" authority. Sean and Greysen stood stark still, Greysen with tired palms in the air, making it clear they had no plans to disobey. She gave them a wide berth, circling almost to the furthest wall—the one nearest the sofa—before Sean called out, "The Glock!"

He found the gun frozen in a deadly aim at him. "Easy, Rockefeller," Sage said without registering that she'd just called him by the moniker she'd endearingly assigned him.

Bam! Bam! Bam! Bam! "FBI! Open up or we'll open it for you," a voice barked with unequivocal promise.

"Coming!" Greysen called out.

"You don't want the FBI to find the Glock," Sean carefully warned. "It would be bad for you. It will be bad for Jadia."

Sage's head snapped to attention. Jadia! It registered, if not completely. Jadia's face flashed and vanished, pushing Sage back to stark reality. Back to a wielded gun. Sage looked at the Glock.

"Stuff it between the sofa cushions," Greysen softly called out.

Sage quickly did as she was told. The men's shoulders fell a bit, but the tension in the room remained. They spun around in unison as heels clicked into a run across the expansive floor to the sofa.

Greysen let out a breath and, with eyes glued to the door, leaned over to Sean's ear. "Thanks for saving my ass back there. Sage was going to kill me."

"I didn't do it for you," Sean whispered through gritted teeth as Sage neared the door. "I did it for her."

Sage struggled with the locks before pulling the custom-built door open. In one eternal second, everything happened at once. She cocked her head, straining to come to terms with the gaggle of granite faces. Two male agents shadowed the doorway. The first was average height with coarse, red hair and flushed skin. The other was slender, short, and wearing thick sideburns. He was the laid-back one, the one in charge. He inspected Sage a long while. Then, in a voice flowing with smooth reticence, he said, "FBI, ma'am."

Sage squinted at glints of multiple badges flashing under the crystal lighting in the crowded hallway. A plainclothesman with receding blond hair and a disposable BIC lighter leaned against a wall behind the horde of agents. His thick thumb rolled over the BIC's wheel, then he lifted the flame to the cigarette dangling his from mustache-hooded lips.

The hinges pitched a tiny squeak under the door's widening swing. *Sss-q-u-e-e-e-k. Bang!*

Sage reached out past Agent Redhead, trying to cover the impossible distance to the smoking plainclothesman. She caught her own madness, then dropped her arm and stammered, "Uh, uh."

Agent Redhead and Agent Sideburns pushed past the doorway, followed by a phalanx of FBI, CIA, and local authorities trailing in their wake.

Sage faltered back, away from the forward pressing pack of agents, away from the onslaught of images surfacing from her memory. As the procession continued, she pivoted 180 degrees, pressing her back against the interior wall, struggling to both understand and erase the minuscule image of the torched woman she had seen in the BIC's flames.

Against the backs of the forward marching agents and police officers, Sage saw a cinematic view of herself, Jadia, and Rockefeller—Sean! They were seated in a dive, eating banana pancakes.

Sage wrenched loose from the wall and lunged into a run. Her heels clicked arrhythmically across the room. Greysen stepped forward at the ready to embrace her, then watched with impotent protest as Sage barreled through the throng of sauntering agents and covered the remaining empty space opening to the kitchen.

She yelled, "Sean!"

Sean stood near the island where he had absconded to find his cell phone. He turned just in time to open his muscular arms and corral Sage in. Greysen stood to the side, swallowing as Sage pressed her face against Sean's chest, her graceful fingers clutching his Zegna lapels.

Sean stroked Sage's locks, his face softening as he looked down at her. The lids of his eyes lifted as he kissed her head. Over her shoulder, Sean's eyes hardened at Greysen. His gaze flicked to down to Sage, as he lifted her chin and cast her a warm smile. "I can't describe my relief."

"Sean, I—"

"Ma'am," Agent Sideburns interjected in a bored tone. "We need you to step away from the suspect."

Confusion scrambled through Sage as she looked over her shoulder and said, "Wha—"

Agent Sideburns gestured to Agent Redhead who gently grabbed Sage by the elbow and pried her fingers from Sean's lapels like dislodging a clawing kitten from her mother's teat.

Concern rippled through Greysen like a tidal wave, and he began to migrate through the throng of federal and local police, trying to get to Sage. Agent Sideburns lifted Sean's hand from Sage's shoulder and twisted it behind his back. A metal cuff opened and clicked shut with disturbing finality. Sage shrugged off Agent Redhead's hold and tottered back, her mouth open, eyes wide.

Greysen threaded around tapering columns, pain stiffening his knee into a lumber as he closed the distance to Sage.

Agent Sideburns reached around to Sean's opposite side to grab his other wrist. The sound of metal clicking was repeated.

Greysen rounded the far end of the island, cupped a corner of the granite, and spun himself into limping trajectory until he was flush against Sage's backside. He gingerly curled calming hands on Sage's arms and spoke low into her ear. "The couch."

Sage's questioning eyes looked behind her shoulder at the Greysen, then fell to the floor where Sean was now seated and cuffed. He, like Greysen, was bruised from their brawl. Sean glanced at Greysen, surprised at the apologetic expression on his face, then he looked at Sage before nodding concurrence. Her shoulders relaxed, and her chest fell into breathing rhythm again. She looked back at Greysen.

"I want to say something to him," she whispered.

Greysen glanced at Agents Sideburns and Redhead, who looked on without expression. He released Sage.

Sean, noting Lori's ongoing absence and remembering Greysen's suspicions—innuendoes that still smarted—returned Greysen's perceptive nod.

Nearly toppling, Sage righted herself as she kneeled close to Sean. "Sean," she said. "I remember how you helped. How you—"

"Ma'am," Agent Redhead warned. "Step away from the suspect, or you'll be in the same shit he's in."

Sage pushed out a breath as she stood. "I will be there for you like you were there for me—and Jadia. I promise." She touched his shoulder. He returned her somber smile and watched Greysen cup a hand under her elbow. As Greysen gently guided Sage away, she heard Agent Redhead begin to cite the Miranda Warning.

Seated on the couch, Sage withdrew into herself and panted like an overheated dog.

"Everything is going to be all right," Greysen said.

Sage stared at the Pusher at length before, "You were there weren't you?"

Greysen blinked.

"You were there," Sage repeated. "When that woman died. Eli."

Greysen stared aimlessly at his throbbing knee before looking back at Sage. "*We* were there," he said. He glanced at the kitchen where Sean was now seated in a plush chair the agents had pulled from the library. Greysen added, "All of us."

Swallowing, Sage studied Greysen.

"Are you all right?" he asked.

Framed still shots of memory began to flash in Sage's mind. Flashes of faces and events flitted across her mind, and with a sharper edge than ever before, she saw images of Anthony Campbell and Manny Cofield at the correctional facility. A car racing down country roads came back to her.

"I guess—I guess I'm Sage Wirspa after all."

"Yes, you are."

Greysen's confirmation brought on a flash. She saw herself with a gun—the Glock. A man with mangled gums lay bleeding before her. She threw one hand over her mouth and clutched her stomach with the other as more pieces of violence, fear, and loss rushed back to her.

"I have to get away from here." She stood as quickly as the memories came, tottering and stepping clumsily over his long legs as she headed to the door.

"Whoa," a local detective said, turning her around. "Bathrooms are that way. Otherwise—"

"I've got her," Greysen said. Against his body's aching protests, he'd leapt up after Sage. He focused on her, squelching anger at the arrogant agent who'd just given him directions to his own bathroom.

"I have to get out of here," Sage repeated. She covered her mouth, suppressing a dry heave.

Greysen looked at her, concerned brows hooding tired eyes. He gimped closer in slow, measured moves. "Local police, New York's Bureau of Investigation, and both Fed agencies are going to want statements. Do you think you can hold on a little while longer?"

She studied him a long while. "Yes," she said finally. She pulled the hand from her mouth. "I'll be fine."

Robust knocks came from the open door before more agents filed into the condo. Greysen glanced that way, then looked at Sage again. He whispered, "Do you remember me yet?"

She looked up at him, trying. "No," she whispered back.

"Why don't we sit back down?" he said.

CHAPTER 66

It was no ordinary arrest. Sean was a prominent attorney in New York and Pennsylvania and a candidate for the presidency. Shell holding companies camouflaged his ownership in boutique prisons gone wrong—kickbacks, nepotism, drugs, and money laundering. And there were those other entities—the ones with global footprints that were equally diseased with illegal transactions. All were linked to Team Swoboda, or more accurately, to *Sean*.

State, local, and federal authorities packed the Forty-Ninth Street condo and clustered in small groups in the hallways and on the sidewalk discussing what was going to be a much publicized case. Local television crews staged for the night's news coverage, while the agents drilled Sage and Greysen who sat on opposite sides of the room. The questioning lasted for hours. During a break, they were offered beverages and allowed to sit together on the couch. Greysen opted for water. Sage was nursing a cup of hot tea when she noticed that a beautiful, leggy brunette had joined the entourage.

"Hello," Ayde Carona said. Greysen lifted himself to stand.

She raised a palm in protest. "No, please. Stay seated. Someone's bringing—" Then she added, "Ah, here it is." A uniformed officer placed a chair near the threesome and left after he was thanked.

Ayde sat down and slid her eyes around the room before landing them on Sage and Greysen. Then she presented her badge.

"I'm Ayde Carona, FBI."

Greysen lifted an eyebrow. "Carona?" She nodded with a half-smile. He gestured to Sage, his eyes softened at her unchanged expression. "This is Sage Wirspa."

Sage remained quiet. Greysen turned back to Ayde, who said, "Pleasure."

"And I'm Greysen Artino."

"Yes. I know who you are. My father keeps pictures of himself and old buddies framed in his offices. You're in a couple of them. Dad told me about what you did for him when you guys were colleagues. My mother speaks highly of you too."

Greysen studied her with narrow eyes and nodded. He smiled. "You're Andres' daughter."

"That's what they tell me," she said. The corners of her mouth perked.

"I'm not sure undercover works for you, Ayde. You look just like your dad, only much prettier."

"I look like my mother," Ayde corrected.

"Plus," Greysen agreed nodding, "I've seen pictures of you and your brother. Andres rarely exposes his family to anyone, but we grew pretty close when we were overseas."

"I know," Ayde agreed.

"Did Andres send you to help?"

"As you know, my father's now a Company man, Mr. Artino." Ayde referred to the code name for the CIA. "The Swoboda file was a clandestine operation initially headed by the FBI. Dad had neither engagement nor intelligence regarding my assignment, and he had no idea you were involved until—" She paused. "Well, until intelligence reached the Bureau regarding the West Virginia house bombing, at which time the

CIA became involved." She reached for his hand and held it. "I am very sorry for your loss, Mr. Artino." Greysen nodded his head once.

Greysen averted his eyes and thought about the day Sage had left to pay respects to Oma and search for the love letters he had written to Cheney nearly two decades ago. He'd been afraid of her reaction to the letters. Missed her. Harbored growing doubt he'd ever see her again.

Overwhelmed, he'd visited Eli's mound, a once-frequent ritual that had dwindled to rarity after Sage had entered his life. But during this particular trek, he spotted a dirty piece of charred metal buried in the silt near the creek. The sighting was a complete fluke. He had bent down to grab a rock to skip across the creek, and there it was. A tilt fuse. And in Greysen's errant opinion, solid evidence of Sean's guilt.

The next day, Greysen's buddies landed from various agencies with a coordinated thud on Eli's property. Remnants of explosive canisters soon after surfaced. And to Greysen, this was more solid evidence of Sean's guilt. He told the authorities how Sean had shown up with Sage and Jadia in the middle of the night, and how Sean had insisted on going to the service station alone the morning of the blast.

Now Greysen knew he had misjudged Sean. Minutes ago, he'd overheard an agent mention Manny Cofield's release from incarceration. Hearing Cofield's name again brought a vestige of recall—a vague but budding recollection that Sean had not been the authority behind his carte blanche visit at the prison the previous year. Greysen's self-perpetuating suspicions that Sean had planted the bomb that killed Eli, fed his belief that his law school pal also had something to do with Oma's death. Once Greysen's misguided beliefs had gelled, his misconceived idea that Sean had a vested interest in the private prison industry was also a given.

Greysen's fresh revelation of Sean's blind naïveté and innocence had come too late to stop the chain of events he'd errantly set in motion. Thanks to him, the authorities held the circumstantial, but none-the-less damning, evidence against Sean. The nightmarish domino effects were well underway.

Greysen's guilt was making toilet soup of his guts. As he chewed on this unsavory imagery, something else gurgled with diarrheic certainty: he utterly, completely, and irreversibly loathed one Lori Swoboda. And he was getting the unnerving sense that the feeling had been mutual a very long time.

Ayde jolted Greysen from his reverie. "The FBI's preliminary investigation yielded indications of transnational activity," she said. "So, of course, the CIA is engaged. This case became of particular importance to my father after he found out you were involved." She arched her brows. "Dad's been telling me the story of how you saved his life since I was a little girl." She twisted a corner of her lips into a half-wistful, half-mischievous grin before saying, "I'm sure it was sanitized."

They exchanged knowing looks and gave in to an irresistible, quick laugh. The private joke about her father's hilarious if crass sense of humor proffered a reprieve, if only momentarily, for Ayde Carona. She'd spent every other second since her arrival trying not to think about how she had walked in with the group of agents as they surged toward the kitchen—and Sean.

Sean must have felt the pressure of someone watching him. He'd lifted his head, searching the crowd. His gaze, gray and brilliant, stopped when he saw her face, glided downward, and then flicked back up in surprise. Their eyes met. A string of reactions morphed on Sean's face. First came a flash of relief. Before she could blink, his expression had morphed into disparaging disappointment as he realized Ayde Carona was an FBI agent. His face hardened into stony passiveness as he'd studied her with abject objectivity. They held one another's gaze until Sean's lawyer squatted in front of him and blocked her view.

CHAPTER 67

All the agents had finally left. The condo was quiet. Greysen looked at Sage. She remained planted on the sofa, and he sat on the cocktail table, leaning toward her, elbows on his knees.

"How are you, Sage?" he asked.

The effects of the drugs on Sage were in a slow fade. Exhaustion tugged at her. Words dragged in her head like a donkey-pulled tiller. She took a breath.

"They've taken Sean away," Greysen said. Sage stared past him, across the living room, beyond the kitchen alcove—all the way through the crystal clear glass. A dark sky was pressing against the floor-to-ceiling windows and sliding glass doors.

"When I woke a while ago," she started, staring with remote bewilderment through the far windows, "I thought it was dawn. But the day is not beginning." She turned her gaze to Greysen. "It's ending."

Greysen leaned into her, held her hand, and whispered, "Everything is going to be all right, Sage. We're going to help Sean …" As he spoke, his lips brushed her ear. The words trailed off, and Sage tilted her ear to his mouth, dipping deeper into the sounds, the experience of Greysen.

She felt the moist, warm air of Greysen's breath. It felt ... intimate. She turned her face into his. The tips of their noses nearly touched. Sage dove into his pupils, searching, probing. Trinkets of faint memory played like pins and needles against her brain.

Greysen watched Sage's full lips part. She sighed low, a scaled-down version of the way she responded whenever he'd—

"The more I hear your voice," she said, intercepting his thoughts, "the more I remember."

He waited.

Sage whispered, "We were lovers."

The words hit Greysen like an eighteen-wheeler. He rested his elbows on his knees, leaning closer to her. He nodded and whispered, "Yes, we were lovers."

Sage looked away from Greysen and swallowed before braving his study again. "And you were my mother's lover."

Greysen looked at his hands, a thumb playing across a lifeline.

"That was a long time ago, Sage. When I met you last summer, I did not know you were Cheney's daughter. I had no idea who you were."

Sage's voice was barely audible when she said, "I know. My mother died almost twenty years ago and, in order to protect me from whoever killed my grandmother, you invented my death and had it published."

"We," Greysen corrected. "We invented your death and, with the help of resourceful acquaintances, an obituary was published."

Sage freed her hand from Greysen and busied her fingers by picking at the piping along the seat cushions. "I'm sorry for what happened back there, Greysen—blaming you for drugging me and aiming the gun at you. I remember taking what I thought were Jadia's tranquilizers because I was having anxiety attacks. Being back in the city, the murders, and fear of someone trying to kill me overwhelmed me.

"I didn't realize I had combined prescriptions. Oma must have thrown her own pills in with Jadia's, something she did when preparing to dispose of expired medications. I wasn't paying attention and, well, you know the rest." She hand-raked her hair and planted unwavering eyes on Greysen.

"If I had known you believed Sean was behind the bombing that killed Eli and the home invasion that left Oma dead, I would have never agreed to your scheme to lure him here." She hesitated, her mind racing back a year and a half to the prison visit. "Sean is loyal and relentless in friendship, Greysen. You should know that."

"I'm going to do everything I can to get him the best representation."

"Even if Sean is cleared, it's nearly impossible for his record to be expunged. You can't reverse the damage you've done to his reputation or his standing with the Bar."

Greysen inwardly recoiled from Sage's rebuke. The image and shock of Sage pointing the Glock at him flashed and tightened around his throat like a constricting python.

"Oh," Sage said, breaking the ensuing silence. "I almost forgot something." She reached into her jacket pocket and slipped out a crumpled envelope. "This is one of the letters you wrote to my mother." She handed him a sealed envelope. "The thing is, my mother never saw this one—never read it."

A beat after staring at the envelope, Greysen looked at Sage. "How do you know Cheney never read this?"

"Well, aside from the letter being unopened, she died May 13, 1977. The letter was dated on May twentieth of that year."

Sage fiddled with her purse strap and then said, "If dog-eared corners and worn creases are any indication, my mother read your letters frequently. I stowed a few others between your mattresses. The rest are still in Oma's house."

Sage took in a deep breath. "I really need to rest, Greysen."

The pronouncement broke his trance on the twenty-year-old epistle.

Greysen placed the sealed envelope on the coffee table and focused with piercing clarity on Sage. "Why don't we crash out here for the night?" he asked, as Sage stood. He followed suit and waited for an answer.

"I heard you and Sean talking. I didn't understand it at the time, but now I'm copying loud and clear. You both—" She froze. She stared at the stairs on the far end of the wide-open space, and slowly traveled up each riser to the second floor landing. They stretched toward the bedroom hidden behind darkness and walls and yesteryear.

"You and my mother made love in that very room upstairs," she said softly, deep blues back on Greysen. She flicked away from his silence and panned the large room from the foyer to the Tuscan kitchen to the crowning fireplace. She landed back on him. "I'm sure you and Cheney made love in most every spot in this place." An all-telling silence fell on them like a heavy weight.

Greysen scanned the furniture and walls, the fireplace, the stairs. The plan—his and Cheney's plan—had been for them to stay in New York. In the condo. Together. "Maybe I shouldn't have brought you here," he said.

Sage didn't say anything. Instead, she languidly walked upstairs and returned a few minutes later with the small travel bag she'd found earlier in the walk-in closet draping her shoulder. She also toted a leather, leopard-print purse that she had found on a bare shelf in the closet—the very place she had scoured several hours ago. But she'd never looked up. The purse was in hand now and she'd already inspected it for ID, credit cards, and cash. All was in order.

At the base of the stairs, Greysen inclined his head at Sage as she descended the risers. "I'm going to a hotel," she announced.

"It's almost midnight, Sage," Greysen said, stepping closer.

Sage walked around him, heading for the couch. She dug in between the two large, plush seat cushions, fished out the Glock, and inspected it before leveling her eyes on his. "I'll be fine."

Greysen wasn't sure about that. Sean's erroneous arrest meant whoever killed Oma was still at large. His eyes strayed to Sage's bag where she had stowed the Glock, and he thought, *Maybe Sage was right after all—she will be okay.* Still he wanted her to stay. "Carrying a concealed weapon is illegal in the state of New York, you know."

Sage threw him a smile. He was still soaking it up when she stepped past him and headed across the lengthy expanse toward the door. Greysen's gimp followed Sage's clicking heels. She managed stilettos like she handled the Glock—with confidence, grace, and well-honed skill. Greysen didn't want to see any of it walk out that door.

"It took me a while to figure it out," he called across the short distance between them.

Heel clicks stopped. Sage hesitated, and she slowly turned around. "Figure what out?"

He stepped closer. "Why I fell in love with you. It was your ability to grasp the nettle. You don't shrink back from the tough stuff. You take on problems head on. Did you get that from your mother? Probably." He took another step closer. "But, Sage ..." A half-step closer. There was no more space left between them.

"I fell in love with you long before I had an inkling Cheney was your mother."

He lifted her chin, a thumb stroking her cheek. "All I'm asking is that you try to remember what we had before either of us knew we shared history with Cheney." Greysen leaned in and rested his forehead on Sage's. They both closed their eyes.

After a long wait, Sage whispered, "Okay." Then she opened the door and listened to one last *sss-q-u-e-e-e-k bang* as it closed behind her.

CHAPTER 68
NOVEMBER 1995

Lori Swoboda wheeled past the expansive double mahogany doors into the firm's Manhattan office, stormy and unstoppable. "Where's Ayde Carona? I have to see her now," she said, after she had whizzed across the anteroom. Her voice bellowed beyond the astonished receptionist down the long corridor, carrying with it her fierce intent. "I have something just for her. Where is she?"

Instantly the hallway filled with curious spectators. The receptionist was still scurrying around a massive workstation and struggling to pull down a too-tight skirt. She called out, "Uhm, Mrs. Swoboda! Mrs. Swoboda! With whom do you have an appointment? Mrs. Swoboda!"

"Shut up, Deanna. Since when do I need an appointment?" Lori Swoboda careened from one open door to the next, knocking on closed doors, and even disrupting an ongoing conference by elbowing it with a big thud as she swerved past the door.

"Extraordinary" described Lori Swoboda in every way. This statement was especially true in regard to the strength of her mind, will, and broken body. Her insistence on bypassing motorized wheelchairs and sticking to a manual version paid off in strong, beautifully muscular arms and torso, and mastering speeds that she knew a motorized chair would never reach. Her wheelchair of choice? A sports variety used in quad rugby for its speed and agility.

Two of the more senior partners approached Lori Swoboda from opposite sides of the hallway. The first one to reach her waved a low hand, directing her into his office. With grace and practiced precision, she maneuvered the wheelchair in a pivot that rivaled the best military left-face turn and rolled into his office. The second partner trailed in her wake and closed the door behind him.

"Good morning, Lori," the first partner said, sliding into one of four high-back leather chairs stationed at a round table in a corner of the room. The second partner joined him after pulling aside a chair to make room for Lori to roll up. The oversized furniture made the men look small. Lori's presence filled the room and made them look smaller. She stayed in place, staring at the vacant space at the table with narrowed eyes. All at once, she flicked glares at the men, shifting from one to the other, freeze-framing them in her mind. They stared back at her, marveling at her ability to command an audience. Her smooth skin and natural blonde hair gave away no secrets of her age. Her attire was indicative of a woman with custom-tailored taste and the means to support it.

"I am in no mood to be toyed with today. Let's keep this simple. My only business is with Ayde Carona."

The partners looked at each other in a way that suggested mutual confusion, and then a silent but mutual urging for the other to speak first. Finally, the first one cleared his throat, and then said, "Lori, Ayde Carona no longer works here. She resigned immediately after—" He paused, giving his partner a glance that could have been interpreted as a call for help. A call that received no reply.

"After the trouble," he finished.

"You haven't seen trouble yet. Where can I find her?" she said. Her face was cemented with solid determination. "I have something I'd like to give her for her reading pleasure." She reached into a compartment of her wheelchair and slid out a sleek, black patent leather hand clutch. From it she pulled out an envelope neatly fitted into a transparent plastic sleeve. Judging from its mint condition and sepia color, the partners correctly assumed the documents in it to be both dated and well preserved. They also noticed Sean Swoboda's script. The letter seemed to be addressed to a Cheney D—

Lori flipped over the envelope, blocking their prying eyes from seeing more. She took a deep breath and stared at the now-overturned envelope in her lap. It was weighted with the same letters she'd found two decades before. Sean had promised to burn the professions of love and apology but, hours before his arrest, Lori discovered them in a safe he'd kept concealed behind an office bookcase in their Central Park West home.

She had discovered the safe was there a few years ago. Lori hadn't given it much thought until she saw Sean and Ayde at dinner, and even then, she delayed acting on any impulses. After an indeterminate amount of time, she paid one of New York's most skilled and highly sought-after locksmiths a handsome sum to discreetly crack the safe. A slot on his jammed calendar hadn't opened up until the day of Sean's arrest. Nauseating chagrin clawed at Lori after she slid the contents from the safe. The toxic letters Sean had written to Cheney—letters he should have never written at all, letters he'd sworn on their wedding night to destroy—were intact and breathing foul, mocking air in Lori's spurned face.

In a flash, Lori picked up the envelope and waved it at the partners. She made no effort however to subdue the wave of hot jealously erupting with every word that followed.

"Ayde Carona is difficult to convince. I knew this when I saw how she looked at my husband during last year's Christmas party. Knowledge of an outsider in Sean's life will help Ayde understand his true nature—just as it helped me to understand." Tears brimmed her eyes, but didn't drop. This was also the end of her discussion on the matter. There was no way Lori was going to reveal that Sean and Ayde had gone to dinner, and that Sean had later lied about it, reaffirming Lori's long-held suspicion that her husband reciprocated Ayde Carona's advances.

"Give me Ayde's forwarding address," Lori demanded.

"Ms. Carona left no forwarding address," the reluctant spokesperson replied.

Lori Swoboda scoffed. "You're partners in one of the East Coast's most prestigious firms. My husband chose you. Make no mistake—you benefited far more from that choice than he. The point is, I know you have the best technology and investigative resources available to find Ayde Carona. Get to it."

The spokesperson raised his brows, a corner of his mouth twitching into a small, condescending smile. "Mrs. Swoboda, your husband's services were duly compensated and recently deemed no longer necessary or desired. His severance package was almost as generous as full retirement, had he been employed with us long enough to achieve that honor. As for Ms. Carona, she tendered—"

Lori brusquely interrupted the partner's thread. "Yes, yes. You've already said she resigned—a fact I deduced long before I arrived. I'm here for her forwarding address."

The partners looked at one another, their eyes spelling disbelief. In comical unison, each man returned his respective gaze back to Lori Swoboda as they assumed their formal roles as spokesperson and silent partner.

"Mrs. Swoboda, we do not have Ms. Carona's forwarding address and would not be at liberty to share it even if it were in our possession. I'm sure finding her on your own won't be a problem. She's one of the best litigators in the—"

"She's a woman," Lori Swoboda interjected, "and don't you forget it." She leaned her pretty, youthful face forward and shifted her intense gaze from one stone face to the other in turn. With her blonde hair, shifting squints, dark suit, and commanding presence, she looked like an angry, blue-eyed bald eagle.

"Ayde Carona is wily, crafty, and accustomed to getting her way," she said. "She plays her cards like a pro because she is one. I recognize my own when I see them, believe you me." She tapped the plastic-covered envelope with a forefinger before returning it with care to a compartment inside her sleek purse, and returning the purse to an even sleeker side compartment of the wheelchair, and finally, returning her posture to ramrod straight in the wheelchair.

Lori Swoboda back-rolled into another impressive pivot until she was facing the doorway. The silent partner jumped up and loped to the door, opening it just in time for Lori to slip through. Right then, she silently dubbed the two partners, the Dynamic Duo.

"Gotham City's finest," she said aloud.

"Come again?" the spokesperson asked her back.

"Never mind," she said. She tapped the wheel of her chair, collecting her thoughts. She and Sean had symbiotically coursed through nearly two decades of marriage without the need to tease out kinks because there had been none. If she had to mark a connubial turning point, she'd place a big, fat, red X on the 1993 calendar—the firm's Christmas party. That one infinitesimal instant when Sean's pupils dilated after alighting on Ayde Carona's long legs.

Like historical buildings being razed for glitzier edifices, down had gone Lori's plans to discuss the prospects of private prison investments with her husband. So she went out on her own—nothing new there— and began developing relationships with people who controlled federal and state detention centers. She learned the lingo and ruthlessly postured through the correctional system's political, financial, and social undercurrents until she herself was the sluice gate. Nothing rivaled the power and narcissistic rush she felt with proprietorship, especially because absolutely no one knew Lori Swoboda was the owner.

The disadvantage of building layers of fictional corporations and commissioned middlemen between Lori and the prisons she owned was slow communications. By the time news of Manny Cofield's machinations reached her, Sean had become a victim of them. In truth, Lori mused, Sean was a victim of his own stupidity. Lori had initially supported his attachment to the Wirspas because of how well Sage had branded the Philadelphia law office: how well Sage had branded *Sean*. And there was Jadia, that beautiful girl who had been brutally raped. But business was business. When Sean received Marcia Clark's offer to join the O. J. Simpson prosecution team, Lori dropped her support of the Wirspas like a hot, rotten potato. Why Sean had remained attached to the Wirspas, despite her urgings not to do so, still remained out of Lori's grasp, and now far beyond her interest.

Instead of standing next to Marcia Clark in an LA courtroom, Sean had called her in the middle of the night from a payphone in West Virginia hick town, whining about the pandemonium that had taken place while he was at one of the prisons she clandestinely owned. Worse, the judge Sage had called was getting ominously close to finding out Lori's secrets. That the community pillar and political mastermind Mrs. Sean Swoboda wanted the Wirpsas to untether her husband, leave the state, and get the hell out of her way. She had orchestrated Anthony Campbell's early release to expedite their exodus and intercepted Sage's letters to block interference from the meddling judge.

Then Manny Cofield went berserk in the prison, undermining Lori's authority. The penalty for stirring such immutable chaos for Lori was death. Cofield had been granted a stay from that punishment only because she needed him. She had both paid and threatened him with great effect to kill the judge and, subsequently, to come out of hiding and confess to all the prison related murders. In exchange, Lori manipulated Cofield's early release from prison, and had to suppress a strong instinctual urge to keep him there because, as much as she disliked the man, she needed him for one more piece of business: to decommission Ayde Carona.

Instead of delivering on Lori's edict to kill Ayde Carona, Cofield tried to sniff out Sage Wirspa, and he'd deliberately killed her grandmother in the process. Lori was no Wirspa fan, but she was less a fan of insubordination. Well, Manny Cofield was—as of yesterday—no longer a problem; Lori Swoboda would deal with Ayde Carona woman-to-woman.

Rediscovering the letters Sean had written to Cheney had equipped Lori with a way to jab a sharp knife right into Ayde Carona's heart. After all, who knew better than Lori how the slow, anguishing demise of one's spirit begins with your lover's betrayal.

Returning her attention to the Dynamic Duo, Lori pivoted to face them and said, "Sean made one mistake a long time ago, and it accounts for everything else that went wrong in his life: he didn't stick to the plan."

The men watched with singularity as Lori once again deftly pivoted the chair 180 degrees. She headed toward the harried receptionist. In her wake, attorneys, paralegals, and admins crowded in doorways lining the long corridor. Her audience marveled as she halted to a near screech at the double mahogany doors. Deanna rounded her desk to see what was going on. Lori jockeyed a wheel in a spinning tip to face her audience.

"Fill the room with your intelligence," she boomed with alacrity, parroting her husband's favorite line from *The Paper Chase*. "And stop gawking at me like I'm a freak. I *had* an accident. I am *not* the accident. I don't even *own* the accident. It just happened. Don't let it bring you to idiocy." *Although for most of you, it is already too late,* she thought.

She punched the huge nickel-plated handicap button mounted on the mahogany paneled wall. She had demanded the partners install this after the accident, and like her husband, they did as they were told. Her audience remained captive as the great mahogany doors slowly opened with dramatic pageantry. Lori Swoboda wheeled through the massive threshold, leaving the firm in wide-mouth wonder.

She was wrong about one thing. Their gawking awe had nothing to do with her accident or the majestic way she piloted the chair. Rather, their shock rode on a wave of the hottest office scuttlebutt. Apparently Lori Swoboda had strategically developed tightly woven relationships with the NYDA as well as state and federal judges presiding over her husband's indictment. With impeccable timing and panache that only a mastermind could engineer, she provided her new friends with a preponderance of irrefutable evidence of her husband's involvement in fraud, money laundering, larceny, murder, murder for hire, labor racketeering, and other egregious activities affronting state and federal laws. She crammed the courts with Sean Swoboda's now infamous celebrity in a way that guaranteed him to be fodder in one of her very own prisons.

"Geez," one of the associates said to a paralegal as they filed back to a sea of cubes hidden beyond Partners Row. "It's too bad Sean Swoboda doesn't have O. J.'s luck."

CHAPTER 69

JANUARY 1996

A wintery blast whistled its way around the Boston home where Jadia and Thomas lived. Jadia sat quietly at the table and finished a stack of banana pancakes while he made a stack of his own. With a dish towel draped over a shoulder and spatula in his hand, Thomas began flipping the row of flapjacks. The griddle sizzled, and the cakes rose high and fluffy. The trick—and his favorite part—was folding in whipped egg whites. He'd planned to make batches for Thanksgiving and Christmas breakfasts, but with all the varying wake-up times and diet preferences lingering in the house, he had abandoned that idea despite Sage's furtive urgings. He'd known what she was up to. She was trying to prove the banana pancakes improved Jadia's condition. Not only was the premise unfounded, it had quelled his appetite for the pancakes. Otherwise, the holidays had gone remarkably well. Thomas's parents, Sage, and even a couple of his friends from Philadelphia had visited in November. Sage and his parents remained through Christmas and well past the 1996 New Year.

Reflecting, Thomas spun the spatula around in his hand. Sage had been perfect. Saying and doing all the right things at all the right moments. And her cooking—Thomas had to admit it was nice having a kitchen break—he'd loved it. It freed more time for him to spend with Jadia and his parents. There was a sweeter perk: Sage owning the helm gave the home the air he felt Jadia most needed. A mother's touch. Healthy memories.

And there was something else. Sage herself seemed different, lighter. *She wasn't gayer. No, that wasn't it,* Thomas thought as he flipped the pancakes and tried to put his finger on it. Outside of being around Jadia, Sage wasn't necessarily happy. Instead she was ... content? Or maybe calm? Yes, maybe that was it. Sage wore a calm he hadn't seen since before the tragedy. The calm he'd fallen in love with. The same Sage-calm that had mothered his child. It was almost as if nothing had changed. Almost.

In that tiny space of "almost" lay infinite reasons Thomas would not fully trust Sage again. Retrieving Jadia from the middle of nowhere in the middle of the night had taught him well. To this day, Sage had not explained it, and Sean Swoboda had yet to own up to what happened. Sean was supposed be their attorney. *Attorney? Geez. The man behaved more like a wild horse, whinnying and gallivanting around West Virginia hills without reason or rhyme. And president? Forget about it. The guy was suspect down to the moment he was indicted on nearly every count in the book. No surprises there.*

What knocked Thomas off his feet and had his jaw clenching until he saw her pretty face at the airport, was that Sage was had still been blindly tagging along Sean Swoboda right up to the minute of the attorney's arrest. The authorities' public exoneration of her was the only reason Thomas had not banned her from seeing Jadia. He would have canceled his stateside return altogether and had his parents join him and Jadia in London had it not been made clear that Sage was not involved with Swoboda's shenanigans. That she was only Swoboda's innocent client. Sean Swoboda's services had been employed to address Anthony Campbell matters. Campbell had died over a year, so why were Sean and Sage meeting? And why had their business taken place in the apartment her mother had shared with Greysen Artino? Why were the authorities growing more and more doubtful that Swoboda had anything to do with the bombing that killed Greysen Artino's girlfriend? And who was *Greysen Artino?*

Thomas shook his head. It was all so incomprehensible. If it hadn't been for Lori Swoboda's complimenting, protective, almost maternal words about Sage's innocence, he would have believed as he did at first—that his ex and the attorney were having an affair. Now he didn't know what to believe, and he doubted he'd ever understand it all.

He used the spatula to lift a corner of the last remaining pancake in the pan before stacking it on the heap already mounted on his plate. Jadia's glass was empty, something he hadn't noticed until his hand was on the coffee carafe. He aborted the coffeemaker to grab a carton.

"Your wish is my command," he said, replenishing Jadia's glass. He kissed Jadia's forehead before heading back to the counter. He eyed the pancakes, thinking about the packing he and Jadia needed to do. Tomorrow they were headed back to London. In a reluctant sigh, he grabbed a fork from the utensil drawer. The warmth of the pancakes rose to his face, then he reached for the plate and heard—

"Dad?"

Thomas froze. The fork slipped from his fingers and fell on the edge of the counter with a muted clink, then rattled itself in a dramatic fall down layers of drawer handles before noisily bouncing and tittering to a stop on the Mediterranean floor.

Silence.

That quiet stretch of five or six seconds felt like a lifetime that began beautifully with Jadia's birth and festered like an open sore inside him after her kidnap and rape. Until this very moment, the onslaught of rotting decay had not let up. The divorce. That unexplained dark week when Sage had taken off with Jadia and his undying suspicions that she'd taken their precious, hypersensitive daughter to see Anthony Campbell. The layers of distrust that had built between them like soap scum until they were no longer able to co-parent. The undesirable but necessary decision to secure full custody of Jadia. Sage's subsequent breakdown and his inability to help her. All of it, cankers oozing somewhere unreachable inside him until this moment when finally, the one and only panacea had arrived.

With his back to Jadia, Thomas pressed his closed lids tight to hold back tears. The psychiatric and counseling team repeatedly warned him not to overreact to any progress he might detect in Jadia. He controlled his breath, if not his shaking hand, as he slowly turned off the stove and returned the hot plate, heavy with pancakes, to the counter. He turned to his daughter.

It was impossible to see her and not think of Sage. The curl of her hair—shiny, black. The expectant eyes—daring, playful, and deep sea blue. The skin—creamy with a hint of gold that lingered through winter as if blanketing the colder months with a sheen of summer. It seemed the only thing Jadia had gotten from him was good sense. And yet his daughter was her own person. The amazing, infinitely unique Jadia. A quick chuckle spurted from within him as an easy smile found its way to his lips.

"Yes, sweetie?" His tone was higher than he'd intended, but he could not suppress his relief, gratitude, and love—his happiness.

Jadia looked at him, her Mediterranean blue eyes glinting under the kitchen light. "May I have more pancakes, please?"

CREDITS

O. J. Simpson Trial Timeline, http://usatoday30.usatoday.com/news/index/nns053.htm, O.J. Simpson Civil Trial.

CPSIA information can be obtained
at www.ICGtesting.com
Printed in the USA
FFOW03n0656020615
13884FF